The Wishing Lake

Mark Robinson

Copyright © 2011 by Mark Robinson

Cover design by Mark Robinson
Book design by Mark Robinson

All rights reserved.

No part of this book may be reproduced in any form or by any electronic or artificial means including computer storage and retrieval systems, without permission in writing from the author. The only exception is by a reviewer, who may quote short excerpts within a review.

All characters and organizations in this book are fictitious. Any resemblance to real persons or organizations, living or dead, is purely coincidental.

First Published in December 2011

ISBN: 978-1-4709-8366-6

'We shall see that at which dogs howl in the dark, and that at which cats prick up their ears after midnight.'

- H.P. Lovecraft

Table of Contents

1. A Lost Heritage
5. A Hidden Place
15. An Image of Life
33. The Wishing Lake
41. Eternal Home
53. A New Discovery
69. The Waters Edge
79. A Shadow Falls
91. Keepers of Memories
105. In Remembrance
121. Recollections of the Past
133. Eclipse
149. The Kilportach Enigma
157. Session 1
165. The Rabbit Hole
179. Still Water Secrets
187. The Watcher in the Dark
205. Reunion
213. Grimorium Votum
229. The Cloud Painter
243. People of the Past
251. Session 2
263. Reminiscence
275. Records and Requiems
283. Quietus
295. Farewells

A Lost Heritage

I sometimes call them 'hidden places'. Tired buildings where nobody lives, crumbling ruins where nobody goes. Places that have a soul, if you will. Like they are waiting to be found, yet hoping not to be.

As I write this, I have but yesterday returned from one such place. I will admit, it feels strange to be home. I can hear the whir of my ageing computer, the humdrum babble of suburban families scurrying past my windowpanes. It's all so normal, so mundane, yet I'm actually pleased to be seeing it again. Or perhaps not.

The thing is, when I was there; in the 'hidden place' that I will tell of shortly, something happened to me. Something so odd, so unutterably irregular, that I can truly refer to it only as 'something'. Yes, my sanity was always in doubt, but I jeered at the doctors who told me so. What could they possibly have known of me, save for their textbook recitals of illness? Still, I can write with the knowledge that I am not mad. For I may have stared into the eyes of madness during my time in that unwelcome place, but that is all. No, I am definitely not mad.

It started though, as always, with a desire for answers. My birth certificate calls me 'Leonard Clarke', but I never really had a family. I remember my Father, but that is all. Even he died when I was just a child, leaving me funnelled into foster care with naught but tears and blurred memories. I don't even know what happened to him. As for my Mother, she is simply a photograph. I'm looking at it now; faded yellow and hung on the wall; long black hair and a homely smile. There's a necklace glittering above her dress; a silver mermaid with long hair and an etched tail. A single photograph, that's all I have.

It's perhaps no wonder that I found an interest in researching my family history. I have no desire for a family of my own, but the stories of those who came before me have always preyed upon my mind. So, this last year, after searching through countless archives of files, I managed to find my Father's name. It was odd that now, some thirty years later, I was finally seeing the man I remembered but faintly from my childhood. They may have been simply old census documents, but they were in essence the closest thing to his existence living on.

I spent weeks; months combing through the archives. My evenings were turned into restless searches and endless printouts of differing records. With that and my work, this small home office quickly became the only room in the house I lived in. Listening now, it's strange to hear the repetitive tick of the GrandFather clock in the hall. At the time, it was the only sound in the house, save for my fingers thumping this keyboard against the flicker of the screen. But if I'd only known then what my searching would find, I'm not sure if I'd even have started to look.

The first time I knew that something was wrong, was when I couldn't find myself on the genealogy websites. My Father was there, and so was my Mother, but nowhere was I on any of the records. I know when I was born, I had my birth certificate to prove it, but it was like I didn't exist. Furthermore, a Brother I didn't know I had appeared on the census records with them. Why was I never told about him? It all felt so wrong, like I was looking at different people who just happened to share the same names as my parents. I made sure though. Made sure it was the right people.

But then their child, Edward, was certainly my Brother. He was born but two years before I was, and showed up on each record as the son of Lucas and Ethel Clarke. But it said that he was their *only* son! Where was I? Had my mind sank so far into imbalance that I forgot my very own kin? Impossible. But then, why was I never told?

The strangest thing though, was yet to come up. I still remember the evening when I discovered it. I was sat here as I always did; a small halogen heater placed at my feet, the clock stretching to half eleven at night. I was tired, the record lists on my computer screen blurring into an endless muddle. But then something woke me up. It seemed that, to my surprise and somewhat disturbance, my family all died on the exact same day.

I didn't believe it. But I double checked; bought records from every website I found, and each one told me the very same thing. On the 31st November 1981, my Mother, Father, and even the Brother I had just discovered, were all listed as having died. What could have happened? Images stirred in my thoughts; visions of accidents and fires and murders. I knew at once that something was wrong. I have slight memories of my Father dying, but as a small child I was never told why. I was simply torn away from my life, with my only real memory of the time being pain.

The record was worrying, yet oddly fascinating. There was even a place of death listed, the place where my whole family lost their lives. A town called 'Kilportach', it seemed, in southern Ireland. I'd never heard of it. It wasn't even listed on some of my maps. But I did manage to find it, eventually. A small town, surrounded in nothing but fields and marshlands, the next town more than ten miles away. It seemed so secluded.

I tried to think, to make sense of my findings, but I quickly found that I could not. Sleep had never came easy to start with, not with these headaches and 'things' that I see. I don't even know if I could call them headaches, but that doesn't matter. I was up all night anyway, rereading the records and racking my brains. Why was I not on any records and files? Who was this Brother Edward, and why did I not know of him? And how did my family all die on the same day, in some isolated town in the middle of nowhere? I knew at once that I had to found out.

It wasn't long before I left for Ireland. I wanted to see this place for myself, to explore it's graveyards and people and buildings, to see what more I could discover. It was easy for me, after all. I worked from home and had no life-draining rota to live my life for me. The customers could wait, anyway. Indeed, that was all there was to it. I locked the door to this house and left, and was on my way to the town of Kilportach.

Would I have still gone there if I'd known what was waiting? I do not know. But how can one honestly know, foretell what will happen as they live their lives? Even in a day as mundane as normal, you have no idea what is waiting for you just mere seconds away. But none of that matters.

I am writing these memoirs as much for my own sake as for any willing reader. The things that happened in that awful place are as hard to correlate as I dare undertake. Without writing them, it would be impossible. Or perhaps that is simply the nature of my mind. Either way, I hope to recount my experiences, cast them in ink as to grant them physical form. That way, perhaps I can better understand them. Then in time, when merciful death finds his way even to me, my words here will become my voice.

Perhaps it has already happened. Are you reading these no doubt weathered notes after their writer has passed away? If so, then feel free to make up your own mind. You may not like everything you read, and I don't expect you to believe my tale. Yet I will say one thing. Though the things I saw were doubtlessly unreal, there existed a sense of reality to them, which was more existent than what is known to be 'real'.

What follows is a log of my time in Kilportach, from the time I arrived to the day I departed. I do not know if truly this exercise will help, but it is all I can do. For even when my pen has finished the last page, I doubt I will be further to a full explanation. All I know for sure is this; I witnessed something in that Irish town. Something that although of this world, could be only described as outside of our existence.

A Hidden Place

Even the train to Kilportach was odd. I had travelled to Ireland on a modern ferry, linking up with a crowded train to the major city of Cork. It was your standard affair; sleeping businessmen woken up by rowdy chatter and crying children. I stared out of the window for most of the way. Some rather stunning views.

Cork station was busy and suitably shiny, filled with travellers and non-stop announcements. There must have been hundreds of different people, all standing on platforms bogged down with luggage, waiting impatiently for trains to arrive. I begun to wonder where they could all be heading.

My platform however, was different. I couldn't find it at first, resorting to having some gel-haired assistant show me where I was meant to go. It seemed to be at the end of the station; a single line leading into nowhere, set apart from the rest of the building. A broken bench sat daubed with graffiti, and an overfilled bin spilled onto the platform. I was the only one waiting there, as well. The assistant had told me Kilportach was a 'request stop', and so I'd have to tell the conductor on-board that I would like the train to stop there. Usually then, the train would just hurtle through the town before the people aboard could even see it. Was it really so remote?

Still, the train arrived, late as expected. What I didn't foresee though was the state it was in. The previous train ran with a sonorous purring, the seats small yet amply comfortable. This one, contrarily, was the opposite. It's threadbare seats shook as it revved up, and it's paintwork was faded, showing visible rust. On the windows, degenerates had etched small drawings and symbols; scribbled names and peppered expletives. There wasn't even an on-board speaker; the conductor actually stood in the aisle and shouted the name of the upcoming stop. The brakes screeched.

It all seemed dead, somehow. The aisle was empty, the only other passenger a grimy old man, talking to a bottle on a seat in the corner. I already wanted to leave the train, with thoughts of it breaking down coming to mind, leaving me stranded in the wilderness outside. I tried to relax though; there was still another hour until it would get there. I knew already though, Kilportach was going to be one of those places. A 'hidden place'.

I had of course questioned my decision to come, but it was far too late to abandon the thing. I had in my suitcase a number of folders, each with details of the family members I had found whilst trawling the databases. Yet I knew that even should I find them there, it would be nothing more than a crumbled grave or monument with their name. But still, I found more interest in objects and things than in the company most people seem to keep. I understood them more.

It was 7 pm when I finally reached Kilportach. The brakes on the train once more screamed; the conductor standing and shouting loudly as to make himself heard over their noise. The old man with the drink was now sound asleep, his bottle empty and clasped in his hands. I walked past him on my way to the door, the stench of alcohol filling my lungs.

Outside, it was twilight. A single wall lamp flickered in front of me, the name of the town displayed underneath it. I stood still for a second, allowing the train to rev up behind me, then disappear into the night. I was finally there. The station was tiny, just one platform and nothing else. A plastic board was stuck to the wall, with a timetable visible behind a smearing of dirt. It seemed the train I was on only came twice a day.

I realised then that there was nothing around me. A rusted gate led out of the station, and straight into successions of muddy fields. A trampled footpath led into the distance, but nothing else was visible. There wasn't even a light or a signpost, and if it were any later in the evening, I doubt I could have seen anything at all. It was as if the station was out of place; dropped into the middle of a row of fields, many miles from civilisation. The whole place already felt wrong to me.

I checked again that I had alighted the train at the correct stop, and of course I had. This was indeed Kilportach; the single train-line disappearing across the fields and into nowhere. But it was all just flat, open earth; the idea of there being a town there at all difficult to comprehend. But I was there, the day growing darker each minute, the next train not due until late the next morning. I turned to the exit, stepping on the sodden and empty field, and wondered just where I could find some life.

Someone called to me as well, from the station platform as I turned away from it. I thought at first that the drunk on the train had secretly alighted and was shouting out to me. But there was nobody there. There never is.

I ignored it, and continued to trudge through the fields before me, following footsteps pressed into the mud from previous passengers leaving the station. There was a cold breeze, and slight drops of rain were starting to spit in intermittent spurts. I glanced over my shoulder, and saw the station standing alone in the field, looking more like a ruin than a railway station. I continued to walk. My shoes were gradually buried in earth, squelching water now seeping through them with every step I took. This was hardly a footpath into a town. Not even a farmhouse would surely choose to stand at the base of such sludge.

But there really was a town there. After a while, the field began to undulate, gradually steepening and leading down until a wooden stile sat alone at it's end. At the other side, dim lights could be seen from amongst the trees; and a rough stone footpath led no doubt into the town itself. I scraped my shoes on the stile before climbing; the legs of my trousers now soaked with the wet soil from the field. But no matter, I thought, soon I would find the guest house I'd booked into and start my research the following morning.

This guest house, which sounded like more of a B&B, was one of only two hotels I found whilst arranging my travel to town. The other one, though seemingly larger and more prestigious, proved impossible to contact at all. It was listed online and in the phone directory, but I was swiftly told when trying to ring that the number was not in use. Likewise, though a street address was found on the Internet, no website or email was apparent to me. Anyway, I managed to find this other place, 'Hawthorn House' as they called it on the phone. I just needed to find it.

Thankfully, it was one of the first buildings I encountered. After leaving the stony footpath, I found myself standing on familiar pavements on the edges of Kilportach itself. In front of me stood a small T-Junction, an old water pump stood in it's centre. Behind it, a wooden sign stood crooked and weathered, the street names all but faded away. Clumps of houses dotted the landscape, and the road was cracked and somewhat narrow, with nary a street-lamp to light the way. It seemed quiet, lifeless even, like the people were all huddled up in their homes, leaving the street sides barren and empty. Yes, this was definitely a 'hidden place'.

I followed the pavement around to the right, and was greeted near instantly with a hand-painted sign, swinging in the garden of the B&B. Usually, one would think such signs serve as advertisements to the homely service of the guest house in question. This one was just a sheet of wood, two holes drilled as to hang it to a post, with untidy handwriting reading *'Hawthorn House, Bed and Breakfast'*. It wasn't exactly a welcoming sight, and the house itself was not much better. It looked depressed, with dirty curtains and no lights on, the garden overgrown and the windowsills flaking. It was as if nobody lived there at all.

Still, I placed down my suitcase, and gave a few knocks on the flimsy feeling door. There was no answer. Is there ever? I tried again, knocking louder, the door so thin it felt like I was seconds away from breaking it down. Nothing.

To my surprise, I tried the door and found out it was open, leading straight into a makeshift reception, complete with a desk and cash register. I walked in, then closed the door. There was a heavy odour of damp in the air, a fact made stronger by the dirty beige wallpaper which looked like it could peel off at any second. A number of paintings where hung on the walls, generic landscapes and boring abstracts. I walked to the desk.

Behind it, a closed and notably filthy doorway hid muffled noises coming from behind it. Someone was watching TV. On the desk itself, jumbled papers were clumped together, and the old till sat perched on the edge, looking like as though it weighed half a tonne. At the other side, a curious glass case was home to a taxidermy blackbird; perched on a twig with faux moss surrounding it. Next to it, a brass desk bell was waiting to be pushed.

It gave out a loud, unhealthy sounding ring. Almost immediately though, the sound of the TV behind the door was muted, and the stumble of footsteps was heard in it's place. The door opened. It was an overweight woman in a stained old apron, her hair in a bun, light brown and greying. Rounded glasses were wedged on her face, and her skin was red and pimpled like rosacea.

"Ah, so our guest is here, is he?" she said, her tone hearty and actually welcoming.

"Leonard Clarke. I rang about a room?"

"Of course, of course. Your the only one here tonight. I was waiting for you to get here."

She marked something down on one of the pieces of paper. She seemed friendly, but I was never so trusting. I didn't know what to think about being the only guest, but I suppose I should have expected it. The place was a dump.

"Let's see", she said, examining the paper. "I can put you in the best room we have in the place. Great views up there."

"Thanks."

She opened a drawer and removed a key, then asked me to follow her to the stairs. They were narrow and covered in a shabby carpet, each floorboard moving as I placed my foot on it. The woman led the way.

"What was it you were here for again, my dear?" she said as we climbed the stairs in front of me.

"Family tree. I'm doing my family tree."

She paused on the stairs as they turned a corner, a set of awful wall ducks hanging up behind her. She turned to me.

"Clarke Family?" she asked.

I nodded, and she continued to lead me up the stairs. At the top, a thin corridor was stretching out, the ceiling low and the floorboards bare. Patches of wallpaper were missing in places, revealing a crumbling and cracked plaster. The whole place smelt so damp and musty. She took me to the last room on the right, a white painted door with the number 4 stuck on it.

It was a square bedroom with a double bed taking up most of the smallish room. A rickety wardrobe stood at it's foot, as well as the usual kettle and dresser. I put my suitcase down on the bed. I was going to speak, but the woman opened the curtains for me and beckoned me over to the window.

"Come on, you have to see the view from here."

It was still twilight outside, and I could just about make out successions of marshlands stretching as far as the eye could see.

"That's our namesake. Our history, that is", she said.

I glanced at her, then back at the view of the marshes outside. They were vast and rolling, covered in pools and vegetation, with birds fluttering overhead. The heavier bog looked thick and deep, as if walking too close would surely result in being sucked down under it's merciless grasp.

"The Kilportach bog land", continued the woman, also looking out of the window. "Years ago, people would work out there. Dig out the peat, that sort of thing That's why the town was built, you see."

In the middle of the bog, a number of men where gathered around a single floodlight pointing downwards. Behind them, a tractor was stood with a digger attachment, it's headlights on and lighting the area.

"What are they doing?" I asked.

"Bog people", she bluntly replied, backing away from the window. "They say there could be hundreds of them, buried out there in the peat. Looks like they found another, eh?"

"What, you mean bodies?" I stared across the peat bog before me.

"Well, they're more like mummies, I think. You didn't know?"

"Know what?"

"Never mind dear. Some people come to the town just to see them, that's all. It was in all the papers, you see. Look, read about it if you want."

She pointed to a leaflet on the bedside table. The photograph of a mummified body was displayed on it's cover, underneath a headline of *'The Kilportach Bog Men'*. It seemed to be some sort of information booklet.

"Anyway", said the woman, "I think I should probably leave you to it. I'll cook you some breakfast in the morning, OK? What sort of time do you want it?"

"Oh, whenever you like".

"Alright dear, just let me know."

The woman said her goodbyes to me, then left the room, closing the door. I went straight to the window, looked out once more across the bog land. It was getting darker, the only real light coming from the tractor and floodlight in the middle. The men were still there, all seeming to be searching for something in the peat. It was strange to imagine; hundreds of bodies laying preserved on the edge of a secluded, Irish town. Strange, yet somehow fascinating.

Still, there was nothing more to see for tonight. I closed the curtains, and turned on the light in the room.

The first thing I did was hang my clothes in the flimsy wardrobe against the wall. It stunk heavily of mothballs, and the bottom drawer was jammed up completely. But still, at least there were hangers. All I brought with me were a few sets of clothes, anyway. That, and my folders full of genealogy details, which I promptly laid out on the dressing table top.

The only other thing was my bottle of pills. It was a new bottle, more than enough to last for a week. I hated the things, but I knew that I wouldn't get far without them. In fact, I could already feel the first few throbs starting to squirm around up there. I knew it would happen as soon as I heard that voice, the one calling my name in the station. It usually started with something like that. Damn headaches.

The room I was in was hardly a help. It was far too warm and unusually stuffy, with layers of dust collecting in corners and across the cheap wooden furniture. There was nothing in the room, the travel kettle the only thing which told me I was still in the 21st century. Nothing else, not even a TV. Not that I'd have watched it, anyway.

Above the bed, a short poem was bordered with a floral pattern, and hung in a small square photo frame. It seemed to be religious, and so usually I wouldn't bother, but it's content struck me as interesting.

'Pause traveller, and bethink thee,
How holy, and yet how homelike this place
Time that thou spendest humbly here,
shall link thee with men unknown
who were once of thy race'

It was unusual to see a Christian poem with such underlying metaphysical tones. I have never had time for their dogma in my life. The poem however was suitably curious, especially considering that outside the window, I'd be sharing my night with countless bog bodies. In essence, they were 'once of my race' as well. What happened to them, I wondered?

I could have easily thought about it for quite some time, but a familiar sting soon intruded my mind. One of my headaches. It was always the same, a dull throb which suddenly attacked the nerves, forcing me to squint as it shot down my face. The 'signs' were there as well; the ring in my ears and the nauseous blur in my eyes. I called them the 'signs' because when they appeared, I knew that I had to take a tablet.

I went to the bathroom for much needed water. What a hole. The bath was dirty and heavily stained, the taps on the sink making awful noises as the water dribbled out of them. I felt sick. Still, I took a mouthful of water, and downed the tablet with a forceful gulp. I always feared they would stick in my throat, they were such an irregular shape and size. It was all OK though. I worked next on focusing my eyes. On the bathroom windowsill, a glass clown ornament was standing alone. I focused on it, my vision gradually losing it's tremor, returning back to a settled normality.

I knew however that it would take an hour for the headache to fully settle. There was no point in staying awake. I climbed into bed, turning off the lights apart from a small lamp beside the bed. In a way, this dim light made the room look better, as it hid the grimy wallpaper, and obscured the ugly décor. There were a lot of shadows though. I hoped they would not play tricks with my mind, for the pulse in my head made it easy for twisted forms to appear in the dark. I'd seen things before.

One thing which helped to tire my eyes was the bedside leaflet about the bog men. If anything, I thought that reading it could take my mind away from thoughts of this squalid building. The front cover was certainly interesting enough. The body in the photo was bent and crippled, the facial features remarkably preserved. The woman mentioned the bodies were featured in newspapers, but I had never heard of them. I seldom read the news, anyway. There is little more discouraging than digesting the vapid opinions of political ingrates. I hated it.

Either way, the leaflet soon took my whole attention, and the pill I took was slowly working it's way into my head. There was another photo of a body inside, as well as a non-scale drawing of the bog, with markings where bodies or items were found. I laid back in bed, and took in everything that I was reading.

'The existence of bodies in Kilportach's peat bog has been known for nearly all of it's history. During the heyday of the bog and town, workers reported discovering remnants of previous inhabitants having worked the bog. After much interest and speculation, an archaeology team was called to the town, and the first bog body was pulled from the peat.

Since then, four more bodies have been discovered, and the bog was placed under archaeological care, in hope of uncovering all of it's secrets. Over the next couple of years, the team hopes to examine the entire area, and remove any more mummified remains from deep within their marshland graves. Locals have speculated the number of bodies could easily reach into the hundreds, though official word has not been confirmed. All we know is that Kilportach bog is one of the largest in the country, and the cause of death and reason for burial here is the real mystery of these bog people'

It was not long before I felt my eyelids closing, and although I was interested in studying more, I knew I was going to fall asleep. The pills always did that to me. Indeed, it was not long before I found myself drifting involuntarily in and out of sleep. I put the leaflet down, telling myself I'd finish it later.

I don't think I dreamt while I slept. I usually didn't, my nights were far too restless to grant the mind any time to form them. On occasion, a very lucid dream would challenge these largely dreamless nights, but not often. As a rule, such dreams would present themselves just like they were memories, although their existence was surely unreal. They existed inside, and yet outside of my mind.

For that reason, I do not believe I was dreaming on my first night in the B&B. Although what happened was certainly characteristic of a dream, the senses were notably sharper than what a simple mental image could grant.

I had already woke up a couple of times, and had managed to fall back into sleep by thinking of beginning my research tomorrow. One time though, I wasn't simply awoken by an aching muscle or recurring thought in my mind. Something in the room had woke me up.

Of course, it was far too dark to see anything, but I had the distinct sensation that something was sitting on the end of the bed. I could feel the weight pressing onto the mattress, with whatever it was remaining still even if I moved my legs and body. It took a few seconds to fully accept it, but the feeling soon settled that somebody else was in the room with me. An animal? An entity?

I quickly sat up and reached for the lamp, and only wished that I had managed to find it. For what happened next I am still unsure. The thing on my bed was of physical form, and it seemed to pounce or fall onto me as soon as I went to press the light switch. For a second, I saw something. It was a shape rather than a tangible mass; just pure black and heavy feeling. I fell back, finding myself unable to even move my head or body. I tried to shout, to throw it from me, but it's strength was far too great. It pressed something to me, over my face. I could hardly breath, like a pillow or towel was forced across my nose and mouth, restricting air. I writhed, felt my lungs tighten and spasm.

And then, I was awake. As soon as it had started, it was over. I sat up in bed, catching my breath in deep, automatic wheezes. I lunged for the small bedside lamp, switching it on and dazzling my vision. The room was empty.

An Image of Life

When morning arrived in that bothersome room, I found I did not want to leave the bed. Daylight had long since pierced the windows, lighting up the scores of dust which hovered around in it's airspace. I was so tired. But still, I knew I would have to get up at some point.

The headache was gone, but what happened last night was still preying on my mind. I was already aware of this type of dream, where you cannot move and try to scream out, but find your body to be paralysed. I had also heard of a similar phenomena, where waking and dreaming are mixed together, and the dream momentarily 'appears' in the real world. Perhaps that was all it was, just a tired mind affected by it's headache and environment. It felt real though, horrifyingly so. I could feel the presence on the bed, see it's shape as it tried to smother me.

For the time being, I tried not to dwell on it. The bathroom was hardly fit to wash in, but I put my thoughts aside to make sure I was at least presentable. I found that the mirror near the sink was scratched, like someone had scraped it with a key or coin to lessen it's reflectiveness. Thankfully, it was not too damaged, and I could see enough to comb my hair. While doing so, I quickly noticed a small red marking on the side of my neck, like I'd caught it on something or bruised it somehow. I was sure that wasn't there before.

Either way, I was happy to be once more surrounded in daylight. I opened the curtains to the view of the bog land, and opened the window to let in some air. The peat bog outside was truly huge, far more so than I had imagined last night. It was as if this town was the last place on earth, and all that remained was untamed land fit only for shrubs and animals to live in. I thought of the bodies, too. The idea of them buried there under the peat, preserved like the one in the leaflet I read. It was understandable that people would come here to see them.

I looked at it for a little while longer, then decided to show myself downstairs. I was not looking forward to breakfast though. I was still tired from last night's episode, and the thought of eating from the kitchen in that place did not inspire any hunger. Besides, I'd always hated eating in the close company of strangers.

Still, I managed to eat a small fried breakfast while sat in her lino covered kitchen. It was edible, I suppose; the egg overdone and the beans watered down. It did settle my stomach, though. The kitchen itself was as I'd expected, bare walls stained with years worth of cooking, piles of pans in the sink to wash. The woman was there, too, drinking coffee whilst saying good morning and watching me as I ate her food. Most of it was banal small talk and nonsense, the sort of chatter most people engage in to make them feel like their presence is wanted. I just nodded and swallowed the food. She did say one thing interesting, though.

"I was thinking of places for you to go, dear. To do your family research, and such."

"Yeah?"

"Let's see now... there's the old cemetery of course, and we have a museum in the town if it's open. And of course the bog land. You must see the bog land."

"I will. Thanks."

I had already planned on visiting the cemetery. I didn't know of a museum though. Frankly, the town itself was at this point no concern. I was here to find what happened to my family, who they were and why they died. I decided to ask her.

"You haven't heard of a Clarke family living here, I take it?"

"I only took over this place a few years back, my dear. I've heard the stories, of course, but nothing else."

"What stories?"

"Oh. Nothing, dear. Nothing"

I had no idea what she was talking about. I just finished the breakfast in front of me, then thanked her for cooking it. I didn't really feel like talking to her any longer, as my 'dream' last night was making itself known with the tiring effects of sleep loss. I took a sip of the weak coffee she had made for me, and massaged my temples for a second, my head still feeling a little tight.

Before long, she had taken my plate and added it to the pile of unwashed dishes, and I was about ready to leave the building. I picked up my folder with the family records in it, thanked her again, and made for the door.

"Oh, I nearly forgot", she called out just before I left. "You should speak to Doctor Kenny while he's in town. Might be able to help you."

"How so?"

"Well, they brought him in from Limerick to look at the bodies. They wanted to know if the people lived here, before they were buried in there, you know. Might be worth seeing him, you think?"

"Maybe. Where can I find him?"

"We only have the one doctor's surgery, dear. He'll be in there, should you decide to look in."

"Thanks".

I doubted a doctor here to look at the bog bodies would have any interest in a family researcher, but her gesture seemed to be meant in kindness. Anyway, she had at least given me a bit to go on, and I was looking forward to exploring Kilportach properly. I said my goodbyes, and left the B&B.

Finally, fresh air. It was a drizzly morning, the skies looking like any minute they would open up and drench the town. I walked down the road from the guest house, and wondered where I should start to search.

Before long, another crossroad split the roadway, revealing a row of terraced buildings leading in a slight downward slope. Occasionally, hand painted signs would be hung in gardens, or plaques and signs stuck to house walls. They seemed to be shops, yet appeared little more than converted houses with crude signs and small display windows. Most seemed closed, anyway.

I was looking for a way into the town centre, where I assumed I could find tourist information and begin to ask for details there. The further I walked down those empty streets though, the more I realised how barren this place was. There was no sign of a main row of shops, just twisting pavements and clumps of buildings, which all looked cramped and huddled together. It was more like a village than a town.

I had hardly seen anybody, either. The majority of streets I turned to were empty, and were it not for the occasional car passing by, I would have thought the whole place to be a ghost town.

Eventually, however, I discovered what I guessed was the centre of the town. It was a single street, flanked at each side by shop displays, with a narrow road running through the middle. There were still very few people on the streets, but a handful of shops were clearly open, and a couple of people were going into them. I began to walk along the pavement, already imagining my ancestors having been there. I had no idea where I would find them, though.

Most of the shops were standard fare, save for their signs and window displays appearing as if they were still in the 50's. That said, to say that the town felt stuck in the past would be describing it as actually existing in time. Indeed, it felt more as if it had simply stopped, like the people there just lived out their lives, unaware of the world outside. Most shops I passed seemed sleepy and empty, like an antique shop crammed full of items, and a chemist emitting an odour of antiseptic.

Near the end of the row of shops, a swinging sign hung on the wall of a small, square looking shop front. It was a tourist office, various leaflets displayed in the window, and a rack selling local books by the door. I didn't hesitate to go inside.

It was oddly dark, lit only by a single, dim light bulb in the middle of the room. A number of tables stood peppered with leaflets, and an old oak desk was sat at the back, a lit candle standing upon it. Behind, a large map of the local area was hanging against the wood panelled wall. In the corner, straightening out the books and leaflets, an elderly lady turned to greet me.

She had a black bonnet covering her hair, and a matching black dress all ruffled and ornate. For anything, it looked like a Victorian mourning dress, and the thought crossed my mind it was possibly for show. She stood crooked yet without a stick, and bore on her face a friendly smile, beneath a healthy collection of wrinkles.

"Here to see the mummies in the peat bog, are you?" she said before I had time to speak. "Been a lot of you coming through lately, there has."

I explained to her what I had came to Kilportach for. I spared the majority of details, of course, simply saying who I was and that I was there to research my family tree. As I spoke, she hobbled across the dark tourist office, and sat on a cushioned wooden chair in the corner.

"I see. Well, I always said that only three types of people come here any more. Most come the see the peat bog bodies, and others come looking for ghosts and memories. And so you're the third type, as it seems your looking for memories here."

"I suppose."

"I've lived here all my life, you see. It was always like this though. Always quiet."

She didn't need to tell me. Even this tourist office was barren and defunct, with not a computer or modern display in sight. The candle on the desk stood still without flickering, the air heavy like an old library. Even the old lady seemed out of the past; her clothes and mannerisms a far cry from your usual tourists' welcome. Thinking about it though, I was surprised the office was even there. The town was dead. Still, the office was the only place I'd found with any signs of life. So, I decided to ask the old woman.

"You said you'd lived here your whole life? Have you ever heard of a Clarke family living here?"

"I don't know. Oh, I could have told you a few years ago. I used to know everyone here. Now though, I just don't know. You forget things you know, when you get to my age."

"Don't worry about it."

"The town used to be a special place, you know. People said it was sacred ground, and they came here looking for inner peace."

"They did?"

"But when the bodies showed up, that's all people cared about any more. Look there, read about it if you like".

She pointed to one of the leaflets on the table. It had upon it a landscape of a large, natural lake. Above it, a headline read *'Kilportach: Myths and Folklore'.* I picked it up, put it in my pocket to read later on.

"Take as many as you like", she said. "Something could help you, you never know."

"Thanks."

I didn't really see anything that could help, but knowing this place was here if needed was at least something I'd already found out. So, I had another scout through the leaflets, and then thought I should explore some more of the town. I said my goodbyes to the old woman, and headed for the door. On the way out, I noticed a poster stuck to the wall.

It had upon it a photo of a doctor, short combed black hair and neat, black beard. Beside, it a few lines of text read;

"We are pleased to welcome Dr Aaron Kenny from Limerick to our town. The Neurobiologist will be here next week to study our curious peat bog mummies. All enquires to the local surgery, where Dr Kenny will be based whilst here'.

It was the doctor the B&B owner had mentioned. She didn't say he was in Neuroscience. It was something I had briefly found interest in, mostly due to these deathly headaches I had suffered for so long with. I was always sceptical though, finding most men who try studying the brain to be more interested in petty behavioural traits. I detested psychiatry, but the brain interested me. Perhaps Dr Kenny would be worth a visit, after all.

First though, I continued to walk through the quiet street and look through the windows of the remaining shops. There really was nothing there. The only shops which were open at all sold basic commodities for those who lived there. Everything else was either closed down, or selling cheap and useless items of little interest to anyone. There was a pub though, standing at the end of the row of shops, a crossroads spread out in front of it. A large old sign was hung on it's wall, with the words '*The Wishing Lake*' displayed above a painting of water. Unfortunately, the place seemed to be closed.

I turned right at the crossroads, leaving the main street and into a downhill, terraced row of houses. At this point, I didn't really know where to go, the only places I knew of being the cemetery and museum she had mentioned in the guest house. Thankfully, there was a road sign, although it only pointed back up to the town and across the street to the doctor's surgery. With no other ideas, I decided to follow it, just in case this Dr Kenny was there. After all, there was a chance I'd find out something from him.

Walking through the streets, it was difficult to imagine the place being 'sacred', as the old woman had told me earlier. I wondered what she had meant, guessing she was talking about religion or some ancient folk belief. The place felt far from sacred, however. If anything, it was like I'd thought, a 'hidden place' by all accounts. The sort of town that no one knows, that small maps cover with a tiny dot, and large maps don't even mention at all. The sort of town that is forever sleeping, hiding secrets in all it's recesses, which would only be known should the town awaken. In that respect, it probably was a 'sacred' place.

Before too long, I reached the end of the small backstreet, and was greeted by the sight of a rectangular building, with a sloping roof and small car-park in front of a short hedgerow. Above the door, embossed letters were stuck to the wall, spelling out '*Kilportach Surgery*'.

In the car-park, two men were standing and talking to one another. One of them definitely looked like a doctor, mostly due to his familiar, long white coat. I didn't want to walk straight into the surgery, so I approached the men to ask for advice. Immediately, the doctor turned to face me.

"Sorry", I said, realising there was likely nothing here to help me with my research. "I was just walking around the town, and-"

"Is this him, I wonder?" interrupted the doctor. "Are you the one staying in Hawthorn House, by any chance?"

I had no idea how he knew who I was. However, before I managed to say a word, he extended his hand to me with a large smile. Of course, I told him, with added confusion surely showing in my voice, that I was indeed from the guest house he mentioned.

"Bridget told me you'd be coming. Family tree man, right?"

"Bridget?"

"Bridget Brady, from Hawthorn House? Ah god, she rang me without asking you first, didn't she?"

"Looks that way."

"That woman! Ah well, I'm Dr Kenny anyway. She did mention she had told you about me. So, how can I help you?"

I told him I was sorry to interrupt; that I had only came because I didn't know where else to go in the town. I felt slightly uncomfortable being there. Still, the doctor seemed to be friendly enough, and before any more was said between us, he asked me come inside the surgery.

His beard was shorter than on the photograph, and although he was tall he was moderately overweight. I got the impression that he thought my research was more advanced than it actually was, and that I had came with the specific intention to seek him out for advice. Because of this, I didn't really know what to say to him.

Nevertheless, he led me through the doctor's surgery and into his office at the back of a corridor. Switching on the light, I was met with a large yet untidy room, with numerous equipment and tools on display. A bench at the back housed an old computer, and a sofa and bed were covered in white sheets, silently awaiting an ailing patient. Strangely, this room was the only thing I'd seen in Kilportach which didn't look ancient or long forgotten. Even so, it was still far from cutting edge.

Dr Kenny switched on the computer, then asked me to take a seat on the sofa.

"I don't pretend to be an expert in genealogy, you know", he said. "But I have some records on here you might like. It's to help my own research into the bodies. We want to find out just why they were buried here, and what sort of local connection they had."

"I see."

"So, what name is the family your looking for? I'll run a little search on here for you."

"Thanks. It's Clarke. They all died here on the same day, in 1981. There was my Mother and Father, Lucas and Ethel, and my Brother Edward, who I never knew. I wasn't on any of the records though, like I was never even born. And as for why they died, well I don't know a thing. I hardly even remember my parents, really. So, well, that's why I'm here. I want to find out."

"Jesus, it's a mystery then? Well I don't blame you, my man. This damn town if full of mysteries, if you ask me."

"How so?"

"The bodies. You have seen the bodies, I take it?"

"I just got here. I was told about them, that's all."

"Well, would you look at that. You haven't even seen the bog people yet! Come on my man, you have to see them before we do anything else. It'll be only a minute, promise. Come on."

He left the computer and beckoned me over to another door at the back of the office. It had on a plaque with a 'no entry' sign, and looked deceptively innocent for what it was hiding.

I have experienced many times the sensation of a 'jump'. By this, I mean the sort of shock that brings out a gasp and skip of the heartbeat, like when taken by surprise by a horrid sight. Such a feeling came strongly when in that room.

It was not so much as morgue as a collection of beds, all laid out in rows and lit by harsh, overheard strip lights. On every bed, a different mummy was lifelessly laid; not looking like people, but more like dolls or sculptures. In total, there must have been ten or more bodies in there, all placed on beds and with paper labels tied to their limbs. Dr Kenny walked into the room.

"And here they are. The real inhabitants of Kilportach, if you will. Not so long back, people were coming here just so they could see them. Amazing, aren't they?"

It was hard to take in that what I was seeing were actual human remains. They were not like bodies in funeral homes, or even medical research cadavers. It was like they were simply frozen in form, and beneath their malformed, dead exteriors, they could still see and think like we do. Not only that, but the majority of them seemed be writhing in pain. Their faces were all contorted and twisted, with some looking as though they were screaming or frightened. Others were damaged; their bodies buckled and distorted, with one or two being only a torso.

"The leaflet I read said only 4 bodies were found. Were there really so many?"

"Oh yeah. Since the time the town became famous for these guys, we've been finding more and more out there in the peat. The townsfolk think there's hundreds of them."

Because they were mummies, the bog people's bodies were not displaying the decomposition of normal remains. Most had leathery, dark brown skin, rumpled yet otherwise perfectly preserved. Likewise, the majority of bodies had full heads of hair, stained from the peat yet remarkably intact. In one way, the sight of these mummies was strangely unnerving. In another, however, they were clearly fascinating.

"Look here, I'll show you something", said Kenny, standing behind one of the bodies and peering down at it. I joined him, standing mere inches from the mummy of a bent, frightened looking bog man.

"See here", he said, pointing carefully at the mummy's head. Above it's temple, the skin was broken and the skull cracked, revealing a hole which opened up into the brain area. "See it? Well, they're all like this."

"What do you mean?"

"Every body we found in there was killed in the same way. A hit to the head. Look, see this."

He placed his hand on the mummy's head, showing sections of colourless matter stained to the side of the skin.

"Brain tissue", he continued. "From where he was struck with something, you see. But the weird thing is, like I said, every single body has the same head wound. They were all killed in the exact same fashion, then all dumped in the bog outside town."

Such a brutal cause of death surely explained the expressions on the bodies, but it was definitely a mystery. I bent over the bed, looking closely at the damaged skull of the mummy that Kenny was showing me.

"Were they murdered, you think?" I asked.

"Very likely. For what reason, we don't know. But it's one of the reasons they brought me here. To try and find out why."

I had a look at some more of the bodies. In the corner, a female mummy was actually sitting up in the bed, the body leaning against the wall at it's side. Another was laid with it's mouth wide open, teeth still present and looking as though it was wanting to scream. The most frightening thing, of course, was that whilst the bodies were thin and deformed, their preservation had granted them a unique sensation of life.

Dr Kenny was pleased that he had shown me the bodies, and continued to chat about them after he had taken me back into his office. After a while though, he returned to the PC from before, and brought up on screen a collection of records.

I had hardly even sat down on the sofa when my headache quickly returned. It was unexpectedly rapid, and yet as quick as a blink or a single heartbeat. A heavy sharpness fell through my mind. It was the type of experience which is difficult to recount, with at least a partial amount of time being doubtlessly spent unconscious.

As I remember it though, I called out to Dr Kenny. My speech was slurred though, and I could hardly hear the words I was saying for a dense throb in my ears and thoughts. It was like a ringing sound, but dull and static like white noise from the radio played into my ears. I didn't feel sick, but confused and actually light in weight.

As I recall, I felt myself blink and immediately woke up in a different room. I was laid on a bed, Dr Kenny sitting near to me tapping away on a computer. I sat up shocked; realising that I must have temporarily lost consciousness.

"Ah, your back", said Dr Kenny, spinning around on his office chair to face me. "Good God man. How do you feel?"

I didn't really know how to respond. I must have mumbled, still being drowsy from whatever caused me to pass out. I didn't feel nausea, just the sort of tiredness you get from waking up prematurely. I didn't speak, just sat on the bed. Kenny told me what happened.

"So, you mentioned something about your head, but when I turned around, you were gone. Out cold. I brought you in here right away, of course."

It was a mid sized room, dominated by a large MRI scanner against the wall near to the doctor. I had no memory of anything; just sitting on the sofa after seeing the bodies, and almost instantly feeling in pain. I sat for a minute, took in some deep breaths as per Kenny's instruction, and also sipped at a glass of water. The headache was gone, but a slight tingling was still present above my eyes. I had no idea what had happened.

"You weren't out for long" said Kenny "But God, I would have thought you'd told me!"

"Told you what?"

"I found these, while I lifted you onto the bed there." He picked up my bottle of pills from his desk. I had kept them in my pocket in case I needed them. They must have fallen out as he brought me in there. "You could have at least said something, you know."

"Why? I take them for headaches. I brought them with me in case one came on."

"Jesus, they're not just headaches though right? These are anticonvulsants, for your seizures and the like. But then you still go passing out on me. Maybe these aren't strong enough or..." He started typing on the computer.

"I don't suffer from seizures. I was given them for headaches, like I said."

He stopped typing. "Well, what did they say to you? When they gave you them, I mean? They're supposed to for seizure disorders, like epilepsy and the likes. Do you suffer from anything like that?"

I was already confused from having passed out. Then he started to ask these questions, telling me the pills I had taken for years were something to do with serious seizures. I had no such thing. In fact, I had hardly even visited a doctor's surgery, save for a few original visits to get the pill prescription in the first place. Truthfully, I hated going to doctors, and tried all I could to avoid having to. Still, I was concerned that I had so quickly lost all consciousness. Were the headaches getting worse? I thought it must have been from last night's experience, or something to do with the mummies and town. But I was lying to myself.

"No", I said. "I've always had trouble with headaches and such, but no epilepsy. Nothing like that."

He got up, and placed his hands around the back of my head, pressing in fingers and uncomfortably examining.

"I see", he said as he prodded my skull. "Well those tablets are pretty serious things, you know. And now your saying you don't know why you were given them?"

"Yeah. The doctor just handed them over. They work. Or most of the time they do, anyway. I just get on with it."

"What do these headaches feel like then?"

He finished examining my head, and sat back down on the chair. I had not asked him for a medical check up. I would have been happy just to leave the surgery or talk about my research as I'd first intended. I'd never sought doctors before about my headaches. I would just take a pill and hope it would go. I didn't want want opening or tests being done. The last thing I wanted was cutting open whilst docile students experimented on me. Still, for the time being, I had little choice. However, I was at least a bit concerned that the pills I was taking were designed for such serious ailments.

"The headaches?", I said. "Well, they're usually throbbing, as you'd expect. But they also blur my eyes and thoughts, like I can't focus on anything. I see things too. Hear things, as well."

"What do you hear? Do people talk to you? Say things to you? And you say you see things too? What kind of things?"

"Slow down. I'm not schizophrenic. The things I see aren't in my head. It's shadows and things, that's all. Like a kid's bad dream. I don't care about it."

"OK. Well look sir, I can tell you aren't comfortable with talking about it. And that's fine. I just thought that, seeing as I'm quite a experienced neurobiologist, you might have wanted to see me about it. While were both here, I mean."

"Not really."

"But sir, did your doctor really not do anything before he gave you those pills?"

"He asked some questions, if that's what you mean. But I didn't want to know anything about it. I just wanted something to stop the headaches. Nothing else."

"I see. And did you use a machine like this, at all?" He pointed to the MRI scanner which took up most of the room.

"No."

At this point, I was irritated that Dr Kenny seemed to be working for a diagnoses. Sure, I could understand the concern on his half; I had just passed out for no real reason and I'd be lying if I said that didn't alarm me. I was just not used to such direct questioning.

"OK Mr Clarke", he said. "Well to be honest with you, when they brought me here I thought I'd be having some patients to see, you know? You've seen the place though, it's a ghost town. Looks like they really did want me just for the bodies."

"Mmhm."

"Look, if I were you Mr Clarke, I'd get an MRI done as you quick as you can. You said these headaches were bad, right? And well, we both saw what just happened to you, plus the severity of that medication. It's only right, you know?"

I knew that he was right. I hated the thought of having real tests done, to actually succumb to the will of a doctor, but I started questioning myself in that office. Dr Kenny was seemingly renowned for his work, and it was hardly as if the place was packed with other patients to see. Plus, the headaches were definitely something I would, if given the chance without the scores of rigmarole, be rid of in an instant. As I begun to fully awaken from whatever had happened to me earlier, I realised that I should at least speak with Kenny about his opinion on the matter.

"This MRI", I said. "What's it do, exactly?"

"It just scans your body, or in your case, your brain. Gives a good picture of what's inside there. Like an X-Ray if you like, but safer and higher quality".

"I see. So how do I get one done? If I wanted to, that is."

"Well like I said, I'm alone here with no patients but the mummies. Usually, you'd have to see your GP and book an appointment and all that. But look, if your concerned about what's going on up there, I'll do it for now, if you like."

"Now?"

"Oh, only if you didn't have somewhere to be or anything."

He seemed almost excited at the prospect of running me through his machine. I wasn't sure though. It wasn't that I was afraid of the outcome, or even worried about pain or discomfort. In truth, I didn't care about any of that. But I had lived with these headaches since I could remember, and tried my best to simply ignore them. Even the pills were sought out of desperation, usually I would not have even thought of seeing a doctor about them. It got so frequent though, that I knew I would have to get something done. So, reluctantly, I got the pills. From there it was just a simple matter of handing in a sheet for repeat prescriptions. Now though, Kenny was offering a real diagnoses. I wasn't really ready, nor in the mood, for any of it. However, I realised that when I really dug inside and ignored my cynicism, that perhaps having the test was the right thing to do.

"I'm not too pleased at the thought of it, doctor. But no, I have nowhere else to be right now."

"Well look, it doesn't hurt or anything like that. Hell, you won't even have the results of the thing until tomorrow. Today, all you have to do is lay still on there."

Kenny explained a bit more about the MRI, before asking me to wait as he cranked up the machine. He said it was an old one, but that the image should still be of good enough quality to see if anything was amiss. It was something I had actually given some thought to; exactly what was wrong up there to give me such pain and confusion. I never imagined I would actually know, however. In a way, I begun to sense a feeling of interest, the concept of seeing a picture of my brain impossible not to find fascinating. With this in mind, I climbed on to the MRI bed without hesitation, or a word to Kenny.

Before he switched it on, however, he grabbed a piece of paper from the desk.

"I forgot to tell you by the way. I found a bit of data for your family tree. It's a strange thing, though."

"What did you find?" I said whilst laying out on my back, the circular mouth of the machine behind me, waiting to feed me into it's centre.

"Well, your right enough that the whole Clarke family died on the same day in '81, but they weren't the only ones who died it seemed. Looks like the week before it happened, somebody was murdered in the town. Moreover, another man was registered dead on the same day as your parents. Coincidence maybe, but a lot of deaths in one day for a small town, especially one as damned quiet as this."

"So someone was murdered? Who?"

"Ah, let me see." He ruffled through the pages. "Here it is. A man called Shane Cullen, it seems. Lived in the town. His body was taken to this very surgery after they found him murdered. No murderer found either, or not that I could see."

"Odd. And what about the other person who died, on the same day as my family?"

"That was strange as well. They didn't give a name for him on the record. I take it he was only visiting town or somehow couldn't be identified. Something happened though, that's for sure."

"Heh, no joke. And thanks."

Kenny smiled, and went to the side of the MRI machine to send me into it's scanner. He was just about to press the button, when I interrupted him with another thought.

"Sorry, Dr Kenny? Did you find my name on that record at all? Like I said, I couldn't find myself when I was searching at home."

"Sorry, Mr Clarke. You weren't on there at all. Neither registered born or died, either in Kilportach or elsewhere. I agree with you, it's very odd. Actually, who I am kidding? It's bloody mysterious, that's what it is!"

"You said it!"

It was enough to give me food for thought as I entered the old MRI scanner. So in the space of a week my family, as well as two other people had died in the town, including one who was murdered. I instantly began to think elaborate plots, tried to imagine just what could have happened. I was also concerned with why I was still not on the registers. My own mind was as good as useless; I knew nearly nothing about my upbringing. I only remembered my Father, and even then not a great amount. My birth certificate states I was born in England, but I must have been here with my parents at some point. It was like an entire chunk of my childhood; the part of it spent in Kilportach no less, didn't exist in memory or record.

I laid back whilst thinking of it, and allowed the bed to propel me into the scanner. A slight mechanical sound ensued, like belts and gears smoothly purring as I disappeared within. I can't say that I was happy to be there, but I had already agreed to go through with it. Inside, the spherical tube was lit by a blueish light, which faded away as I closed my eyes to concentrate on my research. I felt nothing, and all I could hear was a slight humming noise and Kenny typing away in the office. I was not afraid of what the scan might find, but more concerned about how they would 'treat' it.

The Wishing Lake – Mark Robinson

The Wishing Lake

It was midday when I got out of Kenny's surgery. The MRI was painless enough, just a lot laying still and thinking to myself. He said the results would be there in the morning, and so clearly I should come back and see him then. It was an unexpected experience, for sure, but at least Kenny had given me the first real clues towards my family research. Of course, I was no closer to finding anything, but knowing of the murder and mystery death was something concrete I could look into. I wondered if they could be related, somehow.

For the time being though, I had ventured back onto the main row of shops and found the pub now showing an open sign. Outside, an A-Board was standing with chalk writing, saying simply *'Open – Food served till 2.30'*. I wasn't really hungry, but I imagined the pub would be a good place to meet the people who lived in town. I decided to have a look inside.

As I opened the stained glass door, I imagined the place being empty and dark. I was right, as well. A number of wooden tables were sat on the carpet, yet not a single customer was eating or drinking. I could smell food though, so I knew the place was open. I walked to the bar, the usual selection of spirits and beers displayed in a colourful line behind it.

It took a while, but the bartender finally noticed I was there, and came into the room from an open door at the back. It was a woman, about 50 I'd say, sporting a blue dress and collection of jewellery. She had long, straight black combed hair, and a pale white complexion like she never saw daylight.

"Afternoon", she said. "How can I help you?"

"You are open, right?"

"Ha, yeah, we're open. I know, not exactly lively in here, is it?"

She gave me a menu and asked what I was drinking. I went all out and ordered a Tullamore Dew, large, and took the menu to a table to read. Most of it was standard pub food material; the fried breakfast, the pie and chips. I didn't feel like eating any of it, but I thought I'd order something anyway. It was few minutes until she came back, and by that time I'd wet my throat with the whiskey and put my episode with Kenny to the back of my mind.

"So, decided what you'll be having?"

"Just a sandwich, I think. Chicken, please, with salad."

"Coming up!"

I was surprised to see the place empty at midday. Even in the quietest of town's I've visited, pubs still manage to pull in the people when it's lunchtime and they're serving meals. It was almost disheartening to see the pub empty, even though I'd usually prefer it to be so.

The place itself though was crooked yet comfortable. An open fire danced healthily against the wall, and a number of photographs were hung showing the town and it's people in days long passed. It was old looking and filled with character, like it had at one time been the heart of the town. Above the bar, carved wood lettering spelt out the name of the pub; *'The Wishing Lake',* and below it hung many old pewter drinking mugs.

It reminded me of the leaflet I had picked up earlier from the tourist office. It was about Kilportach's myths and legends, and also had a picture of a lake on the cover. While waiting for the food to arrive, I decided to unfold it and glance at it's contents.

'Famous as the home of the mummified bog men, Kilportach is a town which although quiet, has more than it's fair share of myths and folklore. Originally the site of a Celtic settlement, the town was built to house the families of those who worked in the surrounding peat bog. It grew with the Christianisation of Ireland, and gradually the Celtic roots of the town were all but erased by the spread of the Church. Even so, the town was still steeped in tradition and folklore, and no amount of modern Religion could fully stamp out the old tales of it's forebears.

Perhaps the most famous surviving myth relates to the lake in the north end of town. Known as 'The Wishing Lake', this ancient lough is believed by some to fulfil the wishes of all who visit it. Townsfolk would tell the lake of their troubles; often throwing in coins or gifts to assure their issues would be resolved. It soon became a place of pilgrimage, with people looking for spiritual peace coming to Kilportach to visit the lake.

The legend is believed to have originated with the Celtic people who first settled here. According to oral tradition, the people who lived here suffered ill fortune, with bad crops and illness befalling their community. A beautiful maiden who lived in the settlement saw how bad things had become, and summoned the people to meet her one night, offering to share with them a secret. When everyone was present, she revealed that she was in fact a Selkie; a seal-faery who could be human or seal by simply changing her skin. She said that she was upset at the state of the settlement, and thus would return to her seal form and go to live within the lake. However, she was willing to help anyone who asked her, so long as they left her a gift at the lakeside. The people did this, and so the Selkie maiden often returned, taking her gifts and granting help to all who were kind enough to seek her.

Today, The Wishing Lake has been overshadowed by the recent discovery of Kilportach's bog bodies. However, visitors in town to see the mummies would do well to remember the lake and it's story. It's a place of outstanding natural beauty, and is sure to leave all visitors to it with a profound sensation of peace. And who knows, throw in a coin and the Selkie maiden might see it her duty to grant your wish!'

"Here we are", I was interrupted. "One chicken salad. Is that OK for you?"

"Great, thanks."

I put the leaflet back in my pocket. The woman disappeared behind the bar, leaving me to contemplate the large sandwich in front of me. It was as I'd expected, fresh bread and cold, crispy lettuce; the chicken real and thickly cut, unlike the reformed efforts of supermarkets.

Truthfully, I was more interested in an image which had appeared in my mind whilst reading the leaflet. It was the photograph of my Mother; the only real memory I had of her. On the photo, she is wearing a silver mermaid necklace, standing out brightly against her skin. I know it well; I had kept that photo close to me for as many years as I remember. I would often wonder just who she was, what she would have been like to know? That necklace was the only thing I knew about her, and the old folklore story reminded me of it.

I slowly ate the chunky sandwich, stopping periodically to wash it down with tiny sips of the Irish whiskey. The pub was still empty, with not so much as a background noise to accompany me as I ate. It was bitter-sweet; as I was free from the company of noisy customers, yet there also was nobody there to help with my research. Still, I was at least free to eat without distraction.

That was until the barmaid decided to join me before I had finished eating, of course. She walked from the bar and over to my table, and to my discomfort sat straight opposite me.

"Visiting town then, are you?"

I was already fed up with having to explain to every person why I was there. I realised that this was a close nit ghost-town, and that I was seemingly the only outsider, but I wished sometimes to be just left alone. That said, though a misanthrope I may have been, I knew I would have to retrieve information from the people who lived in this silent town. So, I told her why I'd came to Kilportach, sparing her most of the sordid details.

"So, your family lived here in the town then?"

"I assume so. I don't know anything about it, really. I was only a kid when they died."

"Sorry. Well look, I'm Molly, anyway. I'm the landlady of this thriving establishment."

"Is it always like this?"

"Always has been. People don't really do much in town, not these days anyway. It's all half day closing and early nights. If people didn't come here to see the bog people, I'd probably have closed the place down years back. You've seen the bodies, right?"

"Yeah."

She proceeded to tell me, whilst managing to hardly pause for breath, her own theory on the famous bog people. According to her, the bodies were criminals thrown in the bog after they were executed by the courts. It made sense, apart from Kenny's observation of the identical head wounds on all the bodies. I told her I had no idea myself; that I had found the remains to be suitably curious, but had not guessed as to why they were killed.

"Yeah", she said. "I guess we'll never really find out for sure. So anyway, how's the family tree hunting going? Find anything since you've been here?"

"Only more questions. They all died on the same day, you see. I wanted to find out what happened to them. Anyway, it turns out they weren't the only ones who died back then; there was somebody else...and a murder, apparently. At this point, I don't know what's related and what isn't, unfortunately."

"You don't mean Mr Cullen, do you?" She leaned forward, looking somewhat shocked. I picked out a piece of scrunched note paper from my pocket, where I had written the info Kenny had given me.

"Shane Cullen. That's it. You know about it?"

"Do I know? Good god, I do." She got up, and walked back over to the bar. There, she began to ferret through a drawer. "I used to live in the town back then, you see. Well, I'd just gotten married and we were moving to Cork. Ah, here it is."

She brought to the table a slightly blurred photograph of herself along with two other men. She was much younger, early twenties, and one of the men had his arm around her. The other, dressed in rough overalls with a bald head and glasses, was leaning on a shovel and posing in the middle of the picture.

"That's Mr Cullen", said Molly, pointing to the man by the shovel. "God, this was taken only a few days before...well, you know. We left for Cork on the same day, so it's not like I could ever forget".

"You left town on the day he was killed?"

"We did. It's like it was yesterday, really. The town was in an uproar; everyone shouting and crying and that. And just before we left, we were told what had happened. Mr Cullen had been murdered, found dead near his own home. Christ, I mean who would..."

The photo captured my attention. A frozen moment in time; it would have been taken whilst my family were still in town. It was like a glimpse into what I was seeking; the Kilportach of 30 years ago, before any of them had died. Furthermore, it was interesting to think that the man in the middle, Shane Cullen, was killed only days after posing for the photo. He looked happy, like he had no idea just what was waiting but a few short days into the future. How could he?

Still, Molly and the photo were the first real insights I'd had into what happened 30 years ago. Chances were she had encountered my family as well. I picked up my drink, tipped it back in one sharp gulp, and didn't hesitate to ask her.

"Look, according to this Dr Kenny I saw, Cullen was killed a week before my parents and Brother died. Do you know anything about that?"

"Well, I might do. If you tell me your surname, that is!"

"Oh yeah, sorry." I had been deliberately vague with my info; not wanting to spill the entirety of my story to strangers of whom I had never seen. That said, she was the most help I'd had so far, so I put my natural retainment behind me.

"It's Clarke. I'm Leonard, and my parents were Lucas and Ethel. There was an Edward too. My Brother, I think."

"Edward Clarke? Yeah, I knew him!"

"You do?"

She took the photograph in her hands, and took another poignant glance, as if bitter-sweet memories had just came to her. She then looked over her shoulder, focusing on another picture hanging in a frame on the wall of the pub.

"You see that picture, there, as well?" She pointed.

I stood up, walked to the photo so that I could see it better. It was black and white, showing a small wooden cabin in front of a large tree, standing on top of a grassy hill. Beside it, I could just about see a body of water, reflecting the tree and the cabin within it.

"That was Mr Cullen's shack", said Molly. "He worked in the park near the lake, you see. Well, I used to often see him with young Edward then. He was always playing in the park."

"This is the lake the pub is named after? The Wishing Lake?"

"Yeah. God, the town was so different back then. They'd just started finding the bodies in the bog, and people were coming from miles away."

She got up from the table, stood at my side and joined me in looking at the photograph. She seemed to be pleased by telling me her memories, like the kind of person who would jump at a chance to show you their family photo albums. I usually hated hearing other people's lives, but at that point I didn't care. She said she had known my Brother Edward, and that's all I wanted to know about.

"Anyway", she continued, looking up at the lakeside photograph. "I remember that Edward Clarke quite well. You see, there was only two children in the town back then."

"Two children? In the whole town?"

"Heh. Well like I said, the place has always been stupidly quiet. So yeah, only two children. There was Edward Clarke, and another girl. I didn't really know her though."

I was about to speak, but a clock on the wall struck 1pm, it's chime echoing in the still empty pub.

"One o'clock!" said Molly, walking instantly back to the bar. "Mr Clarke, look I'm sorry but I'll have to get the food on for tonight. Tell you what, come back later eh? We can have a good chat."

"Your cooking the food yourself?"

"Landlady, chef, cleaner-upper....God, who could I employ around here, anyway?"

"I guess your right. So I'll come back tonight?"

"Any time."

She seemed agitated by being late with her cooking. What she had told me though was definitely interesting. If there were only two children in the town 30 years back, then I was clearly not one of them. So where was I, if not in Kilportach with my parents? None of it was making sense. However, I had at least found some real information. This Shane Cullen seemed to know my Brother, and another girl also lived in the town, who was friends with Edward before he died. Who was she? And why was this Shane Cullen murdered? My mind raced with ideas and thoughts, but none of it resulted in anything other than more questions. All I knew for sure was that 30 years ago, something happened in Kilportach. Something which led to the deaths of my family, as well as Cullen and this other mystery person.

I had a feeling that Molly could tell me more, and so before leaving I told her again that I'd return to the pub this coming evening. I also asked her about the cemetery, of which she happily gave me directions to.

Leaving the pub, I felt this town was hiding more than just the bodies in the peat bogs. It had a history; the kind of history that never fades, but clings to the walls of it's buildings and street sides. It was the sort of thing one could almost feel, like the houses themselves knew all that had happened, and those memories pulsed from their brickwork exteriors. I could sense it, as I followed her directions towards the old graveyard. It was like all my answers were waiting there, just sleeping and hoping they would one day be found.

•

Eternal Home

I have always enjoyed spending time in cemeteries. They embodied almost everything I found of interest, so many curiosities contained in one place. They are often the sole place of peace in the midst of a city; enclosed in their own solemn atmosphere, set apart from all else around them. Indeed, I would often visit a cemetery by choice, with no graves to tend or funerals to go to. I simply enjoyed exploring their pathways, alone with only the singing birds and marble memories of time.

Moreover, cemeteries usually contained 'hidden places', or even were in themselves such a place. Certainly, in order to be a 'hidden place', an area must be alive with feeling, yet enclosed and seldom seen by the masses. In that respect, cemeteries are easily classified as such. They each contain secret and crumbling corners, ornaments left to the passage of time, and air alive with a poignant ambience.

Kilportach cemetery was exactly as I'd expected. A rusted gate on the outskirts of town led into an overgrown, forgotten graveyard. Most stones were tilted and badly decaying, their epitaphs all but faded away, leaving nothing but deserted memories. The grass was wet and had not been cut for months, and although it was fairly large in size, not one grave was tended with flowers or tributes. Like everything else I had seen in Kilportach, it felt like it didn't belong in a town, but more in a sleepy and tiny village.

I began to trudge though the tall grass and gravestones, looking for any names of my family, or indeed anything that would help me at all. A hot feeling seemed to ring in my head; like the cold air hitting me after the whiskey. I knew I shouldn't have drunk it, not so soon after what happened with Kenny. Still, I was in the place I had most wanted to see, and so the thought of another upcoming headache was swiftly put to the back of my mind.

A number of larger graves stood out above the rest, familiar statues of angels and crosses, embossed with names of what I assumed were the rich or important in the town. So far though, nothing had struck me as belonging to my family. Of course, most stones had hardly no writing visible, and those which did were badly faded. That said, I was still enjoying my cemetery visit.

One thing which always struck me as interesting was that every gravestone was from a different time frame. Standing over a grave, I was standing in the same place as relatives had gathered, where emotions were high and tears were shed. Furthermore, graves were like capsules in time themselves. They were filled back in and then forgotten; never disturbed or seen again. Underneath, it was forever the date they were dug and filled in, like six foot cocoons where time didn't flow.

Such abstract thinking was likely what drew me to visiting cemeteries in the first place. My foster family; the Ford's, whilst providing a home and decent upbringing, were intellectual savages. To them, life was not meant to be thought about; it was above and beyond their level of reason. They viewed life as a social blueprint, a somewhat odious check-list of experiences, where everyone should just strive to tick the boxes. I hated it, even as a child. I had no interest in social politics or rat races. Life was short and designed to enjoy. I knew this first-hand after losing my parents. Because of this, my relationship with the Ford family was strained from the offset. I would not say I hated them, but I did not respect them, even then.

I forever tried to get away, to hide from their insistent ethical interference. This is probably what got me started with the 'hidden places', and the cemeteries followed soon after. More so, I found that whilst in the midst of loss, people were often at their most genuine. The people I saw weeping by gravestones were likely not bothered by the concerns of my fosters, and rightly so. I always felt more at home with objects than people, anyway.

Kilportach cemetery, though, was nothing like the ones I would visit back then. It was uncared for, forgotten by the people and left to crumble. I had found nothing of help nor of interest, just weathered memorials and damaged stones. My head was hurting too, that hot feeling gradually resulting in tiredness, my eyes feeling heavy and difficult to focus. A headache was coming on.

I stopped underneath a tree to rest, leaning against it and taking deep breaths. I comforted myself with thoughts of returning to Molly in the pub later on, or attempting to feel the energy of the cemetery like I usually did when I came to them. As always though, the onset of the headache dominated my thoughts, quickly resulting in a nauseous sensation which writhed in my stomach and my mind. Thankfully, the air was cold; I could feel it enter my lungs as I inhaled, momentarily calming the coming pain.

It was not long though, before it started to happen. I heard someone call my name from behind, and when I turned to find there was nobody there, the familiar shooting pain fell across me. For the time, I stayed underneath the tree in the graveyard, not wanting to move and worsen the throb. I took a pill, of course. But it would take a while to settle in properly, and until then I could only stand there and wait.

At one point, I looked up after staring down at the ground, and saw what I could only describe as a 'thing' in my mind. It was stood in front of one of the gravestones, like a grey light or formation of mist, elongated yet without a shape. I found it hard to concentrate on, my eyes darting around and blurring, like I was not supposed to be looking at it. It definitely felt like it was 'there' though; a few hundred feet from where I was stood. I couldn't help but stare towards it, even though it hurt my eyes to see it.

There was a flash, too. A bright white flash before my eyes. After, I realised I couldn't hear anything. It was like the breeze had stopped completely, the birds had stopped signing, the grass stopped swaying. I'm not even sure if I was breathing at all. I just continued to look at the shape, tried to focus as it stood by the headstone.

When my hearing came back, but a few seconds after I had realised it gone, I heard something speaking from inside. I will not say it was in my head; as it felt more like it was in my whole body, the muscles twitching as it rumbled throughout them. I don't know what it was saying though. It was like many voices, all shouting or talking at once, like they were trying hard to make themselves heard.

I remember I felt a distinct sensation; that of sorrow and a sudden sadness. It was accompanied by the usual goosebumps in the back, and came on without a warning or reason. However, whilst standing and staring at that motionless thing, I felt at once unsettled and unusually depressed.

I also must have fallen, maybe even lost consciousness again as I had in Kenny's office. For the next thing I knew I was knelt on the ground, my arms outstretched and supporting my body, as if I had fallen face first to the ground. I looked up, and everything was back to how it was. There were no voices, no shape by the gravestone. My head still throbbed though, bringing with it a nauseous feeling which simmered restlessly in my stomach. I took in a few breaths, tried to focus my eyes as I usually did with these episodes.

I am not aware of how long I spent there on the ground, but I can clearly remember being properly 'woken up'. It slowly came to my attention that someone was behind me. At first, I thought it was the shape from before, and I quickly turned round with a frightened gasp. But it was a person. A real person.

A woman. She was standing under the tree behind me, looking down at my pitiful condition. I pushed myself upwards, got to my feet with a slight throb of dizziness.

"You OK?"

I had to force myself to speak, my breathing still heavy and my head still pounding. In fact, I wasn't sure that I hadn't lost consciousness again, or indeed whether I was even awake.

"Yeah", I said. "I'll be alright in a minute. I think. I just need to rest, or something, that's all."

"You look pretty rough. You feeling ill?"

"I just need to sit down, like I said."

I tried once more to take deep breaths, as to stop myself from throwing up. The woman just stood and looked at me. She had very light blonde hair, which looked almost white or pink at first glance. It was long and curled, falling across her face. She wore an ill fitting, tan brown coat, and below it a pair of short black shorts; her legs bare save for a set of brown boots. She stood still, stared at me as I focused my eyes, still feeling a little languid and faint.

"If your that bad, I'll show you somewhere to sit down, OK?"

I had no idea what she was meaning. True, I had noticed the cemetery had no benches, but I was planning on simply sitting under the tree as soon as she saw fit to leave me alone. Of course, she seemed to have other plans.

"Come on, you can walk, right? Follow me then, I'll show you."

She stood for a second more simply watching me, then beckoned me to follow her as she started to walk. I am not in the habit of following strangers, and my headache shot pain through my mind at the very thought of walking around. Of course, though a deep sigh and head-shake came with it, I felt helplessly compelled to follow her advice. I was hardly in a state for anything else. At least she could help should I pass out completely. Or so I thought, anyway.

So, I slowly walked behind her, through the uncut grass and rows of gravestones. She didn't speak, just traipsed through the cemetery. I was unsure whether she was trying to be friendly or not, or indeed where she had came from in the first place. When I first entered the abandoned cemetery, nobody was there at all. In fact, being on the quietest edge of town, I had not even heard a human voice, even in the distance, since finding my way there. Who was she?

After a while, she came to a stop by a large stone angel statue. It was up on a ledge, displaying an angel peering upwards, holding onto a large cross relief. She was dressed in a loose and well carved dress, and bore on her face a doleful expression.

At the side of the monument, some steep steps led down to a thick looking wooden door below. It appeared to be one of those walk-in crypts, an expensive and rich underground structure, built only for the most wealthiest of families.

"Here we are", said the woman, before beginning to walk down the steps in front of her.

"What?"

"Just come on, will you?"

My mind was already muddled from the headache, and now she wanted me to walk into a crypt. I didn't trust her.

"Why down there?" I said as she fiddled with the hefty and strong looking door.

"Are you coming in or not? You'll see when your inside."

It was unbelievable. She had mentioned taking me to a place I could rest, but an underground crypt was quite bewildering. Incredibly though, she produced a key from the pocket of her coat, and actually opened the door in front of her. She asked me once more to come inside, and then disappeared into the blackness. I will admit, my curiosity got the better of me. I assumed that she must have worked in the cemetery, and her gesture of kindness was at the expense of respecting the dead she was supposed to look after. It was all so bizarre.

Still, I was not about to simply walk away. Carefully I stepped on the old stone steps, and begun to walk to the door below. Above the stairs, affixed to the ledge that the angel stood on, I paused to read an epitaph carved into marble.

'Erected by her loving & sorrowful sister
in affectionate memory of Catherine Elder

Died 18th October 1901

She opened her mouth in wisdom,
and on her tongue was the law of kindness'

The grave was clearly untended and forgotten, being likely that no family still lived to see it. I had often passed these elegant tombs, the kind of memorial which stands above all the other stones in the cemetery. I had even looked at the doors to the crypt, imagined just what was lying beyond. But I had never even dreamed I would find myself inside one for real. If anything, it actually helped to take my mind from my headache.

That said, nothing could truly prepare me for what I discovered behind that door. I had imagined a darkened and musty room, filled with cobwebs and a decaying coffin. But upon reaching the bottom of the stairs, and peering into that underground tomb, I was met with an instant and marked sense of sheer astonishment.

It was a small square room, lined with crude brickwork and falling earth, a heavy scent of decay in the air. To my amazement though, it was not simply containing a coffin or even the usual funerary objects. It was fully decorated.

There was a bed in the corner; a fold-up type with a thin, hospital like mattress. There was a wooden table against the wall, filled with papers and stacks of books, a folding chair placed underneath it. Many shelves jutted from the walls, each crammed full of ornaments and items, looking like they could fall off at any second. There were china figures, cups and saucers, even vases with flowers in them. On the desk, a lamp was lit with a bright light bulb, casting the room in a harsh, yet still shadowy glow.

"Close the door, then", said the woman. I agreed, closing the heavy door behind me. As I did so, all noises of birds and the outside breeze were instantly muted behind it's weight.

"What is this?" I asked, actually feeling a little unsettled.

"You wanted a place to sit down. This is it.". She sat on the bed, the springs creaking as she did, like they were old and thus uncomfortable and damaged.

"No. I meant this. This place, what is it?"

"Oh, I live here". Her tone was short, like she didn't care to make small conversation or explain her every move. I knew how she felt, but I was still in a state of curious awe.

"You mean you work in the cemetery?" I said.

"No. I just live here. Look, sit on there if you want." She leaned over and pulled out the chair from under the desk. Of course, I didn't hesitate to sit upon it. The pill was starting to take effect; the shooting pain in my face gone, leaving only a heavy feeling in my head.

"Stay as long as you want", she continued. "Just let me know, right?"

I didn't know what to say. She said nothing more, just picked up a book from on top of the bed, and lounged back as she started to read it. I could have said a thousand things; near shouted out at this place's bizarreness. But I didn't. I just wanted the headache to go away, and for that, I knew that I needed to sit still.

I did however take another look around the room. The lamp behind me seemed to be wind-up, a key shaped handle extending from it. At the foot of the bed, an untidy pile of clothing was laying in a heap, and a number of drawings were hung on the wall. They were mostly pencil, all depicting fairies or bird like creatures.

In the corner of the room nearest to the door, I was taken aback by what I saw there. It was the coffin, stood upright and leaning against the wall. It seemed in relatively good condition; solid oak and with brass or gold handles. It looked so wrong propped up in the corner.

Still, I didn't need any more confusion or annoyance. The woman was silent and reading her book, and so I bent over, putting my head in my hands. I closed my eyes, and the headache quickly started to ease. It was so quiet down there, with not even the falling crumble of earth daring to disturb it's stillness. With that and my eyes closed, it was like nothing even existed at all. All I could see were the shapes in my mind, and a moist, earthy odour began to fill my lungs.

I remained like that for quite a while, staying as still as I could until my head returned to somewhat normality. She hadn't spoken to me during that time. When I opened my eyes, she was still slumped on the bed, occasionally turning the page of her book, and nothing more. It was one of those rare moments; a moment where I didn't know what to think. Did she really live down there? The bed and the clothes made me think that she did, as did the collection of ornaments and drawings. But it felt all wrong, so much so that it actually worsened my nausea.

It was around that time when I noticed it. Truthfully, I can hardly believe it took me so long, but most likely my headache had taken over all of my thoughts. Indeed, I had to look twice to make sure that the dingy, eccentric room was not playing tricks with my eyes. But it was definitely there. Around her neck, she was wearing a silver mermaid necklace. It was the exact one. The one that my Mother was wearing on the photograph.

"Hey", I said, breaking the silence. "That necklace. Where did you get it?"

"This?" She put down the book and sat upright. "Someone gave it to me. Why?"

"I...I know it. Who gave it to you?"

"Just someone I knew. I take it your feeling better, then?"

She didn't sound like she wanted to talk. That necklace though, it was definitely the same. Even though it was likely a different one, it was still unique in style. I had never seen the same one in anything other than the photograph. It was like my past; my only reason for being there to start with, was drawn to me by my simple presence in town. Or perhaps it was just mocking me. Either way, I had to know. This woman, and the situation of which we met, were far too unusual to not find alluring.

"Look. Yeah, I'm feeling better now. Thanks for letting me sit down here. You said you lived here?"

"Yes. Anyway if your feeling better, I'll let you get on your way."

She stood up as to walk to the door with me. I stood up too, knowing I needed to get through to her.

"Sorry. I couldn't ask you something, could I?"

"What?" She turned around to face me. "I don't really want to. I just thought you looked ill, so I brought you here to rest. I didn't want a conversation."

"Me neither", I replied, laughing inside as she sounded just like myself. "But you brought me in here. The least you could do is tell me what this place is, right? Don't worry, I have no interest in social chitchat either. Anything but."

"Heh, OK". She walked past me, sat back down on the bed. "My name's Amelia. I live here, like I said."

"Why here?" I sat back on the chair.

"I just do. I won't lie to you; I just don't like most people, OK? I choose to be here, to stay away from it all."

"Why?"

"Stop asking why. There's nothing wrong with me, if that's what you think. I don't ask to be liked."

She delivered her words with an angered tone, but what she was saying was strangely identifiable. I had to get her to talk somehow, to share what she knew about this town and my past. She had to know something, and that necklace was proof of it. Moreover, I agreed with what she was saying. I may not have been as extreme as she seemed, but I understood her cynicism. I was never outward about my feelings, but I didn't encourage my dislikes either. Her assumption that I thought something was 'wrong' with her was somewhat comforting, in a bizarre sort of way. I felt the same way; our whole race was bigoted and seldom accepted people.

"Don't worry", I said, attempting to calm her and get her to talk. "I don't blame you. I agree, anyway."

"About what?"

"Wanting to live away from the world. That's what you meant, isn't it?"

"Not the world. Just people in it. I don't have time for it. All the politics, the social ladders. It's complete crap, and I can't believe people don't realise it."

"Tell me about it. They live their whole lives in...well, a bubble, don't they? And where do they end up, in the end? The...well, the graveyard, I was going to say."

She laughed aloud. "I know. This place is ironic in a way, right? I like it like that though. What's your name, then?"

"Leonard Clarke".

I finally felt I was loosening her up. Not that I was acting by false pretences. It actually felt good to be able to speak what I really thought about topics like that. I did not hate people as she may have done, but I was far from keen on their mediocre minds. At one time, their stupidity would drive me to bouts of deep anger, but I learned to simply accept them as being there. Anyway, she was now talking to me and that's what I wanted. It wasn't long before she came out with something interesting.

"Clarke, you say?"

"You know my surname?"

"The Clarke's used to live here when I was a child. Are you from the town?"

"I'm here looking up my family tree. You knew the Clarke family? Then tell me."

She stood up, walked to the pile of clothes by the bed, started searching around.

"I had a photo somewhere. Probably can't find it now. Anyway, I was only a kid. I used to know someone called Edward Clarke, though. He lived here in the town."

"That's who I'm looking for! He was my Brother, although, I never knew him for some reason. Your telling me you actually knew him?"

"I just said I did."

She threw her clothes around looking for the photo, then shook her head and stood back up.

"Can't find it right now. I had a picture somewhere, never mind. Anyway, this is probably a different Clarke family."

"Why?" I stood up, walked over to her so that we were both stood in the middle of the room.

"Edward Clarke didn't have a Brother. Besides, they're all dead. I didn't even know until years later. They didn't think a kid worth telling, I suppose."

"What happened to them?"

I was starting to get aggravated. Every answer I received just led to more mysteries. She knew Edward, and said that he was an only child. But had I really come looking for the wrong Clarke family? Impossible, I thought. It had to be right, something was just missing; something which explained why I wasn't there. How could I have a birth certificate but not be registered on any records? I wondered if Kilportach really did hold the answers.

"I don't know how they died", continued Amelia. "Anyway, why would I tell you? If your here to research things, find out yourself."

"I would if I knew where I was going. It's not like most people are capable of helping, right?"

"Your right there. People only ever want to help themselves."

"I know, your right" I said. "I'm not asking for your help, anyway. Just something to point me in the right direction. I mean, you did know Edward Clarke, didn't you?"

"Yeah. Look, why don't you go to the Wishing Lake? That's where it happened, apparently."

She once more climbed onto her bed, this time laying out fully on it, and picking up the book from before.

"What, you mean that's where he died?"

"So I was told". She opened the book. "You want to search around, go and have a look there. I don't know anything."

At last, I had gotten some information from her. That said, I felt she still knew a lot more than what she was saying. But I didn't want to ruin my chances of getting more info; so I decided against badgering her any more, when it was clear she had grown tired of talking. I wouldn't have liked someone asking too many questions to me, either.

But I did have something I could now say I'd found out. Plus, my headache had all but gone. I said my goodbyes to Amelia then, and thought it best to leave the tomb. I was not sure whether my headache would return, and was thus wary of exploring any more today. But I had made a start, and had already found out new snippets of info regarding whatever happened in the town. There was a long way to go though, I knew this for certain.

Either way, I opened the heavy crypt door and was more than pleased to feel fresh air again. It had crossed my mind why she approached me in the first place, but when leaving the tomb, I was glad that she had. Still, it was definitely a mystery. So, after leaving the tomb, and just as I was closing the door, I called back to her for a final time.

"By the way. Thanks, Amelia."

A New Discovery

My second night in the B&B passed without complication. I decided against returning to the pub, finding myself not in the mood for more drinks and stories from Molly. I could always go back the next day.

That's not to say I slept too well. I spent most of my time taking notes, correlating what I had learnt so far and where I could try to visit in the morning. At that point, everything seemed to be related to Edward. Molly from the pub said that she remembered him, and that he was one of only two children in the town back then. So then this other child was probably Amelia, who claimed she knew Edward from when she was young. She was also wearing that wonderful necklace; the silver mermaid from my Mother's portrait, and obviously knew more than she was willing to tell. And then there was this Shane Cullen, the man who was murdered, and of course the question of what killed my family.

Anyway, I made up a list of things to do. I would revisit Kenny first of all; I wanted to know if he'd discovered anything after that unexpected brain scan. Afterwards, I'd go to the pub and see Molly again, and hopefully find this 'Wishing Lake' I'd heard about. I may not have found a lot on my first day; but one thing was for sure; Kilportach was already full of mysteries.

My head was still full of the day's events, even long after I had fallen asleep. Thankfully, nothing untoward seemed to happen, and morning came without another headache or nocturnal disturbance. I didn't get up until fairly late though; finding it easier to actually sleep in the early morning than through the night. I don't know why.

That said, the promise of another of the B&B's breakfast's was not exactly tempting me to get out of bed. The owner was friendly enough I suppose; but the state of the place told another story. Indeed, when I came in last night she was not even there, the reception desk empty like the place was abandoned. Later on though she knocked on my door, asking if I wanted cups of tea or dinner. I risked the tea, but didn't fancy her cooking again so soon. Still, she didn't make a fuss about it, just disappeared back downstairs and left me alone to my notebook. I was still the only guest there, as well.

Of course, when I finally got up and got myself dressed; I could already smell the scent of bacon downstairs. Still, I thought it would be a good time to talk to her, if only to see what she knew about the people I had encountered the day before.

Something had happened though. Almost as soon as I entered the kitchen, my eyes catching the soggy breakfast on the table, Bridget burst into conversation.

"Ah, there you are", she said, "You haven't heard, have you?"

"What?"

"They found another body! Pulled it out late last night apparently. Jack phoned me first thing this morning about it. I just had to tell you!"

"You mean another mummy, from the bogs?"

She nodded her head, visibly excited that this had happened whilst her 'guest' was staying in the B&B. I was taken aback, but instantly interested. I remembered seeing a tractor in the bog when I first arrived at the guest house. Could it have been digging out the body, even as I slept but a short distance from it?

"You have to go see it", continued Bridget. "Jack said they've got it on show in the bog. You can go have a look and see what it looks like."

"I definitely will."

"You do that, dear. I might even go have a look myself, later in the day, of course. But still, don't you think it's exciting and all? They just keep on finding them, like there really are hundreds in there. Jack was ecstatic when he rang me about it."

"Yeah, I admit it is quite something. I saw some of the bodies yesterday with Dr Kenny. I can see why people come here to see them".

I started to eat the breakfast in front of me. Whether it tasted bad or not, her news had temporarily filled my thoughts. There was no doubting that the bodies were a spectacle, and the fact that more were still out there was incredible just to imagine. I had not yet seen the bogs up close, but this news was sure to make me go there. I already imagined a fresh bog body; laying in the wet marsh it was discovered in, bent and crippled like the ones Kenny had shown me.

"By the by", she continued before I could attempt to speak. "I'm sure some new visitors will show up now, you know. To see our new find, I mean. You never know, some of them might help you."

It was true that the body would likely bring visitors. Truthfully, I would have liked to see the town with a few more people, even if I had no reason to talk to them. As it stood, the whole place was far too close nit and quiet; I felt like the only outsider they had, and so all their eyes were instantly upon me. I hoped this new mummy would change that perspective, thus allowing me to snoop around in peace.

I finished the breakfast and thanked her for it, washing down the final mouthfuls with the lukewarm coffee I had nearly forgotten about. Just before leaving, I decided to ask her a question I had thought of, with the smallest of chances she would be able to help.

"Have you heard of a woman called Amelia, by the way? It's just that I met her yesterday, and was sort of wondering if-"

"Don't worry dear", she interrupted. "Most people here know about her. She's harmless, apparently."

"Right, harmless. So what do you know about her?"

"Well, I don't think there's much to say, my dear. She's like a hermit, something like that. You sometimes see her walking about, but she never talks to anyone. Bit of an oddball by all accounts."

"I don't care about that. Do you know her personally?"

"No. I don't think anyone really does. Honestly, I'm surprised you managed to see her at all. She actually spoke to you, you say?"

"Yeah."

It was annoying that Bridget was not prepared to discuss anything other than Amelia's eccentricity. I wanted to know if her story was genuine, whether she really did know my family as a child. Perhaps it was folly to expect such response; people were usually loathe to discuss any person they viewed as outside their 'box'. I was more than familiar with that kind of intolerance.

Anyway, it was worth a shot to see if Bridget knew anything. I thanked her again for the breakfast and drink, and swiftly left the B&B.

It was better weather than the day before. The sun was actually visible today, yet although it made the town look warm, there was still a cold chill in the air. Even so, the town centre was still as empty as ever, most shops closed up as they were yesterday, with just a handful of people walking around. I got a feeling that the town ran on a sleepy routine; like the shops always woke up at the same time, remained open for a only a few short hours, then comfortably closed for yet another day.

At one point I passed a hardware shop, the door locked up and a closed sign hung on it. Outside, two tables at the side of the large glass windows still had upon them tools and utensils, left out all night on the side of the pavement. It didn't appear to be just a mistake though; it felt like the owner left them out in trust, with the locals likely knowing him personally and the town empty from dusk until dawn. Indeed, it was like the town was run just for itself, the shops opened only for those who lived there, with no pressure of competition or image.

Leaving the main street, I tried to find my way to the bog so that I could see this latest find. As before, the streets soon jumbled into twisting terraces and I found myself unsure of just where I was going. Strangely, I found that the road signs didn't point to the bogs, an odd omission considering their supposed popularity. Instead, signs pointed just to the centre of town, and all other streets led round in circles and into silent suburban cul-de-sacs.

Eventually though, I found my bearings. The street I was stood on steeply descended, giving a spacious view of the of the outskirts of town. I could see the bogs there, spread out for miles against endless countryside, like the town just stopped and the bog took over. I made my way down the steep road towards it.

It was a longer walk than it looked at the top, but before too long I reached flat pavement which led straight into the peat bog area. It was almost like a seaside promenade; a pedestrianised street flanked by railings stood against the endless marshland. There were even information boards with pictures and text, and a few litter bins and wooden benches, all sat looking out at the peat bog fields.

It was obvious that any funds for the town's tourism were spent entirely on this part of town. It was a contradiction to everything else, like one clean room in an otherwise derelict house. Of course, the bogs themselves were a natural haven; sprawling wetlands filled with greenery and many circling, singing birds. There were no buildings to spoil the landscape, just swaying foliage giving way to glistening pools and undulations. I could easily imagine the extent of it's secrets.

I wasn't alone there, either. Unlike the rest of the town, a number of people were gathered on the street, standing around something I couldn't quite see. Getting closer though, and joining the group of around 15 people, I was quickly greeted by a macabre yet fascinating street-side display.

It was the new body, laid out on a narrow hospital trolley, clumps of wet peat still dripping from it. As before, a distinct jump shuddered inside me when I first caught sight of it's frightened expression. It's eyelids were closed, it's mouth wide open in a permanent scream. The skin was stained dark brown and rumpled, and the skeletal legs were bent upwards, frozen in an eternal discomfort. I also noticed that the arms were stumps; seemingly lost or cut off above the elbow.

I couldn't take my eyes away from it. Unlike the bodies I had seen in the surgery, this one was surrounded in the peat it was found in. I instantly began to imagine his fate. What brought him to this place where he died to begin with? It was strange to think that this object of attention was at one time a living human being. He would have had no idea of his future, that many years later his preserved body would be pulled from the bog and ogled at in public. It was enough to really make me think.

In fact, so entranced was I by the sight of the freshly found mummy, that I didn't even pay attention to the other people around me. It was not long though until someone put their hand on my shoulder, forcing me to turn from staring at the body. It was old woman from the tourist office.

"Sorry to bother you, Mr Clarke, was it?" She was dressed in another old fashioned outfit, this time a dark blue floral dress, complete with matching, ruffled handbag. She also wore another bonnet, more colourful than the one before, but still obscuring all of her hair.

"Ah, hello there."

"Mr Clarke. I hope you don't mind me asking, but I was just talking with a friend of mine. Have you perchance visited the town museum yet?"

"Oh, not yet. Sorry."

"I see. Well then, just a minute". She looked behind her and beckoned somebody over from the crowd. A man approached with short blonde hair and glasses, sporting a smart business style suit.

"Oh", she continued, "That's right. I have something to show you later, if you're interested. Might be of help for your family studies. Come to the office if you ever have time. You know where it is."

"Great. Thanks".

"OK. Now then," she turned to the man with the glasses, "Jack, this is the man she was telling you about. I'll leave you with him, OK?"

At that, the old woman smiled and left me with her acquaintance, then began to walk to the front of the crowd. I quickly glanced around at the bog body again, then turned to the man in front of me.

"Hi, Jack Daly", he said, extending his hand to mine.

"Leonard Clarke."

"Leonard, I see. Bridget was telling me you're a family researcher?"

"You mean Bridget from the B&B?"

"Yeah. We're friends and she mentioned you were staying there. Thing is, she didn't say what you looked like, so I asked Catherine to point you out!"

It was clear immediately that these people all knew each other. I remembered the name Jack mentioned at the B&B; and had wondered then who she was talking about. So Jack and Bridget were friends, it seemed. Moreover, he was obviously acquainted with the tourist centre woman, who he had mentioned was named Catherine.

In a way, the familiarity of all the townsfolk reminded me one of those awful 'neighbourhood watch' streets, where everyone poked their nose into the lives of those who lived there. As it stood though, I needed to meet as many people as I could, despite my distaste of their supposed gossip.

"So Bridget told you about me, did she?"

"She did. Well look, I don't think we can talk much now, but all I wanted to say is this. I'm the curator of the museum here in town. It's not a lot, but we have some records and files you might like. Pop round sometime if your passing, yeah?"

"Sure. Where will I find it?"

"The museum? It's just down there, really". He pointed across the street we stood on, past the bog body and to the end of the paved area. "It's just a small building, used to be an office for the workers in the peat bogs. You might find something in there to help you. Who knows."

"I'll try to come take a look sometime. Thanks a lot."

I made a mental note of the museum's location. Any news regarding genealogical files was of definite interest, and the museum would surely be intriguing anyway. I was also curious as to what she had found at the tourist office for me. When I went in last, it seemed nothing more than a badly lit room full of tourist leaflets of little use. Had she she really been looking for something that would help me? I doubted it, but I wondered what it could be anyway. I'd call in later after dinner, I told myself.

I looked at the body for a little while longer, before the chatter of the people fell to a hush as a figure appeared beside the body. It was Dr Kenny, dressed in the same white medical uniform and holding in his hands a clipboard. He stood by the back of the hospital bed, looking down at the mummified body. I remembered then; I needed to see him as soon as I could.

Still, there was no time for that at the moment. Kenny soon began to speak to the small crowd, raising his voice to make himself heard, forcing the people to stand still and listen. He began by introducing himself, then recited figures from the clipboard about the number of bodies found. It seemed to be miniature presentation; a small lecture for the townsfolk who had came to see the fresh bog mummy. After a while, he put down the clipboard on the bed, and began to point out the oddities of the remains.

"As you can see", he said. "The arms of this person are missing entirely. Now, this could have been due to a number of factors, but formations of tissue around the bone are telling us they were actually removed by force. Not only this, but the body has the same head wound as the others, as well as other signs of a struggle. It is thus very likely that this person was murdered, his body then thrown in the bog to dispose of, along with the many others we have found. The big question, of course, is why this would happen?"

I felt a noticeable shiver when listening to Kenny. I had always found myself thinking deeply, and the sight in front of me only heightened this trait. There was something unsettling about knowing the body was murdered. The expression on it's face was made even more alive; the pallid scream quite possibly formed from his final gasping breaths in this world. It was like some sort of cruel mistake; the body was supposed to have rotted away, yet the earth had preserved his every feature. It was almost like he had wished to be found; so that he could once more show the world his torment.

"And so", continued Dr Kenny. "Another bog man has been pulled from below us. Will he be the last we find in those marshes? Well, I'll leave that up to you. Either way, the body will be on display today, so feel free to take a closer look whenever you find the time. My colleague Dr Ryan will be here to answer your questions, so please, come and take a look."

Another man was present with Kenny, who took over speaking as Kenny stepped down. Then was my chance to speak with the doctor. Although I could have listened to the rest of the presentation, I didn't want to lose sight of Kenny. Those MRI results were something I wanted as soon as I could, if only to get them over and done with. So, I pushed past the crowd and walked by the body, reaching the doctor as he approached a white van.

He seemed to be actually pleased to see me. A quick handshake followed my greeting, and I congratulated him on the speech he had given. Of course, I didn't mull around with small talk. I just wanted to know if he had found anything on the MRI I had done yesterday.

"I did", he said. "I was going to ring you at the hotel, but you know, I got carried away with this."

"Wait, you actually found something on the scan?"

"Yes. Look, are you busy? I'm just heading back to the surgery for a bit. If you come along, I'll show you what I found."

Of course, I wasn't busy. The plan I had made for the day was pointless, seeing as already things had changed on their own. Besides, the results of this scan had been preying on my mind, especially after the increasing headaches. I quickly accepted the doctor's advice, and he offered me a lift in his van to the surgery.

I was all but silent on the way. I didn't predict that this would happen, but I got rapidly nervous about the result. Throughout my life, I had always tried to forget the headaches, to just take a pill and hope they would go away. The last thing I wanted was to be thinking of them, giving them attention and thus inflating them. I just got on with it; laying down until the pain subsided, then carrying on with life as usual. But now, I was sat in the van being driven to the doctor's, and I was finally going to find out about them.

I wanted to ask Kenny there and then, but he said nothing and I didn't ask him. I felt he wanted to actually show me, give me X-Rays or scans he had printed and tell me what was wrong up there. I didn't even want to know, not really. But I had allowed him to give me this MRI scan, and so I didn't have a choice but to find out. Still, I told myself it would all be gibberish, just medical blabber and a new course of pills. Still, I didn't want to argue.

It wasn't long until we arrived. During the trip, the only thing we spoke of was the mummy and it's fate, he didn't even mention the result until we got there. Was he trying to soften the blow? I wasn't sure. Soon though, Kenny switched off the engine, got out of the car and allowed me to follow. Without so much as a word of the scan, he led me once more through the empty surgery, and into the office where the MRI machine was.

"Right, take a seat then", he said as we entered.

As I did so, I felt my heart beating in my ears. I hated that feeling, and it was accompanied then by a deepening breath. I usually didn't get overly nervous, my emotions usually stopping at apathy, but this was different. I had thought a lot about getting this result. During the last headache, whilst sat with my eyes closed in Amelia's 'home', I had thought of almost nothing else. At that time, I just wanted to know what it was, even if it turned out I could do nothing about it. Later though, whilst lying in bed in that musty old room, I felt I didn't really want to find out at all. I just wanted to forget that I even had the headaches, and told myself the doctor would only worsen things.

Now, of course, there was no turning back. Kenny reached onto his desk full of papers, and removed a picture of which he handed to me.

It was a black and white scan of the side of my head, showing the brain in all it's detail. I had obviously seen such pictures before, but never one of *my own* grey matter. It felt, perhaps expectedly, peculiar. I soon noticed though that not all was perfect on the image. Near the top of my brain, a bit above the eyes and near to the back of the skull, an aberration was clearly visible. It looked like a like a dark smudge or smear, like a part of the image had not came out in the scan. It was fairly large, and it's shape appeared spherical yet irregular, like a dried stain where a liquid was spilt.

I felt myself swallow. I had never been too bothered by the threat of illness, but seeing it for real made my whole body sink. Something was wrong up there with my brain. I was staring at it, and it in turn stared back at me. It was a rare sensation for myself, but I actually felt physically unnerved.

"What is this?" I said to Kenny.

"OK. So that's the left side view of your MRI scan, right? Well like I said, I thought we'd be finding something."

"This...area here, you mean?" I showed him the part of the picture I referred to.

"Correct. Well Mr Clarke, I'm not sure there's really an easy way to explain this. Honestly though, I still can't believe you didn't get this done sooner."

"Just tell me what is it. Please."

"OK, OK. But it's not easy without seeing your prior medical records, you know. I mean, have you ever cut your head, or fallen badly, or something?"

"No. Not that I know of."

"Right. Well, this sort of thing doesn't just happen, you see. Usually, it would take a quite serious trauma to see such a result."

"I haven't had anything like that. Look, what is that shape on the scan? Just tell me, will you?"

"OK. Well look, it appears you have suffered from a traumatic brain injury, Mr Clarke."

I said nothing. The words he said just fell from his tongue like he was used to saying such things every day. To me though, it was part relieving and part confusing. I had wondered for years if a term existed to describe the headaches I was having, and there it was. But it didn't make sense. I had never had a trauma to my head, nor to any part of my body. I knew that Kenny was a professional, but I still wasn't sure about what he was saying.

"So, what's that mean?" I asked.

"Let me show you". He took the picture from me, held it up and pointed to the aberration. "This part here shows where an intracranial injury occurred. Basically, that means that something caused a trauma to that part of your head. I often see this after vehicle accidents, or particularly bad falls or violence. It can't be caused by anything other than direct trauma, you see."

"But I haven't had anything like that. Nothing at all."

"Well that's what I don't understand. You see, this TBI has been left untreated. Some of the brain tissue has actually died surrounding the remains of the original injury. There's no way that such a trauma could go unnoticed, Mr Clarke. In it's original state, it would have been a medical emergency."

I wasn't sure what he was trying to say. I had never suffered from a fall or head injury; let alone any medical emergencies. If that were so, I would have instantly known where the headaches were from, and not wondered what had caused them for all these years. One thing was for sure though; the scan Kenny held was proof that something was wrong. My brain tissue was dead and damaged; the obvious cause of the experiences I'd had. I could have stared at the scanned image for hours, but Kenny put it down and continued to ask me unwanted question after question.

"If you can't remember what caused it, it's possible your memory has become repressed. Sometimes you see, bad memories are blocked out by our brains in order to let us carry on with life. Do you think that could have happened to you?"

"No. The only part of my life I don't know about is before my parents died. But I'm not expected to, surely. I was just a child."

"I see. And yet you also told me you don't remember your Brother. And the memories of your parents deaths are obviously repressed. Mr Clarke, I think that's what were looking at here. I really do."

One thing I hated about doctors was that to them you were only a subject. I writhed as Kenny mentioned my family. They weren't a family of people to him, just another set of clues on his way to hooking me on treatment. In a way, I was pleased he had uncovered this 'thing' in my scan, but I wasn't happy at the coming consequences.

What truly hurt though was the realisation; there really were parts of my life that I knew nothing about at all. It was the reason I was there in that excuse for a town. The only memories I have of my parents are faded pictures and a single photograph. I had a Brother who I didn't even know, a fact I was sure was almost impossible. As much as I hated my life being dissected; Kenny really had hit on something. Could this injury have occurred as a young child too? What happened to me before my family died?

"So, what are you going to do about it?" I asked. "I'm not too keen on most treatments, you know."

"Don't worry. Those pills you have are about the limit, short of actual surgery, anyway. The only complication is what caused the injury, and how severe it was. You see, there's still a chance of long lasting damage here."

"But like I said, I really don't know what could have done this. Honestly Doctor, it's a bit of a shock as it is, you know."

"I understand that. And really, there isn't a great deal we can do at this point. What I'd recommend though is seeing my colleague Dr Ryan. You may have saw him at the bog land earlier, with our latest discovery?"

"I did, yes."

"Right. Well Dr Ryan is a clinical psychologist. It might be useful to discuss this with him, to see if you can remember what caused the injury. Also, his screening will allow us to rule out any further effects of the damage here. In some cases a TBI can cause, well, mental disturbances, you see. So it's for the best if we arrange an appointment."

I refused before he could even finish speaking. Psychology was where I drew the line. I might have agreed to the MRI, might even have accepted new pills from Kenny, but I refused to deal with a psychologist. I detested the profession; having seen it for decades as little more than a grand and very damaging scam. I knew full well that what were termed as 'disorders' were little more than brainwashing and stigmatized labels. I wanted no part of it, and I didn't need it.

"Sorry, Dr Kenny. I think I'd rather not see him, if you don't mind."

"Well, it would definitely be to your benefit. All he would do is ask you some questions, that's all. And If he thinks it's worth it, you might be able to attempt regression hypnosis. It may help you remember things. What do you think?"

The idea of 'remembering' was obviously an interest, but I still wasn't going to see the other doctor. As Kenny had just confirmed himself, the psychologist was only concerned with questions. I felt a clench of anger by just imagining them. I had no intention of telling personal information to this man, all so that he could label me mad and probably sell me yet another drug. Indeed, it doesn't even matter how you answer their questions; they will still come out as saying you are ill. My eccentricities were mine alone; and I would not be told I was 'wrong' because of them.

"I know that doctor, but still, I really don't feel like seeing your colleague. I'm grateful you've found the cause of these headaches, really I am. But I don't want to go any further with it."

"OK. It's your decision, Mr Clarke. You can always change your mind and come back. I promise it's nothing for you to worry about. But without the screening, that really is all I can for you, I'm afraid."

"That's fine. I'm relieved to have seen that. At least the next time I get one of the headaches, I know what it is that's making it happen."

I wasn't lying that I felt relieved. There had been times when I was sure I was mad; that the headaches and things I saw where not in my mind at all. But now I knew that they really were. I didn't crave for a full on cure, I only wanted an understanding. And so, I knew that I had a 'traumatic brain injury', a medical term for what I was experiencing. I might not have known how it came to be, but at least I knew what it could be called.

That is not to say that I felt uplifted. The shock of what I had found out was worrying. How many years had I lived my life with this blackened blotch inside my brain? Had it influenced my personality, changed the way I viewed the world? There was no doubt I always felt removed from people, but I always took it as sheer cynicism. Mr and Mrs Ford, my foster family, had always tried to mould my life, and I stood as strong as I could against it. Could my difference of views really be caused by my injury?

I didn't believe it. Even long after I left Dr Kenny, and aimlessly walked through Kilportach's main street, I couldn't make myself believe it was so. I remembered first thinking up 'hidden places', and knew it was from 'me' and not this brain oddity. At that time, I had slammed the door on my oppressive fosters after some superficial argument. I must have been 12 or 13, I suppose. A long time ago. Either way, I discovered a Holy well hidden in a parkland. It was covered in leaves near an untrodden footpath, away from the other kids and people in the park. I was the only one there. It was crumbling away, a solitary idol balanced on it's top, a faded prayer card left at it's base. I remembered the feeling of sheer stillness, of utter peace and removal from the world. I called it a 'living place', then later a 'hidden place'.

From then on, I would always search for similar places. They were the secret corners of towns and parks, the nooks and cranny's that all had forgotten. 'Hidden places' always spoke to me, their energies being that of watchful, cognizant entities. I could spend many hours in them, escape from everything that was not a part of their aura.

No, I was definitely not mad. I would not let Kenny's diagnoses get to me. It was my choice to have the scan, and my choice to refuse his psychologist. Still, I found myself walking up and down the main street, not looking in the shops nor even where I was going. I was just thinking of that MRI image, wondering how such and injury could have happened. I was not so worried about it being there, but more that I'd lived with it and didn't know. Either way, the next time I found myself having a headache, I would at least have the security of knowing why. I was grateful to Kenny for that, at least.

A number of people were shopping in the town. It still wasn't busy, but it seemed as I thought; the new bog body had brought the locals out of their homes. I paused on a bench, watched as the world passed by a for second, then gathered my thoughts as to where I would go next.

The Wishing Lake – Mark Robinson

The Water's Edge

In my mind, a number of links were beginning to form based on information from the people I'd met. I may not have discovered anything concrete, but what I had found were a handful of townsfolk willing to share their stories with me. Jack Daly had met me at the peat bog, stating his museum had selections of records which he thinks may help in my research. Then there was Molly at the pub, likely expecting me to come back in for another meal and reminisce. And Catherine, the lady from the tourist centre, who told me she had something to show me whenever I happened to pass the office.

I decided it best to start with her. If nothing else, the piles of leaflets in the building would fill me in on more local tales. I got up from the bench I had gathered my thoughts on, and headed to the tourist office in the main street.

It was still as dark and unwelcome as it was before. On the desk, another solitary candle was lit, helping to illuminate the dark panelled walls. I was still amazed that such a building could serve as a tourist's first stop in town, the selection of leaflets untidily stacked and the place devoid of modern signs or systems. At least it enveloped the feeling of the town.

The old woman welcomed me in with a smile. She was sitting on the chair in the corner of the room, seemingly lost in her own daydream. I asked her about what she wanted to show me.

"Oh yes. You see I was thinking about your stay here. I was sure we had something with your name on it, so I had a little look in the drawers. Now then, it's a newspaper clipping. I put it on the desk for you, over there."

A small newspaper cutting was sitting on the desk, it's paper yellowed and slightly creased. I went to pick it up, then decided to ask her a few things first.

"By the way", I said. "Are there any visitors coming into town now? To see the new bog body, I mean."

"I would like to think so, wouldn't you? If we're in the papers, people will come. They always do, you see."

When I first came into the tourist centre, Catherine told me she had lived in Kilportach all her life. I realised she couldn't remember small details, but she gave me a feeling of knowing the town, like she'd seen it change and knew it's people, albeit from many years ago.

"I hope you don't mind me asking these things. But I'm starting to learn things about my past. Now then, have you ever heard of a man called Shane Cullen, or a woman calling herself Amelia?"

She sat up straight on the wooden chair, like I'd said something to spark her interest.

"I have, my friend. Shane was the son of a dear friend of mine. Oh, I'm sorry. It's terrible, isn't it?"

"I'm Sorry..."

"Ambrose Cullen was the Father of Shane. He was, well, let's just say I admired him a lot. He was a vet, caring for all of the animals in town. Yes, he was a wonderful man. But when Shane... well, I don't think he ever really recovered."

She was clearly upset at recalling these memories. I wanted to know why Cullen was murdered, but perhaps asking her was not the best plan. It was poignant to think of her as a young woman, if only in her memories which were no doubt painful. I didn't want to trouble her though, so I thought it best not to press the subject.

"Thank you, that's a help. And what of this other person I met, Amelia? Do you know anything about her?"

"There is someone called Amelia, yes. Terrible woman, by all counts."

"Terrible?"

"Oh, well I shouldn't put it like that, of course. I've never met her myself, you see. But no one has a good word to say about her. I think she might have a great many problems. Best to stay away, I think."

"I see".

It was interesting to hear Catherine's opinions. I wasn't sure if these Cullen's were related to my research, but they seemed like a known and upstanding family. So why then would Shane Cullen be murdered? Also, both Catherine and Bridget were openly wary of Amelia, her presence known yet not accepted. I still didn't know what to believe, but would keep myself naturally distanced.

I thanked Catherine for her information, and reached for the newspaper clipping on the desk. At first, I thought I was seeing things, such was the nature of it's content. But I stared for a second and realised that yes, what I was reading was actually in front of me.

'Today marks a sad day for Kilportach, as police confirm the deaths of Lucas, Ethel and Edward Clarke. The family of three are thought to have entered a cavern near the town's 'wishing lake', when a freak cave-in trapped them inside. Another body was also discovered, of which no identification has been made.

Lucas Clarke was a prominent sign writer, having lived in Kilportach for much of his life. His intricate work for local business can be seen in many a shop in our town. He married wife Ethel in 1973, who that same year gave birth to their son Edward. The family lived in the Lusca Row area, where residents described them as 'a pleasure to know'

It is still unknown why they entered the cave, which was not part of the public area surrounding our famous lake. The area has since been sealed off, and police investigation is ongoing as to why the family may have entered. Suffice to say, all of Kilportach are deeply shocked at hearing news of this tragic accident.'

It was fascinating, exactly the sort of thing I was looking for. I was holding in my hands the very information I had hoped to find in this sleepy old town. Real news. It's content was doleful yet somehow perfect, like it was there just so I would one day discover it. But even though it was faded and creased; there were answers written on that paper I held. Answers which made sense, calmed my mind.

I soon realised though, that something was wrong. I skimmed across the clipping again, and knew I'd really just found more questions. I actually felt a little bit sick, like the strain of trying to work it out was making my whole body turn against me. But I couldn't help it, it was there in front of me. I tried to think.

If Edward was born in 1973, that would make him 8 years old when he died. This was in tune with my original research, making Edward two years my senior. So then I was born two years later, but in England and not Kilportach. But if they died in Kilportach in 1981, where was I? I was not even mentioned on the article at all, not before or after my family died. Had I been given over to my foster family before the accident occurred? I couldn't see why such a thing would happen.

I knew I needed to increase my research. This unknown body found with my family was surely something to do with them, and I felt that Cullen and Amelia were too. They had to be. I turned to Catherine, feeling a little dazed from having read the clipping, but still managed to ask her more.

"Sorry, but do you think I can keep this, just for a bit?" I said.

"Oh, but of course. Keep it. It's only going to be put in the drawer, anyway. Your more than welcome."

"Excellent, thank you. Also, by the way... what do you know of this wishing lake? I was thinking of maybe having a look, but I don't know much about it, you see."

"You have read the story, I take it? Well, the lake is just outside of town. It's a beautiful place, really beautiful. Before the bodies in the bog were found, people would visit our Wishing Lake. They said prayers to it, you see, believing the legends."

"Can you tell me how to get there?"

She explained how to find this fateful lake, and I wrote the directions on a scrap of paper. I knew I had to go there, even if just to see the place where my family had died. Of course, I knew it would only a be a body of water, maybe even overgrown and abandoned, but I just had to see it. I thanked Catherine for the clipping and directions, and left the office with a heavy feeling in my chest.

It was the sort of sensation that I usually felt when I found myself deep in inner thought. It was almost like a hypnotic state, where my breathing felt smoother as my brain ticked over. I was actually surprised to not have another headache, so much information had quickly came to me. Perhaps Kenny's diagnoses had settled whatever was bringing them on. I hoped so, anyway.

    Following Catherine's directions took me swiftly out of Kilportach. Yet like the train station I first stepped out on, all that surrounded the town were fields and bog. A muddy road led through open countryside, eventually entering an avenue of trees, a 'public footpath' sign leading the way.

    It was strange to think that these untamed fields were essentially part of the town itself. Looking behind me confirmed that I was not a great distance from the buildings I'd left, yet it felt like a different place entirely. Usually, I would have thought such land would be quickly bought up, and paved over to build more 'social housing'. Kilportach however was consciously slumberous, most likely sitting undeveloped since the day it was first turned into a town.

    The sodden footpath soon opened out, revealing a small hill covered in grass, a large old tree stood still at it's summit. A dilapidated building was standing by it, the wood it was built from rotten and perished. I recognised it; it was from the photograph Molly showed me. Shane Cullen's cabin.

    That meant the Wishing Lake was close by. I climbed the hill, stopping for a second to examine the building. A rusty wheelbarrow was standing near it, and the windows were boarded up in chipboard. The whole thing looked to be leaning slightly, as if the soft earth had subsided below it, causing the wooden panels to come loose. If anything, it was sad to look at, knowing that it was all that remained of the man who was murdered in the sleepy town.

    Behind the cabin, I stopped by the tree and looked out at the horizon. At the other side of the hill, a huge lake glimmered against the hiding sun. It was silent and still, like a sheet of glass with not a blemish upon it. At the other side, endless hills and fields spread out, revealing a view that enticed the eyes. For anything, the lake looked mute but still communicative, hiding shoals of coloured fish in depths replete with the memories of many old things.

By the waters edge, a thick rope fence prevented entry. On it, a multitude of coloured ribbons were tied and blowing the breeze. They stood out against the reflective water, almost as if they were waving or dancing. Could they have been people's wishes?

In fact, I was so taken in by the immediate energy which struck me in that place, that I didn't notice someone else was there. The figure was standing with their back towards me, hands resting against the rope fence, looking out towards the lake. As I walked down the hill and got closer to them, the person turned around.

It was Amelia. She seemed to be wearing the same clothes as before, apart from a different, longer black coat. I was slightly shocked to see her there. The place was deserted and out of the way, and I hadn't expected to see anybody.

"What are you doing here?" she said as she saw me.

"Someone told me how to get here. This is the Wishing Lake, isn't it?"

"Yeah."

I noticed she was still wearing the mermaid necklace like my Mother's. It reminded me then of the Wishing Lake story; the Selkie maiden who lived in the lake, granting wishes to those who left her gifts. I wondered if the story had any truth in it, whether people really did throw things in the water. More than that though, it felt too poignant to see the necklace there. That was the place where my family had died.

"I'll come back later", said Amelia, starting to walk away from the lakeside.

"What?"

"I'll come back later when you've gone. I don't like being here with other people."

"Wait. I wanted to ask you something, actually."

She turned around to face me, making eye contact and looking slightly annoyed.

"No. And definitely not here. Do it later."

"Why not here?"

"Because I said so. This is a hidden place, it's not meant for you asking your questions."

It was unbelievable. I might have known the lake would be a 'hidden place' before I saw it, but to hear her call it so was astonishing. 'Hidden places' were something I made up myself; it was my own term and my own concept. Yes, the Wishing Lake was definitely a 'hidden place', and she was calling it the same term.

"What did you just call it?" I asked.

"Like you'd understand. A hidden place is somewhere special, OK? But people aren't supposed to go there and talk."

As before, her misanthropic personality was making her difficult to get anything out of. She made me feel bad though, as she continued to remind me only of myself. I too would hate it if someone barged into one of my own 'hidden places', and started asking questions about it. The whole idea was that they were secluded.

"Actually, I do understand", I said. "And I'll leave. I just came here to see where my family died. I didn't know it was a 'hidden place' until I got here."

"So Edward really did die around here? Like I said to you?"

"Oh that's right, you said didn't know, didn't you."

I handed her the newspaper clipping I was given from Catherine. She stood for a minute, glossed over it with some speed, and handed it back with a glum expression.

"I had no idea about this." She walked past me and once more to the rope fence overlooking the water. "Like I said, they didn't think a child worth telling. But a cave-in? There aren't even caves around here! Where the hell did they go?"

I joined her at the rope fence, pleased that she seemed to be willing to talk, if only about her reaction to the clipping. I was close to the lake, it's silent water looking deep and untouched, like even dead leaves knew better than to soil its surface.

"The world really is a horrible place", she said, looking out to the water. "Crushed in a cave...Edward. Why did no one ever tell me? They think I didn't care or something?"

"Well, something's wrong about it all. The whole thing. I wasn't mentioned on the article at all, and yet I'm sure I would have remembered something like this. And then just a week before this happened, a man called Shane Cullen was murdered in the town. Honestly, I never expected to find so much mystery here."

"I remember Shane Cullen". She turned to look at me. "He was actually kind, not like the other people. I don't want to talk about him, though. Not now."

"That's fine." I knew she was unlikely to talk for long. Honestly, I too would have liked to explore the lake alone, but meeting her there was an interesting chance. Both Bridget and Catherine had spoke badly of her, but I wished to know her connection with my family. It would be hard though, I knew that.

"You really didn't know how the Clarke's were killed?" I asked. "Someone must have said something, surely."

"Well they didn't. And I don't read newspapers or things like that. All I knew was that they were dead. Someone told me later that it happened at the lake. But that's all. This is the first time I've heard of that clipping you showed me. And your right, it is all wrong."

"How so?"

"Like I said, there aren't any caves around the Wishing Lake. I know, I come here all the time. There's just what you see, the lake, the trees. There's never been a cave or any of that stuff."

There had to have been, and I was more willing to believe the report than anything Amelia was talking about. But still, she actually knew my family in person, and seemed to be hiding a great many stories. That said, it was definitely hard to imagine a cave there. It looked as if the landscape had never changed; a grassy verge leading to the old rope fence, then nothing but deep and expansive water. But if there were no caves around the lake, then what was the article referring to? At that point, I just couldn't trust Amelia's words.

"Anyway, I'm going", she said. "When I come here, I just like to enjoy the solitude"

She turned again and begun to walk away. I knew this time I would let her go, if only so that I could examine the lake without her eyes following my every move. Before she left though, I just had to to ask her something.

"Why did you call this a hidden place, by the way?" I said in a raised voice to make her stop in her steps. She turned around, took a few steps back towards me.

"I guess it's possible for you to have found these things out. Your meant to be researching the people here, after all. Me and Edward Clarke used to know each other, right? Well, we used to call thing's 'hidden places' back then, or he did, anyway. I don't know where he got it from, probably from Shane or his dad or something. There's nothing more to it. That's all."

She didn't say another word, but turned again and quickly walked away, leaving me standing alone at the lakeside. I could have easily shouted out to her, but I didn't. I just watched as she disappeared over the hill, back towards the path to the town. I stood still, not so much shocked as guilelessly perplexed.

I was adamant that 'hidden places' were my own invention from my childhood. Hearing otherwise was hard to believe, like being told that your memories were false or your beliefs were fabrications. I turned to the lake, swiftly entering a deep daydream as I peered at the water and thought about this.

If Edward knew about 'hidden places', did I get the initial idea from him? He was my Brother after all, despite the fact I could not remember him. And if he himself did not create it, who was the one to give birth to the concept? It seemed like the memories of my past were far more confused than I had assumed. If Amelia and Edward looked for 'hidden places', then surely I must have done so with them. But she said Edward was their only son, and all of the records seemed to confirm this statement. I was starting to think I'd been sorely mistaken. I was not the son of Lucas and Ethel at all. Could some kind of horrid mistake have put me together with those who shared my name? I couldn't even trust my own fuzzy memories, for what was to say they were not just dreams?

I had a strong urge to look at my birth certificate, a copy of which I had brought with me to town. I knew full well what was on it of course, but I just needed to settle my mind. I sighed, looked out at the water with tired frustration. Was my 'injured' mind so far obscured that I thought I'd created something I'd not? I was beginning to realise just how little I could trust my own thoughts. And Kenny's MRI had not helped a bit.

I shook my head, tried for a minute to quiet my mind and concentrate, even if just for a short amount of time. I put my hands on the ribbon covered rope-fence I stood by, and imagined the story of the old Wishing Lake.

It was amazing to think of people leaving gifts to the Selkie who was said to live in the water. I wondered how many antiques and relics were laying forgotten on the bottom of the lake? I imagined hundreds of coins and items, covering the bed of the undisturbed water, glimpsed at only by the fish who lived there.

There was definitely a presence surrounding the place, a mood which spoke and at the same time stayed silent. Many bodies of water shared similar feelings, with the ocean in particular compelling to visit, like between the monotonous crashing of waves, it saw and remembered all of time. I often felt that 'hidden places' involving water were aware of what that they housed in their murkiness. But they knew to always keep it secret, realising that should we glimpse at the world below, the whole concept of all that we knew would change.

The same was true of the Wishing Lake. In the story, the Selkie returned to live in the lake, only coming to the surface to grant the desires of those who had asked her. I wondered just how such a myth was started, how a lake awash in willing solitude was said to be home to such a creature.

I decided to stay at the lake a while longer. There was very little room to explore it's corners, the fence restricting access to it and flanked at each side by trees and forest. I wasn't expecting to find the cave though. Yet even so, the idea that this was the place it all happened filled me with a mixture of dread and sorrow. I wasn't sure of what to believe, but an energy flowed there which pierced the senses. The very epitome of 'hidden places'.

A Shadow Falls

By the time my second day in Kilportach ended, a light yet constant rain had fallen over it. It started soon after I left the lake, catching me unaware as I trudged back through the field and into town.

The start of a headache was there, as well. For some reason, I was concerned about it, perhaps just paying it more attention after Dr Kenny's discovery. Though really I think it was my new-found fear; the idea that what I remembered and didn't were more mixed up then I ever assumed. But still, it was the normal early signs of a headache; a dull pain accompanied by a slight auditory delusion. I thought somebody was standing behind me, and that their lips had just parted, as if they were about to say something. I was alone, of course.

Either way, I decided not to waste the evening by simply lying in bed and taking pills. The more answers I found the more questions arose, and I needed to find out as much as I could. Therefore, despite the fact I knew it would make my head worse, I made my way back to the town's small pub.

It was almost as quiet as it was before, but at least a few others were inside that night. It was still mostly empty though, with only a few sat by the bar and drinking without making much noise. There was no idle chatter nor music inside, just the occasional clinking of glasses set to the sound of the rain outside. I passed my eyes around for a second, then found Molly the barmaid talking to a man on a small table by a window. As I approached her, she turned to greet me.

"And here he is look, the man himself! We were just talking about you."

She offered me a seat on the table with the other man. He was sat in front of finished plate of food, and was sipping from a gradually emptying pint glass. I took a seat, said a brief hello to the man, and tried not to concentrate on the coming headache. The man I was sat with was about my age, his hair greying yet curled and somewhat wild. He also had a neat grey goatee, and wore a loose but smart looking shirt.

"Are you eating tonight, Mr Clarke?" asked Molly.

"No, thanks. Just a soft drink tonight, I think."

I knew I should have had something to eat. But I also knew that eating with a headache would only cause the nausea to take it's full form. I did not want to fall ill in the pub, and so although not eating would surely make me tired, it was probably for the best at the time.

Molly went to the bar and returned with my drink; a mild orange juice in a half pint glass. I took a few sips, the coldness not helping the coming throbs. But still, at least it quenched the thirst. After a second, Molly sat down at the table next to me, and introduced me to the new face.

"Adam here is new in town as well, Mr Clarke. I was just telling him about there been two guests here at once! Amazing, eh?"

"If you say so".

"Oh, believe it", said the man. "I came here as a child once, with my Father. It was like this back then, as well".

"I see."

"I'm just here in town to, well...to see it again, you could say. It could be my last chance, you see."

"I'll just go check the kitchen", said Molly, getting up and leaving me and Adam to talk.

"Why your last chance?" I said, after taking another small sip of the juice.

"Cancer. Inoperable as well, apparently. So, you see, I want to do and finish up as many things as I can."

He did not look ill to the naked eye. If anything, he looked more healthy than many other people I'd seen in my life. Then again, it was not his outward appearance that was dying. Even so, a particular block often formed in the mind when confronted with one who was terminally ill. Curiosity prodded me to ask all about it, but I knew full well that he would not be willing to talk about such things. Instead, I was interested that he came to the town as a child, and was only now returning to bid the deserted place farewell.

"Have you seen the bog bodies?" I asked. "It was only this morning that a new one was found. Pretty amazing, actually."

"Please, don't." He swallowed a large gulp of his drink. "I know the place is famous for them, but they're just not for me. I try to stay away."

I suppose it was understandable. The bog bodies held a morbid charisma; an image of death far different from what we usually encounter. Perhaps for a man with terminal cancer, peering face to face with death would not hold the curiosity it did for others. I personally would never feel this way, but I understood if he did so.

"So, I understand your looking up a Clarke family tree, right?" he said.

"I am. Did Molly tell you about me?"

"Actually, it was that woman from the hotel your staying at. Bridget Brady? She was in here a while ago."

"Oh, she was, huh?"

It seemed Bridget from the B&B was the textbook gossip in Kilportach. She had spoke to both Kenny and Jack Daly about me, and was now informing strangers in the pub about my reason for being there. I had hardly spoken to the woman save for pleasantries in the guest house, yet she clearly enjoyed telling everyone I was there. Honestly, I didn't like it.

"Yeah, actually she was looking for you, I think", he said. "Said she had found something to help you. I don't know."

"Oh right. Well, I'll see her later on, anyway."

I would have wondered just what she had found, but something else had arrested my thoughts. The headache 'signs' were starting to show, and I knew I needed to take a pill. It started with the usual ringing in the ears, and I knew that soon my eyes would start blurring. I hated it happening in public places, even more so whilst sat with this stranger. I felt a sickening pulse in my stomach; racing up my windpipe and resulting in a light-headed nausea. I needed to get away.

"Sorry, excuse me for a minute, OK?" I said to Adam, quickly getting to my feet and trying to find where the toilets were.

To the left of the bar, a corridor stretched out behind the pub, a picture of a pointing hand on the wall showing the way to the gents toilets. The floorboards were uneven and moving beneath me, which at that time only worsened the headache. Sometimes, even small movements gave cutting pains from behind my eyes, and that night was no different. Before I managed to find the toilet, my eyesight had managed to lose it's focus, and the heavy pain in my mind had heightened. It was amazing how quickly it happened sometimes.

Thankfully, the toilets were empty and largely noiseless. An uncomfortable florescent light hung on the wall, and a number of cubicles spread out beside it. I put the pill into my mouth, gulping a mouthful of water from a tap to help force it down. For a second, I just stood, looked down into the aged looking sink, and wished the medicine would kill the pain quickly.

The bathroom was clean, at least. The walls were fitted with lime green tiles, and a number of paintings hung upon them. They were mostly of areas around Kilportach, like the peat bogs and the Wishing Lake. I tried to focus my eyes on them, but the harsh light was not helping. Instead, I continued to lean against the sink, and simply closed my eyes.

I am not sure if I fell asleep, or whether the pills had just brought with them their drowsiness, but I'm sure I was not fully awake. For when I opened my eyes to a still throbbing pain, I realised the light had been switched off. The room was dark save for a frosted window, letting in a dim light from whatever was outside. I knew at once that something would happen. It always did when the headaches struck; like my mind had trouble processing the world whenever the pain started to show. At that moment, a strong urge came over me to leave the bathroom.

Sometimes, I would see things during those episodes; faces reflected in mirrors and windows, shapes which moved in my dim bedroom. On other occasions, I would not see anything physical per say, but feel or sense their presence instead. That feeling was strong in the bathroom that night.

I was shocked that the light had abruptly switched off, and stood in the middle of the nearly black bathroom, the dark actually helping the throngs of pain to succumb to the tablet. At first, I was feeling as I usually did as the pill got to work and resulted in drowsiness, but I soon felt that the air had turned heavy. It was like many eyes were upon me at once, like unseen figures were standing in the corners, where I could not make out their form. I felt at once my skin turn cold; my arms and neck come out in bumps and raise the hairs with chilled awareness.

For no longer than a second, but feeling like many; I found my feet would not move from their place. I am unaware of exactly what stopped me, but I felt that should I so much as twitch, those shadowed hands would lunge towards me in a scene akin to a child's bad dream. I was aware of the sink and mirror behind me, yet did not feel fit to turn and look, knowing too well the horrific expressions my mind would render in their reflections.

My feet soon found their bearings however, and the sight of movement in the back of the room soon had me running towards the door. I did not look back nor guess as to what; but something definitely moved there in the gloom. I could feel it approaching.

Indeed, as I opened the door into the well lit pub, it felt like the light which pierced inwards had caused the shifting entity to vanish. It was as if I had opened it just in time, before the fingers of that man or beast discovered a way to pull me back inside. Instantly though, the fear subsided in the lights of the pub. Everything was the same, a few solitary drinkers and Molly behind the bar. Had I really just experienced a presence in the bathroom? I did not even want to think about it.

I then noticed that the table I was sat at was empty; the man from before being nowhere in sight. I approached Molly behind the bar. She was polishing glasses and stacking them neatly on a shelf. When I sat on a barstool, she turned to talk to me.

"Alright, Mr Clarke? Adam went back to his camper van I think. Said he'd had enough for one evening. You OK? You look a bit white."

"Oh yeah, sorry. I suffer from headaches. I took a tablet. Makes me a little tired, that's all."

"You want a glass of water or anything? Just say if you do, OK?"

"Sure."

I sat for a while lost in my own thoughts, then accepted her offer of a glass of water. It was bottled, and she poured it into a glass for me just like it was a more expensive drink.

"Here you are then. On the house!"

"Thanks"

The cold water did help me to relax; the feeling of it sinking into my stomach helping to reverse the nervous sensation I felt in the bathroom. The headache was reaching it's medicated climax, just a dull ache left in back of my head, bringing with it heavy eyes and a prickly heat. But still, the worst of it was over. In fact, knowing the cause of the headaches seemed to actually help me cope. Of course, none of it made any sense to me, but the 'traumatic brain injury' Kenny had found was at least a term I could hang on the pain.

I took a few sips of the water in silence, watching as Molly got back to polishing glasses behind the bar. I knew it would not be long until she opened conversation with me, and I didn't speak until she did. She stacked two or three glasses on the shelf, then put down her cloth and turned to face me.

"So, found anything out yet? About your family tree and that?"

"I found some things, yes. Of course, It only leads to more questions, really."

"I bet. You had me looking through my photo drawer there, after I showed you that picture of Mr Cullen. Hang on, I'll show you another one, actually."

I had a feeling she would show me another photograph. She opened the drawer with a kind of excitement, as if she always waited for people to visit of whom she could show her memories to.

The photograph she gave me was again black and white, showing a close up of the cabin near the lake. It had beds of plants sat by the door, and the wooden walls were painted with floral murals. Outside, two men were sat on deckchairs smiling, and another man was nearly out of shot in the background. I recognised one of the men as Cullen, he was dressed near identical to the other photo; rough overalls and a pair of circular glasses. The man next to him had a dark sweatshirt, combed over dark hair and a pair of jeans.

"I took that one", she said. "It's outside Mr Cullen's cabin. That man in the background is my ex-husband. And the one sat next to Shane I don't really know. He was a visitor in town, I think."

"I see."

"I think he may have been friends with Mr Cullen. I remember them talking together a lot. He was interested in the lake's folklore, thing's like that as far as I remember."

She picked up the photo and held it close to her, her eyes open wide like the people on it were alive with movement and talking to her. She smiled slightly, not out of amusement but from obvious sentiment, and carefully put the photo back.

"It's a perfect picture, isn't it?" she said. "His cabin looked so wonderful back then. He really took pride in all of his work. I just wish I'd listened to him, sometimes."

"Bad memories?" I asked, noticing a clear sadness in her voice. Of course, it was non of my business to ask, but my thirst for stories of Kilportach's past overrode my usually apathetic emotion.

"Oh, don't you worry about it. It's just that I left this town too quickly, thinking I'd found some shining prince. Mr Cullen always said I'd be better off at home, but why would a young woman listen to that, eh?"

She got up and immediately picked up her cloth, getting back to polishing the small pile of glasses. I drank my water back in one large gulp, half wanting to engage her in conversation but knowing I should really just sit and wait. It was interesting though to see her photo; as I remembered passing Cullen's cabin on the hill near to the Wishing Lake. It had nearly collapsed, the structure looking decrepit and weak, like after Cullen's death it was simply forgotten. It was almost sad to see it in the picture, alive with flowers and painted murals.

I also wondered about the other man, whom Molly said might have been a friend of Shane Cullen. If he knew him, he could have known me or family as well. I decided to ask Molly, if only to stop her from dwelling on her melancholy.

"The other man on that picture you showed me, what was his name?"

"Oh, I don't think he ever told me. He was only in the town as a visitor, like I said. Actually, I think he might have spoken to young Edward's parents too. I don't think it's anything to help you, though."

She was probably right, and although she confirmed my assumptions that the man may have known my family, a single visitor was of little concern.

I was going to ask her more about Edward, but the door to the pub opened with such violent force that both myself and Molly turned round immediately. It was Jack Daly, the man I had met earlier from the town's museum. He was drenched in rain; a frightened expression pressed onto his face, gasping with breath like he'd just been running.

"Bridget's gone missing!"

"What!?" shouted Molly, leaving the bar and approaching Jack. I too got to my feet, took a few steps towards him. The open door let in the now heavy rain, soaking into the carpet and blowing a noticeably cold wind inside.

"She rang me up, at my home...she was...she said someone had broken into the hotel! I got in the car but she...the door was open, but she wasn't there!"

"Wait, broke in? What do you mean?" Molly sounded confused and unsure, standing close to Jack and grasping his arm.

"The door had been forced in, the lights on, but she wasn't in there! I've looked all over I have but I-"

"Hey, calm down" I interrupted, seeing his breath was quickening and his eyes moving erratically. I walked close to him, Molly giving me a worried glance and letting go of Jack's left arm. "Tell me what happened."

"Oh yes, you...your staying at Bridget's hotel aren't you? You've got to help me look for her!"

I felt a sharp quickening of my pulse; an audible heart thump in my chest as the weight of what he was saying hit me. But I knew there was no time to think or ask questions.

"Mr Clarke", Molly turned to me. "You have to help! I just can't believe...I'll phone the police."

"I've already phoned", blurted Jack. "But god knows how long they'll take to get here. Clarke, will you help me look for her?"

"Of course."

It was one of those moments of heightened sensations; where the usual thinking and feeling of the mind are swept aside by stronger, reactionary senses. There was something about him rushing inside, of the backdrop of rain and chilled nightfall, that sent primal emotions throughout my body. Something was wrong, seriously so.

"Alright, well look, I've searched the town centre, the shops and the lake. We need to go check the graveyard and the bog land."

"Right."

I didn't have time to think about anything. Jack turned round and ran outside, not a word on his lips or a blink in his eye. I looked at Molly, took a final breath of the inside air, and quickly walked outside the pub.

"Find her, Mr Clarke!" shouted Molly as I left.

My clothing was immediately drenched throughout; this gelid downpour pelting the skin and jumping up from the pavements it pummelled. Jack shouted at me to check the bog, then ran off almost slipping on the road, his arms flailing and his jacket billowing. I had not seen a man so insistently worried for quite some time. Whatever she told him on the phone must have been more horrid than I dared to think. Of course, he was clearly friends with her, and it was natural that he should jump into action upon this most bitter of nights.

I made my way the peat bog area, not running like Jack but pacing quickly, the rain forcing my eyes to squint as I splashed through it's bouncing puddles on the pavement. The streets were nearly completely unlit, save for the glow from nearby houses reflecting in the non ending rain storm. It made me feel acutely unsafe, the feeling of someone walking behind me burning holes into my back with every step. I imagined the burglar still at large, knowing that a man out in such bad weather could only be searching for his captured victim. Really though, I didn't understand it. Who would break into that dingy guest house? There was nothing in there but dust and old furniture, and even then the place was empty and unused. Indeed, I was the only guest.

Even so, the idea of the woman having vanished from in there was as unsettling as the night was cold. Had she simply ran to escape the intruder? I could not imagine the sense of fear that having a stranger force in your door must have entailed. Even though I only met her a mere two days back, I felt an odd feeling of concern for her as I passed my eyes around the empty streets.

By the time I reached the peat bog itself, my hair and clothes were in such a state that I felt rain trickling across my skin, filling my shoes and pouring out upon every uncomfortable step I took. I had questioned my unthinking willingness to help, but knew that refusing to go with Jack might have rendered my presence in a worse light than it was. This was a town in which the people all knew each other, and such an event was clearly unusual and therefore a shock to those involved.

That said, the place I walked into was dark and unfriendly. The peat bog's were an endless ocean of night, the only light being from distant buildings, carried on shadows to where I was standing. I forced myself to advance, but slowly; my hands held out in case I should fall, my eyes working hard to adjust to the darkness. I was foolish not to ask for a torch, but decisions made in the spur of the moment seldom cover all eventualities. At that time, all I could do find my bearings, and try not to lose myself in the blackness.

That feeling returned, as well, without even the need for a headache to accompany it. The thought of the bodies laid close in the bogs brought a whisper of dread across my mind. Something about it affected me; the hairs on my body expecting an unearthed hand to be reaching out for them in the dark. I could hear the rain fall into the bog; hissing as it landed in bubbling peat and bottomless pools. The wind too brought a myriad of voices, dreadful whistles which echoed in the glacial air of this marshland graveyard. If I was not there for such a serious matter, I would have turned and left without a single thought.

But even the most abhorrent of feelings could not prepare me for what I discovered. The reaction was not a 'jump' per say, but a sheer collapse of mental reasoning. I remember a manifestation of doubt, quickly rising with repugnant panic and a startled realisation. It wasn't an image from my damaged brain, nor a moving shadow in the ghostly bog land. It was there, in front of me; real and cold.

Bridget. She was stone dead, laying in a heap by the metal fence which prevented access to the bog itself. In a single second I felt a rush of horror, like someone was screaming silently in my ear; telling me I shouldn't have seen such a sight. I didn't even know what was going on. I felt a hundred people standing in the dark, rushing towards me with unexplainable shrieks as I stood in the blackness and simply stared. But everything was still, unmoving and voiceless.

I got to my knees. It was definitely Bridget, the talkative woman from the B&B, the first person I had met in this loathsome town. Rain water had drenched her clothes and skin; making her hair stick to her head as she laid face down in the puddling water. I kept expecting her to move or speak; or even to disappear entirely and reveal herself as a cruel mirage. But everything I saw was far too real. I got hold of her hand; ice cold and limp, all signs of a pulse long faded into nothing. It felt like another force was present, not life as we know it but a abstruse presence. It was like it could see and sense my dread; and hovered with a contagious longing over the lifeless Bridget I was kneeling by.

The true horror, of course, were the coming consequences. An image of Jack entered my mind, searching the cemetery as I knelt there, still desperately searching for his friend. How could I tell him of such a discovery? I couldn't, I knew that. Yet even so, I could not stay kneeling and staring forever. Police would soon descend on Kilportach, and it was I who would have to tell them the news. And then what of myself? As the only guest in the B&B, I would not only find myself without refuge but placed right in the middle of a death enquiry.

I had found a dark thing in that old peat bog. So heinous, in fact, that I could not even begin to think, to will myself into standing back up. It was a moment where thought does not just become shocked; it shuts down reasoning altogether. I was motionless, aware only of my breathing and the insoluble horror which pulsed throughout me. I just knelt, the rain penetrating my skin and clothes, and peered hopelessly, timelessly, at what laid before me.

Keepers of Memories

Sleep had never been easy for me. I would wake up most nights pounding with thoughts, unable to force myself to relax. But that night was different. I knew at once I would be up all night, if not from emotion then from sheer circumstance. I didn't even entertain the notion of sleep. Not on that night.

When I finally left my morbid discovery, I met up in town with the police car Jack had sent for; it's flashing blue siren out of place in the otherwise pitch dark main street. Thankfully, Jack himself was not in sight, and I was able to tell the bearish officer what I had found in the dark of that peat bog. He was blunt and somewhat impolite; yet after the obligatory radio chatter decided to believe me and go the bog. I went with him, in the car, the headlights lighting up the bogs and making Bridget's body stand out on the paving.

From there, he called for an ambulance and more police cars, and turned back to me with a forceful authority. I had never liked the police to begin with, and this one especially was uncivil and hard-featured. He spoke as if addressing a child or simpleton, his tone not conjuring a sense of respect but more of a writhing disfavour within me. I waited with him for the ambulance, all the time not taking my eyes away from the waterlogged corpse slumped out in front of me. I even noticed the presence of blood, lit up in his headlights and diluted in the rain, puddling around the body and street. My initial shock may have wore off, but the sight of her laying there still made me uneasy.

When the ambulance and police car eventually arrived, I was swiftly whisked back into his car and taken to give a statement with him. I felt at once sick and also apathetic; I knew such things were a formality but was still not pleased with prospect of such. I tried not to speak to the officer on the way, instead just looking at the night outside and replaying my finding of the body in my mind. I wondered if Jack had been informed, and just hoped the police man who broke the news was more humane than the brute I was sat with.

Even so, the statement was generally painless and quick. The police station sat on the outskirts of town and was almost entirely without character. I sat in a harshly lit square room, a tape recorder placed between me and the officer, and simply recounted my grim experience. He asked more questions than I would have liked, but I answered them all, if only with one syllable.

It was not long before I was free to go, and was offered a lift back into Kilportach, the time now stretching to almost midnight. I was glad to be rid of the authoritative officer, and stepped out of his car into the silent main street, the rain still falling but slowing down.

And so it was over. I was once more alone in the lifeless Kilportach; the distant sound of the occasional car the only sign that I was still awake. The street felt even more dead than before. I had witnessed abhorrence in it's murkiest corners, yet only I seemed to retch with disturbance. The town itself sat mute and uncaring, it's people yawning through daily existence, unaware of the horror to befall their neighbour. Only I was present to stumble in that gloom, uncovering nothing but a grisly remnant of whatever happened in that unkind town.

For the rest of the night, I did very little. I returned to the pub where Molly allowed me to rest, and ended up simply sat with her in silence. She had heard the news from Jack himself; who phoned inconsolably for but a second to inform her of what I had found. Molly was upset, and sat with me in the closed up pub until long after she would usually retire. That said, there was little I could find to say. I was more concerned with wondering what had happened. What had she saw in those final moments, what had led to her losing her life?

Kilportach was not the sort of town where I expected such incidents to even be heard of. It seemed to be the kind of place where years would pass in humdrum cycles, each stone and pebble remaining unchanged. Indeed, each person I'd met knew of Shane Cullen's murder; it was fresh on their tongues despite it happening all of 30 years ago. Yet what happened that night was so swift and violent; the phone call to Jack about a break in, the rain-slicked search through passionless streets, the corpse laid fresh and waiting to be found.

It all felt so odd and out of place, so much so that I was sure Molly had a hard time comprehending it's reality. She did eventually speak to me though, yet only to say she was going to bed. At that, she left me alone to rest in the pub; my only companion the embers in the fireplace. The smell of alcohol lingered in the air, and an open window let the night air penetrate it's stuffy atmosphere.

I didn't sleep, of course. In fact, even when morning pierced the pub's net curtains, I was still sat upright and awake with thought. I did not want to leave Kilportach yet, but I felt my research would surely start to suffer. To start, I was now without a 'base' to return to, as it was clearly impossible to stay in the guest house after what had happened there. And so what could I do? I knew I needed to retrieve my belongings, but where could I put them, apart from the pub? I knew at once I would have to find somewhere else.

That morning, I waited until Molly came down the stairs, and thought to leave the pub and get my suitcase. But after her sombre sounding greeting of 'good morning', she quickly got onto the phone to Jack. By this time my eyes were heavy with grogginess, and it wasn't until Molly spoke to me again that I fully found myself feeling awake. Apparently, Jack wanted to speak to me on the phone. I had no idea what he could want, and moreover I knew not what to say. How could I speak to a man who's friend I'd discovered dead in the cold last night? I just didn't know how.

When I took the receiver, the voice on the line was quiet and mournful, yet underneath the obvious tears he sounded able to retain his strength. The shock must have been tremendous for him. However, the true scope of what I found last night did not hit home until I heard Jack speak.

"She was murdered, Mr Clarke. Murdered."

"...What?"

"I don't know...I just, I mean, the police said she...she'd been shot."

I could have said a thousand things, but none of them had the strength to turn into words. A murder in Kilportach? I couldn't imagine it. And yet, as the police car's headlights pierced that darkness, I remembered the bothersome sight of blood. Images quickly flashed in my mind; a gun held cruelly to Bridget's flesh, a shot heard only by the peat bog bodies. I couldn't even start to envision what happened, what could cause someone to murder a person like Bridget? It didn't make sense.

"Oh, Mr Clarke", continued the distraught Jack on the telephone. "Could you come to see me, sometime if you can? I just...well, I'd like to see you. Please."

"Of course. Where can I meet you?"

"I'm at the museum. It isn't open, I mean, I couldn't...but, please, when you have time, come and see me. Can you do that?"

I wondered what he could want to see me about, save for simply someone to talk to whilst recovering from the news. I did recall though, in a brief yet now sombre memory, that Bridget had wanted to see me only the day before. The man called Adam had told me this, saying he saw her come into the pub hoping to find me there. Could it have something to do with that? I doubted it, not seeing how Jack would care about my trivial research in the face of what had hit him last night.

Still, visiting Jack was the only real thing I could do that day. I did however go to collect my suitcase; and Molly was kind enough to let me put it in the pub until I found somewhere else to stay. The guest house itself was cheerless and forlorn; a length of police tape covered it's door, and an officer stood preventing entry. If anything, it's untidy garden and and dirty windows felt for the first time to radiate feeling. No matter how badly looked after it was, the structure still wept in lament for it's owner. It knew that she was not inside, and therefore knew it had lost it's essence.

Somewhat annoyingly, the police man outside would not let me in to retrieve my belongings on my own. He instead insisted on going himself, bringing down my briefcase and documents and handing them over with aloof disinterest. Thankfully, it seemed to be all there, and I took it at once back the pub where Molly placed it in a back room somewhere.

Before leaving, I glanced a look at my birth certificate; my earlier feelings of having found the wrong family requiring the need for confirmation. Sure enough, I was the son of Lucas and Ethel Clarke, and was born in 1975 at St Margaret's Hospital, Essex. This meant nothing to me, of course, but it proved that I was right in first place, the Clarke's of Kilportach were my parents. So then I must have discovered 'hidden places' from Edward, and must have lived in Kilportach at one time. But then where was I on the day they all died? The paper confirmed that all three of them were in the cave, but made no mention of their other son. Had I really already been given up to care?

Thinking about it helped me to return a level of normality as I walked through the town. But it wasn't the same. A direful thought kept piercing my mind; that someone had murdered Bridget Brady. A murderer walked in the streets of Kilportach, a person who, should I have been in the guest house with her last night, could have attacked me as well. Of course, there had to be a motive for such a crime, but I just couldn't think of it. Bridget was clearly one prone to gossip, but other than that she seemed friendly and genuine. She was definitely not the sort of person who brought such anger or hatred towards her. She didn't seem to be, anyway.

I arrived at the museum around an hour after the phone call. The peat bog avenue was heavy with police, and a white tent was erected where I had found the body. I didn't speak to the police as I passed, wanting to avoid any further questions or intrusions into my business in town. Besides, a number of forensic officers seemed to be searching near the tented area, and I was sure they didn't want me stopping their work.

The building where the museum stood was small and square, with white painted brickwork and a flat roof. Above the door, a square wooden sign was screwed to the wall, the word '*Museum*' carved into it. It certainly didn't look anything special, appearing more like a storeroom or workshop than a museum. Moreover, it's position was odd for a tourist attraction, it stood alone by the grassy verges of the bog, facing away from the town behind it. In fact, it was likely that many a visitor would miss it, and the lack of signposts was evidence it didn't crave their custom.

I knocked on the heavyset wooden door, and waited for Jack to open up. I glanced behind me to the endless peat bog; where a large heron stood in a pool of water, waiting for movement within the wetlands. As the bolt of the museum door was unlatched, it took to the sky and left Kilportach. I turned to find Jack standing in the doorway.

"Mr Clarke, come in. Please."

His eyes were red and swollen from tears, but he still dressed smart in a suit and tie. He locked the door again behind him, and welcomed me into the tiny museum. At the back of the room, a desk stood against a wall covered in leaflets, and in front of it a small collection of gifts. Jack walked slowly behind the desk, but was clearly not really prepared to talk.

"Sorry, Mr Clarke, Leonard, was it? I just wanted to...well, I don't know. Look, I'm sorry for having to involve you in this. I am."

"You didn't, I just wanted to help. And I'm sorry, I really am."

He must have known that it was me who discovered the body, a realisation which made me feel an irritating guilt. Yet even so I could not guess as to the emotions he was experiencing. He seemed to almost regret inviting me, finding that when we were face to face he lost the ability to focus and speak.

"I wanted to see you", he continued slowly. "But it's something that she, well, I don't know that I can. I'm sorry about this, but I thought I was ready."

"That's OK".

"Could you come back later? I just...just need to gather my thoughts a bit. You could look around in here, if you wanted to."

I just wanted to know what he brought me there to talk about. That said, looking in the town museum was something that had been sitting on my list to do. I told myself I had to carry on with my research, even if the town goes into shock at this murder. Therefore I didn't hesitate to accept Jack's offer.

He reached behind the desk and turned on a light switch, bringing dim lights in various cabinets dotted around the room. He said I could take as long as I wanted, that he would need some time to gather his feelings before speaking to me about whatever it was. I once more gave my condolences, and began to look around Kilportach museum.

At each side of the desk an open doorway was standing, each leading into the two main galleries. Above the right hand door the word '*The Wishing Lake*' was written, and above the left '*The Kilportach Bog Men*'. In the reception room itself stood a few small cabinets, mostly containing china saucers and pottery, as well as a couple of old tins and bottles. It was standard fare for a small museum; the items covered in visible dust and displayed with functionality rather than charm. Nothing particularly stood out in there, it was just a humble row of cabinets, with items most likely donated by the townsfolk. They weren't even labelled; just locked inside and laying dormant for visitors to pass them by. They were not so much cabinets of curiosities, as simply cabinets of leftover memories.

Yet there was always a feeling attached to old items, something abstract but not unreal. If a spirit could be said to exist in the living, then that same soul surely lived within antiques. After all, something as simple as an ornament could easily survive for many human lifespans. It could travel through time and be touched by many, knowing all that has passed since the day it was made. I therefore felt that such antiquities were, save for their lack of a heartbeat or breath, living things in themselves.

I wondered if anything inside the museum could be of any use to my research. I took another look in each of the cabinets, then went through the door labelled *'The Kilportach Bog Men'*. It was yet another square shaped room, the floor wood panelled and the walls painted white. However, the contents inside were a stark contrast to the wearisome reception room that I came from. Against the left wall was proudly displayed what could only be the museum's greatest exhibit. It was a bog body, staring out from the walls of a large glass cabinet, illuminated by an overhead spotlight. It's arms were clasped around it's chest, the skin dark brown and heavily crumpled. It was not as well preserved as some of the others; there were numerous patches where the skin had peeled, revealing the stained skeleton underneath. But it laid in a position of unnatural contortion, the legs twisted round and bent opposite to the torso. I could almost feel an ache in my back from just seeing it.

However, the face on the body lacked the horrified expression of the latest one I saw fresh from the bog. Instead, his mouth was closed in solemn rest, his eyelids closed as if asleep. Nevertheless, a large hole was visible in the side of his head, almost identical to all the others. The skin was broken, the cavity irregular and jagged looking, as if the skull was cracked underneath the remaining skin. Like the others, the hole was in the top side of the head, a little above the eye socket and three or more inches in diameter. It was difficult to see what could have caused it.

On top of the glass cabinet, a few pieces of paper were neatly displayed, each with the headline '*Reference Only – Do Not Remove From The Museum'*. They seemed to be giving a brief history of the bog body I was standing in front of, as well as information about it's archaeological significance.

'The Silsbury Man was the first bog body to be found in the peat bogs surrounding Kilportach. He was unearthed in the first day of an archaeological study of the land, and is thought to be over 2000 years old. Originally known as 'Kilportach Man', his name was changed as more and more bodies were found in the bog lands. He was thought to be a man in his early 30's, and showed signs of having worked in rough, physical conditions. John Silsbury, who discovered the body, described it as 'the most spectacular thing I have ever seen'.

There is great debate over the reason for Silsbury Man's death. His body shows signs of a violent struggle, including strangulation and a fatal head trauma. It is very likely that Silsbury Man was murdered, and some have speculated the nature of death to be ritualistic. This hypothesis seems increasingly likely as more bog bodies are found in Kilportach. At the time of writing, every bog body has the same head wound, and all show signs of struggle or strangulation. At the present time, of course, one can but wonder what caused the untimely and brutal death of the Silsbury Man.'

It was infinitely fascinating, but the focus on head wounds on all of the bodies was making me aware of my own discovery. My head was presently without any pain, but I knew it was only a matter of time. I still wasn't sure that I trusted Kenny, but the MRI image could tell no lies. I had a 'traumatic brain injury', a term which had endlessly circled my thoughts ever since it passed from his lips that day. It sounded awful, like a step away from being told you are 'brain damaged'. Yet I knew full well I had no such thing; and the concept of such was loathsome to even think of. Of course, I was not prepared to lie to myself, but the label of having a TBI was still a shock to accept in it's fullness. I still wasn't prepared to see his psychologist, though.

Anyway, I quickly put it out of my mind, and returned the small exhibit room I stood in. Apart from the bog body, the room had collections of tools and jewellery, all found in the bog during the excavations. There were many elegant necklaces and brooches; most of which in nearly perfect condition, all hung to the wall and displayed on shelves. The tools were mostly spades and forks, used for cutting and digging the bog, all rusted away and pocked by woodworm. They gave the room a sensation of agricultural history; of people bent over and digging the peat, working hard until the sunset robbed them of light. It was, in many ways, what gave birth to the town.

Back in the reception, Jack was sat reading a letter behind the desk. His eyes were still swollen and visibly reddened, and he didn't even look up as I walked in the room. It was clear he wasn't ready to talk, and I wondered if he would not ask me to come back another time. Personally, although I had very few close friends, I knew I myself would not be willing to talk to anyone following such a death. I was surprised he had invited me there at all.

Sensing his grief, I did not speak to him, going instead through the opposite door with a label of *'The Wishing Lake'*. It had the same shape and décor at the previous room, but was lit by an overhead green filtered light. This soft glow gave the room an energy, taking the eyes some getting used to, but standing out and certainly unique.

At the back of the room, a long glass cabinet housed hundreds of items, all cramped together rather untidily. There were old coins, child's dolls and wooden carvings, watches, mobile phones, and even waterlogged books and photos. In the middle of the cabinet, a small piece of paper was stood on a stand, reading *'Assorted items found in the lake.'*

It was fascinating; exactly the sort of discarded items one expects to find in 'hidden places' such as the Wishing Lake. Many such places had them buried within them. I had nicknamed them 'trinkets'; like unusual shells in uncharted coves, or graveside ornaments in unused cemeteries. They would tell of a time when others had been there, leaving not just there imprint, but their items behind as well.

Of course, the wealth of objects inside the case were of far more interest than the usual findings. Being from the Wishing Lake, it was likely that they were used as offerings; thrown into the lake as a wish was made. This gave their already palpable aura a further sense of allurement for me. I wondered what wishes were connected to them; what troubles their owners told to the lake as they cast them into the waters below. In a way, it felt wrong that the objects were out on display; like the wishes had been pulled out from the lake, and put under lights for people to stare at. On the other hand though, each item was individually fascinating.

On the wall to the left of the large glass cabinet, a number of children's drawings were hung, each displaying a crayon picture of a Selkie. Some were far more detailed than others, and each was signed with the name of the child, as well as their age in thick black crayon. One in particular stood out to me. It showed a woman in front of the sea, removing the seal skin from her face like a mask. The drawings were unusual to see in a museum, yet they each represented a different child, having visited the town and learned of it's folklore. I thought it was an interesting touch.

On the other wall in the room, opposite the drawings, a painting of water was drawn onto the wall itself. It was detailed and colourful, showing a wave and a rippling blue covering nearly all of the wall. In it's centre, neat printed writing gave another version of the story of the Selkie and the Wishing Lake.

'One of the area's oldest folk tales, The Wishing Lake now sits quiet and alone, surrounded only in natural forestry. According to legend, a Selkie living in an early settlement was saddened by the misfortune of the people. She broke her secret to those she lived with, saying that the seal they had seen in the water was in fact her when in her seal-skin. However, she was going to give up her life in the village, only returning to grant the wishes of those who would visit her at the lakeside. To do this, she instructed that they leave her a gift by the lake, in order to make sure she listened to their wish. The greater or more luxurious the gift; the more likely she would be to shed her seal-skin, and grant the desires of whoever had asked her. Even to this

day, people who visit the Wishing Lake throw in votive offerings to the Selkie who lives there.

The origins of this myth are unknown. Studies of the town have found evidence of glacier caves in and around the area, and some are believed to have at one time ran underneath the lake. Other than this, the Wishing Lake is no different from other loughs in southern Ireland, apart from it's high content of votive deposits. This story has many different versions also, making finding the origin of the folklore almost impossible. Some versions state that the Selkie told the people what gifts she wanted, and was even responsible for stealing items and placing them in the lake herself. Either way, this story remains the most popular in Kilportach, and the tradition of offering gifts to the lake continues even now.'

So there really was evidence of caves under the lake. Amelia had previously said that there were none. This confirmed what the newspaper said as true, my family was killed near the Wishing Lake, when one of the glacial caves fell in. It was in one way a relief to know this; to at least understand that there *were* caves in town, and it's possible my family went inside for curiosity's sake alone. It all made sense, I could have simply been at home that day, and was swiftly taken to foster care after the news was broken to me. Such shock could clearly lead to confusion, and even memory repression like hinted at by Kenny. I felt a unique feeling of clarification; as if a blockage somewhere had been cleared and my mystery was starting to flow into proportion. Yet I still itched with the desire to know, to find out more, as much as I could about what happened 30 years ago.

In the reception, I decided to speak to the forlorn Jack. He agreed this time to speak with me, still visibly shocked but trying to remain as strong as he could. Before talking, he reached once more behind the desk and switched off the lights to the exhibit rooms. It was strange to think that the museum was opened momentarily just for me; that I was the only guest it would see all day, perhaps even for a week or more. That said, the reason I was there was because of Jack, and as he started to slowly open up to me, I felt a shuddersome realisation. Somebody in Kilportach was a murderer.

"You see", said Jack. "After I met you in the crowd there, when they found the bog body...Bridget came here. We looked at the records, just out of interest and nothing more...to help you, I suppose. Well, she..."

"Take your time."

"No, it's alright". He picked up a bulky envelope from the desk, and handed it to me. "She wanted to find you, but couldn't. So, well...she wrote you a letter. I'm sorry, I had to read it, again and again. That's why I couldn't speak...I wanted to see it again."

"Wait, what is this about?"

"We found something in the records for you. Good god...to think only a few short hours and...look, the letter will tell you. I can't, OK?"

"I understand."

It was difficult to follow Jack's train of thought. In fact, I didn't feel comfortable opening the envelope in front of him. If it was from Bridget like he said, I couldn't just stand there and read it in front of him. Instead, I thanked him for letting me see the museum, and told him I would read the letter later. Truthfully, I had no idea how to talk to Jack, and knew that inside he was not really ready to discuss the matter. So, after taking his envelope and giving more condolences, I left Jack in the tiny museum, and once more ventured into Kilportach.

I was sat on a bench near the town's main street when I decided to open the brown envelope. Inside, a handed written note was folded around a large and rusted key. The note was written in a blue ink pen, the writing neat if slightly slanting. A peculiar feeling seemed to rise from the paper; the chilling knowledge that what I was holding was written but hours before her death. It was almost as if she was still communicative, her note to me spoken from inside the grave, her words still clinging to the world with life. I put the key inside my pocket, and slowly read the personal letter.

'*Mr Clarke,*

I've left this in your room because I felt it easier to write this than tell you. I was thinking about your family research and went to see Jack at the town museum. Jack's the person you met at the peat bogs, he's a wonderful friend of mine and runs the museum all by himself. If you haven't been yet, then you have to go see it. There isn't much there really, but it's still all very interesting. Anyway, I was telling him all about your reason for being here, and we got onto looking through the old museum records. Well, believe it or not, we found something that could really help you. It's a bit strange, hence I thought I better write it rather than try to explain!

We found an old police document regarding the murder of a man called Shane Cullen. Nothing like that ever happens in Kilportach, so this was a really stand out case. Anyway, it seems that a suspect for the murder was a man called Lucas Clarke. It gets weirder, too. It says that Clarke was staying at Hawthorn House, my B&B, with his son. Now I can't vouch for that either way, as I hadn't taken over that place back then. But it's so odd. The Clarke family definitely lived in Kilportach, so why would they stay in a guest house in town?

I know this might be a shock for you. In fact, I'm sure it will be! Anyway, there was just one more thing, regarding the key I put in the envelope. It was in the museum, and Jack and I both thought it didn't belong there. We think it's the key to Shane Cullen's old cabin, which I believe is somewhere out of town (not sure). If you can make use of it, then please do so. Jack says the cabin is derelict, anyway.

Anyway, best of luck with everything else, and I hope your enjoying your stay in my B&B!

Sincerely, Bridget.'

I read the letter three times in my head. I thought at first I was imagining the names on the paper, like wishful thinking mixed with delusion. But it really was there. Lucas Clarke, my Father, a murder suspect. I couldn't even start to figure out my feelings. It had to be wrong. It just had to be. She even admits it; this Clarke was staying at her guest house, which wouldn't happen if he lived in Kilportach. But then, what did it mean? Were there two Clarke families in the town? It certainly made sense. What if the son he brought with him to town was me, and the other Clarke family are not related? My mind began to fight itself, fall into a kind of expected despair as I realised I still knew utterly nothing.

I sat for a minute, tried to cancel all incoming thoughts. It was impossible, of course. I had the key to Shane Cullen's cabin, meaning I could actually search inside and hopefully find just what happened to him. It was worrying though, for what if it were true, and he really was murdered by Lucas Clarke? No, I refused to believe it.

I had more questions than I knew how to deal with. All I knew for sure was that I needed to act; to step up the pace of my research in town and find out what happened once and for all. And yet of course, a new morbidity now hung over it all. Who killed Bridget Brady, and why?

In Remembrance

The death of Bridget and her subsequent letter had cast a despondency over my research. The guest house was now the scene of a kidnap, the bog lands the place I discovered her murdered body. A police presence hovered in the streets of Kilportach; their cynical eyes watching every small movement. Additionally, her letter had smashed at the very core my understanding of what happened in town. My Father was listed as a murder suspect, having killed Shane Cullen whilst he stayed in the same B&B I did. None of it made sense, and the rampant pulse of unanswered questions battered my head into sheer confusion. Really though, there were only two possibilities; either my Father was the suspect in question, or there was more than one Lucas Clarke in town.

I cleared my mind before continuing my investigation. I went into a very old fashioned newsagents, buying a bottle of chilled water to drink. Somewhat lost in thought, I paced up and down the still desolate main street, trying to straighten things out in my mind. I did however run into Adam, the man I had met in the pub on the night of the murder. As before, I was surprised at the colour in his cheeks and complexion, considering his own admission of illness. We didn't speak long, but he confided in me that he'd heard the bad news.

"I could hardly believe it", he said. "The place is so quiet, I can't even think of something like that happening here."

"I know."

"It's always been a really nice town". He glanced around the empty streets. "I thought so, anyway. They're such rustic and friendly people, don't you think?"

"I suppose. I don't know what could have happened, honestly, I don't."

"We'll likely never know. And it had to happen when I decided to visit, eh? Should have expected it!"

We shared a laugh together, even if unusual in the face of the topic. But both myself and Adam were outsiders in Kilportach; each there for our differing reasons. Bridget's death may have been a great shock, but our reasons for being there could not stop because of it. Actually, I decided to ask Adam; if only out of wishing to change the subject, about how he was enjoying his visit to Kilportach.

"Oh, well it's mostly just me saying farewell, you know?" he solemnly confided. "I'm staying in an old camper van, just out of town. And...well I'm mostly just looking at these old streets again, but from an adult's perspective this time, you see."

"Yeah. You were a child when you came last, weren't you?"

"That's right. I came with my dad on some business turned holiday thing. He had some friends here, wanted to catch up with them, and he treated me to the vacation as well. I can still remember how terrible I thought it was back then!"

We laughed again, with Adam saying that Kilportach was certainly unchanged, with even the shops the same ones as he remembered. I could believe it, and shook Adam's hand with a genuine friendliness as I wished him the best with his poignant holiday. And we parted ways, leaving me with a few seconds of forgetfulness, before sinking once more into memories of the tragedy. I shook my head, told myself again that I couldn't dwell on it, and tried my best to carry on with my own reasons for being in the town. So, putting my thoughts into action, I headed towards the tourist office, with questions forming in my mind to ask.

I remembered Catherine telling me she knew the Cullen family. I wondered if she would be willing to talk, to tell me more about Shane and what happened to him. When I went inside, she was standing behind the dingy desk at the back, dressed once again in a now more fitting looking black dress.

We began by exchanging sympathy's at the events that had happened in town, before I asked if she had the time to talk. She did, and before I begun to ask my questions, she struck a match and lit the stumpy candle on the desk.

"I always like this on", she said. "Even when I'm just alone. There's no reason, it just brightens the old place up a bit. I think so, anyway."

Catherine always seemed to be a humble old lady. She had seen Kilportach change through decades; knowing the streets which in turn knew her. I didn't hesitate to show her the key. I guessed that if she knew the Cullen family, the fact that I had a key to his cabin might inspire her to talk of them. I handed her the key and mentioned what it was, and she looked at it with an almost enchanted expression.

"This is really his key?" she said.

"So I'm told, yes."

She examined it some more, holding it close with squinted eyes, then handed it back to me. "Your planning on going into his cabin? Well, you'd be first one to go there since before it all happened. It's always been empty since then. You are going in, aren't you?"

"I am. But, do you know what's in there?"

"Knowing Shane, it will be exactly as he left it". She sat once more on the chair in the corner, where she had sat each time I had spoken to her. "Untidy, mostly likely. But filled with character. That was young Shane all round, really."

"You knew Shane Cullen and his family, didn't you? Could you tell me anything more about them?"

"I can, my friend. They were very good people, both of them were. Ambrose was Shane's Father, but his wife died whilst Shane was only a baby. Yet they worked together as a team, helped each other with all that they could. And Ambrose was such a dear friend to me. I always remember when he took me out. Oh, it was only the little pub in town, but it was wonderful. A candlelit dinner, just the two of us."

"And Shane?"

"He always wanted to become a gardener. Of course, Ambrose wanted him to be a vet like he was, but Shane just loved to be outdoors. Well, he found a job at a park just out of town; cutting grass, planting flowers, everything he loved."

"A park? Where about is that?"

"It isn't there any more. Oh, it's such a shame, isn't it? They closed it down, and all his flowers just wilted away. It looked so lovely when

Shane took care of it. But there's nothing there now. Actually, it was near the lake, not far from...well, his old cabin, you know."

It was hard to imagine a colourful park being near the Wishing Lake as it was now. All that was there was overgrowth, hiding even the lake itself beneath it's reach. To think that at one time a park was there; filled with flowers and freshly tended earth. It was sad, in a way. Just like his derelict cabin that waited for me, all Shane's life had been forgotten; covered in the wilderness he once strove to tame.

Of course, the thing I really needed to find out was the situation regarding Shane's death. I always felt he was somehow connected to my family, but Bridget's letter was a different matter entirely. I still didn't believe my Father was responsible, but the thought of it just wouldn't leave my mind. If it turned out I was wrong in my family research, and my Father was not the same man I thought, all I had found out would be for naught. I needed to know; and so far Catherine was by best option to do so.

"When Shane died, do you know anything about what happened?"

"I try not to think of it", she said quietly, her eyes removed from looking at me and swiftly towards the floor. "I think he was just too nice. Just like dear Ambrose, in a way."

I didn't know what to say, and knew even less about how to word it. Catherine seemed once more to return to her memories, staring at the floor as if the images of those she spoke about appeared to her from below. I simply stayed still, and allowed her to speak in her own time.

"He used to love that lake, you know. Both he and Shane did. Oh, how myself and Ambrose would speak about it. Long into the night, sometimes."

"The Wishing Lake, you mean?"

"Yes, my friend. Now I wouldn't say they believed the myths, but how they were both fascinated by them. I used to argue sometimes, you know. Why would a Selkie have nothing better to do than grant wishes, I would say!"

"I see. But do you know anything about why Shane might have been targeted? It just doesn't make sense to me, you see."

"Of course not. He was known, and liked, all over the town. It was just a pointless, horrible thing, done for completely no reason at all."

I got the idea that Catherine was not truly willing to discuss this in detail. I thus decided it was best not to push her, in case I needed more information from her in the future. However, it was clear from what she had said that Cullen likely had no enemies in the town. Could he really have been murdered in sheer cold blood? It was hard to believe.

I decided it best to leave the tourist office. I had gotten as many memories as she likely wanted to tell me, and I truly wanted to check Cullen's cabin. Before leaving though, Catherine stood up as I was about to open the door. I paused, turned once more to face her.

"You will go in there, wont you?" she said.

"Shane's cabin? Of course."

"Please, if you should find the painting in there, you will bring it to me, will you not?"

"What painting?"

"Oh, I am sorry. A painting by Shane of myself and his Father. I was quite a few years younger on it! Oh, if it's still there, please say you'll let me see it again".

"I will. No problem."

"You are a kind person. It would mean a lot to me. You know, Ambrose always said I looked grumpy on it. But my best memories are from those days."

Honestly, I was unsure about taking items from the cabin, even if it was just a derelict wreck. But Catherine clearly cherished her memories, and I felt she was starting to open up with her stories of the old Kilportach. Still, I doubted very much that her painting would be there. I already imagined the place to be empty; filled only with dust and rotting timber. Still, I knew I would soon be finding out.

On the way to the cabin through the deserted town, a niggling thought kept prodding my consciousness. What if I did find something in there which confirmed my Father was his killer? It struck me that even though hard to believe, the possibility of it was definitely real. The memories I had of my Father were as small and blurry as any childhood image. Indeed, the most vivid memory was simply of him taking photographs of me in a small garden. I didn't even know where it was, or what was happening on that day. So how could I possibly know for sure that this man really was not Cullen's killer? I couldn't.

When leaving the town and heading towards the lake, I caught sight of Dr Kenny coming towards me, walking with another man. I wondered if he was the psychologist he'd mentioned; the one he wanted me to see for therapy. He looked OK, I suppose; but the idea of seeing him was still out of the question. As they passed me, Dr Kenny muttered a simple hello, of which I friendlily acknowledged. Somehow though. I felt that if the other man was the psychologist, Kenny would waste no time in telling him about me and the MRI. Doctor's so called confidentiality always made me cringe. Still, I was not in the mood to concentrate on my headaches. In fact, since Bridget's death I had not had another pain up there. I knew it wouldn't last though, which was actually worrying considering I had not yet found a place to be alone and sleep.

As the final row of houses ended, an old street sign stood covered in nettles, pointing the way back into the main street, and towards the bog and cemetery. It was then I got the idea to revisit Amelia, if only to see if she was still in her graveyard 'home' from before. More than that though, I remembered her saying that she knew Shane Cullen as well, and wondered if she would share more information should I tell her about the key to his cabin. Indeed, Cullen and Edward were the only people Amelia spoke of in a positive light. If she was genuine about her childhood in Kilportach; she would probably be interested in going into the cabin. So, I would use the key as a bargaining chip, so to speak.

That said, my enthusiasm waned as I entered the cemetery, and was once more stood in the uncut grass with the crumbling, forlorn gravestones around me. There was not another person to be seen in the area, a factor I would usually see as beneficial, but not after all that had happened in town. It may have been just the fuzzy memory; the cemetery tree making me remember the headache and the 'thing' I saw, but I wasn't so sure. It was silent save for the chirping birds, the faded memorials standing weary by clumps of nettles and tall brambles. There existed a stillness which made me feel somehow unsafe by simply walking through it. It was like the sensation that someone was there; walking behind me with mute footsteps and vanishing when I peered over my shoulder. I usually loved the atmosphere of a cemetery, but it all felt different that day in Kilportach.

It was understandable, of course. Somebody in Kilportach was a murderer, their presence hovering in the minds of all who lived in the sleepy town. There was no telling who this person was, or what was their purpose of targeting Bridget. It could have been anyone, and they could have been hiding anywhere in town. Even the cemetery.

Therefore, upon finding the statue above Amelia's 'home', I paused with a gnawing and bothersome distrust. She had openly admitted her dislike of people, and lived secluded in a small graveyard, away from all collective sight. She was, in many ways, an oddity; and one whom I definitely couldn't exclude from being involved in Bridget's death.

I soon realised however my growing hypocrisy; and refused to envisage her as anything based on timorous speculation alone. I had always hated the sheer speed at which people disregard another's validity, simply because they are different to them. I had never fit into their 'roles' myself, and therefore knew that even I will have been vilified by the small minded masses. For all I knew, Amelia was closer to my own world-view than anyone else in Kilportach. Still, I felt unsure; hesitant even, at purposely knocking upon the door to the crypt.

Even when I did find the nerve to do so, there was perhaps expectedly no answer from her. I stood still for a second and listened within, but could not hear a noise inside. Again, I loudly knocked, this time shouting my name as I did, realising she would likely not open up for anyone. No answer. I thought at this point I was wasting my time, and turned to walk back up the steps to the cemetery. As I did though, I heard the door unlock, and heavily open. She really was there.

"What do you want?" she said as she opened the door behind me.

"Ah, so you are in there after all. I have something you might be interested in."

"What?"

I reached into my pocket and removed the key, then walked a step down towards Amelia. "This. It's the key to that cabin near the Wishing Lake. Shane Cullen's old hut, right?"

There was a moment of contemplative silence. She looked at me uncomfortably in the eye, then extended her hand hoping to take the key from me. I pulled it back, put it in my pocket. I felt an elongated second of apprehension; it was like she didn't know whether to speak or to slam the door back into my face. After a while though, she audibly sighed, then looked at me once more in the eyes.

"Alright. Come in then, I suppose."

She closed and locked the door as I stepped inside, and I was once more standing in her hidden abode. The room itself looked the same as before; an untidy bed and paper filled desk; selections of shelves jutting from the walls, covered in many ornaments and drawings. I knew then I hadn't simply imagined it, exaggerated the room's contents from having been in there with a terrible headache. No, it was all real. There were hundreds of decorations on the shelves, piles of clothes and objects on the floor, and that same wind-up lamp on the wooden desk, lighting the area in an eerie radiance. There was a sense of unreality present in the room, like it's airless humidity excluded it from existence inside the realms of the known. It felt wrong, but also luridly fascinating.

Amelia slumped down onto the bed. She was wearing this time an old looking white blouse, as well as a rather ripped beige skirt, long and covering all of her legs. Around her neck, she still wore the same mermaid necklace from before. I stood in the middle of the stuffy room, once more taking the key from my pocket.

"So where did you get that?" she immediately said.

"Well, you've heard of the murder that happened in the town, haven't you?"

"Murder? I heard some sirens the other night, but I didn't know what it was about. Wait, your telling me someone actually got murdered?"

"Someone called Bridget Brady. Know her?"

"Of course not." She stood up from the bed, pulled out the chair from under the desk, and nodded as to silently tell me to sit on it. I did so, and she sat back down on the creaky mattress. "I don't know any of them, really. Not any more. But seriously, one of them actually killed somebody? I didn't think the town was cut out for things like that!"

She showed a noticeable lack of emotion at the news. Of course, she didn't know of the person in question and had no reason to show personal grief, but I expected more than a simple acknowledgement. However, although it's possible that I was simply naïve, she seemed to me to be telling the truth about not knowing it had happened. I was still apprehensive though.

"I didn't think it possible either", I said. "But it happened. It was the person who's guest house I was staying in too, believe it or not."

"And what about the key? It's really Shane Cullen's?"

"Yeah, so I'm told anyway. That's why I came to see you. You knew the man, didn't you? As well as Edward Clarke and his family. I'm looking for answers, you see."

"Answers? You've got them, haven't you? It was you who told me how they died in the cave-in. Even I didn't know that. What more do you want from me?"

"Look, I know. But there's something else happened, and I'm not so sure any more."

"About this murder thing? Listen, if your playing detective I don't want to know. Don't involve me in other peoples problems, OK?"

"It's nothing to do with that. You might even be interested in this yourself. And believe me, I only want to know about my past, that's why I came here. So, will you hear me out?"

She leaned back on the bed, let out another extended sigh. "Go on, then. I'll listen."

It was then my chance to tell Amelia what I had found. I wasn't sure I was right in doing so, but I didn't hold back on explaining my findings. In a way, it was automatic; I was relieving burdens that had grown inside me, explaining my confusing research in words. She seemed to be listening, as well. So, I told her about how I wasn't on the records, how I couldn't remember my own Brother, how I knew nothing about my parents. I also explained my latest discovery; that Lucas Clarke was a murder suspect and how nothing seemed to weave into sense. I could have rambled for hours, most likely. However, it was not until I mentioned her necklace; explaining that my Mother wore the same one on a photo, that Amelia finally interrupted.

"What?" she said, sitting up straight from her reclined position, her hand instinctively reaching for her necklace. She hesitated to speak again, and looked me as though she was confused or suspicious of my story. "Your right, that is strange."

"What is?"

"Well, I suppose I should tell you", she sighed. "It was Mrs Clarke who gave me this necklace. Oh, and it's a Selkie, not a mermaid."

It was astonishing. In a breath, I leant swiftly forward on the chair, my eyes fixed firmly on the silver necklace she wore Somehow, I felt I had known it all along. It really was the same one. The hair was identical as on the photo; the etched tail bearing the exact same design. It was my Mother's necklace, the very one I had stared at for years in that photograph in my house. I felt at once startled, and yet also relieved; as her admission was certainly unexpected, but it served a purpose far greater than it's intent.

"Hang on a minute", I said. "This is the same person we're talking about, right? Edward Clarke's Mother? Ethel?"

"Of course."

"That's amazing". I stood up from the chair, on the verge of pacing around the room as I usually did when thoughts overtook me. "So then I really was right, all along. For a while I thought that I'd got the wrong people, that this other Clarke was my real Father. But now I know that it has to be-"

"Wait up", she interrupted, now standing up as well from her bed. "Don't go so fast. Now I'll admit, your story was pretty impressive. But if you want my opinion, your totally wrong."

"What do you mean?"

"Like I said, the Clarke's only had one son. Edward. He was my friend when I was a child, I think I should know."

"But...no, it's impossible". I turned to face her. "You've just said yourself that's my Mother's necklace. And my original research said Edward was their son. But they were my parents as well!"

"Your wrong. Look, you said that you weren't on the records, right? So that's proof that they aren't your family. Have you never thought that it could be the records that are wrong? Edward Clarke was their only child. I'm telling you."

"Alright, alright. But you admit it, don't you? It doesn't make any sense."

"Not really. It's obvious if you ask me. That other Lucas Clarke was your real Father, and you were the son he came to the town with. That's all, nothing else to it."

"I thought that as well". I took a few steps away from her, feeling the tension of debate starting to build. I stood facing the coffin propped up in the corner, it's morbid appearance not doing much to ease my growing unease. "But then what about the necklace? If the Clarke's from Kilportach aren't my family, then how would I recognise it was my Mother's? I know the records can be wrong, I do but, well honestly, I don't know any more."

"Hey, do you want me to show you something?" she said.

"What?"

"Come on", she made her way to the door. "I think you should see this."

I was not about to refuse. I did wonder though what she wanted to show me. If anything, it seemed she too was interested in what I had told her, but I couldn't be sure. However, seeing as she knew the people in question, it was possible she may have had a personal interest in the situations surrounding their death. I was still a bit unsure of her though, although somehow I found her interesting, despite our shared unsociable tones.

I wordlessly followed her outside of her converted crypt, and back into the abandoned looking cemetery. It was strange how noisy it seemed at first; the utter silence of the crypt having muted all sounds from the outside. Usually, I found the sounds of a cemetery to be nothing short of serenely tranquil, but at that time I could hear everything around me.

Amelia proceeded to lead me though the gravestones, eventually stopping near a line of trees, which formed the back end of the cemetery. Between the trees, numerous cracked and discarded headstones were thrown in the thickets and left to rot. Some had even sprouted new life from them, with clumps of moss and roots claiming them as their own.

It made me believe that this cemetery really was no longer used. The stones had been unearthed and then deserted, leaving only flattened and unmarked earth where the town's ancestors rotted below. It was almost reminiscent of Kilportach's bog bodies, expect that their discoveries were scientifically important. In the cemetery though, those loved ones buried in unmarked graves would cry out not to be unearthed. Their gravestones were removed and with them their identities; leaving only the trample of feet above them, oblivious to what lays beneath them.

In front of the trees with the damaged headstones, a large sandstone obelisk was standing alone, a carved cross rising from it's top. On it's face, decorative writing was etched caligraphically, and painted with black as to stand out.

'Sacred to the memory of
LUCAS CLARKE
Died 31st November, 1981

Also of
ETHEL CLARKE
and their beloved son
EDWARD CLARKE

They shall mount up with wings like eagles.
They shall run, and not be weary'

Seeing the names chiselled in stone made me feel an instant, salient emotion. It formed in my chest, like two large bubbles meeting as one, speaking in unison of poignancy and curiosity. The grave was, in many ways, the singular object I had expected to find. Yet it was not communicative, standing dormant in unanimated time, unwilling to rouse from it's nested inaction.

"So this is it, huh?" I remarked to Amelia.

"Yeah. I visit it all the time. I mean, they're still here, in a way, aren't they?"

"What do you mean?"

"Under the earth, right now, all three of them are laid there. So your not just visiting a gravestone, the people themselves are there. Or their...physical forms, you know?"

Many people would assume her statement to be outlandishly morbid or even incorrect. I however fully understood her. Metaphysical thought came naturally to me; entering my mind far easier than the shallow things most people filled their heads with. I always saw things in a different light, and it was no different with Amelia's statement. It was exactly what I was thinking myself; almost as if she had captured my thoughts. I imagined the passage of earth beneath me, through rocks and worms and moist, soft soil. I could almost see them laying under there; three splintered boxes on top of each other; three motionless bodies peering upwards. The once living forms of those people I searched for.

"I know", I said. "So these are the people that may be my family."

"Well, like I said, I think you are mistaken there. I mean look; Edward Clarke was their only child, and he is buried right here along with his parents. There was never anybody else. I would have known, wouldn't I?"

She was right, of course. I remembered Molly mentioning that only two children lived in the town then; and they had to have been Edward and Amelia. Thinking of this, the only thing that made sense was Amelia's proposal; the murder suspect Lucas Clarke was a different person entirely. He was my Father, and the son he came to town with was me.

But there was something else. It was something perhaps less 'real' than the stone, but it manifested with the same sense of corporeality. There were too many oddities to know for sure that I had been looking into the wrong Clarke family. Her necklace was one which stared straight at me, and the other was the matter of 'hidden places'. She had said previously that her and Edward had looked for and named things as 'hidden places', and her description of them was identical to my own. The Wishing Lake was indeed such a place, and it was fascinating to hear her refer to it as so. Knowing this, it seemed impossible that the Clarke's on the gravestone were *not* my family. I decided to ask her.

"You remember calling the lake a 'hidden place'? You said that you and Edward used to call things that?"

"Well, yeah. What's that got to do with anything?"

"I have called things 'hidden places' myself for years. It was something I thought I made up myself. They're the sort of places nobody goes, hidden and filled with unknowable feelings. Like the Wishing Lake. That's it, isn't it?"

She stepped back, paused for a minute beside the gravestone, once more making irritating eye contact with me.

"Hidden places are like that, yeah. I like them myself, thanks to Edward." She smiled in the direction of the old obelisk. "It's impossible you'd know that though. I mean, I think Edward got the idea from Shane Cullen."

"So then, those people have to be my family, don't they? I just can't make sense of it. Are you sure they didn't have another son?"

"I don't know", she sighed with underlying sensation of annoyance. "I suppose it is possible, but why would I never have seen him, eh? I don't know why you can't remember yourself, anyway."

It was almost embarrassing to admit that my TBI was preventing me from remembering my own dilemma. I thus didn't even mention it to Amelia, instead simply affirming that I couldn't remember with a definite air of 'avoiding the question'. Really though, it was worrying. If I could find the secrets buried from my supposed injury, perhaps this confusion would not exist. In a way, it was like my mind held it's own 'hidden place', that black blotch showing on the MRI, the place where my memories were laying in wait.

"I just can't remember", I firmly said. "I mean, why do you think I'm here? Look, if Shane Cullen had something to do with this, maybe I'll find something in his cabin, right?"

"Don't ask me." she said. "I was too young to know anything when it all happened, anyway. I guess it's possible that..."

"What?"

She turned away from the Clarke's gravestone, took a few steps forward, peering into the damaged stones in the trees.

"I suppose", she said. "Shane Cullen could have told you the same thing as he told Edward and me. You could have got 'hidden places' from him, and so it just feels like it's a coincidence, that's all."

"Ah, you mean if I was here with the other Lucas Clarke?"

"Yeah. What do you think?"

"It makes sense. I'd never thought of that, actually. You know, I really think I should visit this cabin of his. He seems to be right in the middle of all this."

Speaking to Amelia had given me new food for thought. From hearing my story free from confusion, she was able to ponder and theorize about it without the mental fog I encountered. What she said made sense; and seemed to, if only for a few seconds, clear my mind into new understanding. Furthermore, seeing the names of the Clarke's on the grave was a cold and essential reality check. Any callow illusions of their deaths being a mistake were swiftly put into perspective. They were dead; the entire course of their earthly lives reduced to an unread and deserted stone. There was nothing more.

It was not long before I left the cemetery and headed towards Shane Cullen's hut. Strangely though, Amelia said she wanted to come with me. She said that should I find something in there, she wanted to see it with her own eyes. Furthermore, she confessed that she found my rather muddled research to be engrossing; and as someone who knew the Clarke's as a child, found reviving their memory to pique her interest. So, as I walked through the outskirts of Kilportach, my journey was shared by the eccentric Amelia.

I felt uncomfortable with it, in a way. The realisation that the town hid a murderer was still sharp inside my mind, and Amelia's reputation was already tainted with venality. My thoughts flitted and fought with each other, building to an involuntary tight feeling in my stomach. Yes, I may have only been going to a wooden cabin with her, but it was still a drastic difference from simply speaking to the woman. I felt at one second that she was trustful and genuine, and at another that she was problematic and unstable. Furthermore, there was the fact that the Wishing Lake, and the hut which stood nearby to it, was even more secluded than the rest of the town.

Still, Amelia was likely there for her own reasons, the same as I was there for mine. The only real question is what we would find, if anything, hidden inside the old building of Cullen's. I felt that this man was important to my research; perhaps even the central point of which the events were all connected. I didn't expect to to find much in the cabin, but I knew I was finally on the right path. Moreover, I thought that perhaps Amelia's presence would help to make sense of anything I did find. For now though, Kilportach faded into the distance, and the Wishing Lake began to glimmer, against the backdrop of the cabin on the hill.

Recollections of the Past

Placing the key in the rusted lock created a peculiar, anxious feeling within me. The cabin was alone and drearily slumberous; it's boarded up windows like closed eyelids, lost in dreams of it's long dead owner. By opening the door, it was like I was waking it up; forcing what was inside to discard it's trance and hopelessly return to the modern day.

The key turned with relative ease. Amelia stood uneasily close to me, so near that I could feel her breath as it rhythmically pulsed beside me. I didn't like it. I just turned the key in the lock, heard an arthritic clunk from inside, and reached for the white, circular door knob.

"Wait", she said before I opened it. "Shouldn't we look around outside first?"

"What? No, come on, let's go in."

She backed away from me, and began to silently look at the cabin's exterior. I paused, deciding it best to not annoy her, and leave the door until she was ready.

"There used to be flowers here", she said. "And up the walls, there were drawings and things."

I remembered the cabin from Molly's photo. It was nearly unrecognisable now; all traces of the murals and growing plants reduced to nothing but untamed weeds. There existed a feeling of loneliness about it, like it sat in dejection at being forgotten, unseen by the other buildings in town. Perhaps it was just because it stood near the lake, but I felt that the wooden cabin hid answers; as if it's closed up windows were not actually dreaming, but remembering old things.

"When I go to the lake", continued Amelia. "I always stop here for a little bit first. It reminds me of the old Kilportach, before thing's were complicated."

"The town was different back then, wasn't it?"

"Oh yeah. Of course, people would say my childhood memories are just glorified and the town hasn't changed, but they're wrong."

I turned from Amelia and closely examined the cabin's surroundings. Catherine said that a park once stood nearby, and that Shane Cullen used to work there. Looking now, the hill I stood on was barren and empty, the tree near the cabin thickset and old, like the only thing remaining of a time gone by. There was nothing else there, no evidence of anything apart from nature.

"You know", she said. "If it wasn't for the bog bodies bringing people in, I'm sure the town would be dead completely. The people who live here just can't see it."

"I can understand that."

I turned back to the key in the door. Mental images swiftly appeared; the door would be opened to piles of history related entirely to my own research. Truthfully though, I didn't expect to find anything in there. In fact, I was slightly worried at the cabin's safety; it was visibly decaying and heavily weakened, the subsiding earth causing the wood to bend and fall away. The last thing I wanted was to be injured in there, especially with my only help being from Amelia. Still, it was impossible to change my mind about it.

"Come on", I said. "Let's go in."

"Right."

The door swung open with little effort, revealing a colourless, dingy room, the air immediately heavy with dust and mould. In the middle, an oblong table was standing empty, a single chair sat at it's end, covered in cobwebs and layers of dirt. Against the wall stood an ornate wardrobe, built from dark brown wood and carved with flowers. Apart from these, the room was empty.

"I knew it", I murmured as I walked on the loose feeling wooden floorboards. "Nothing here."

"Look", said Amelia facing towards the wall on the opposite side to the wardrobe.

It struck me at first with a sensation of geniality, a single patch of colour in the lifeless room. It was a painting, framed and hanging on the bare wood wall, depicting the portraits of a couple. The man was smiling with a hearty warmth, his arm wrapped tightly around his partner. He wore a pair of rounded glasses, and his hair was side parted and light brown in colour. The woman had black hair tied in a bun, and wore bright, silver and ruby earrings. Her eyes looked outwards with a longing stare, and her lips sat only on the cusp of a smile.

I soon realised that I recognised the woman. It was Catherine from the tourist office, meaning this was the painting she had spoken about. It was fairly large, painted with thick yet precise brush strokes, and whilst not a masterpiece in terms of skill, still encompassed the unique aura of it's subject. I knew at once that I had to take it to Catherine.

The rest of the cabin was seemingly bare. The occasional cockroach scuttled on the floorboards, and thick layers of dust had built in the corners. My illusions of finding stacked information or definite answers were swiftly put into their true perspective. The only thing in there were rotting floorboards and a heavy door of decay. There was nothing else.

Even the wardrobe doors were stuck, with Amelia trying to violently force them and giving up with a noticeable annoyance. I think she too thought something would be in there. Indeed, I decided to ask her, whilst still stood trying to open the wardrobe, just how this place looked when Cullen was alive.

"I can't remember the details of it, you know", she said. "But it was full of flowers and things, as I remember. Paintings, flowers, all that sort of thing."

"And Shane Cullen was friendly towards Edward Clarke and yourself?"

"Yeah. Most people seem to see a kid as someone so removed from them that they can never approach them. Shane was different though, he used to talk to me and Edward all the time. I'm not sure if he was right, thinking back, but at the time, he was like our 'friend', in a way"

"What sort of thing's did you speak about? With Edward as well as Cullen, I mean?"

"Why does it matter?" she pulled back on the wardrobe, forcing the door to open up. A visible plume of dust erupted, revealing a nearly empty wardrobe, housing only a small shoebox in it's corner.

"We were just kids, that's all. Yeah, there was the 'hidden places', but other than that it was just normal kid stuff."

"I see. Anyway, let's have a look at this."

I reached inside the wardrobe and retrieved the shoebox. It was around this time that I felt the 'signs' which would soon lead to something completely unexpected. At this point though, it presented itself as nothing more than a sharp pain in the centre of my head. It was like a thin knife had been pushed inside, running through the flesh with a momentary, yet distinct discomfort. I flinched back, almost dropped the box.

"What's wrong with you?" said Amelia.

"Nothing."

I opened the box, tried for a second to ignore the obviously approaching headache. It was amazing how quickly they could manifest, sometimes. That said, the contents of the box did help to capture my thoughts, stopping me concentrating on the pain if only for a few seconds.

A piece of paper, yellowed and covered in what looked like mould, was folded around a polaroid photograph. It was a man with combed-over dark hair, dressed in a business suit and stood by the window inside the cabin. I recognised him from Molly's photograph. It was the man who was sat with Cullen on her photo, the person she said was a visitor in town. Why would a picture of him be kept after so long?

"Do you know this person?" I asked Amelia, who stood close at my side so we could both see the photo.

"I don't think so. Looks like it was taken in here, though. Must have been one of Shane's friends, or something."

"Molly from the pub showed me another picture of him, said he was a visitor in the town. Not much help, either way."

I turned over the photograph, revealing on the back a smudged line of text, written by hand in a black ink pen. *'Lee Buckley, 1981'.*

"Lee Buckley, eh?" I remarked, putting the photograph into my pocket. "Anything else in here, you think?"

"I doubt it. Looks like all the things were taken away" she sighed. "In a way, I actually expected to find the place still full of his things. Stupid, right?"

"Not really."

It was at this time when, without any warning, the 'sign' I had turned into a frightening reality. It is difficult to convey in words an experience which only half existed in consciousness. It was like waking up from a lucid dream, and thinking for a second that it really happened, before realising that the bed was beneath you. During moments like that, a fogginess forms in the centre of the mind, making it feel both deftly confused and actually physically heavy. That same sensation overcame me in that second.

The first time I realised something was wrong was when I realised I was on the floor. I was laying, looking upwards at the worm-eaten ceiling, my back stretched out against the floorboards. At first, I assumed I had been asleep for hours, and all that I experienced was in fact a memory now fading away with the act of waking. After a second though, I realised that I once more passed out, and had no idea what had happened to me.

I sat up sharply, catching sight of Amelia sitting on the chair at the end of the table. She breathed a sigh of what I assumed to be relief, then stood up and joined me as I slowly got to my feet.

"What the hell happened there?" she blurted out.

"Wha...look, did I...wait, what happened?"

"You just collapsed on me! I thought you'd had a heart attack or something, you scared me to death!"

"How long was I...how long?"

"I don't know, about quarter of an hour or something. I mean, I straightened you out on the floor there. I didn't know what else to do!"

I could hardly believe this had happened again. Just like in Dr Kenny's surgery, I had lost consciousness without any warning and with no memory of what happened to me. I felt groggy as if I'd slept all night, with my head now pulsing with a dull headache, and my stomach turning over with nausea. It was frightening. It felt like I had no control of my body, that such a thing could happen again and end up causing a serious problem. I walked to the chair Amelia had been sat on, and fell into it with a painful rigidity.

"Are you alright?", continued Amelia. "I mean do you have some sort of illness or something? Why didn't you tell me!"

I knew that I had to tell Amelia. If anything, she had now helped me with the headaches twice, even if her comforts were lacking in delicacy. For a second though, I just sat and concentrated on my breath. It had happened so fast I could not focus on it; still thinking I was half asleep or maybe even in a dream. There was something about losing all awareness, something which felt uniquely daunting. It was as if I had travelled out of my body; returning only with muted memories of some far off, immemorial darkness. I didn't like it. It made me feel decisively unsafe.

Still, I managed to tell Amelia, albeit slowly and after much recuperation, about the headaches I had suffered from. I told her about the MRI, the 'things' I had seen, and the eventual diagnoses of traumatic brain injury. While I told her, she stood at the end of the table, her hands leaning against it, and simply listened. I was surprised she did not interrupt or speak; something I felt most people would do when confronted with such a woeful admission. When I had finished telling my tale, she stood for a second and looked at me, before finally responding to what I had said.

"So, when I found you in a bad way in the cemetery, that was to do with one of these headaches?"

"Yeah. Like I said, Kenny wanted me to see a psychologist, but I couldn't go through with it. But I don't know what happens, they just...come on."

"I see. Well, I'd say your right about the psychologist anyway. They'll just make you worse."

"I know. I just hate the idea of it." I stood up from the chair, my headache still throbbing yet not as strong as it could be. I did however take a tablet, getting one from my pocket and forcing it down my throat without water. It would help, but for how long I could never tell.

"Oh, nearly forgot", said Amelia. "I managed to open the bottom drawer in the wardrobe whilst you were out."

"Anything in there?"

"Have a look". She reached into her pocket and removed a piece of lined notepaper. On it, a handwritten letter was neatly written, the writing style old fashioned and calligraphic.

"That's all that was in there", she said. "See what you think."

I was not really in the mood for reading; my eyes still slightly fuzzy and my mind overwhelmed with what had happened. One thing I always told myself though was to avoid focusing on the headaches. Doing so only amplified their feelings, in the same way that thinking about your heart will make you aware of it beating inside your chest. So, after a few more words to Amelia about the cabin, I walked back to the chair and sat down, trying to focus on the letter in front of me.

'Shane,

Thanks for allowing me to meet with you in Kilportach. It will be wonderful to finally see the place with my own eyes, not to mention putting my ideas to work. I have waited a long time to finally visit, and knowing you'll help me is a truly great comfort.

Anyway, I've been getting our findings ready for when I come. As I said, I am sure that the recent unearthing of 'bog bodies' are directly related to the gifts at the lake. Just think about it. Those bodies are dated at over 2000 years old, meaning they are the people who originally lived in Kilportach. Now, what reason would primitive settlers have to kill so many people? It just has to be the lake! I'm sure of it. Those bodies are the gifts that were left to the Selkie; offered to her at the waterside. It has to be. After all, was it not said in the book you sent me that Selkie's were often seducers of men? The settlers were simply giving her what she wanted. That way, she was sure to grant their wishes. (Couple this with the original book, and we're definitely onto something).

There's more, too. If what you said has truth in it, we could be really onto something interesting. You said that in another version of the tale, the Selkie stole gifts or told people what she would like. If this is so, it means she chose only certain people to be offered to her at the lake. This means one thing; the bog bodies are not just random people. The settlers chose them especially to sacrifice; they thought the Selkie had wanted them for herself. Therefore, this is where we need to research. What made them choose only certain people, and did those chosen go willingly to their deaths?

I do hope you'll continue to help me with these enquiries, Shane. You have been of a far superior help than any number of books could be. I just hope that when I arrive in town, we discover the truth of the matter together. So, all being well, I shall meet you as discussed a week on Thursday. I already feel excited at the prospect of seeing the town for myself!

Yours Sincerely,

Lee Buckley'

The letter was not what I had wanted to see. It contained nothing more than a slew of questions, and at the same time answered none of my own. Still, it's content was interesting on it's own; a small peek into the life of Shane Cullen. So it seemed he was helping this Lee Buckley with some research into the Wishing Lake myths. I had also never thought of the reason the bog bodies met their end. Thus, his hypothesis struck me at first as outlandish, but there was no pretending the bodies were not a mystery. Anyway, the letter was not of direct help to me, and for that reason, I did not dwell upon it for long.

I did not really feel like leaving though. My body had sank into the rickety chair, and I didn't feel like standing up and worsening the throbbing ache in my head. Truthfully, the fact I had lost all consciousness again was filling me with an involuntary dread. I knew at once; I had to see Dr Kenny again. The idea of passing out without fair warning was both dangerous and uniquely upsetting. I was lucky that Amelia was there to help that time.

In fact, it wasn't long before she helped even further, with the empty cabin enlightening memories of her time in the town as a child. She was pacing around on the dust laden floors, presumably waiting for me to move or say something. I didn't, of course. After a while, she stopped in her tracks, turned to me and spoke with instant spirit, as if she had mentally snapped her fingers.

"Of course. Edward must have gotten 'hidden places' from Shane! Just like I thought."

"How so?" I raised my head from it's growing daydream, momentarily awakened by her assertiveness.

"I just remembered him calling the lake that. It's weird how memories come back when standing in places like this, isn't it?"

"You mean Cullen called the lake a 'hidden place'?"

"Yeah." She walked up to me, leaning on the table. "We used to often go there as kids, you see. Well Shane definitely called it a 'hidden place', with all the same descriptions that Edward did later. So yeah, I'm sure of it."

The Wishing Lake was definitely a 'hidden place', judging by my own definition of the term. So if what she said about Cullen was true, it meant I can't have created the concept myself. It was interesting news, though in my state of recovering from the recent episode, it only worsened my growing confusion. I was always sure that 'hidden places' were my own invention and nobody else's. But if Shane Cullen had known about them, as well as Amelia and Edward respectively, then my assumption was clearly a mistake. It didn't make sense, like being told a story you wrote yourself had been told exactly by another writer. I could feel my head twist inside, both with the throngs of headache pain, and from simply trying to make sense of my findings.

"And you said yourself the lake was a 'hidden place', when I was there", I said, moving my chair back ready to stand up. "So, you too got the idea from Shane Cullen as a child?"

"I suppose so, yeah. Me and Edward used to try and find them though; go on little adventures to discover such places. Like children do, you know."

"Well then", I stood up, a feeling of heaviness falling through my head. "I must have met Shane Cullen too, then. Don't you think that makes it impossible for me to-"

"Wait", she interrupted. "Don't start with all that again. You could easily have met Shane when staying in town with your dad. Come on, it's simple, isn't it?"

"Yeah, I know", I lowly replied. "It's just a pretty big hit if it's true, that's all. Look, you really think that other Lucas Clarke was my Father?"

"Of course. It's easy, I don't know why you can't see it."

"Tell me."

She sighed, shook her head slightly, before leaning more heavily over the table, and drawing a circle in the dust with her finger. From there, she began to recite her theory of my story, drawing more circles and connecting them with lines, as to try and join up the threads of my tangled research. I just stood, looking at her dust drawing on the table, and tried my hardest to listen to her theory.

"So, the thing that confused you was the records you found in the first place, the ones which made you come to Kilportach. They were wrong. Think about it; two Lucas Clarke's were in town at the same time. It's easy for the records to get mixed up over the years. That's why you weren't mentioned on them, your record was lost when the two Lucas Clarke's were mixed up. What you found was the family I knew; and you obviously assumed them to be the right people. That's why you couldn't 'remember' Edward; he was never your Brother to begin with."

I stood still for minute and thought about it. It all made sense, and hearing my story from another's lips made me realise just where the confusion had came from. I'd been wasting my time, all along. Of course, there were certain strands which were still unexplained, but it seemed at that moment I could blame myself and my TBI for most of it. The feeling was refreshing, yet also disappointing. My mysteries were making sense for once, but my family research added up to naught. More than that, the Lucas Clarke who stayed in town was a murder suspect for Shane Cullen. What happened with him?

It was not long before we left the cabin. Of course, I first removed the painting of Catherine, intending to present her with it shortly. I also desperately wanted to see Dr Kenny; partly to see the MRI printout again, yet mostly to ask about my loss of consciousness. In fact, the concern I felt towards my headaches was greater than the fear of being alone with Amelia, or of finding the cabin in it's forlorn state. In many ways, the cabin itself was a disappointment; it held no secrets apart from the painting, just countless years of dust and woodworm.

On the way back to town, the sky abruptly opened with rain. Oddly, there was no gradual gathering of clouds, nor even a few small warning droplets. It simply began to fall to earth; so heavy it bounced from the pavement's and curbs, creating puddles with nary an effort. In a few short seconds, my clothes were saturated; the town covered in a dark grey blanket which altered it's very mood and appearance. In the gloom, Kilportach lost the aura of a quaint little town, instead becoming a mournful creature, remembering old rain storms which had fallen across it; lamenting quietly in it's own solitude. It felt far more sinister.

Certainly, the rain that day was so heavy and sudden, that I ran with Amelia to her cemetery home for cover. I held in my arms the framed painting, rain falling smoothly across it's glass, freeing dirt and dust which ran black across it. In fact, I held it out in front of me as I entered the crypt, making it essentially the first thing I took out of the unrelenting storm.

Once Inside, Amelia quickly forced shut the door. Yet again, it's loud clunk closed was followed by nothing; just cold and somewhat unearthly silence. Still, we were out of the rain, and as I placed the painting down against the wall, my clothes dripped freely with freezing water, falling onto the cracked, unclean stone floor. I was pleased to be out of the piercing rainfall, but in some ways the clammy odour of the tomb made my sodden clothes feel even more drenched.

Still, my headache had just about faded away, and I was, for the time being, safe from the elements which ravaged outside. Amelia instantly turned on the lamp, and I slumped down onto the old chair from before. For now, the rest of the world was shut out from existence. There was only myself, the coffin in the corner, and the mysterious recluse who lived in there.

The Wishing Lake – Mark Robinson

Eclipse

The first time I met Amelia, I found myself both curious and taken aback at her furnished tomb and misanthropic personality. When meeting her again at the Wishing Lake, she almost refused to speak to me, our conversation more of a short and apathetic two-way argument. She was an oddity; an eccentric person of whom the town spoke low of, a cynical hermit who didn't try to be trustworthy. For anything, she was the most suspicious of all the townsfolk I'd met; an assertion I shouldn't having taken lightly, seeing as there was a killer in town.

That day though, I was with Amelia for over an hour, as I waited for the rain to ease before deciding to leave her crypt. During that time, the minutes of silence grew weary and thin, the room all but demanding a conversation, or at least a few words to be spoken between us. And so we did. Of course, my only real concern was my family research, but when Amelia began to speak to me, I couldn't help find myself enjoying her company. Well, it was perhaps not 'enjoying' so much, as feeling an arrant understanding with her.

She had broken the silence with the offer of a drink or cigar, saying she kept such things in the drawers and that I could reach in and help myself. I did not trust drinking her liqueurs though; not so much because of their age or appearance, but more of my gnawing distrust of both herself and the townsfolk in general. I had read too many mystery novels where poisoned drinks were downed unawares. Instead, I took up her offer of a cigar, and opened her drawer to find a handful to choose from.

From then on, I occasionally checked on the status of the weather, and engaged in curious conversation with my host who laid sprawled out on her bed. As always, I refused to ask for personal anecdotes; I disliked banal social chatter so much I would not inflict it on anyone. Interestingly, she seemed to be the same. She told me she simply had no time for 'people'; that the pointless things they brought to her life where not in her eyes worthy of her effort. That said, she didn't appear to be overly hostile, rather emitting a sheer disinterest, a somewhat rare ability to see things as they were.

So, as I leaned back on the chair in her dingy abode, the corona shaped cigar filling the room with it's leafy aroma, my own emotions seemed to float along with it. In a way, one would think emphasising with a shared world-view would fill the body with positive feeling. But alas, it wasn't so for me. My own indifference towards society was something I thought of only in passing; I never gave myself time to sit and wonder just why I was the person I was. That being, when Amelia spoke about her willing removal from society, I felt not only a sense of agreement, but involuntary memories beginning to churn.

I could almost see my foster parents forming in plumes of the smoke I exhaled. Growing up in the Ford household, it was evident quickly how removed from their world I was. In the years of adolescence and early adulthood, their incompetence didn't simply burn, as fill me with a sheer, inexpressible fury. Constantly, they would disregard my every ambition, assuming my detachment from social propaganda to be something they needed to be 'concerned' about. I could understand such involvement to be present with a child, but when a man is older he knows what his needs are. Yes, in my case this meant solitude and remoteness, but it was born entirely from my own personality, rather than pathetic psychological excuses.

I could easily have fell into a spiral of scorn, a dark mood massaged by the tranquil taste of the expensive cigar I smoked. Indeed, I had been a 'lover of the leaf' for years; the opiate flavour of good cigars the perfect companion to many a night. Still, a bad mood was not on the cards for that day. Amelia's own misanthropy was far greater than that of my own, and our conversation grew thin rather quickly, prompting me to once more open the door and check on the weather outside.

When the rain finally stopped, I was quick to leave. Her 'home' still held an essence of murky repugnance, the air heavy with damp which lingered in the lungs. I had no reason to stay with her for longer, anyway. So, I took the painting of Catherine from against the wall, and thanked Amelia for the cigar. Before I left, she sat up straight from her laying position, and called out to me as I opened the door.

"Hey, thanks to you, as well. For showing me Shane's cabin, I mean."

"No problem."

"Seriously, Leonard. It meant a lot to me, to see it again. So yeah...thanks."

It was was the first time I had heard her speaking softly; a tone in contrast to her otherwise sharp indifference. Though it wasn't until I had left the cemetery, and was on my way back to the now yawning main street, that I realised how much I was grateful for our interlude. By telling my story to another person, I had allowed myself to put it into perspective, and seen it displayed from another angle. If anything, her version of the truth behind the research made more sense than my own introspection; and whilst walking the paved street of closed up shops, I had no trouble in believing it as true. More than this though, I should have thanked Amelia for staying with me, helping me as I passed out in the cabin. After all, it would have been far more unnerving if I had experienced the episode alone.

Of course, I really needed to see Dr Kenny. For the time being though, I had few options. The tourist office, as well the remaining shops on the main street, had closed their doors and turned off their lights. Interestingly, some shops left items on display outside; the antique shop in particular leaving out a table with multiple objects on it. It even had an A-Board still by the door, an open sign hung upon it, above it's name *'The Rabbit Hole'*. I wasn't sure if the owner had forgotten to remove it, or had simply known that his items would be safe. Either way, I would have to wait until the next day to present the painting to Catherine.

For the rest of the night, I didn't do much but sit in the pub, sharing a meal with Molly and Adam before gradually watching the night grow old. We didn't even speak about anything interesting that night; I think the news of the murder was still on their minds, and so all other conversation was rendered insignificant. I didn't mind, I was pleased to not have to explain that I now believed I was wrong in my research. That said, Adam did tell me of the old Kilportach, saying he remembered the park by the lake from when he visited as a child. Like myself, he seemed to have visited the Wishing Lake and found it's current starkness a little unexpected. Other than that, the topics we spoke of were largely without a tangible subject.

I spent another night in the pub, as well. Like before, Molly agreed to let me sleep in the closed up bar. In a way, I was amazed that the pub did not have guest rooms upstairs, but according to Molly it never had done. Indeed, she said that the upstairs was mostly undecorated, with only her own living quarters being fit to live in at all. It was not too much of a surprise though; Kilportach was hardly bustling with trade. In fact, whilst laying and trying to force myself into sleep, I remembered the recent bog body discovery, and how I assumed it would bring people into the town. But apart from Adam, I had seen very few. It was like he and myself were the only outsiders in the entire town; or even in the entire area. It was so secluded.

The next morning, I decided not to stay around for Molly's kind offer of a cooked breakfast, wanting instead to find Catherine quickly and then move onto Dr Kenny. As far as my research; I wasn't even thinking about where I could go next. If Amelia's theory was correct, the only thing I could try to find out was how Lucas Clarke was involved in Shane's murder. Maybe then I could find out the name of his son, or at least something about the man himself, so that I knew for sure the hypothesis was right.

By coincidence, the only person I could think of to ask was the very woman I was going to see. Perhaps Catherine would be willing to talk after I gave her the painting of herself that she asked for. Still, I knew it was a difficult subject for her, and that she wasn't guaranteed to remember anyway.

Still, my first port of call was the tourist office, and as usual Catherine was sat inside, already on the old chair in the corner, seemingly hypnotized in the silence. As I entered, she realised immediately I was holding the painting, and stood up to greet me with a wrinkled smile.

"My word, is that...you found it?"

"I did". I couldn't help but feel honoured at handing her the painting, as if I had handed her something to reunite her, even if for a second, with the man she loved from her past. In a way, the painting belonged to her, and as I let her take it from my arms that day, it was like the painting itself had longed for the day she would see it again.

"Oh my...oh yes. Yes, it's exactly as I remembered."

She stood still in the dingy tourist office, her arms clasped tight around the large framed canvas. For a number of seconds there was nothing but silence. I could sense her sentimentality. Soon though, she carefully put down the painting, leaning it against the desk at the back of the room, and continued to look at it as she spoke.

"Thank you, my friend. Thank you. Ambrose; no, Shane would have wanted this. I'm sure of it."

"It's my pleasure." I didn't really know how to respond, though I realised I had done the right thing in removing the painting from the cabin it stood in. In there, it was a definite oddity; standing out against the dust and barren walls worn thick with cracks. Now though, it looked almost to be in the place it was made for; beside the person who once posed for it, sat humbly below the flicker of her candle on the desk.

"Doesn't he look wonderful on it? That's how I remember him. Always."

It was obvious Catherine was emotional at the prospect of being in possession of the painting. In a way, I almost felt like I shouldn't have spoken, but simply let her peer at the picture and came back to ask her my questions later. At the time though, I craved information on the other Lucas Clarke, realising that without a lead to follow, I may as well have left Kilportach completely.

"Um, Catherine, was it? Look, could I ask you something about Shane Cullen? I was hoping to find answers in his cabin, but apart from your painting, there was nothing in there."

"Really, there was nothing there?" She turned to me. "That's a shame, my friend. It is. Oh, and of course you can ask me about young Shane. Please, feel free."

"Thanks. Well, my family research seems to be connected to the Cullen's somehow, and I was wondering...when Shane died, what happened in the town afterwards? I mean, they must have questioned people about it, right?"

"Oh yes. Just like now, the town was in shock. Perhaps even more so. There was a lot of things, a lot of theories. But they never found anything about 'why' it happened."

"I see. And what about Shane himself? Did he have any fears or anything like that, as if he had an idea what was going to happen?"

It was funny to hear myself speaking like a detective. I had an image in my mind of the worthless police man who took me for my statement; hoping I was not seen in the same light by Catherine. I detested the police and their methods of questions; seeming to treat every person they met as potential criminals waiting to be 'caught'. Truthfully, I had felt like that ever since the night of the murder. The entire town felt colder now that a police presence was there.

Catherine however remained friendly, taking another look at the painting I brought her, then slowly sitting back down in her chair.

"No, no. Shane was always happy, and always so very friendly. Honestly though, I'm not sure I can remember. He had just had a friend stay with him, I think. That's why it was such a shock to us all. Everything was so perfect, so normal."

I wondered if she meant this Lee Buckley character, the person from the old photographs and letter. According to Molly, they were together a lot, and the letter confirmed that they were interested in the Lake. Of course, this seemed unconnected to the murder or my research, but Lee Buckley was the only person around then of whom I had heard nothing about. Of course, I asked Catherine if she knew him, but she couldn't remember. Politely though, she told me that should the name come up, she would try to make sure to tell me about it.

Leaving the tourist office, I felt I had done Catherine a great service, and an unusual warmth fell over my body. The painting may not have been worth a great deal, and was not even particularly well painted, but to the old lady it meant the world. Of course, I had not gotten the information I hoped I would have, but for the time being I wasn't too bothered.

Next on my list, I headed towards Dr Kenny's surgery. Of course, I knew already that he would recommended the psychologist, but for once I cared not for the obligatory 'push'. More than anything, I wanted to see the MRI again, if only to study it and come up with questions. Unlike the usual headache experiences, the fainting episodes were far more upsetting. I wasn't too concerned about the pain I felt, or even the hideous 'things' I saw. Such aberrations could swiftly be dealt with by simply taking the pills I carried. But losing consciousness was different entirely, and worryingly it was a new experience. Previously, I had never passed out because of the headaches, even though I sometimes felt close to doing so. But within my time in that unwelcome town, I had fully fainted more than once. I did think that it may be related to stress; but I realised that thinking so was avoiding the subject.

Annoyingly, when I finally arrived at the doctor's surgery, I found that Dr Kenny wasn't there. Instead, I was met inside by the other man, the one I had seen Kenny walking with before. Thankfully, he was friendly.

"Dr Kenny? Oh yes, he's about. He's at the peat bogs I think, something to do with the latest body we found. Were you looking for him?"

"Yeah. I saw him a few days ago, and I just wanted to ask him something. Will he be back soon?"

"Oh, just go down there and see him, why don't you? I'm sure he wont mind. He's always complaining that this place is too quiet, anyway!"

"Yeah, he mentioned that. OK, I'll take a walk down there to see him. Thanks."

"Actually", said the doctor as I was about to leave. "Are you Dr Kenny's patient then? There's a Mr Clarke patient at the surgery you see, and-"

"Yeah, that's me."

I knew that Kenny had been talking to the other doctor about my condition. That said, it was possible that I was the only patient in the surgery, as it still looked empty from where I was standing. Of course, the fact that my MRI had been shown to the other staff was not really of my concern. I knew all along that the pledges of confidentiality were taken with grains of salt by doctors. I didn't care about it then though. I just wanted some advice.

"So, your Mr Clarke?" said the doctor. "Well look, if your question was regarding a health concern, I'd be more than willing to help you myself. I can pull up your records on the computer, you see. If you wanted, that is."

To be honest, I didn't feel like walking all the way to the peat bogs, just to be told to go back to the surgery when I got there. This doctor seemed just as friendly as Kenny, and although I was still sceptical of their agendas, I needed more than ever to find some fresh answers.

"OK, that's fine." I said.

"Great. So then, we can do this in my office I think. It's just down here, if you'd like to follow me."

Once more I was led through the empty surgery, the scent of antiseptic strong in the air, the corridors desolate and silent. I had not walked more than a couple of hundred yards though, when the doctor stopped me by a closed private room.

"You saw the bog body from the other day, didn't you?" he asked.

"I did, yes."

"I see. Well in that case, you might just be interested in seeing this thing. I haven't shown anybody yet you see, so I'd appreciate your opinion on it."

I didn't have time to wonder what he meant. He pulled down on the silver handle to the door, and swung it open for me to see inside. It was a small, square shaped recovery room; the usual selection of hospital décor covering each of the white painted walls. In the centre, a hospital bed was raised to an almost seating position, a standard lamp pointing a harsh light onto it. On the bed, the bog body was peering outwards.

It caused another involuntary 'jump', the unexpected sight of the blackish body staring out at me from the middle of the room. It looked wrong, though, like it wasn't supposed to be there. The room was designed to recover from illness, to gradually get back on your feet and leave the surgery in full health. But the bog body represented an opposite to this function. It was out of place; an image of death, of preservation of death, in the midst of a room focused only on life. It was hard to look at, somehow.

"I thought I'd make a little display for him", said the doctor. "In case people came here to see him, you know?"

"I see."

He closed the door, looked at me with a thick smile, and signalled for me to continue following him.

"What did you think?" he said as he continued to walk through the corridor.

"Well, I don't know. I mean, I saw a lot of the bodies when I came with Dr Kenny. It's odd seeing this one displayed like that, if I'm honest."

"Yeah, I guess it could seem a little morbid. But the surgery is empty, if you hadn't noticed. We thought we may as well use it for something, and the research of the body's is the main thing we're here for."

"Ah, so you came here from out of town as well?"

"I'm from Limerick, same as Dr Kenny." He reached a door at the end of the corridor, went into his pocket for a bunch of keys, and fumbled around to find the right one. "The name's Don Ryan, I usually work as a clinical psychologist. They brought me here to have a look at the bodies, if you can believe that."

I should have realised it sooner. This was the psychologist of which Dr Kenny wanted me to see for my TBI. I felt like I'd been intentionally led here, as if the doctor knew I was reluctant to see him and thus tried his best to twist my arm. I was being paranoid, though. If anything, he seemed a lot more 'human' than I had imagined, his light brown hair and clean shaven appearance a far cry from the mad-doctor image I conjured. Still, I felt I needed to be careful.

Inside his office, he offered me a seat on a long, brown leather sofa, and booted up another old PC, which whirred loudly in the small office room. On the walls, numerous medical posters were hanging, and a cabinet at the back held many different coloured files. On the doctor's desk, the old monitor was sat next to a pile of hand written papers, as well as a china phrenology head. Interestingly, the head was the only thing in the room which told me I was visiting a psychologist.

If anything, it was just like any other doctor's room; minimal and covered in documentation, a fold up bed and lamp in the corner.

"Alright now", said Dr Ryan as the computer fully loaded. "All I'm going to do is pull up your records here. Shouldn't take a moment. In the meantime, why don't you tell me what the problem is today?"

"Well, I don't know if there'll be much you can do", I said leaning forward on the sofa. "But it's my head, you see. I had an MRI with Dr Kenny, and he found a TBI on the results."

"Traumatic Brain Injury, eh?" He faced away from me, typing on the keyboard. "Well, your right that it isn't my field in itself. But I'm sure we can discuss something together. OK, I have your records up on the screen here."

I was beginning to worry, even if just slightly. I knew that the doctor would read of my memory repression, as well as my visual and auditory disturbances. I even imagined it would say on the records that Kenny requested I see the psychologist. I felt at once like I didn't belong there.

It was not that I didn't like Dr Ryan, his willingness to see me without delay was unexpectedly cordial. It was just that I felt a staunch dislike for the whole profession of modern psychology. The brain itself was fascinating to me, and many times I had wondered about it's secrets and thought about just what made it 'work'. But psychologists, despite their supposed expertise in the field, seemed more concerned with asinine dogma than anything substantial. Of course, I had never before spoken to an actual practitioner, but had read many times their articles and opinions. Unfortunately, what I saw almost always angered me. It seemed that many thousands of people were fiercely quick to believe their 'diagnoses'. But unlike the MRI scan I had done, there was nothing tangible to see or feel. Their disorders and syndromes did not really exist.

For that, I was nervous at the prospect of talking to the doctor. Of course, I realised I was not there for psychological treatment, but the stigma of his profession wouldn't leave me alone. That said, I managed to retain my composure, and before long the doctor printed out a document, and began to question me about my condition.

"OK, Mr Clarke. So, as you said your MRI scan found an untreated traumatic brain injury. It also says here that you discussed with my colleague a matter of delusions and repression of memories. Is your problem today connected to this at all?"

"Yeah. You see, the thing which made me have the MRI was that I passed out whist seeing Dr Kenny. I didn't know why, but I thought it was just a one off thing, you know? Anyway, yesterday it happened again. There was no warning, nothing, I just fainted."

"Right." He put down the paper on top of his desk, moved his chair a little closer to me. "And so, when this happened, did you experience any pain in your body?"

"Not before it happened. But afterwards my head was in a lot of pain. I get the headaches all the time though, that's why I came here in the first place, you see."

"Sure. Now, are you taking any medication for this at all?"

"Yeah, hold on". I reached into my pocket to remove the bottle of pills. Frankly, I was amazed that so far he had ignored my 'delusions', as well as not mentioned my lack of childhood memories. It actually settled my nerves a bit, that perhaps he would not push his own therapy onto me against my will. Either way, I handed Ryan the bottle of pills, and he squinted his eyes to read the small label.

"Ah, I see." He paused for a minute, then handed me back my bottle of tablets. "How long have you been taking those?"

"Oh, for years. They do seem to work, if a little slowly, sometimes."

"I don't know". He stood up, walked over the cabinet filled with files. He scanned his eyes around it for a number of seconds, then removed a battered and full cardboard file. "As far as I remember from my days as a GP, those can cause orthostatic hypotension. Perhaps that's why you experienced fainting. Now, let's see."

He removed a couple of papers from the file, and walked back to the desk whilst scanning over them. I sat back on the leather sofa, beginning to feel unusually comfortable after my previous apprehension. It was understandable, I suppose. If the pills were responsible for the fainting, it seemed like something easy to find a cure for. It was still strange though; I had never experienced this before coming to Kilportach, and I'd taken the pills in my pocket for years.

"Ah yes, here we go", said Dr Ryan, now sitting back down on the office chair, the paper document in his hand. "The pills your taking are known to cause orthostatic hypotension, like I thought. What this means is that sometimes, say if you stand up suddenly for example, blood flow to the brain may be interrupted. Now, with you suffering from TBI, this is very likely what caused you to faint."

"So the pills are to blame, you think?"

"I believe so, yes. It would usually happen whilst the medicine was still strong in your body, you see. Now, you mentioned frequent headaches, so it makes sense that your body would be full of those substances, from every time you take a pill."

What he said made perfect sense. It was no secret that my headaches had increased as of late; an occurrence I had blamed entirely on stress from trying too hard to solve my research. Frankly, I'd never questioned the reliance of the pills, they had became so much a part of my life that I took them with nary a thought to their content. They were almost an ingrained habit in a way. A headache came on, and I took a pill. They were peace of mind, a convenient cure.

"I'd never thought of it", I said to the doctor. "I just take the pills without thinking about them, you see."

"Don't worry about it. Now, of course, the thing we can try here is to give you a different medicine. If you notice a difference and the fainting stops, then we know for sure what the problem was."

"Great. You can give me different pills, then?"

"Well, I can write you a prescription for some. Hold on a sec."

He opened a drawer in the desk and removed a book of yellow slips, of which he instantly filled in a printed section at the top. I was surprised at the difference in the doctor's I had seen. Kenny had said that my pills were the best available. At this point, it seemed that Dr Ryan, despite my concerns of his usual profession, was offering help more in line with my expectations. Still, I owed my proper diagnoses to Kenny; as without the MRI scan he performed, I would never have known of the injury I had.

"OK, here it is". He handed me the prescription he had written. Like most medicines, it was unpronounceable, but it's name was far different in structure to my regular pills. Of course, I had to ask about what they were.

"They're a lot different from those you have", he answered. "You have to take them as a course, you see. Take one when you first get them from the chemist, then another before bed. Carry on with two a day until like that, you finish the course. Oh, and no alcohol".

"Right."

"Also, don't be concerned if after the first day or so, you actually experience a stronger headache. You see, if the other pills are still in your blood, the new ones are going to work to get rid of them."

I was pleased he'd warned me, but of course I wasn't looking forward to testing it. Still, an odd feeling of calm seemed to come with the prescription; the realisation of trying something new, no matter how similar it seemed in principle. For all I knew, the new pills could, after their initial side effects wore off, stop the 'things' I saw entirely. I doubted it, though.

Before I left, the doctor and I had a small conversation, which mostly consisted of me telling him my purpose for being in the town to begin with. He seemed to listen, and later confessed that he had seen my acquaintance Adam, who came to the surgery to see Dr Kenny. Apart from that, his knowledge of Kilportach was as small as my own, and I didn't expect him to know of my family. He did mention one thing interesting though; and strangely it was about the very thing I had wished he would not bring up.

"By the way", he said. "I wasn't going to bring this up to be honest, but this is just in case you were ever interested. Your record says you have no recollection of where your head injury came from, right?"

"Yeah, that's right. I've hardly no memories from that time at all, actually."

"I see. Well just so you know, it's a textbook memory repression in my experience. Whatever caused that brain injury must have been big, and very painful for you to go through. When that happens, the brain often blocks out the memory; pretends it didn't happen, if you like. Inside though, the memory is there, buried in what we call your subconscious mind."

"I've read about things like that before. I'll admit, it is pretty interesting."

"Oh, it is! Now, I'm not suggesting you go for a regression or anything like that, but I thought I'd say that I do offer the service, if you ever needed it."

"Thanks."

I'd expected far more in the way of 'hard sell'. As it stood, the psychologist had shocked me with his amiability; his readiness to help and be honest with it an unexpectedly pleasant surprise. In fact, an image soon entered my mind as I sat there; that of finding the answers dormant within me. I'd be lying if I said uncovering those memories was not in line with my best interests, as it clearly was. But I was still apprehensive, and that disquiet throbbed in my stomach with unease. It was not even about the psychology any more, but more about what those memories could be. What could be so bad I'd forget it even happened? I once more leant forward on the doctor's couch, and decided to question him about this repression.

"Dr Ryan, I've a question about this regression therapy. Let's say I....you know, had it done. What exactly what happen? I mean, would I recover all of the memories I'd lost?"

"Well, to be honest it's a pretty controversial therapy. I mean think about it, your mind chose to forget the memories it did. In your case, it's something in your childhood which caused your head injury. That's why you can't remember what happened back then. Anyway, under hypnosis you would, yes, recover those memories. I'll warn you though, it's often very traumatic for you going through it."

"I can understand that. But sometimes, I just wish I could remember my childhood, you know? It would stop all this research business in it's tracks!"

"Well, Mr Clarke, it's something for you to think about it, isn't it?"

It certainly was. In fact, I was thinking about it hours to come. Dr Ryan had encouraged me, put me at rest with the idea of regression. Beforehand, I was stopping myself from truly thinking about it. It was there though; putting up a brick wall in front of my face whenever I despaired at the state of my research. The memories, the truth, was already inside me, and with age regression I would see it for myself.

It was still unnerving though, so much that it mumbled throughout my body long after I'd left the doctor's surgery. There were a lot of thoughts, all darting across my consciousness and not giving me time to focus upon them. The idea of 'knowing' though was heavy and constant; the realisation that should I go for the therapy, all of my questions would be answered at once. I would see my childhood, most likely see myself in Hawthorn House, the other Lucas Clarke my Father as I'd thought. Edward Clarke would be nowhere in it, and neither would the cave-in which claimed their lives, or any of the happenings in Kilportach town.

Yet there was something about his warning to me, which rung with a shrill and worrying truth, which formed the majority of this writhing discomfort. The event would be 'traumatic', he said. My mind would uncover what it locked away, stopped me from remembering for my own good. What could it be? I instantly imagined violence and abuse, my TBI the horrid result of some deviant monster in that small B&B. It was possible, of course. I knew nothing about this Lucas Clarke; nor what perverse propensities he carried out on his son. Perhaps I was overreacting, but I didn't even want to think it though. It just came to mind when I thought of 'age regression'.

Either way, there are times when even the heaviest thought can be broken by a meeting with the unexpected. Though frankly, what happened to me that day, when approaching the main street to visit the chemist, was so unexpected I can not describe it as simply a 'shock'. Instead, it was something I'd never undergone before. Something so unworldly, so unutterably horrible, that even now I shudder to awaken the memory. It came with no warning.

It started as I walked through the empty streets, holding in my hand Ryan's prescription. In my thoughts, endless questions regarding regression were debated inside with leaden perseverance. I wasn't even looking where I was going. Entering onto the main street however, I was met instantly with an unforeseen and thus shocking event.

An ambulance, and two police cars, were parked on the road outside the tourist office. Their sirens were silently flashing in blue, and the back doors of the ambulance were fully open. Around them, a number of people were gathered and talking, their faces all covered in visible dread. I picked up the pace, made my way immediately towards them.

Amongst the small crowd of worried faces, I promptly recognised Molly and Jack. Without delay, I pushed past the people and approached them at once.

"Molly, what happened?" I blurted, forcing her to turn and acknowledge my presence. Her eyes were red and streaming with tears, her expression fearful, her body a tremble.

"Good god, Mr Clarke", she whispered to me with noticeable difficulty. "I...I mean she...sorry, look I can't do this."

"Come on, what happened?" I asked once again. She didn't answer. I raised my head above the crowd, noticing the door of the tourist centre was open, but a brutish police man was blocking all entry. Just then, a hand landed on my shoulder. It was Adam.

"Leonard, I thought I saw you there. Christ, you don't know what's happening, do you?"

"No, I've just got here. Is it Catherine? I mean, what's going on?"

He did not hesitate to tell me what happened. It did not come as a shock like I might have expected. Instead, his words fell onto me with an unusual abasement. It was like the qualm felt in a doctor's room, when his words of your ill health were met with despair. As if the words were wrapped in plumbic black, falling through the body with a sombre hurting.

"They say, well...they think it was another murder."

The Kilportach Enigma

Awareness of time ceaselessly slipped away. The noise of talking faded from my ears, the glare of the sirens vanished from my eyes. For an untold number of painful minutes, I just stood and stared at the tourist office door. For all I knew, Molly or Adam may have spoken to me, but I couldn't hear them above my own thoughts.

Yet it was not until the police man moved aside that the horror of the situation truly hit me. A stretcher was carried from the door of the office, a white sheet covering the shape below it. I didn't blink, nor move, while it was in view. It was unthinkable; the sight of it met with an indescribable abjection.

Only that morning had I given her the painting. She lived; felt the glow of her memories and told of them to me, saw herself on the canvas and was filled with wistfulness. She spoke to me, and I spoke to her. Yet now she was gone; immediate, interminably. Proof of the world's dispassionate nature; the end of a story I had only just been told. Murdered.

For the rest of the day, I retreated into the now closed up pub with Molly, Adam and Jack Daly. We didn't speak to each other, though. In fact, the only word exchanged between us was when Adam left due to feeling unwell. It must have been hard for him, to visit the town whilst terminally ill, only to find it in the midst of a disaster.

It didn't even make any sense. Two murders, both of upstanding and quiet residents, the sort of people who you wouldn't wish anything bad upon. Bridget ran a small guest house on the edges of the town, and Catherine had lived her whole life in Kilportach. She was an old lady, filling her days in the empty tourist office, waiting for a single visitor to come in. She was not the sort of person who was targeted for murder. Neither of them were.

For the time being, I sat in the silence of the pub with an untouched soft drink sitting in front of me. Later on in the evening, the police had issued an emergency meeting, urging all the townsfolk to meet in the town hall. I would accompany Molly and Jack there, not only to see what they had to say, but to hear if any evidence had been found at the scene.

Frankly though, the idea of another murder in the town was near impossible to take in at once. It was the same for my companions, as well. We didn't even share a breath together, just sat alone with our own mournful thoughts, unable to correlate the day's loathsome happenings. I imagined Molly was in utter shock; perhaps denying that this evil had even taken place. She was, after all, part of Kilportach, having lived in the town during Catherine's time and most likely shared many a memory with her. As for Jack, I doubted he could even think about it properly. He had lost Bridget only short days before, and was now unable to escape the image of a murderer lurking somewhere in town.

It was that thought, I think, that stayed with me the most. Why would someone murder a person like Catherine? How? I imagined the culprit was unhinged and compulsive, a maniac who acted without a thought, like someone had flipped a switch within them. It was, of course, a frightening thought. None of the townsfolk seemed at all suspicious; and in fact I'd only seen a handful of people in my whole time in town. Even Amelia, the black sheep of Kilportach's residents, had shown herself to be far from what I would consider a likely killer. So then I had no idea who this psychopath was. Were they close at hand, watching even as I sat in the pub, waiting to pick out their next victim?

If anything, such paranoia leant itself well to Kilportach. When walking at dusk towards the town hall, the mood of the town had most definitely changed. No longer did the deserted streets appear to be dead and vacant of time. Instead, the town seemed almost to pulse with gloom; the rows of windows hiding eyes which followed each footstep which passed them by. Shadowed corners held their breath, the lightness black tangibly real, crawling deep inside all who saw it.

This feeling was strongest at the peat bog area. According to Molly, the old town hall was built to overlook the bogs, and was situated just after the promenade style street ended. Interestingly, she said that the town hall was almost never used; there were no events, no fêtes or political get togethers. To the people in town, it was just another unused building.

The bogs themselves, whilst walking through them in the early evening murk, took on a further aura of unworldliness. Perhaps it was because of Bridget's murder, now intensified by Catherine's grievous death, but the peat bogs felt almost to bubble with uneasiness. It was like underneath that dark, wet earth, the swarms of mummified bodies writhed, imprisoned in the moment of their fearsome deaths. For vast and sorrowful were those peat bogs, as if deep underground some idle darkness clawed upwards through the sodden earth, waiting mutely for the day it could rise up into the town.

When we reached the town hall, it was the only source of life and movement I had seen in the area all evening. It stood alone on the barren roadway, further even than the small museum, who now stood near invisible in the coming nightfall. The town hall though was harshly lit; it's arched windows spilling a yellowed light out into the dusk. It was a square shaped, red brick building, two stories high and with a tiled hip roof. There were no signs hanging above it's doors, nor any indication that it acted as a town hall. Outside, a small car park was almost empty, with just a handful of vehicles untidily parked.

I accompanied Molly and Jack inside. The main doors led into a cold reception room, unfurnished apart from a fold-up table and chair. At the back, another door was held open with a doorstop, and led into the main hall where this meeting would take place.

It was a highly polished, wood panelled room, a small stage at the back covered in a closed red curtain. Many plastic chairs were neatly lined up, although only a handful of people were sitting on them. Amongst them, I recognised Dr Kenny and Adam, as well as the woman from a newsagents I went into. Apart from that, around 10 or so people were sitting in silence, none of whom I was familiar with. Amelia was not there, of course.

Myself, Jack and Molly took seats next to each other, near the front row of brown plastic chairs. From there, it was a long 15 minutes until the police showed themselves. The entire hall was unheated and chilly, it's bare white walls showing visible patches of damp. Really though, it was like I'd expected. Kilportach was barely even a town, so it stood to reason that it's town hall building was just as neglected as the rest of the area.

Finally though, a police man entered onto the stage, dressed in the usual garish costume, complete with truncheon fastened to his belt. Actually, it was the same officer who took my earlier statement; an impolite brute with more ego than professionalism. Still, the matter at hand was a grave one indeed, and I was both agitated and curious to hear what would be said.

"Ladies and gentlemen", he loudly began his presentation. "I'd expected a larger turnout tonight, but we're going to begin either way. Now, I've brought you here tonight mostly to warn you, and also to discuss what is happening here in town."

He began to pace up and down the stage, loudly talking as if trying to give a forceful lecture. Frankly, I thought his attitude was ridiculous already. Of course, two murders in such a secluded town was surely a cause for great concern, but something about his appearance and tone made me wonder if he even understood it's solemnity.

"This week", he continued. "Two people who lived alone in Kilportach have been found viciously murdered in the town. The first, identified as Mrs Bridget Brady, was discovered on Tuesday evening near to the adjacent peat bog. The second, discovered only today at her place of work, has been formally identified as Catherine Maguire. Both women were killed by multiple gun shots, their bodies left in the open for the police to discover."

I saw Molly beside me uncomfortably writhe. The policeman on stage was uncouth and oafish, speaking of the murders as nothing more than objects for his investigation. He seemed pompous and untrustworthy, making eye contact with the audience as if to indirectly hold them as suspects. Of course, there really was a murderer amongst the townsfolk, but shouting and chest-beating was not the way to catch them. I had always detested the police's methods. Still, I had little choice to listen to the rest of his speech, if only to hear if anything was found that might lead to whoever was responsible.

"So what do we know?" he rhetorically asked. "Both victims were women who lived alone in town, and were working in the local trade. Bridget Brady ran a small bed and breakfast called Hawthorn House, whilst Catherine Maguire, although retired, continued to work in the town's tourist centre. What we don't know is why these women would be targeted, or what was the motive of the culprit responsible."

It was true that the murders made very little sense. Both Catherine and Bridget kept themselves to themselves, and seemed unlikely to be the sort of people who would attract such misfortune to them. Could it really be that the murderer was simply targeting random women? I didn't believe it. In my opinion, people do not kill without a reason, even if their diabolic motive is seen by the masses to be simply 'random'. There was always a reason, something inside their unsound minds; a needle pricking an erratic compulsion. So then, why Catherine and Bridget?

"Now", exclaimed the vulgar officer on stage. "In any situation such as this, we urge the public to stay indoors, be wary of any unknown visitors, and be extra vigilant if travelling alone. As it stands, we do not know enough to discover the culprit, and urge all people, women especially, to be very cautious until this criminal is arrested."

I remembered researching Shane Cullen's murder, and how the murderer was never actually found. It reminded me of the man I thought was my Father, the Lucas Clarke who was a murder suspect 30 years ago. I wondered just what he had done or said to make the police think he was involved in the crime. Or was he actually the murderer, having escaped from full prosecution and ended up simply as a suspect? It brought back those feelings of my mystery head wound, and the image of a Father unfit to exist dealing abuse onto his young son. More than that though, was the undoubted truth that Cullen's murder seemed somewhat similar to those of today. He too had no reason to be targeted, was a single man and bothered no one in town. Could the murders of past and present be linked? For the time being, I could not think about it. The policeman had not yet finished talking, and I had no choice but give him my attention.

"So, what else do we know? Well, we know that Kilportach has a very low crime rate, and that both victims were known in town, with Catherine Maguire having being born here. The town also suffers from low visitor numbers, with most outsiders of an academic nature, coming to the town to see peat bog bodies. Knowing this, it is likely that the killer is someone from Kilportach, most likely a person who the victims knew. Because of this, we are opening this town hall throughout next week for anyone with information to step forward. Your concerns and comments will be anonymous, and dealt with swiftly by our team of professionals."

By this point, I knew that the police where not saying anything of interest. The meeting was essentially a warning lecture, letting the townsfolk know they were there, and issuing stark advice to stay indoors. It was standard banter, with nothing said about evidence found, and nothing particularly worth the time it took to sit through. Indeed, for the rest of the meeting I switched off from the talk, retreating at once to my racing thoughts about both the murders and my own research.

Though it may have been rather unsympathetic, I quickly found myself focusing on my own mystery, and concluding that my time in Kilportach was surely ending. I had no more people to question on the past, and those I didn't yet know would surely refuse to speak to an outsider after the murders. The entire town would be thrown into turmoil, and likely the last thing on their minds would be talking to me about events 30 years ago.

Yet I did not want to leave the town. Yes, I may have uncovered grave errors in my research, and reached dead ends with all serious lines of inquiry, but I still felt I had much to learn. It was like the town itself willed me to stay, to scratch the itch hid in it's corners, to reawaken a nostalgic remembrance. In many ways, the past was all Kilportach had. It's shops were symbolic of bygone decades, it's people living in wistful remembrance, the town they know existing only in photographs. Even it's tourism was based on the past. The bog bodies were, despite their obvious interest as morbid curiosities, frozen remains which refused to succumb to time's advance. Thinking about it like that, they were the perfect, if bizarre, symbols of the town. Yes, I would stay in Kilportach. It did not want me to leave it yet.

It was soon that I realized, or rather simply accepted, what my best course of action was going to be. I had long left the town hall with Molly and Jack, leaving Jack to go back home while myself and Molly locked up the pub. Yet again I would sleep in the now welcoming feeling bar, albeit with a sense of unease in the air. I could not pretend that Catherine's death didn't bother me. It was a shock, a poignant and repulsive turn of events; which when truly thought of long and hard, resulted in a sinking, hopeless queasiness. It reminded me of life's brittle nature; of the thinnest of all lines which stands to divide existence from the unknown world of 'death'. I just couldn't imagine who could do such a thing.

Still, I knew what options were open for me in the morning. I would ring Dr Ryan, and after putting aside my still gnawing concerns, ask about booking a regression appointment. I was worried about it, of course I was. But I realized, whilst trying to fall to sleep that night, that it may well be my most helpful option. I would finally know, understand what happened to me to make me forget. It was a massive, and thus oddly disquieting thought to endure. But I knew I would go through with it. I had to.

The Wishing Lake – Mark Robinson

Session 1

Ryan's office felt different when I arrived for treatment. It looked the same, the brown leather sofa, the desk and computer; but it's atmosphere, it's mood, had changed. It felt more clinical to me somehow, like I was there for a serious and delicate operation. The scent of antiseptic in the air felt heavier, and the warmth of the office hit me greater than before.

Although for all it's imagery and my obvious apprehension, I felt no longer worried about attempting the regression. If anything, I was looking forward to how it would work, and wondering just what secrets I'd find, nestled away in the recesses of my mind. Moreover, unlike the MRI scan before it, this therapy felt more metaphysical in nature. In that way, it tied in well with my own topics of interest. Where were memories stored? How did we create them? All questions I rhetorically asked myself.

Ryan was just as friendly as before, perhaps even more so now I'd signed up for his treatment. Honestly, I felt that after all my concerns, I'd be far more angered at the prospect of this meeting. Somehow though, the psychologist had managed to put me at rest, as if all my previous discontent was about to meet it's end that day. I was about to see into the mystery I yearned for, unlock it's secrets after decades of repression.

Before starting the session, Dr Ryan explained to me what the therapy was and was not. He said that I'd be placed under hypnosis, which basically amounted to a deep sense of trance allowing the subconscious mind to be reached. From there, he would speak to me and try to recover my memories, focusing mainly on what caused my TBI. Interestingly, he said that during the deepest parts of the session, it was possible I would feel, speak and think in the manner of the age we had regressed to.

Such possibilities filled my mind with awe, not only putting me further at rest but making me anxious to start the therapy. It amazed me that the mind was so large in scope, that when the subconscious was pierced and accessed, your entire existence was dormant and available. I had wondered once, years ago, whether memories were stored in the brain at all. It struck me that if people with missing brain tissue could still remember their past, that memory was possibly located elsewhere. I thus imagined the brain like a TV set, where the channels exist in the air already, and all we do is 'tune in' to them. Could the brain act in a similar way? I never thought I'd see the day when I could put my hypothesis to the test.

As the session was about to begin, I was asked to comfortably lay on the sofa, while Dr Ryan closed the curtain and applied a subdued light overhead. Yet again, the room's character changed. It was not a doctor's surgery any longer, but a dimly lit and secluded room where a journey of some sort was about to take place. I was oddly relaxed, but I could not help feeling my location was imperfect. I remembered the bog bodies which shared the building with me, as well as the morbid realisation that Bridget and Catherine were likely there too. For the first time since entering the doctor's room, I felt a coldness. A momentary doubt.

Soon though, Dr Ryan began the hypnotic induction. He was sitting on the office chair opposite the sofa, and lowered his voice to a softer tone, speaking slowly and deliberately.

I was asked at first to close my eyes, to consciously relax all of my muscles, and prepare myself for the journey ahead. It was similar at this point to self hypnosis tapes, where the general goal seems to be entering the deepest relaxation possible. Ryan spoke quietly, leaving long gaps between his instructional sentences, as to make himself as clear as he could. I was asked to mentally count down from 100, at the same time concentrating on my gradually deepening breath. At first, I was able to slowly count backwards as asked, but after a few elongated seconds my mind began to lose it's grasp on the thoughts. It was, in a way, reminiscent of the minutes before falling to sleep. Thoughts, memories and ideas floated in, hovered for a second in the abstruse blackness, then dispersed back into my swirling subconscious. Soon, I found myself feeling a pleasant light-headedness, as if my mind was fluttering peacefully between waking and sleeping.

"And as you concentrate on that slow, deep breathing", said Ryan, "you can almost see the air you breath, coming in through your nose, and out from your mouth. It reminds you of the old fashioned steam trains, who would sit on the platform on summer afternoons, their engines running and poised for the coming trip."

It was easy for me to imagine it. In fact, I was most pleased that Ryan had chosen such imagery to guide me through this hypnotic induction. Steam trains, unlike their soulless modern counterparts, always seemed to pulse with the aura of discovery. Of course, I could not concentrate on the image too much. It simply appeared in that space reserved for imaginative thinking, like the vision of a place which existed between the worlds of thought and reality.

"You are now aware that you are standing on such a railway platform. In front of you, a very old train sends plumes of steam up into the summer sky. And you notice that the door to the train is open, beckoning you to go inside. You take another, even deeper breath; hold it, and let it go. Now, when you are ready, you walk onto that old steam train."

By this point, I felt myself fully surrendering to the imagery Ryan was suggesting to me. I was no longer aware of feeling in my body, seeming to exist entirely within a spherical world of thought. In the back of my mind, the realisation that I was in the surgery was still evident and noticeable, but I felt I was only there in body, and that my mind had already begun it's venture.

"Now, I want to you to find a compartment in the train, any of which you feel you are drawn to, and lock the door as you enter inside. From here, you take a seat by a large windowpane, and relax into the comfortable chair, just waiting for the train to depart."

Ryan's voice soon took on a different aura, like he was not speaking directly at me, but rather his voice was already 'inside'. Honestly, I was amazed I had not drifted to sleep, but was instead suspended half-awake, like a lucid dream where the world was in flux, changing to fit each emotion and thought. Before long, Dr Ryan presented me with more breathing exercises, and the train in my mind departed the station.

"And as you peer out of the window, seeing endless countryside passing by, you realise that this is a special kind of train. For this train can take you far into the past, returning you in both mind and body to any point at all in your whole life. Even now, as you continue to breath and look out of the window, you may see memories in the fields outside. Memories of you, or of people you know. And you realise as you see these memories, that even now the train is taking you back. Far back, into your past."

What Dr Ryan said was correct. Though they lasted only a fraction of a second, splintered memories from through my life seemed to appear in the back of my mind. Thing's that meant nothing at their time of happening, thing's I'd long forgotten about. I knew then that my memories really were within reach, that all that had passed was still there somewhere, sojourned and waiting for my return.

"You are now aware that the train is gradually slowing down. Slowly, you notice a new station appearing in the window. This is your destination. Take another breath, once more hold it, and exhale. And now in your own time, allow the train to roll into the station, bringing you to a gentle, relaxing halt. When your ready, you may leave your compartment aboard the train, and step out onto your own, personal destination."

I could feel a change in my emotions as I stepped out of the train. In my chest, the deep breathing brought with it a fleeting tremble, like a diminutive anxiousness at being finally 'there'. Although my thoughts were without words or verifiable feeling, I knew that my past was but a short distance from where I mentally stood on the platform.

"This platform is barren, covered on all sides by many trees, their branches creating thick shadows on the track. And amongst these shadows you notice a door. It is alone, made from a material of your own choosing, and closed with a key already in it. You stand by the door, and know that soon, you will turn the key".

My imagination had always been strong, and the image of the secluded station came to me with a particular ease. In a way, it was a dream version of Kilportach's own station, which really did stand in the middle of nowhere, overgrown and abandoned to time. My station though, was pulsing with energy. I imagined the door to be of old, thickset oak, and the myriad of trees to be staring at me, with human features like the Great Deku Tree. I stood by the door, and awaited with eagerness for Ryan's instructions.

"This door will take you into your memories. On the other side, you will find yourself living in the world of your past, in a time just before you injured your head. During this time, I am going to speak to you, ask you questions that you can answer. And remember, nothing you see through the door can harm you. It is an image, a record of something that has already happened. Now, take your time, and stay where you are for as long as you need. When you are ready, turn the key, and walk through the door."

A shiver of apprehension fell over me at once, my heartbeat audible in my ears as I turned the key to the old oak door. At first, I was met with only a deep, blinding darkness. Slowly though, images began to form around me, fading into view with an anxious shiver, eventually covering my mind entirely. At that moment, all of my senses were amplified. I was there, seeing my memories alive in front of me, like old photograph negatives held up to the light.

"So, Leonard, could you perhaps tell me, where are you right at this moment?"

"It's the lake. The lake near the town."

"Good. And how old are you, can you tell me?"

"Eight."

I was unsure if I was simply imagining myself standing by the Wishing Lake, but the 'memory' of it was vivid and real. The actual images were hazy and dream like, but the idea that I was accessing a memory, and not simply my imagination, was distinct and easy to differentiate.

"OK, now we're going to explore what happened to you on this day. Take your time, there's no rush. OK, what is happening around you now? Are you alone? What are you doing?"

"I was speaking to a man...it's...Mr Cullen. I don't know what he's saying."

"Please, try to remember. What were you talking about? Say it out loud if you can."

"I was...he asked me about a hidden place underneath the lake. Said another kid had seen it too....Had I been under there? What did I know about it? He's asking all these questions."

"OK, that's good. Now, slow down, and remember your breathing. In through the nose, hold it, and release. Good. Now, what else was said between you two?"

"There's another man, he's speaking to Mr Cullen. Now he's asking me the same questions, all about the lake. I don't know anything about it!"

"Slow down, Leonard. Take your time. I need you tell me about this Mr Cullen and his friend. It's OK if the memory is blurry, we just need to know little bits about it. Tell me what they said to you; all in your own time."

I had no ability to mentally question the things I was uncovering at the time. The memories swirled and entered my mind, like dreams that I was conscious about experiencing. I was only aware of being 'inside' my thoughts, accessing a part of my childhood that had previously proved impossible for me. It felt odd though, like a childlike fear was present around me; a sort of helplessness crossed with nervous submission. That said, I was still aware of my adult emotions, but they shrunk behind a growing tremor of returning feelings from long in my past.

"Mr Cullen wants to know about a hidden place", I continued. "He said that someone else found it under the lake. He wants to know if I've seen it. Wants me to tell his friend about it. Mr...Mr Buckley, I think."

"That's good, well done. Now let's move forward a little, if we can. What did you do later on? After you'd spoken to Mr Cullen?"

"I went to see my friend. I think...I said about what Mr Cullen asked me. Then...I think we went back to the park. I played on the big concrete tunnel thing, and we had ice creams I think because it was hot."

"Go further on than that. Later on, that evening perhaps. What did you do then?"

"I don't know. I don't...I can't remember."

"Yes you can. You can remember. Take your time, allow the memory to come to you by itself. OK. Now let me ask again, what did you do that evening? What was it?"

I felt what I could only describe as a wave of foreboding, forcing itself into my chest, and pulsating along with my quickening heart beat. It was different from normal anxiety though. It brought with it a shiver of murmuring guilt; as if I'd just been attacked or was in fear for my safety. A childhood emotion. Like the emotion of being 'told off' by an adult. It was strong, taking over my entire being.

"I just...I don't know why I did it!" I said, my voice surely the image of that frightened eight year old that had been summoned from my mind's recesses.

"It's alright, you can tell me what you did. Remember, it's only a memory. Nothing can harm you."

"I said I was going back out, with my friend again. But I...I went to the lake. And where my friend had shown me, I went down under there. I shouldn't have done it. Why did I do it?"

"Don't worry. Just tell me everything about it. You say you went underneath the lake? How did this happen?"

"We found the cave earlier; a hidden place. We didn't go under then, but I told Mr Cullen about it. He wanted me to go under, when I spoke to him earlier. I really shouldn't have. But...I went under on my own. I wanted to see what was down under there."

"And what did you see? What did you see underneath the Wishing Lake? You can tell me."

"It was...a Selkie."

My muscles began to tremble as I laid on the sofa. No longer did I feel relaxed and at rest; instead throbbing with a rueful whimper, as if my words should never have left my lips. For a second, I felt like I could have opened my eyes, prematurely ending the regression. Somehow though, they remained tight shut, the memory vivid yet still unstable, like I couldn't focus without it losing it's sharpness.

"Now now", said the doctor. "We both know Selkie's don't exist, don't we? Come on, what was it you really saw under that lake?"

"No, it was a Selkie. It had to be, I know it was."

"Slow it down, concentrate on your breathing. Don't force the memory out, let it come to you in it's own time. You're under the lake, in the cave. What did you see?"

"I don't know! I can't remember!"

I felt an instant and sharp jolt to my body, like when lying in bed and a muscle spontaneously twitches. It felt like an electric current almost; running through every vein that I had, causing my body to literally jump. The doctor must have recognised this, and swiftly moved on from the memory I still had trouble in making out.

"Let's move ahead now. Moving in time. Remember the clock ticking slowly and rhythmically, taking you forward and further into the future. Perhaps you can tell me what happened next, after you'd been underneath the lake. What happened then, when you went back into the town?"

"It's my fault", I whispered. "All my fault."

"What's your fault? What's happening now? Tell me what you can see."

"It's all wrong...it's all gone wrong. I shouldn't have gone under the lake, I really shouldn't! I mean, if I didn't, if...If I didn't..."

"Calm down Leonard, deep breaths remember. What's gone wrong? What is it that's upsetting you?"

"I killed him."

"What do you mean?" said Ryan, his voice notably louder.

"I don't know, I don't know! After the lake...I got in big trouble, and then Mr Cullen...but then...my dad wanted to take me away. But Mr Buckley...he came back to see me...and I went back, but then-"

In a second, my eyes forcefully and instantly opened. I was awake. At first, I peered at the ceiling with a lack of thought; with even my breath pausing in shock as I found myself back in the surgery. When I realised that I had broken the hypnosis, I sat up immediately on the sofa, my lungs almost gasping for the air around me, as if I'd found myself somehow short of breath. I couldn't think, my mind still replaying a childhood memory that gradually faded as I regained my senses. I had travelled in time, and abruptly returned.

The Rabbit Hole

It is only on nights where sleep is impossible that the true aura of those dark hours becomes apparent. I had returned from the doctor's at around closing time, and made my way back through town and to the pub immediately. For the first time though, it was actually closed. I didn't realise at first, seeing as the door was open ajar and the empty chairs inside were of course expected. But Molly was not behind the bar. Instead, Adam was sat on one of the chairs, a book in his hand and a lamp lit behind him.

Apparently, Molly was unnerved by the policeman's talk, and had closed the bar and retreated upstairs in fear that the murderer would enter inside. According to Adam, she had asked him to stay in the closed up pub until I returned to sleep there for the night. Clearly, the threat of the murderer affected Molly, and I understood fully her hesitance to open the bar to an unknown public.

"Anyway, your here for the night, aren't you?" said Adam, closing his book and switching off the lamp. "Guess that means I can leave you with it."

He shook my hand as we said goodbye, leaving the key to the pub door with me, and disappearing into the dark Kilportach. I swiftly closed and locked the door, and collapsed down onto a cushioned chair, alone once more in the silence of the bar. There was no fire lit on that night, bringing not only a chill to the air but an apparent lack of flickering light in the corner. It was completely black without any of the lights on.

Of course, I didn't even entertain myself with the notion of sleeping on that night. I switched back on the light that Adam had turned off, and sat in contemplation of my time in the surgery. From my chair, I could see the net curtains of the pub's main windows, an endless darkness clinging to their glass.

Throughout time, there has always been a great dread attached to the night. It's as if when the sun disappears from the sky, an aura of change falls over the world. Fairy tale monsters always came out at night, as do the worries of illness and death, which seem almost to thrive in the blackness of nightfall. Kilportach only intensified this essence, as well. There were no brash clubs or neon 'night life' establishments, nor any signs of life from the very moment that dusk approached. I was alone, with only my biting confusion to accompany me.

Dr Ryan had written what I said in the regression on a selection of lined notepapers. I held them in my hand, and read over my responses countless times, desperately trying to piece them together and make sense of the memories I'd so far forgotten. That said, the images I found in the hypnosis session made so little sense to even the doctor, that I wondered if I hadn't simply imagined them.

The biggest shock of the event was that I had gone beneath the lake, the same place that the Clarke's all met their death. This meant only one thing; I had discovered that 'hidden place' before the family went there, otherwise it would already have been caved-in. Furthermore, Shane Cullen seems to have known of it's existence, saying that another child had been there already, and wondering if I knew anything about it.

This was hard to understand. Yes, it made sense that Cullen had instilled me with the origin of 'hidden places', but who was the other child who knew of the cave? Furthermore, the image of what I saw underneath was impossible to remember, even during the hypnosis. I described it to Ryan as a 'Selkie', the mythical creature who lived in the lake. This was, of course, impossible. But then what did I see? Whatever it was, it's memory was so deeply repressed that I still had no idea what it could have been.

The real horror of the regression though came near the time when I frightfully awoke. Although my physical memory of it was somewhat blurred, Ryan's notes let me remember what I said in handwriting that my eyes would not leave. I seemed to relate my time under the lake, with things going wrong in the town and my family. And this Lee Buckley came up again, with me mentioning briefly that he came 'to see me' after I'd gotten in trouble somehow.

After that, I said the words that no doubt raised me from hypnosis, like a piercing alarm that wakes you up in the midst of a peaceful sleep. 'I killed him', I said. How could I have? I was eight years old according to the regression, and hardly an aggressive or violent individual. How could I have been responsible for a man like Shane Cullen's death? It sounded impossible. In fact, I refused to believe it. I had no memory of such a thing, even during the regression I could not focus on it. All I remembered was an intense fear, a knowledge inside that I had made a mistake, that the world was falling in around me. Could I really have murdered Shane Cullen myself?

The only thing which made me doubt myself was that Lucas Clarke was a suspect in his murder. If that man was my Father as hypothesised, could he have taken the blame for his son's wrongdoing? It did make sense, as outlandish as it seemed. Yet all I knew is that something went wrong; something related to my time underneath the lake. Knowing that, it seemed likely that whatever took place with me inspired the Clarke's to go under as well, who of course were trapped inside by the cave-in. So, I was somehow related to Edward and family after all. It was ironic, in a way.

I sat up for hours rereading Ryan's paper, going over the regression in my head and trying to figure out any more memories. I knew at once that trying to sleep was something I would not even attempt that night, and so I helped myself to water from behind the bar and relaxed into the chair for the night.

It was around that time that I noticed a scrap of paper, left on the table next to the chair where Adam had put his book down earlier. It was torn, and contained a small handwritten note written to himself in a black ink pen. *'Meet with Silsbury at The Rabbit Hole, open 10 till 4 tomorrow. Said on the phone he was ready to talk.'*

So it seemed Adam was carrying out an investigation of his own. As far as I was aware, he was referring to the *'The Rabbit Hole'* antiques shop which stood in the main street of the town. Each time I'd passed by it had been shut, but now according to the note was open tomorrow. I wondered what Adam could have been researching, what he could have meant by the person being 'ready to talk'. Intrigued, I put the note in my pocket, telling myself I would visit the shop and see if this Silsbury knew anything to help me. Actually, I recognised the name. The 'Silsbury Man' was the first bog body, displayed in the small town museum. I would try to see him first thing in the morning.

It was not like I had much else to go on; I doubted the townsfolk would want to talk to a stranger after the murders and the police's talk.

For the time though, I quickly got back to my thoughts on the regression. I was in that chair for the entire night, my eyes at times growing heavy and closing, bringing fleeting minutes of sleep to my tired mind. It was not real sleep however, more momentary seconds when I drifted away, then awoke once again to carry on with my thoughts. When I did sleep, I saw only the hazy images of memory; the things I saw in the hypnosis session presented more like recent than distant memories.

It was probably not until almost dawn when I finally slept for more than a few minutes. Before I knew though, it was 8am, and the morning light had pierced the curtains, illuminating myriads of dust which hovered in the room. I was tired, and hardly in the mood to move from the chair, but I knew I would have to get up at some point. I did however wait until I heard Molly coming downstairs before I made a move.

I decided that morning to take on her offer of breakfast, opting for a bacon sandwich and large mug of coffee. She opened conversation with the usual small talk, and I could tell she was avoiding mentioning the murders. I however spoke instantly about my age regression. It was rare for me do such a thing, I usually found that boring others with my opinions was not worthy of either my time or theirs. But that morning, the regression was the only thing on my mind. Of course, I missed out the parts about me 'killing' Shane Cullen, knowing full well that she was friendly with the man.

Honestly, I think most of my rambling went over her head. She was most likely more concerned with the murders and her own safety than to worry about my fractured memories. She did however confirm that Lee Buckley was the man in the photo she showed me, having previously forgotten his name.

After the breakfast, I thanked Molly and said my goodbyes, the drink having woken me at least slightly from my near sleepless night. In the main street, I was initially going to head straight to the antique shop, but passing the chemist made me remember something rather important. In my pocket, the prescription for new pills that Ryan had given me had still not been handed in. Truthfully, I had forgotten about it; having been given the prescription on the same day as Catherine's murder. I knew though I needed to get hold of the pills. There was no telling when a headache could come on, especially after the regression and last nights sleep loss.

The chemist was as old fashioned as I'd like to imagine. A central counter contained many small, square drawers, and on top of it a number of opaque jars were labelled by hand and stored in a line. Behind the counter, varied glass bottles were stacked on shelves, each containing different coloured liquids of deep reds, yellows and blues. There was even an old brass pair of scales, positioned on a table in the corner and weighed down with highly polished weights. The whole place was like a museum.

I was served by a young woman in a white medical coat. Upon handing her the paper with the prescription, she looked in a number of wooden drawers before disappearing into a room at the back. I already imagined them not having the pills in question. For the time being though, I just had to wait. I could hear her scurrying in cupboards at the back, and I stood waiting in slight amazement at the vintage nature of the chemist.

At the back of the shop, a large wall cabinet was lined in glass, containing a selection of medical items and even more coloured glass bottles. There was even an old looking eye chart attached to the cabinet, it's cardboard stained yellow with time and heavily scuffed around the edges.

Eventually, the woman came back with my prescription in hand. She gave it to me in a brown paper bag, again reciting what Ryan said about taking one now and the other before bed. I thanked her for taking the time to find them, and began to open the box they came in even before I had left the chemist.

They were standard to look at; orange in colour with a collection of numbers written on them. They were also small enough to swallow unaided, and I took one immediately, as instructed, before putting them back into my pocket. Of course, I remembered Ryan's previous warning about them. He said that after taking the first few tablets, a stronger headache can be brought on by them, as the remnants from other pills are still in my body. At the time, it didn't worry me. I just hoped it wouldn't happen, I suppose.

After taking the tablet, I did not waste time in the damp feeling weather, heading instead to the '*Rabbit Hole*' antique shop, which Adam had left a note about. When I got there, it was open for the first time since I'd been in the town. The same A-Board and table full of items were outside, but this time the door was actually open. In fact, it was held open by a large iron doorstop, as if trying to entice townsfolk inside the usually closed walls of the shop. I didn't hesitate to go inside.

It was, as expected, jammed full of antique items. In fact, it was so full that the thin aisle in the middle was so narrow, that I had to walk sideways to fit comfortably through it. Against the walls stood dark wood tables, cupboards and beds, and on top of them were hundreds of china items, none of which containing prices or indications that they were for sale. Glass cabinets contained old bowls and plates, and heaps of small collectibles shook with the squeak of the floorboards I stood on.

It was also clearly damp and musty; with a heavy odour clinging to the air, like a room that had been locked up for decades. The green carpet was threadbare and showing the floorboards, and most of the items were stood amongst visible layers of dust. In the middle of the room, a single light bulb was lit in a dirty floral shade, it's dim glow hardly lighting the room which grew darker the further I walked inside.

At the back of the shop, an elderly man was sat behind a cheap wooden desk. He was thin and crippled, a light layer of white hair atop a heavily creased complexion. As I approached him, he looked upwards with the beginnings of a smile.

"Ah, your here. Early as well, I see."

"I'm sorry?" I said.

"We spoke on the phone? I was wondering when you'd be coming to see me."

I had to greet him with an explanation that I was not the person he had spoken to earlier. He seemed rather deaf, leaning forward and occasionally asking me to repeat what I had said. I tried to speak loud without shouting at him, and explained that I was in town researching my family.

"I see." he said. "Well then you'll have heard of me already, I presume? The Silsbury Man, bog mummy?"

"Indeed. You are the one who discovered it, aren't you?"

"That's right. So don't worry, I've had people coming here to ask me questions for, well, as long as I can remember, really."

I was glad that he seemed willing to discuss Kilportach and it's history with me. I did however wonder how accurate his information would be. His deafness and advancing age was already making conversation difficult, though I still spoke to him with the greatest of optimism. I was offered a seat as soon as we began, and I pulled up the chair close to his desk and sat amongst the piles of antiques. From where we were sat, the door to the outside could hardly be seen, hidden amongst the dark wood wardrobes and delicate shelves of china odds.

"So, my good man, what would you like to pick this old brain about, hmm?"

"If I knew where to start, it would be a help". I was half wanting to bring up the regression with him, mentioning my still prevalent fears of Shane Cullen's death and my involvement. I decided though to start elsewhere, thinking I could ease my way into the topics should the old man know of anything to help. I begun by asking him about Lee Buckley, the friend of Cullen who showed up in my regression.

"Lee Buckley...Lee Buckley. Actually, I think I do remember him, yes."

"You do? Great. What can you tell me?"

"Well If I'm thinking of the same person you are, he spoke to me on the telephone before he came to the town. I remember it, yes; he wanted to know about the people who lived here, their behaviours and things like that"

"What for?"

"Oh, I can't remember to be honest, my man. He was a historian, or archaeologist I think, something like that. Came to town researching the bodies. Ah yes, that was was it."

"What?"

"Lee Buckley was the man who thought the bodies were sacrificed, something to do with our old Wishing Lake. Crack pot theory I said, of course!"

I remembered seeing Buckley's letter to Cullen. He had mentioned then that the bog bodies were offerings; killed as the 'gifts' that the Selkie in the lake would ask for. Of course, this was unrelated to why Buckley would speak to me about the lake, or why he 'came to see me' while I was in trouble after going beneath it. Still, I at least knew that Silsbury was thinking of the right person. I sat back in my wooden chair, it's back creaking and evidently weak. I smiled, waited for him to gather his thoughts, and allowed him to continue speaking to me.

"Yes, yes. There were a few theories like that, I'm afraid. It was due to the holes in their heads, you know. I think that Buckley fellow thought the same thing. I put it all down to that god damn Sullivan book. You've read it, I suppose?"

"I haven't, sorry."

Silsbury seemed to be the type who could easily descend into a long winded ramble. Though what he said was clearly interesting, at the moment I cared only for piecing together the haunting regression. Of course, more questions had begun to appear already, and answers were still far out of my reach. Still, I felt that Silsbury was my best bet at the current time. He had not mentioned the murders yet, and was not unwilling to speak to a stranger despite the killer being on the loose. For the time being, I stuck to my idea of listening to his ramble, and slipped in my own story between his own.

"So, what is this Sullivan book that you mentioned?" I asked.

"Oh, it's a lot of old rot, if you ask me. But it's where Buckley and his type get their ideas from, I know it. Look, there's a bookshelf behind you, there's a copy on there I think. Unless I threw it out altogether."

I looked over my shoulder to a white painted bookshelf. It was heavy in dust, and a small number of books were stacked haphazardly in between small china figures.

"Go on, it should be on there", he continued. "You can take it if you wanted to know about that sort of thing. I won't be wanting it, that's for sure!"

I forced a smile, then got up from the chair to look for the book. I had no idea what he could be meaning, although anything related to Cullen and Buckley was at least a step in right direction.

It didn't take long to find it, a blue covered book of many pages, engraved with the title of *'Grimorium Votum: Translated by Samuel Sullivan'*. I flicked though a couple of pages in it, most seeming to be images and stories with an occult or magical theme to them. I took it in my hands, and sat back down on the chair.

"So what am I looking for in this book?" I said.

"Well, that Buckley fellow was into all that. I told you this, didn't I? Yes, well; there's a part in that book about Kilportach, and I'm damn sure that's where he got it all from. Human sacrifices...it's all poppycock you mark my words."

"I see. So anyway, what's your take on the bog people?" I asked the old man, aware that I was starting to veer off topic. "I mean, you discovered the first one. You must have some ideas about them."

"Mummification, if you want my opinion. The people who lived here might have been primitive, but this land was their home, and they knew every inch of those bogs out there. Well, chances are they figured out that the peat could preserve things buried in it. To them, it was a way to ensure they would live forever; to be buried in peat and never rot. That's why there's so many; it was a special cemetery for the people who settled here. That's what I think, anyway."

His theory was definitely more logical than that of Buckley and Shane Cullen. To me, the bodies seemed somewhat of a mistake; the reluctance of nature to allow her usual course of returning the dead to earth. Much like the rest of Kilportach town, the bodies were trapped in a single time frame, as if somehow they were still consciously aware, and clung to this life with their rigid fingers. It was like the town didn't want them to die.

It was all fascinating, as always, and I could have easily spoken about the bodies to Silsbury for many an hour. However, I knew I needed to dig for relevant info whilst the old man was still in the mood to talk. At that point, I felt I'd heard enough about Lee Buckley and Cullen, and moved on to the other matter of the cavern below the Wishing Lake. I wanted to know if this place was known in town, and how I as an eight year old could have discovered it. My only theory was that if Cullen told me about 'hidden places', he also told me about the cave. This made sense, as Edward Clarke was said to have known Cullen too, and it was shortly after that the other Clarke family went under the lake as well. I tried my best to convey this to Silsbury, leaving out the confusing details and focusing only on the bare bones research.

"You have been digging into the past, my man, haven't you?" he said, leaning back in his scuffed office chair. "Anyway, your right on one count. There is a cave under that lake, and a family did indeed lose their lives under there. Tragic, wasn't it?"

"Yeah. But was that cave known about before the accident with the Clarke's? I mean, how did the family know it was there to begin with?"

"I don't know, or I can't remember anyway. All I know is that it hit the town hard, the news of their deaths. It was a strange old time, right enough."

"What was?"

"The murder of your other man a week before, obviously. Everyone was in uproar about it to begin with, then a whole family die the very next week."

"You mean Shane Cullen's murder?"

"Yes".

My stomach sank at the thought of the murder. I remembered again the regression session, how I writhed uncomfortably and told of my guilt. At the time, it felt unquestionably real; I said that 'I killed him' without a thought, like the knowledge of my horrid past was known to me inside all along. But I couldn't believe it. Indeed, when discovering the murdered body of Bridget, I knew that I had never before seen something like it. The emotions were too pure; too raw and unfettered. To me, that alone was enough to dispute the hypnosis.

Thinking of the murders, I wondered if Silsbury was even aware of what had happened in Kilportach that week. He was either avoiding the issue completely, or was literally unaware of what was going on outside of his shop. He didn't seem to be skirting the issue though, making me believe he really was ignorant to the week's horrid events. Somehow though, I didn't want to be one to tell him about it. Sometimes, after all, it is better to remain in the dark of matters which if known could be devastating to you. Therefore, I didn't think it appropriate to bring up the subject. Not at that time, anyway.

"So, um...had anyone been in the cave before the Clarke's went under?" I asked, trying to clear my own thoughts as I did.

"It's possible. Clarke's son went everywhere with that young girl, you know. The daughter of that builder chap, forget his name. Anyway, I think the Clarke's did know about it before going under, yes."

"How so?"

"Yes, I remember it now; very odd if you ask me, actually. As I recall, the family seemed to know that something was going to happen to them. They had someone come to town, about a week or so before it all happened. Seemed they wanted protection, or maybe someone to look after their affairs, should the inevitable happen, you know."

I wasn't sure that I was following Silsbury. It was the first I had heard about a third party being involved with the Clarke's, let alone them predicting their own deaths. I wondered if the old man was not confusing his memories, telling me stories of other families who existed only in his faded thoughts. It did seem rather strange to believe that the Clarke's were prophetic of their fate. In fact, I was sure Silsbury's memory of the events were distorted. Why would the family go under the lake if they knew what dangers were waiting in there? Furthermore, why would they bring in an outside influence to guard them or look after their affairs? It didn't make sense. Although, if true, it would mean that another unknown character was present at the time of the events in town. Could they have been involved in my own time under the lake?

"Wait", I said, trying to fish for more info from Silsbury. "Who exactly was it that they brought in to protect them? It's the first I've heard about anything like that."

"Well like I said, they might not have wanted protection really, just someone to be there should thing's go wrong. I don't know anything about it, really. I just remember people saying they were scared of something, just a short while before the lake cave-in happened. It's all just coincidence, probably."

He was most likely right. Unfortunately, this information didn't help me directly with understanding my regression treatment. I did however wonder if this 'other' person, if really there, was not somehow related to my time under the lake. I was sure at this point that whatever I saw down there inspired the Clarke's to investigate it themselves. In my regression, I noted that my Father wanted to 'take me away', but then Lee Buckely came to visit me resulting in a further unexplained event. Could not the person Silsbury referred to be my own Father telling the Clarke's of the lake? It made sense on two counts. First, Buckley's visit may have been to ask my Father to speak to the family. Secondly, two Lucas Clarke's in the same residence could easily have resulted in the original mistake, linking the two families together.

Knowing this, I felt like I was once more seeing the past in tiny slithers from Silsbury's lips. He seemed genuinely interested in telling the stories, and apart from his deafness and tendency to mumble, felt to me like a friendly old man. Perhaps it was that which made me forgo my anxiety on the subject of Cullen's murder. It circled in my head like a living thing, prodding me to think and concentrate on the horrid things I said in the childhood regression.

"Mr Silsbury", I said. "I hope your don't mind me asking this, but about Shane Cullen's murder...do you know who was responsible, by any chance?"

"I've been asked these things before, my man. And I don't, I'm sorry. They say it is usually someone they know, don't they? That's my best bet."

The problem which such a deduction method is that most people in Kilportach seem to have known Cullen. I was no expert in solving mysteries, and the murder of Cullen made as little sense as the recent deaths I had witnessed myself. Why would somebody murder Catherine? She hardly seemed to step outside the tourist office, and existed entirely in her own mind of memories and candlelit shadows. Nobody in town seemed suspicious to me, and I had little intention of digging for motives. I just wanted to know about the deaths of the past, to clear my mind and make sense of my story.

It was about this time when my talk with Silsbury was interrupted by the sound of footsteps in the shop. We both turned to face the narrow aisle, and I noticed that Adam was making his way through the jumbled antiques.

"Oh, Mr Clarke", he said, squeezing through the aisle and approaching the desk. "I didn't expect to see you here. How are you?"

"I'm fine, thanks", I greeted Adam, standing up and shaking him by the hand. For the first time since I had met him though, he looked physically ill and paler than before. I wondered if it was simply the effects of the macabre news in town, or whether his illness was gradually, sporadically weakening him. Of course, I was not the kind of person to bring up such things with him.

"Your the man who spoke to me on the telephone?" said Silsbury, standing to meet and shake hands with Adam.

"Indeed", he replied. "I hope I wasn't interrupting you two."

"Not at all", I said, backing away slightly from the now crowded corner of the shop. "I was just about to go, anyway. Mr Silsbury, thanks for everything."

I was not in the mood for another conversation with Adam at the moment. Truthfully, what Silsbury had told me was enough to think about for a while as it was. Moreover, I did not want Adam to figure out that I had read his note about the shop in the pub. I needed to remain civil with the townsfolk as much as possible.

I held the Sullivan book in my hand, and thanked Mr Silsbury once again for allowing me to borrow it. As I turned to leave the shop, Adam noticed the book I was carrying.

"What's that, Mr Clarke?"

I showed him the book, feeling slightly apprehensive seeing how much Silsbury had derided it. Adam took one glance, smiled, and handed it back to me.

"Samuel Sullivan, eh?" he said. "I remember reading something from him as a kid. Too spooky for me though, I'm afraid!"

"Not a fan?" I smiled.

"Not really, I was brought up with that sort of thing though. My dad loved it! Oh by the way, if you like thing's like that, have you seen the Holy well they have in Kilportach?"

"There's a Holy well? I never knew."

"Ah, you need to go and have a look. You'd like it."

He went on to ask Silsbury for a piece of paper, and drew for me a rough map of where the Holy well was in the town. I was most thankful for it, seeing as 'hidden places' like Holy wells where exactly the sort of things I liked to visit. If anything, I thought that a visit might take my mind from the words of the regression which still played over again in my mind. So, I thanked Adam with another handshake, and made my departure from the untidy antique shop.

Silsbury seemed to be a man I could return to for information many a time. Already he had given me food for thought, and presented me with this Sullivan book which I truly looked forward to reading into. Of course, the biggest questions posed by Silsbury were why Buckley would ring him on the phone prior to his visit to Kilportach? It made little sense at all to me, and apart from the matters of the bog bodies, seemed rather enigmatic from my point of view. Furthermore, Silsbury mentioned the Clarkes bringing in a person to help them with their affairs; saying they were scared and predicted their demise. Again, this seemed so vague and somewhat unlikely, but Silsbury seemed to be speaking truthfully. I did remember Dr Kenny saying that an unknown body was found at the same time as the Clarkes. Could it have been that person? No. I was overreacting again. I was sure of it.

Still Water Secrets

As I stepped out of Silsbury's musty antique shop, and was hit once more by the chilled air of the town, I was struck almost at once by a heavy feeling of nausea. It presented itself as a jagged stabbing pain, falling thereafter into a sickening churn in the abdomen. I tried to ignore it and walk along the main street, but the cold breeze soon failed to sooth me, as an agitating, itchy sweat swiftly accompanied the queasy sensation. It had to be the new pills. I felt awful.

Still, I did not have a headache like I probably would have before the pills, and no amount of nausea could live up the fear of passing out like before. Somehow though, I didn't feel like sitting and reading the Sullivan book; feeling much better by keeping moving, if only by aimlessly walking around. Thankfully, I did have a place to go.

Adam's map, drawn on a bit of ripped scrap paper, showed the bog area with the museum and town hall. Further on, he had drawn an 'X' and marked out the well, which seemed to be on the corner of a field even further out than the old town hall. It was no wonder I had not discovered it beforehand.

Before leaving the main street on my way to find the well, I noticed that the tourist office had been decorated with police paraphernalia. Familiar tape with the words *'crime scene'* were plastered around the doors and windows, and a large A-Board was positioned outside, a garish yellow backdrop displaying a black printed, harsh message.

'Can you help us?

MURDER

On Thursday 8th September, 2011, at approximately 3pm,
a female was fatally shot in this building.
Did you see or hear anything?
Please call us on...'

It was oddly disturbing how impersonal the police investigation appeared to be. The earlier talk was brash and offensive, with the force more concerned over asserting their authority, rather than catching the murderer in town. That said, I did notice a heavy police presence that day, with more than a handful of uniformed officers combing the streets with clipboards and mobile phones. I was curious as to whether they had discovered any leads, but was deeply cynical as to their competence. I tried to avoid them.

Indeed, I didn't stay around in the main street for long, heading straight towards the bogs, my stomach still turning and hot with discomfort. I could have easily rested on a bench or street side; caught my breath and waited for the feeling to go, but I refused to let it get the better of me. If it really was just the effects of the pills, I was not so worried so long as, in the end, they worked as they were supposed to. Nothing was worse than the headaches, after all.

I can still remember when I first started suffering from them as a child. It was long before I was old enough to arrange a doctor's visit on my own, and so my only outlet to the pain and visions was to talk to my foster parents about it. Though obviously, they didn't want to know. To them, all complaints of illness were faux attempts to get out of school or chores, and I never dared tell them of the 'things' I see. Furthermore, Mrs Ford claimed to be a Christian and would likely take the news that I 'saw things' badly, so even then I learned to keep my mouth shut. So, I had to live with those headaches all through my childhood, being forced to live out the life of a school boy whilst suffering silently with my own agony. If the new pills managed to take that away, I would be grateful, even enough to ignore their side effects.

It was a long walk from the pedestrianised bog land to the field where Adam had noted the Holy well. After the town hall, the paved area abruptly ended, revealing nothing but endless bog and uncut fields on every side. It was one of these fields; with a trampled footpath and old wooden sign advertising a hike, that I trudged my way through to find the old well. It appeared to have once been agricultural land, but was in it's present state a jungle of grass so tall it reached right up to my waist. I was heading away from the endless bog land, and walking towards the distant trees which formed the untamed surroundings of Kilportach town.

It was within these thickets where the Holy well was waiting. Regrettably though, I could not find myself as inspired at finding this 'hidden place' as I usually would have been. The humid ache in my stomach was not letting up, and despite my deep and purposeful breaths, I was still prickling with an uncomfortable sweat. There was even the first of my usual 'signs', the glimpse of something in front of my eyes which defied the notions of being consciously real. It was like the 'thing' that I saw in the cemetery, an ethereal form of no known shape, floating amongst an opening in the trees. As before, I couldn't focus my eyes upon it, finding it almost painful to look at, as if trying to look at the sun without glasses. It was no different from my previous experiences, the only difference being that instead of a headache, I was suffering from a sharp and nauseous feeling.

As I slowly approached the shape in the trees, an intense sensation of being looked at fell across my back, like somebody was walking behind me. Yet as I tried to ignore this and continue onwards, I realised that the shape had vanished before me. It was there, and then it was not. Had I imagined it? Certainly a shadow or woodland animal could not have created such a 'thing', but my my own mind could surely conjure up anything. Even so, I felt a spectral aura was present in the trees, holding it's breath and watching me as I stumbled amongst the thistles and weeds.

The well itself was easy to find. It was larger than most Holy wells I'd seen, standing tall and alone in the midst of the woods, built from a dark and crumbling stone. It was pyramidal in shape, with an arched doorway set in the middle, revealing a black and endless well below. At it's top, a circular Celtic cross carving was faded with time and covered in lichen, and a weathered statuette of the Virgin Mary was stood to the left of the arched well entrance.

It was a perfect example of a 'hidden place'. In fact, the first time I had used the term was when I discovered such a well as a child. Kilportach's well though was something different; truly secluded and forgotten by man, it was seen only by the eyes of timberland animals, unaware of the energies dormant in the structure. Or perhaps they felt it too. The stones; although old and touched by decay, murmured with a forlorn semblance of life. The deepness of the well was coated in shadows, almost moving with the passage of clammy air, as if rising with whispers of bygone times.

Such was the nature of 'hidden places'. They waited for those who would discover them, replete with an energy so unique it could not be found in the lore of books. And it was that atmosphere; that residual mood, which made itself known to those who chanced upon them. They existed within, and yet outside of the world at large, like tiny places so remote that even time flowed differently around them.

It was the perfect place for me to finally sit down. I leant against a tree near to the well, and sat on the grass with a pacifying sigh, hoping to alleviate my still present sickness. Honestly, I wasn't looking forward to taking the second of the new pills before bed, assuming that if they should not agree with me, another would make the symptoms worse. Still, I knew that I had little choice in the matter, and it was true that despite my ill feelings, an actual headache was absent entirely. Yet I still felt I could throw up or pass out again, my stomach pulsating and my whole body seeming to grow tired from simply sitting there. Perhaps it was exhaustion, but I didn't believe it.

I saw it again, as well. The shape from before, appearing in between the trees, just to the side of the Holy well. At first I thought it was a person, and I almost stood up with that familiar 'jump' sensation. But the shape did not move, nor appear to look at me with eyes akin to those of our own. And as before, I found I could not stare at it for more than a second or two. Doing so strained my eyes and senses, and forced me quickly avert my eyes. Perhaps the shape was not really there, but seen instead through inner sight, or some kind of nauseous hallucination.

Either way, it was there for around a further two minutes, and during that time I sat by the tree, not so much afraid as drowsy and unable to act. Yet like before, the shape soon disappeared without sound nor movement. I looked at it; took my eyes away as to rest their aching, and then found that the shape had vanished again. This time though, I did not feel faint as I did in the cemetery. In fact, when I noticed the shape was no longer there, I stood up at once to investigate where it had been.

Of course, there was nothing on the ground between the trees, save for dead leaves, thistles and goose grass. In fact, the woodland had become noticeably silent; with even birds seeming to sing less than they were a minute ago. The breeze was still, the trees unmoving. It was like this a lot in 'hidden places', of course. Even though some were in the midst of a city, they always managed to exist in a bubble where the babble of life did not care to wake them. Still, the woods that day seemed unusually quiet, as if any second a gust of wind or chance rain storm would shatter their muteness.

I did think of reading the Sullivan Book there, but after glancing through a couple of it's thin, small printed pages, I felt I was not in the right frame of mind. Instead, I returned to the well to inspect it further, trying to enjoy the essence of the place and forget the ceaseless sickness I felt. In a way, it did help; I was able to avoid focusing on the pain and wonder about the Holy well's history. The statuette of Mary told me that the well had been Christianised, most likely when Kilportach and rest of Ireland lost it's roots to the spread of the Church. Most probably, this old well was originally part of the Celtic settlement who lived in Kilportach. It was interesting to imagine it; those crumbling stones having seen the town change, and survived through countless generations of people. And yet now the old well stood alone, no longer on maps or tourist routes, lost to the the town and it's deathly bog bodies.

It was around that time, when I had knelt by the well to inspect it closely, that I noticed a small book next to the statuette. It was lined with a thick and plastic covering, although years of rain and changing weather had still managed to warp and stain it's paper. Upon opening it up, I saw that it was in fact a guest book, complete with an introductory page, written in a smudged yet neat handwriting. Unfortunately, the majority of the book was empty, with only a handful of scribbled entries, hard to read and fading with time.

That said, there was something written in that waterlogged book which caught my eye with somewhat of a startle. Thinking my queasiness was misleading me, I held the book to the light so I could read it more clearly. To my wonderment, I found that I was not in fact mistaken. It was clear in front of me; written in black ink and blurred with rain water.

'Welcome to the Holy Well of St Teresa. Visitors are reminded to maintain the sanctity of this sacred place, and thus no votive offerings should be left at the well side. Therefore, please take a moment to write your prayers and comments in this book, and leave with the light of the world in your heart. Amen.

26/07/1981

name: H. W. Phillips

message: Wonderfully peaceful, a sanctuary.

18/09/1981

name: A. Gainsborough

message: I have twenty-three tiny wishes, but I probably won't remember them all, so I put them all together into one...I'd like to spend more time here.

24/11/1981

name: Ethel Clarke

message: Beautiful, as always

24/11/1981

name: Ford

message: Thank you for bringing us here, Ethel. Such a lovely monument to our Lord. I do hope everything goes well for us both. Thank you.

I read the passages multiple times, still thinking that I was seeing things or that the paper's decay had distorted the words. It was clear enough though. Clear enough to read and understand. Not only had Ethel Clarke came to the well, but someone named Ford had visited with her. The Ford family, of course, was the name of my foster carers.

It made no sense, instantly scrambling all of my thoughts and returning them sheer disorientation. Was I the son of the Clarke's in Kilportach after all? My previous theory had made so much sense; garnered understanding in a way that I put such theories into the back of my mind. But it was impossible. Unless formed by a cruel and sour coincidence, how could a Ford family come to town and meet with the very person I was researching?

My mind convulsed and physically hurt, throwing back questions I hadn't asked since first setting out on this horrid journey. I literally couldn't understand anything; simply standing by the well and staring towards the earth below me. I told myself I'd just give up, get a train back home and forget the town, forget the people and the unending research. I felt so bad that it made sense to do it. I couldn't stand much more of this fragile 'holiday'; sleeping on the sofa in a pub and walking through the streets of multiple murders. Was it really worth it, in the end?

I didn't have time to think about it. For the next thing I found myself consciously aware of was the lack of daylight surrounding the forest. I opened my eyes, and knew immediately what terrible thing had happened to me. I was laid on the floor, the cold earth warmed by my body upon it, the Holy well standing alone behind me. I had fainted again, and this time for far longer than before.

An instant sense of dread fell upon me. I stood up quickly, my head feeling heavy yet not painful, my muscles aching like having slept for hours. The day had gone. It was almost pitch dark in the woodland clearing, the sky above me lit with stars and the gaze of a large and unearthly moon. How long had I been unconscious for? All I knew then is that I felt unsafe. There was something about it; the mute shadows caught between branches and sky, the chill breeze; damp and lightly whistling. It was like I was surrounded by watchful things, who although without eyes still saw inside me, and reached silently outwards with a brumal shiver.

What had happened to me? I stood rooted to the spot, the Sullivan Book now laying beneath me, having fallen to the floor as I lost consciousness. My stomach still burned with an gnawing sickness, and my whole awareness was taken aback, unable to comprehend what had happened and how long I had been laying out there. I was lucky I had not injured myself, having no recollection of anything apart from standing in daylight, then waking in darkness. Honestly, I was unnerved by it. If I could no longer control my own consciousness, what dangers could I find myself falling into? My chest sunk with a depressing guilt; a self depreciating sense of failure at having no memory of falling down. There was also anger. Although it presented as a pounding confusion at first, it was anger at it's heart. The new pills had so far done nothing to help me, and had only intensified the previous experiences. I felt like I'd been robbed; conned into taking them from a man who just wanted a tick on his 'patients' quota. Inside though, I knew that Ryan was not to blame. He was genuine, I knew that.

Nonetheless, I found that whilst standing in the nocturnal woodland, I could focus on little else but primal emotions. The feeling of danger quickly escalated, and memories of the 'thing' I encountered before rushed back to my thoughts with new levels of concern. I came to notice every sound of the forest, and feel both alone and at the same time surrounded by entities old and curtained in darkness.

It was perhaps a childish emotion at heart, but an overwhelming wish to run away fell across me. It was like in a fevered, murky nightmare; where you run from an untold and ancient terror, yet never manage to scream nor escape from it's gaze. At that time, I felt like simply breathing was enough to make me visible to those who watched me, like there really was something out there in the gloom.

It wasn't long before I'd made up my mind. I bent down, picked up the Sullivan Book in both my hands, and ran into the darkness towards Kilportach. I still felt awful, and the pound of my running made my stomach jolt and throb along with it. Though once I had started, I dared not pause nor look behind me, the unfeigned panic which rapidly occurred not letting up nor allowing rationality. In the distance, I could see the lights of Kilportach town, though the path before me was entirely black. For the time being though, I tried not to focus on the possibility of falling, or of finding another gruesome discovery hidden in the dark of that obdurate bog land. I just wanted to get back into the town, to return to light as quickly as possible.

The Watcher in the Dark

The looming lights of Kilportach town felt, for the first time, to be bustling with life. I imagined the warmth of Molly's pub, the flickering street lamps and loitering police, and settled my mind from my childlike panic. I was still quite a walk from the main street though, but I began to slow down and catch my breath the closer I got to the old buildings in front of me.

    Crossing the bogs was the worst part of it. A presence clung to that endless marsh, as if during the hours of evening silence, the earth itself could be heard to speak from below. I rushed through, daring not to stare for long into the darkness, remembering Bridget's B&B and my awful discovery nearby of her murder. The bogs were definitely alive that night though; the bodies sensing the lights of the town, and thus craving the day they would be unearthed; to once more walk amongst their kin.

    My anxiety only begun to calm when I reached the houses on outskirts of Kilportach's high street. Those steep pavements were lit with harsh street lighting, and behind the curtains of many a home, shadows of life could be seen to go about their evening. I wouldn't go as far as to say I felt safe, but knowing that the living where close at hand was in many ways a comfort to me. In a way, I begun to view my startled retreat from the forest to be a moment of madness, yet I knew that inside it was not so. For it was always the same; our childhood fears could be rekindled by a subtle shadow or mumbled voice. Such 'jumps' build up to a single point; a point where we lose our usual reasoning, and fall back to the restless emotions of yore. Thankfully, the signs of life around the outskirts helped me to quench those timeworn sensations. I begun to think, to slow down, and once more rationalise.

    That is not to say I felt physically better, though. In fact, after catching my breath and regaining a regular, steady heartbeat, I decided to grudgingly take the second of the new pills. I stood beneath one of the amber street lamps, and forced myself to swallow the tablet which had already done more harm than good. I just hoped that Ryan was right about them, that an initial worsening of the symptoms would lead to a ceasing of them altogether. I wasn't sure though; I still felt as as if I could throw up any second, and the earlier running had hurt my head and almost brought on another of the headaches.

I consciously forced myself to not think about it. Instead, I told myself to concentrate on the oddity found in the Holy wells guest book. Just why would my fosters have came to this town, if I did not live here as I originally assumed? It seemed that my research was right in the first place; I was the son of the Clarke family, and yet didn't show up on the genealogy records. It made sense on some counts, and still not on others. Furthermore, the regression gave me little that could help in this matter, focusing more on the time I ended up with the TBI, rather than the case of who my family was. That, and the frightening assumption that it was I responsible for Cullen's death; a part of the mystery I tried to focus on as little as possible. Even so, I felt like I was getting nowhere.

For the time being though, I found my thoughts were quickly disturbed when I reached the pub and found it closed. I was a fool, and had all but forgotten Molly's decision to close the pub in response to the murders. The last time I spoke to her, she was worried about running such a place, and inviting the killer in, unknown to her. Previously, Molly had known I was coming back to sleep in the pub, and would leave the door open for me to return. Even Adam was inside last time, waiting for me to come in for the night, so Molly wasn't left alone inside.

But on that night, that door was already firmly locked. Could it be that Molly was left alone and locked up impulsively in fear for her safety? It certainly made sense. That said, I felt an instant sense of concern for Molly; knowing that she was likely safe yet wondering if she'd seen something to worry her.

Either way, my knocks on the door of the closed up pub resulted in naught but an echo in the night air. I waited, peering out at the dark main street, where not even a prowling policeman was present amongst the gloom. There was no answer from the pub, of course. I wondered if Molly was even inside, and realised that even if she was, she knew not know who was hammering on the door at this hour. Indeed, I knew I would not see the inside of the pub that evening.

So then where could I safely go for the night? I knew I could not stay up all evening, especially with what had happened and the way I felt. My legs twitched and ached from running away, and my abdomen still pulsed with a nausea which hadn't let up for hours. I needed to lay down; to at least try to fall asleep, even if just for a few uncomfortable hours.

There was only one place I could think of to go, and it was hardly high on my list of comforts. That said, a final unanswered knock on the door made me realise I really had no choice. I had to act, to find a place to rest my legs before they just gave out from underneath me. Right then all that mattered to me was seeing morning, and hoping to last the remainder of the night without throwing up or fainting again. So, after peering once more through the open curtains of the pub window, I turned once more away from the main street, and walked towards Amelia's crypt in the cemetery.

Of course, there was no guarantee she would let me inside, or even be prepared to open the door. It was one thing to visit the old cabin together, but allowing me to sleep in her makeshift home was another matter entirely. In fact, I was sure I was wasting both my time and hers. Not only that, but whilst I trusted Amelia more than I did before, I was not sure how I felt at the prospect of falling asleep with her in same room as me. Somehow though, I could not stop myself from walking forward. I had reached the point where I felt so bad, that I was almost upset with myself for inhabiting such feelings. My entire body ached as I walked along; not only from the still unrelenting nausea, but from seemingly every muscle in my legs and back. I just needed to rest. It was all that mattered.

When I finally reached the unused cemetery, there seemed to exist a ponderous mood, an ambience which hovered across the silhouettes of old gravestones. A solitary street lamp stood near the gates which formed the graveyard's perimeter; it's faint light penetrating the dark just enough to see mere inches ahead. It was still difficult though. I kept walking into the many headstones, feeling the soft earth of graves beneath as I accidentally stood upon them. And the further I got from that dim street light, the stronger the feeling I detected became. I do not know if I could call it a presence; for such personification would surely grant it the illusion of being alive. Instead, it was more of a rhythmic flutter, like the energies present throughout the day had been intensified by the mask of night. In addition to this, the further I walked from the light behind me, the darker; and thus harder to navigate, the old graveyard became.

Thankfully, the ornate statue of Amelia's crypt was one of the larger stones in the cemetery, with it's raised position standing out against the backdrop of a sky deprived of stars. Indeed, the woman in the statue; grasping the cross and staring to heaven, took on the role of a shadowed overseer, watching me as I slowly fumbled towards the tomb she was stood in guard of.

When I reached the door, I hesitated to make my presence known. In that second, I felt abruptly sicker than I had all night, knowing that should any trouble emerge, I was not in a state to deal with it properly. And yet, after standing by the door for over a minute, I realised I had no option but to try; to at least give Amelia a chance to help. She had came to my aid once before, after all.

I inhaled the cold, wet air of the night, and gave three sharp, loud knocks on the door. As expected, there was no answer. Not even a whisper of movement could be heard from inside. I tried again. And again.

After numerous knocks, a light shuffle could finally be heard from behind the door, followed by a few faint thuds of activity. She was in there at least; that was something. I knocked again, this time breaking the graveyard's silence by loudly declaring who it was that had woken her. Still, there was no answer from Amelia.

"Come on", I said, not bothering to knock on the door again. "Look, you've got to let me in, OK?". I was beginning to lose my patience with her. If she was not going to let me inside, I would be forced to collapse in the cemetery itself, my legs already feeling ready to give way at any second. Truthfully, I could have screamed aloud, or even curled up and held my head in my hands, as the tiredness and nausea became more and more agonising.

To my surprise though, Amelia really did open the door. I had clearly just woken her up; her eyes looking heavy and a creased nightdress being all that covered her. But still, she had heard my knocking and opened the door, and that alone was enough to raise my mood. I stood, bent over slightly with the bubbling stomach ache, and made direct eye contact with the angered looking Amelia.

"Seriously, what do you want?" she mumbled, still holding the door firmly in her hand, ready to slam it shut at any second.

I had to speak fast, to explain my situation. Of course, I had no time to waste with petty explanations, telling her simply that I'd passed out, and was feeling awful due to the new medication. I must have rambled, finding it hard to explain in detail just what I required from her at such a late hour. She didn't interrupt though; letting me tell her all I wanted to, whilst she stood in the open doorway of the crypt.

"Well look", she eventually replied. "You do look pretty ill, you know? OK, I mean...I suppose you can come in. For a little while, anyway."

I couldn't begin to thank her enough. It was odd, bizarre even; but her eccentric crypt was as welcoming to me as any hotel or guest house I'd stayed in. It was shelter; away from the cold of the advancing night, silent to the noises of traffic and animals. I felt uniquely relieved when she invited me in, then closed the door firmly behind, as if to seal off her 'home' from rest of the world.

Of course, I did not feel much physically better. Thankfully though, the crypt was cold, and after putting down the Sullivan book on the desk, I sat down and took the weight from my tired legs. In fact, as I sat there, hunched over with my forehead resting in my hands, I felt the muscles in my legs wearily twitching; a sensation which although born from discomfort, presented itself somewhat with a feeling of easement. Still, I sat as still as I could in the old folding chair, taking in deep breaths of musty air and trying to force myself to settle.

The crypt was lit by the same wind-up desk lamp, creating an atmosphere independent of what time of day it was outside. I also noticed my Mother's necklace, no longer worn by Amelia herself but hanging on a nail above her bed. It glistened slightly from the light of the lamp, almost tempting me with the thought of fate, of my visit that evening being predetermined. If anything, the sight of the necklace created inside me the sentiment of familiarity; a single reminder of my past, my reason for coming to that isolated place.

Amelia laid back down on her bed, not uttering a word to me as I sat and refused to move an inch. I think I closed my eyes, most likely drifting in and out of sleep without consciously knowing my thoughts or emotions. I felt hot, even though the room was damp and cold, and a layer of prickly sweat soon formed across my forehead and arms. The nausea had actually settled down, most likely from sitting still and not moving, but I still felt exhausted and confused at the prospect of my earlier experience.

"Your really feeling bad, huh?" said Amelia in a softer tone than before. I opened my eyes, taking my head away from my hands and sitting up straight so that I could look at her. She was laying on her bed, slightly sat up and wide awake; her white nightdress wrinkled and not very modest.

"Actually, I'm a little better, I think. Thanks."

"Good to hear. By the way, what book was that you brought in with you? Anything interesting?"

I got the feeling she was just trying to cheer me up, to take my mind away from my sickness like most people always try to do. That said, there was a chance she had seen the Sullivan book, or even that she may be genuinely interested in reading it's passages on Kilportach. Either way, she seemed less misanthropic than before; her voice more calm and her whole persona more pleasant to be around. Perhaps it was just because she was tired, or that I'd grown to know her, and trust her, far more than I had on previous meetings.

"Have a look", I said. "The book's on the desk."

She got up, yawning and slowly getting to her feet, then walking to the desk and taking hold of the book that Silsbury had lent me.

"Oh god", she laughed. "Reading this now, are you?"

"You know that book?"

"I read it years ago, yeah. I didn't know it was still in print though. What do you think of it?"

"Actually, I haven't read it yet".

She flicked through a couple of pages, then took it to her bed and sat down to search it in greater detail.

"I remember this", she said. "I used to love it when I first read through it. I guess it wouldn't be as good to read through now though. A bit over the top, you know?"

"Like I said, I really don't know." I took in another deep, purposeful breath, feeling a new twinge in my stomach, accompanied by a surge of irritating heat.

"Wow, I can tell how bad you feel from just looking at you", said Amelia, closing the book and putting it on her bed. "And your saying you passed out again, like before in the cabin?"

"Yeah, just like before. These new pills I got seemed to have made things worse. I should never have let him talk me into taking them."

"They were for your headache things, right? Like what you were telling me about before?"

"That's right."

I remembered how Amelia had stayed with me when I lost consciousness in Shane Cullen's cabin. I had told her all about the headaches, even about the 'things' I see and all of the signs of a coming attack. Interestingly, she didn't seem to judge me for it, nor pass any horrid socio-psychology aimed at trying to 'understand' the cause of my condition. For this, I actually felt quite safe talking to her about it. Indeed, she was clearly of the same philosophical mould as myself, and people of such a cynical world-view are seldom those to judge or sneer. Fears of the townsfolk's motives still haunted me, but I knew then that Amelia, despite her eccentricities, was one of the few I felt to be trustworthy.

"OK, look", she continued, sitting up on the bed and looking straight at me. "I suppose I could let you stay here for the night, if you really were stuck for a place to go. It won't be comfortable though, you know that."

"I know. And yeah...thanks, Amelia. I don't want to be a nuisance or anything, you know. It's just I've too much on my mind to think properly these days. So thanks a lot. Your a lifesaver, in a way"

Of course, for many people, sleeping on a cold floor would be too uncomfortable to even manage. For me though, nothing was worse than being hot on a night, especially since right then I was out in a sweat without even having to lift a finger. If anything, the cold stone floor of the crypt was a perfect place to soothe my nausea. Yes, the hardness would bring pain to my back and legs, but that was hardly a concern for me at the moment.

It was not long in fact before I took up Amelia's offer to sleep there, and she even put down a small bundle of clothes for me to create a makeshift pillow. Honestly, I was taken aback at her hospitality, but was not in the mood to bring it up in front of her. Soon though, Amelia switched off the wind-up lamp, and climbed back into her own creaking bed, quietly saying good night as she did.

Almost instantly, the darkness of the crypt without any light transformed the entire mood of the room. An alien atmosphere swirled in the black, a spirit which spoke of a place grown strange with the alteration of it's purpose. I could hear Amelia lightly breathing, and if I focused my eyes on the gloom in front of me, I could just about make out the shapes of the furniture. Yet of all these things, it was the coffin in the corner which unsettled me the greatest. That preserved oak casket, propped up like some kind of unwanted botherment, was foreign to me and unusually unpleasant.

Ultimately though, I was aware of the immense sadness of the graveyard; the silence inside the converted crypt, shrill with the voices of it's countless neighbours. I had long been accustomed to the whispers of nature, but the ambience of that chilly tomb was more than the sum of it's aesthetics and whereabouts. There was something else, something that we, as the living, could not understand. A pulse, of sorts, which vibrated above our consciousness.

Thankfully, I did manage to fall asleep. In fact, I remember the dream I had on that night with a detail seldom present in the majority of dreams. Occasionally though, I'd have a dream which would stay with me for years, implanting itself inside my mind as a valid experience worthy of being called a memory. In a way, they were the dream equivalents of 'hidden places'; locations visited ethereally in sleep, alive with unique and strong energies. And yet once seen, they could never be returned to, save for in their remembrance as real to recall as any genuine memory.

My dream on that night was similar to such an experience. Although unlike the majority of dream locations, I found myself returned to an actual destination; a place I had visited on holiday years ago. It looked different, of course, wrapped in that kind of morphic pliancy that can only be formed in the world of sleep. But it was the same place; the small town I visited on a solitary holiday well over a decade ago. It was by the sea; a vibrant townscape alive with the mirth of many holiday makers. For me though, the presence of the ocean was not a place to sunbathe or take time away from some hectic home life. Instead, the tides and waves of that endless ocean were to me a potent and powerful healer. I stayed in a small and family run guest house, and spent most of my days exploring the coast and the recesses of cliff-top pathways. There were many 'hidden places' to see in that town, their aura intensified by the ever present voices of the sea. Although even to this day, I felt a certain loneliness to those waves; a semblance imprinted in the many shells and rocks that I still own now, all these years later.

It was that loneliness which I felt in the dream. It was like the sea was attempting to speak, to confide in me who understood the knowledge that those ancient waves imparted to us. I just stood, looked out towards the vanishing ocean, a feeling of being alone with the world falling across my comprehension. After a while though, I heard the footsteps of another behind me on the stony beach. I did not turn around, keeping my eyes focused on the sea as it rhythmically lulled me into a trance. But the person got closer, walking behind me until eventually their footsteps ceased close to my back.

What happened next I am not sure. In the dream, the person behind me reached out to touch me, either putting their arms around my chest or otherwise touching me with their hands. Yet it was in that moment, the exact second when their body came into contact with mine, that I abruptly woke up with a startled gasp.

For the first few seconds, I was sure that I felt the person from my dream standing over me as I laid on the floor. In fact, I could almost make out their shadow above me. I could not see clearly though, but I definitely felt a sensation of company, as if someone was holding their hands above me, or staring intensely into my eyes.

I sat up slightly, thinking at first that Amelia had been trying to wake me up for some reason. But as I stayed still; holding my breath, I realised that I could hear her breathing from the direction of her bed. So, if it was not Amelia, then who had been standing there, perhaps even watching over me as I slept?

I did not move for a number of minutes, gradually losing my drowsiness and thus separating the dream from reality. But I still sensed that someone was in there with me, another person who was not Amelia, standing mutely in the blackness of the crypt. I tried to focus my eyes to see, tried to soften my breathing as to hear them moving. But there was nothing there.

It must have been another couple of minutes before I decided I'd simply conformed to confusion. I was no stranger to what doctor's called 'night terrors', where indescribable feelings of fear are formed from nothing but a malfunction of emotion. Such an experience was similar to what I was feeling on that night; the sudden gasp as I woke from sleep, the momentary pausing of normal awareness. Usually though, a 'night terror' was defined by a moment of thoughtlessness; a primal feeling of fear or panic, which subsided soon after with the arrival of rationality. My experience on that night was different. It was more real, more grounded in what we call reality for any dream to have conjured it up.

Another minute passed. There was no way I could simply lay back down, go back to sleep as if it were simply a dream. The sensation I felt would not subside, no matter how much I rationalised or told myself it was just in my head. Yet it was not until I tried again to focus my eyes, that I realised I truly was not alone in there.

Amongst the blackness of Amelia's crypt, I detected a mass which hovered close to me; a shape outlined amongst the furniture and items. Strangely, I found that I could not focus on it, despite it's appearance as as a simple shadow, an unidentified blackness present in the room. I think it was then when I realised it; the 'shape' from before had returned to my side, refusing to let me rest or sleep until whatever it wanted was finally satisfied.

But what could it be? I had seen it before in the cemetery and Holy well, fluttering statically amid the trees, formless and painful to focus my eyes on. Was it a side effect from the TBI? A spirit? An entity awoken with thoughtless emotion, forced into existence from sheer envy of the living?

No, it was something else. It existed on the boundaries between the real and imaginary, both tangibly existent and entirely invented. I had created this 'shape', this feeling myself; and what happened next on that loathsome evening, only hastened to convince this realisation.

I had just about thought of everything it could be, from Amelia having gotten up in the night, to the murderer skulking in the most muffled of shadows. But at the second I envisaged it being formed in my mind, something happened of which I still tremble to recall. A voice, resounding in the dark without warning nor breath, entering my thoughts with a distinct and shivering 'jump'.

"Why do you not see me?", it said. At first, I subliminally assumed it must have been Amelia, before realising the voice was not of hers, nor of anybody else in the town I had met. In fact, I could not tell if it was male or female; it's tone opiate and somewhat monotonous, like two or three voices had morphed into one. I sat up straight, feeling for a second in leave of my thoughts, unable to respond or work out what was happening. Soon though, my mind overflowed with a frightening awareness that something was in the room with myself and Amelia.

"Amelia", I called out, my voice quiet at first through an anxious distrust of the black form in front of me. I needed to speak louder, though. "Amelia. Hey, Amelia!"

She did not wake up, nor stir in her sleep. I called out again, thinking this time of standing up and shaking her to force her to awaken. I did not want to move though, to walk through the mesmeric shape, even if was only inside my mind. It was then that it struck me; if the shape itself was imaginary, could the voice be also a figment of my mind? I remained quiet, leaving Amelia fast asleep and waiting for the shuddersome voice once again. As I expected, it 'spoke' as soon as I began to imagine it.

"Why do you not see me?" it said once more. Again the voice was tiresome and oddly hypnotic, like numerous murmuring tongues had joined to assemble in a troublesome chorus. To my ears, it sounded both inside my head and within the room; yet I couldn't ascertain as to it's exact location. The shape; or rather the opaque silhouette which hung in the room, did not seem to project the words from it's own immediate direction. Instead, the voice seemed to be coming from all around me; both spoken internally like my own thoughts, and at the same time carried on the musty air of the room.

"What do you want?" I quietly replied, feeling at once both afraid and curious. I knew that I could have woken Amelia, and this in a way was what I hoped would happen. Either way, I sat on the floor, upright yet still in a reclined position, and tried not to focus on the undefined shape which hovered in front of me.

"Her necklace", said the voice. "Does it not haunt you with memories?"

"The Selkie...well, yes. Yes it does." It was hard to raise my voice above a whisper, but I felt oddly compelled to respond to the voice, even though I knew not who, or what, it could be.

"It is the same necklace, isn't it?" it continued, the tone of voice without emotion and entirely colourless. "The one around her neck, on your only photograph."

"My mother's photograph? I don't know". I tried to look into the dark of the room, to see if I could make out the shadow of the necklace hanging above Amelia's bed. Of course, I knew the first time I saw the necklace that it was indeed the same one. It was identical.

"So how do you recognise that necklace?" said the voice. "If Ethel Clarke was not your Mother?"

"How do you know these things?" I raised my voice slightly, sitting up straighter and trying to make eye contact at the shape. It hurt my eyes just like before, despite the lack of light surrounding it. What on earth was it?

"I know you", it replied. "I know all. That necklace belonged to your mother Ethel, Amelia even confirmed it with you. So tell me, what is it that makes you deny it so?"

"What do you mean?"

"I think you know". It sounded as if the voice was changing. It was taking on an aura of bitterness, even of sarcasm. "Edward Clarke went below the Wishing Lake, did he not?"

"Yes. Yes, he did."

"And yet you also walked into that cave, didn't you?"

"You mean..."

There was, at that moment, an audible pulse throughout the room, like a heartbeat or low drum rhythm. It made no sound, yet throbbed inside my body with an uncomfortable spasm; almost as if the air had gained physical mass and forcefully struck me.

"Yes", continued the troublesome voice in the room. "You have known since you came here, haven't you? Now tell me, where did your hidden places come from?"

"What are you saying? Wait, you mean, from...Shane Cullen?"

"Yes, yes. Amelia also knows of them, does she not? And Edward Clarke, her childhood friend?"

"I know what your trying to-"

"Tell me", it interrupted. "Who's name was inscribed on that guest book you found, amongst the old Holy well?"

"You mean Ford, right?" I writhed on the floor, wanting to stand up fully and confront the entity, but feeling unable to compel myself into action. I was surprised Amelia had not woken up, and was amazed I had not felt nauseous or experienced a headache because of this 'visit'. Indeed, I was unsure if the voice was in the room at all, or whether the entire thing was imagined, the voice being nothing but a projection of my own consciousness as it struggled with the events in Kilportach. Either way, it did not stop talking, seeming to inhabit a human quality, and thus able to think and understand.

"Yes, Ford", it said. "Your foster family. You hated them, didn't you? So why did they do it? Why did Lucas and Ethel send you to them?"

"I have no idea! What are you trying to say?"

"You are not on the records, are you Leonard?" it continued, it's tone most definitely accusing and acerbic. "Your family history ends in Kilportach, when the cave under the Wishing Lake crushed your parents, does it not?"

"Well, that's why I came here, yes."

"But your parents only had one son, and he was smashed by the cave-in along with them. So you are not only absent on the records sheets, but from the town, the people, and even your own family?"

I was about to speak, but was confronted with another somewhat painful pulse of air throughout the room. I closed my eyes, feeling a hot tremble rush through my body, like a momentary shut down of the nervous system. I shook my head, opened my eyes once more.

The shape had moved. It was closer, appearing but inches from where I was sitting, the silhouette darker than the rest of the room, seeming to be solid and undeniably real. I didn't look at it, forcing my eyes towards the floor. It was a figment of my mind, a dark blotch in my head like the MRI image of the brain injury. That's what I told myself, anyway.

"Who on earth are you?" it said, louder than before. The voice was dark, lower than anything a person could manage, and seemed for once to be coming from inside myself, rather than emanating from the actual shape. "You claim to be a mystery, a man without a past nor family. So did you visit this place...or have you always been here?"

"I know", I replied, my voice calming back down and focusing more on the growing images inside my thoughts. "But it's not right. Not possible; I mean, they're all-"

"Perhaps that is why you cannot see me", it loudly interrupted. "Because you will not look into the truth, into that which you have known all along is real. Tell me, did you not remember when you first came here?"

"What do you mean?" I felt a change in my heartbeat, a quickening, deepening of it's rhythm; similar to times when a build up of feeling is involuntarily called on in moments of apprehension. I did not feel sick, just stuck in the very moment when a jump tremors across the body.

"Did the town not speak to you, let you feel it's presence? Did those bricks and roadways not breath along with you? And those endless peat bogs...did they not whisper in congruence as you passed them by? Whispering your name...Edward."

    I was punched in the stomach, or at least it felt as if I was. I lunged forward; for a second almost losing control of my senses and running to the door or to Amelia's aid. My back prickled up like a cat in the moonlight, sending shivers of discomfort across all reaches of my skin. And I looked at the shape. Through it.

    It hurt, burned the back of my eyes and tightened the muscles, like I'd switched on a light in the middle of a terrible headache. In a matter of seconds though, I actually saw it; that of which I had previously been unable to look at. It was a swirling current, a moving darkness which seemed like water or as if I could reach and put my hands straight through it. And things were moving within that blackness, old things imprinted in the faces of time, crisp with colour like vivid dreams.

    At this point, I do not know if I saw 'inside' the shape, or once more lost consciousness and fell prey to my thoughts. All I know is that what I saw; the images surging lucidly within that darkness, were undoubtedly real. They were memories, as graphic as those I had seen in the regression, but coming this time with speed and clarity, as if I'd somehow broken a block in my mind and the thoughts rushed outwards like a burst dam.

    I saw my mother, sitting in a chair in a bright, sun speckled sitting room; clean polished floors and expensive ornaments filling the large and high ceilinged room. Around her neck was the silver necklace; the Selkie of which hung inches from me, above the bed of the sleeping Amelia. The memory was bright, yet seemed to be painted in brighter colours than the real world has ever shown us. In that respect, it was like a dream, where even the most mundane of things can be turned into a centre of powerful emotion.

    In my hand, I held a small black camera, of which I took a few snaps of the room itself then turned to my mother, sat motionless in the chair.

    "Come on", I said, my voice once more that of a young boy. "You said I could take your picture, right? Why not now?"

"Oh, very well", replied my mother. She seemed preoccupied, her tone of voice not that of mirth but of a clearly sorrowful depth of thought. "But don't take too many, will you dear? It's the only film we have, after all."

I realised then what I was doing. My mother was wearing the very same dress as displayed on the photograph I had hung in my home. That and the necklace, of course. So, it was I who took that singular picture; that one memory which haunted me through to this very day. It was odd, in a way, that I did not previously remember. I often wondered who had taken the picture, what happened on the day when it was taken. And then I saw it.

But not all was as enlightening as those first flashes of lucid memory. When I took the photo, the harsh white light of the flash blinded me, fading the memory into the distance, moulding it with enigmatical thoughts that circled within my dazzled awareness.

Numerous bursts of memories followed, most of which staying only long enough to realise that they were of my own past. They faded quickly, returning to a mass of coloured shapes which then formed into more and more quivers of my childhood.

"Edward!" shouted my Father, grabbing hold of my arm in the small, untended back garden. "You understand nothing about it. You've got to promise not to go there again. Never speak to that man, you hear me?"

"I didn't. I really...I mean, I couldn't."

"Mr Cullen is dead. Dead! You hear me? Your lucky, we all are, that I'm prepared to do something about this. So don't you ever go near there again, right? You've got to promise me."

"OK...I promise".

At this point, the memory vanished not into a swirling shape like before, but into a complete and unmoving darkness. After a second, I realised that I was back in the crypt, still sitting on the floor, sweating profusely. The shape had backed away, hovering instead where it was to begin with, somewhere in the middle of the unlit room. I went to stand up, to confront the shape with a mixture of anger and poignant release at what it had shown me. Before I could manage it though, I heard it's monotone voice once more; this time throbbing inside my head, as if every word was leaden and heavy.

"You never had a Brother, did you?" it said. "There was no mistake on the records. No mystery to dig for answers. You are Edward Clarke, aren't you?"

"I...I am. But how?" I raised my voice in confusion. "If you can tell me these memories, then tell me how! How am I...I mean, what about the cave in?"

"Is it not obvious? You survived, and were sent immediately to your foster family. But to the town, and all of of it's people, you died as well under that lake. Why? Well, perhaps they didn't want you to live."

"Oh yeah, and whys that?"

"You forget so quickly. Or perhaps you are still unable to recall. It was you, was it not? You murdered Shane Cullen. You set into motion the chain of events, which ended in the deaths of your parents and almost yourself."

"No!" I shouted, standing up and facing the shape. "That is not what happened. It can't be...it just can't, OK?"

In the space of less than half a second, I found myself standing in the middle of the room, surrounded in a bitter and bright white light, stinging my eyes and forcing me to squint. At first, I thought the shape was showing me another memory, but I swiftly recognised that it had disappeared.

Amelia was standing by the desk, having switched on the light after waking up due to my incessant shouting. I do not know if she looked worried or angry, but it was definitely clear that she was disturbed by my no doubt maniacal appearing behaviour. For a number of seconds, I stood still, staring mostly at the floor but also to where the shape was hovering. Of course, the room was empty, as if nothing that night had broken it's silence save for my own irrational outburst.

I took in a breath, inhaling the hot and damp feeling air, and looked at Amelia straight in the eye. Somehow, although I knew not how to even begin, I had to explain to her what had just happened to me.

The Wishing Lake – Mark Robinson

Reunion

When Amelia switched on the light in the room, she unwillingly banished the formless shape which haunted my memories on that night. In a way, she had woke me from a kind of involuntary regression, a waking dream of heightened emotion; fuelled by realisations that were difficult to comprehend.

One thing was certain though. The memories I saw, those lucid patterns which spoke to me as I peered into that amorphous shape, were more potent than anything I had seen in Dr Ryan's hypnosis. For I knew then; in the instant when I found myself once more as a child, that the things I had witnessed were incontrovertible truth. Yes, I had thought many times about the nature of my identity, but I never truly believed it could be so.

Really, of course, it was only a 'name'; a title given to me by my parents which meant nothing outside of an arbitrary identification. Yet for a second, as I stood in the light like an animal caught in a car's headlights, I felt like all I had known was wrong. I was Edward Clarke; a person who was thought to be dead and buried, killed in a cave-in and reduced to a memory. But I'd survived, been given a new name and new foster family, and brought up with my past congealed in repression from my bothersome and unexplained TBI.

Inside, although I knew that I was still the same person as I'd always been, I experienced a feeling of being outside of existence. It was not a negative or depressing emotion, but more of a weightless and illusory sensation. And the more I stood in the light of the room, the more I understood that the 'shape' was indeed a projection of my own repressed memory. Had the new pills loosened the TBI somehow, leading to a sudden flow of constrained awareness? I felt a lightness of both body and mind; like somehow the memory had never been truly repressed to begin with. It was like I'd known it all along; that amongst my upbringing with the authoritative Ford's, I was mutely aware that something, somewhere, was not as it appeared.

The hardest thing, of course, was that Amelia had unexpectedly roused me from the memories, and I now stood still and in shock in her crypt. I had to tell Amelia what had happened, and what I had learned but minutes beforehand.

It was difficult. In fact, at first it was almost impossible. I sat on the chair, Amelia assuming I had suffered a headache or some other painful episode, and began to think of the words to tell her. But how could I? How could I tell her that I was Edward, the boy she remembered from her childhood, the one she visits the nearby grave of? I assumed such an expression to be impossible, and even if I managed to find the words, Amelia would never believe my story.

Because of this, an uncomfortable silence fell over the crypt, with myself sat lost in my own writhing thoughts, and Amelia stood looking over me, both angry and concerned at the same time. The room itself felt different too. An expectant air was present throughout, as if time itself had grown weary of my inaction, and now stood in watch with baited breath, for the moment these childhood friends were reunited.

In the end, it took Amelia to break the silence and ask me for the twelfth time what had happened, before I even managed to mutter a word. Yet when I did, I felt oddly as if I could not stop. I blurted out instantly 'who' I was, then started to tell her about the shape without hardly pausing to take a breath. I must have spoken; rambled, for minutes, with Amelia sitting on her bed and listening to me with widened eyes. At first, she said not a word; allowing me to recount my experience without sparing the details of my maddened apparition. It was only when I finally paused for breath, finally realised the extent of my rambling, that she decided to challenge and respond to my story.

"It's impossible", she said, her voice somewhat quiet as if she too was unsure of what to say. "Your just dreaming, tired, or...something. You were feeling ill before, remember? So there you are. You had a bad dream."

"Yeah", I forced a smile. "Like I didn't think of that. Look, when I saw into that shape, I saw memories. My memories, OK? It was like...like the regression I had at the doctor's, but different. And I know it was true. It just was."

I was aware that to anyone other than myself, I most likely sounded unbalanced or crazy, unable to discern between reality and dream. I didn't care though, not at that time. I just wanted to tell her what had happened, even if only to recount my experience in my own words spoken aloud. Honestly, I wasn't concerned whether she believed me or not. I just needed to settle my own mind.

"Alright", continued Amelia, standing up now and appearing agitated. "So if what you say is true, then why is Edward buried in this churchyard then, hm? Oh, and what about your birth certificate. It doesn't say 'Edward Clarke' on it, does it?"

"No, it doesn't. And I didn't say everything made sense, did I? Lots of things don't. But I did survive that cave-in Amelia, I must have done. I know it now. I always did, I think."

"You make no sense." She looked as if she could start to pace up and down at any minute. "I mean you honestly think you survived, do you? Well, it's impossible. And your wrong."

"How do you know? I mean think of it this way, I went under the lake as a child, right? I saw this in my regression as clear as day; I went under and came out before the cave-in happened. So then...I most probably went back in with my parents, and that's when it happened. I got the TBI during the accident, which is why I couldn't remember it happening. Come on, it makes sense, doesn't it?"

"Well, I don't know. Why would they think you died if you didn't? Your saying that your name on that gravestone is a mistake?"

"Well look, I...I don't know". I sighed, staring at the floor in a surge of confusion. "But look at it this way, you think I would just come out with this stuff if I thought for a second it wasn't true? I've never been able to remember these things. That's why I came to Kilportach in the first place, for gods sake!"

"OK" she loudly said. "I'm not saying your wrong. I'm not, right? I just...I mean come on, you think I'd just take news like that in my stride? I can't believe you! It's just not possible."

"It is possible", I stood up, took a look at the necklace hanging above her bed. "Think about it. What about your necklace, the one my Mother is wearing on my photo. Or about 'hidden places'; how we both know about them, most probably because of Shane Cullen telling us.

And what about the records, the ones that don't mention me on them and equate my family with Edward instead? It's obvious now. It's because 'Leonard Clarke' never existed, did he? My name was Edward all along. Edward Clarke."

Amelia paused, opened her mouth as if she was going to speak, but shook her head as the words refused to come. She then turned to the necklace, took it from the wall and examined it in her hands.

"This was given to me just before...just before it all happened, you know?"

"The cave-in?" I asked softly, detecting a lull in Amelia's angered tone.

"Yeah. I saw her wearing it, and mentioned that I liked it. Well, the very next day she gave it to me, just said I could have it as a gift. A few days later, and..." She shook her head, obviously stirring her own troubled memories; things she had not remembered for years, perhaps.

"I'm sorry. Look I didn't mean to bring back any bad memories, you know. I should have realised."

"Don't." she replied, raising her voice once again to her usual tone. "It's not like I need those memories 'bringing back'. I think about it a lot, actually."

"You do?" I sat back down on the chair, feeling I was calming, or rather reaching an understanding, with Amelia.

"The first thing I remember was a lot of shouting, people running around, thing's like that."

She sat on the bed, put the Selkie necklace around her neck, and looked at the floor, similar to what I was doing myself. I could definitely feel a change in her emotions; swiftly losing her cynical appearance and thus becoming immersed in her truer feelings.

"It was night-time, and I knew immediately that something was wrong. But nobody would tell me. It wasn't until the next morning when they told me something had happened, and that Edward, my friend, was gone. But they said nothing else, assuming I didn't want to know or was too young to understand. What a load of rubbish. I can still remember, I was scared. Just...scared, for some reason. And you weren't there any more, nobody was."

"Wait, so you believe me now?" I asked, realising Amelia had referred to me as Edward Clarke. I got up from the chair, moved to her bed and sat beside her. The bed was uncomfortable, the mattress old and the springs worn out. With two people on it, it felt almost as if it could have collapsed.

"I do", she quietly said, a change resounding in her voice, as if it was strained under the onset of tears. "I want to, anyway. I mean, imagine us meeting again after all this time. Is it really true?"

"I've seen a lot of odd things since I came here, Amelia. Bog bodies, murders...you name it. But that shape, it was something different. It was there when I first set eyes on Kilportach. It was my mind you see; my memories trying to speak to me. And now I've seen it. So it's true, yes, even though I can barely believe it myself."

I was not used to speaking softly, comforting people of whom I could tell were welling up inside with emotion. Such situations always made me uncomfortable, angry even. Yet I think I shared in Amelia's feelings. We were, in a way, childhood friends, despite me having no memory of her and having previously viewed her with an air of suspicion. But I definitely felt different that night. Tired, but awake with the swell of poignancy and realisation.

Indeed, the atmosphere of the converted crypt seemed yet again to change around me. For as I sat there, next to Amelia on her aged mattress, a unique warmth seemed to emerge in the clammy air I breathed in deeply. It was almost as if; for a second or two, the universe was entirely synchronized, with myself and Amelia side by side in accordance with the whims of and reaches of our memories. For the first real time since before Bridget's murder, I felt an odd, but completely genuine sense of comfort.

"When I first met you", she whispered, breaking the growing and heavy silence. "You'd seen that shape then, as well, hadn't you?"

"Yeah. I didn't know what it was, of course. I just felt sick, like I could pass out, you know."

"And I brought you in here. I don't even know why. I usually ignore everyone, try the best I can to stay out of their way. The last thing I'd do is show someone this; my little 'home' of which they'd never accept."

"What are you saying?"

"You didn't die", she said, the beginning of tears most clearly audible in her voice. "Just like I wished."

"You did?" I said, trying my best to force a smile. "What, you mean at the lake? Come on now."

"Look, under there." She nodded in the direction of the desk in front of us. "There's a record player, right? Get it out for me, and the record, as well."

I wasn't sure what she was trying to say, but I agreed to her wish and knelt on the floor, removing the item. It was a small, portable gramophone, in good condition apart from scratches on the front and sides of the dark blue cover. It was clearly old though; like something out of the 1930's complete with a silver needle and handle. There was also a record, it's sleeve creased and fragile looking, stained yellow with time and ripped in the corner. On it, black text contained only the name of a record company, and also the name of a single song. It was written in an italic font, and gave no mention of singer nor band. Only a title; *'The Great Selkie of Sule Skerry'*.

"It's the only record I have", said Amelia as I knelt on the floor, examining the impressive gramophone machine. "But it's my favourite, so I don't really mind."

"I see". I took the record out of it's sleeve, seeing that it was in pristine condition, with nary a scratch or smudge upon it.

"I listen to it whenever I'm about to go to the lake. And yes...I told that 'hidden place' my wish. To see Edward Clarke again, I would say."

"I...but surely..."

"Yeah, don't worry", she smiled. "It's a coincidence. But seriously, your that boy? It's unimaginable, and it's amazing."

"Honestly, I thought my feelings would be different somehow", I said, realising that this was the largest discovery I'd ever found out about my past. But I didn't jump with euphoric joy, nor shake with fear or confusing anxiety. I just felt different. Healed perhaps, but different.

"Anyway", said Amelia. "I have an idea about all this. Want to hear it?"

"Of course."

"Put the record on, and we can both go back to sleep until morning. Then...well, we can think of what still doesn't make sense for you, right?"

"I see", I smiled. "And yeah, your right. I doubt I'll be able to sleep again though."

"You'll see".

At that, I followed Amelia's careful instructions on winding the gramophone and playing the record. I put it up on the desk, placing in the record and using the handle, before switching off the wind-up lamp just as the music began to play.

Back on the floor, I laid on my back and closed my eyes, listening to the crackly sound of the old and haunting gramophone. Almost instantly I felt at ease; a relaxing pulse entering my body with each breath I took of the music filled air. And the lyrics seemed to speak to me, the haunting female vocalist not simply singing, but forcing the air to tremble in tune with the story she told in ethereal song.

Of course, even after the final words were spoken, and the gentle crackle of the record faded into the night's own silence, I was still as awake as I was before. If anything, the song had done little to settle my mind, save for the initial relaxation at the wonderful singing and soft piano. But the story of the song kept me firmly awake; almost as if I was seconds away from another memory presenting itself. I just thought of the lake, the cave beneath it of which I entered, and wondered just what happened under there which made me forget my own identity?

In the end, I gave up on trying to get to sleep. Amelia was silent, and apart from the occasional sound of her breathing, I could have easily been laying there on my own. Yet instead of turning over and attempting to sleep, I decided instead to use my time to think about what had happened that evening.

What haunted me the most though was not my revelation, but the new questions which came from what I had learned. To begin, there was that which in essence prevented me from having remembered my 'real' name any sooner. On the records, in the cemetery, and on the lips of all of Kilportach's people, Edward Clarke was killed in the cave-in. What had happened to make this so? How could I survive and yet still be assumed to have died along with my mother and Father? Moreover, my birth certificate; the one remaining accuser to the truth of my memory, referred to me clearly as Leonard Clarke. Were my new memories wrong after all? No, they could not be. So then, how could I possess an official document that calls me by a name I was not original given? This was even stranger when I considered that the certificate lists my birth at a later date. In fact, it is 2 years later than when 'Edward' was born.

So many things still made no sense, and for every question I could answer with my memories, another unanswered one appeared in it's place. Could it simply have been that I experienced madness, delusions brought on by Ryan's pills mixed with fatigue and unending exhaustion? I didn't want to believe it.

I turned over on the cold stone floor, wishing for the minute that morning would come, so that I could leave Amelia's hidden home. And yet I knew not where I could venture next; the idea of telling Molly my experience not something I fancied trying to explain. But I suppose I had to, somehow. Even so, I could think of no options to continue my research, assuming my spontaneous memory that night to be the largest discovery of my journey. In a way, I just wanted to go back home.

Grimorium Votum

Behind the heavy door of Amelia's crypt, the concept of time was reduced entirely to hands on the face of watches and clocks. There was no glint of morning sun, no dawn chorus loud enough to reach the walls of that sunken tomb. For that reason, I awoke with my head pounding with dullness; a leaden feeling of inaction most prevalent on dark and winter mornings. In fact, if it were not for Amelia telling me the time, I could have probably slept well into the afternoon.

Had I dreamt my experience the night before? The gramophone on the desk told me otherwise, as did the necklace Amelia wore, forcing me to remember the discarnate voice which had spoken inside me. Even so, my head hung with a fog characteristic of lucid dreams, and the experience I had refused to settle; still circling above and within my thoughts.

I did notice one thing different though. Amelia, after opening the door to let in fresh air, appeared to have lost her previous bitterness altogether. In fact, we soon found each other lost in conversation, talking quite freely about the last night without any cynicism or disagreement. Perhaps we had simply recognised the fact; that even though we had barely met, we had known each other in our distant pasts. Indeed, I even found myself talking freely and candidly; something I usually avoided doing with even the closest of acquaintances. My emotions however, were put on hold, allowing me to sit on her rusty bed, opening up about just what I 'felt' regarding the new memories I was constantly reminded of.

It was an odd experience. In essence, all I had remembered was that in my childhood, I had a different first name to that I now went by. Put that way, it didn't seem like a big deal at all; maybe even an expected part of being forced into a unrelated foster family. No, it's importance was not in the name itself, it was in the sheer and quickened understanding of so many strings in my original research. In that respect, I felt unusually uplifted on that morning; a mixture of the brisk air from outside and the end of so much of my prior confusion.

As for Amelia; she said that knowing I was Edward had hit her hard and was thus difficult to believe. Of course, the boy she knew 30 years ago was not recognisable in myself today, but I was amazed, touched even, at some of the thing's she had to recall. In particular, she told me how we would stage our own 'adventures', leaving the town and getting lost amid the fields and bog lands in search of 'hidden places'. She then used to draw the things we imagined, and I would tell her intricate stories I imagined about the places we discovered.

"They really are some of my best memories", she said. "I mean, I can still remember the first day we first met. I bet you can't though, can you?" she laughed.

"Ha, I wouldn't have thought so, no".

"I never really saw the point of friends", she said. "Even as a kid, I could see that my peers were all shallow and boring. So I purposely avoided them, went off and did my own little thing. That's when we met."

"How so?"

"It was at the old primary school, in the next town over from Kilportach as there isn't even one here at all! Anyway, I was among this small clump of trees at the end of the playground. I thought they were haunted, right? So anyway, you came up to me and I turned round so fast, thinking you were the ghost I was hoping to see! I think...yeah, we tried to make the ghost appear together then, but of course nothing really happened."

"That's amazing", I said, trying to force my own mind to bring up the memory she was talking about. I couldn't do it, but I did manage to conjure images; blurred and impossible to focus on, which may well have been from that very day. They were like the rare times when memories would appear in the mind for no reason at all; perhaps whilst performing mundane chores or when trying to fall asleep at night. They were there, though; recorded in time even though I could not push myself to bring them forward.

"So anyway, what happened next?" I said.

"Oh, well we must have found out that we both lived in Kilportach, and then that was it, I suppose. Heh, when I think about it, there was only me and you in the whole town back then. Only two children. Imagine it."

I remembered when Molly first told me that the town was home to only two children. Actually, thinking about it now brought up the chilled rush of goosebumps across my back and arms. It was as if something in those timeworn streets had beckoned me back to their quaint sidewalks; and had known all along that my boyish feet would stand upon them decades later. To Kilportach, of whom life was preserved eternally underneath it's sodden earth, Edward Clarke had simply come home.

I spoke to Amelia for around an hour, and during that time our misanthropic world-views were put to the back of both our minds. I told her things that had happened in my life, speaking without the usual hatred which foams whenever I'm asked 'personal' questions. I suppose in a way I felt comfortable with her, and put all of my earlier distrust aside in order to lose myself momentarily in banter.

After a while the morning grew thin, and although we could both have talked all day, I realised I really should be looking for what to do next. The questions that still remained unanswered were the things which I now needed to solve; though of course I had no idea how to go about it. So, after leaving our small talk for more serious topics, I asked Amelia if she knew of anything to help uncover these somewhat vague 'missing links'.

We must have thought about it for another half-hour, with myself going over the topics aloud and Amelia trying to piece them together. There was the matter of my birth certificate, the concern of the gravestone inscribed with my name, and of course the still unknown reality of whatever I saw under the lake. And among all this was a guilty conscience; a sickening feeling about something of which I could not even begin to remember. It was the matter of the killing of Shane Cullen, and how for some reason I troubled myself with the piercing assumption that I was to blame. To make it worse, I kept this particular problem to myself, not wanting to worry or upset Amelia with the idea that I may have been his murderer.

One thing was for sure though, and that was the fact that the questions I asked were almost impossible to find answers to. By the end of our discussion, both myself and Amelia were more confused than before we even started to think about it. In truth, I assumed already that the questions were true mysteries, and by that I meant something impossible to solve. Even so, I was near taken aback with the vested interest that my new companion seemed to grant my research. In fact, it was around that time when she made a suggestion, which otherwise would have surely resulted in me spending the whole morning in her crypt.

"Like I said, feel free to go up to town or whatever", she said. "I mean, we can think about what to do next separately, then meet back up here later on. If you wanted to, of course."

"Your probably right", I sighed. "I don't think I'm up to telling the townsfolk about my new memories, though."

"Well don't then. I just thought you might have wanted a walk about or something. See if you can think of anything. Then just come back whenever your ready. I'll be here, you know that."

It was clear that I needed to leave the crypt, if only to properly stretch my legs and take in the fresh air of outside. If anything, I could do with a drink and perhaps some breakfast which it didn't seem Amelia was able to provide. There was also the matter of the town itself; the investigation into the murders often pressing my mind to check for an update. So, after saying my goodbyes to Amelia, I decided to walk up into the town, and thus leave her alone with the questions I asked, hoping she really did think of an answer. Before leaving, I remembered the Sullivan Book on the desk, and took it with me as I left the crypt, intending to read it later that day.

The fresh air of the cemetery hit me immediately; the cold breeze and scent of the morning a comforting change from the airless crypt. It had clearly rained throughout the night, and the sky was still heavy with clouds which looked as though they could open up at any second. The ground beneath me was soggy and drenched, and by the time I'd left the overgrown graveyard, my trousers were already soaked through to the skin. Even so, I had always found the scent of rain to be an oddly soothing thing to inhale. It woke me up, anyway.

In the town itself, the main high street was completely deserted, with not even the presence of a single policeman trawling for clues or standing in guard. If anything, it felt even quieter than before, with the tourist office especially dormant; as if the bricks it was built from had not yet been told that it's owner was never coming back to open it. Looking at it, a distinct chill instantly filled my body, forcing me to hurry past, and further into the empty street.

One thing I did not do was take another of Ryan's new pills. I had no doubt that they were responsible for the dissipating of my mind, and thus at least somewhat to blame for my midnight experience. Of course, it was not that I didn't want to unlock more memories, but something about taking another did not sit comfortably with me that morning. If a headache came on, I'd just have to deal with it.

While in the main street, I called into the newsagents for a drink and breakfast, purchasing a sandwich and bottle of water from a very limited, pre-packed selection. Still, it was enough to give me the energy needed to settle my mind on the task at hand. And so for the first time since it happened, I thought long and hard about my 'name' and what, if anything, it meant to me personally.

Of course, I had never had a family life to begin with, and thus my knowledge of a change of first name was hardly as shocking as it otherwise could be. In truth, I got the feeling that it was the Ford family who called me Leonard, and hence refused to even mention my 'real' name prior to them fostering me. I wouldn't put it past them; they were the kind of people to ignore anything which did not agree with their blinkered world-view. But really, what was the point in giving me a new name to begin with? I see nothing wrong the name Edward Clarke, and if that is truly what my parents named me, why would anyone think of changing it?

That said, there was the matter of my enigmatic birth certificate, giving both a different name and a birth date two years out of synch. Thinking logically, it could be that the name I was actually given was the one on the certificate all along. That being so, it would have been my parents who renamed me Edward, and the Ford's who decided to revert to the original Leonard. Either way, the name change was a big new step in my research. With it, my conversations around the town could start to make a great deal more sense. And at that point, the thing I really wanted to know was why; and how, I survived the cave-in below the lake.

Whilst eating the rather bland sandwich I'd bought, I became aware that the streets of Kilportach had taken on a different appearance to me. It was nothing to do with the drizzling weather, nor the elegiac semblance which hung in the air due to the shock of the recent murders. Instead, I begun to see Kilportach as the place I grew up in; the patch of earth and concrete roads where I departed on my first adventures in the world. Usually, a person's home town would change so much as to render it unrecognisable to come back to, but I felt Kilportach was once again different. It's streets were unchanged and burdened with awareness of their own inertia, like their cracked brickworks had grown drowsy with time's advance. And yet amongst that tiredness they still managed to see; to remember all that had passed throughout them. Old businesses and shops, old cars which crossed those entwined roads, old people of whom at one time lived. Kilportach remembered them all, and myself as well, when I came to think of it.

Yet it was odd that even as I strolled the streets, I could not myself recall my childhood having taken place in that empty town. It seemed that the scope of my returning memories was limited only to specific times; those of my time underneath the lake and the resulting chaos of which ensued. And so Kilportach felt as foreign to me as it would have done to any visitor; with perhaps even the town itself being loath to bethink my sullen story.

After the sandwich and water were finished, I begun to walk in the direction of the pub, and encountered my first signs of life that morning on the main street. It was Jack Daly from the museum, walking and talking to Dr Kenny, dressed in casual clothes and not his doctor's uniform.

"Mr Clarke", exclaimed Jack as he spotted me. " I haven't seen you for a while. Are you OK?"

"I'm not too bad thanks", I replied, not prepared to break loose with details on what had really happened to me.

"Good to hear", joined in Kenny. "I hear you saw my colleague Dr Ryan as well. I told it could help you, right?"

"Yeah. It wasn't as bad as I thought. Thanks."

I felt I wanted to ask Jack about how he was coping, and whether there had been anything found out about the murders and their culprit. It was hard however to bring it up, and seeing as Jack seemed more upbeat than before, I did not want to shatter his recovery. That said, it was not long until he did so himself, and brought up without warning the topic of Bridget and the darkness which had befallen the town.

"I started to clean out the B&B", Jack said as I accompanied him and Kenny on their street-side walk. "Honestly I don't know what will become of it. It's sad to think it will just be another empty building, after all the effort she put into making it work."

"Yeah. Actually, it was the only hotel I could find open in the town, if you can believe such a thing!"

"Oh I can", he forced a smile. "That's why Bridget took it over when the previous owner died. She always wanted a business of her own, you see; and that guest house was just the perfect idea. There used to be a bigger hotel as well, but it closed down just as Bridget opened up."

"Ah, bit of good luck then, eh?" I tried to remain as positive as possible, aware that Jack was likely still battling with the shock of Bridget's death.

"I know. Ah, that reminds me actually, there was something I-"

"Hey", interrupted Kenny, bringing our walking to a standstill. "Sorry guys, but this is where I part, so to speak."

We were standing on the other side of the main street, amongst an uphill bank of terraced properties and a narrow, single carriage road.

"Oh of course", said Jack, shaking hands with Dr Kenny. "It was good to talk to you, anyway. Thanks a lot."

"No problem", said Kenny. "And you Mr Clarke, nice to see you again. Glad to hear your doing OK, you know?"

"Thanks."

Dr Kenny left myself and Jack, walking into the row of houses and disappearing from our sight. Afterwards, Jack turned around and headed back into the town, explaining that he had simply accompanied Kenny as he went from the surgery to someone's home.

"So anyway", he said as we once more approached the main street. "As I was putting things into boxes and that, I found an old guest register from the previous owner. I've been wanting to tell you about it ever since I discovered it."

"How so?"

"You remember when, well...before this all happened, myself and Bridget found something in the files about a Lucas Clarke staying in Hawthorn House? Well, it was true. I found his details in the old registry books. Thought it might interest you."

At this point I knew that the other Lucas Clarke was not in fact my Father. Even so, he remained a mystery that I couldn't ignore. The chances of two people with the same name being in a town like Kilportach were slim to say the least. Moreover, there was the matter of a Lucas Clarke being a suspect in the Cullen murder. Knowing this, it was probable that the other Lucas Clarke and son were the key to many of my remaining confusions. If I could focus and find out about their time in the town, I was sure that I could find my answers amongst them.

"What exactly did the registry book say about them?" I asked.

"Well most of it was just your usual affair; name, date, that sort of thing. But there was also a note with it. Pretty weird, to be honest."

"A note? What do you mean?"

"Honestly, it's best if I show it to you. But it seems that the owner of the guest house at the time had a few concerns with the man and his son. Now I'm not saying anything is true or not, but it's probably worth you taking a look, what with your research and all."

"Of course. So look, when can I see this? Have you got it on you?"

"I'm afraid not. Look, why don't I drop it off at the pub for you later? It's back at the museum right now I'm afraid."

It was annoying that Jack did not have the note on him. Instead, I asked him to give me the gist of it's contents, but he seemed somewhat reluctant to tell me anything about it. I was intrigued though; so much that already I began to imagine the sort of things that could have been written. Was the other Lucas Clarke acting suspicious in some way?

Could it truly have been him who was the murderer of Cullen? I just needed to see it, at that point just to ease my mind.

So, I agreed to let Jack drop the note off for me, of which he said would not be for a few hours due to something else he had to do. Again, it was a bother that I couldn't have seen it sooner, but I needed to be grateful and any and all information. I needed to visit the pub anyway, if not just check up on Molly and Adam then to arrange another night sleeping in there. In fact, we were standing almost in front of the pub when Jack and myself went our own ways. He headed back towards the bog land and museum, and I thanked him once more for telling me about the note, then watched as he vanished into the empty streets of terraced houses and narrow roads.

The pub itself was still tightly locked up. I did think of knocking on the door right then; checking in with Molly after being unable to enter the pub to sleep last night. For the time being though, I decided to leave it, and her alone. Jack would be coming back later with the note, and with any luck the pub would be open or at least I'd have ran into Molly elsewhere. Truthfully though, I wasn't keen on another night spent on the floor in Amelia's crypt, and so the lure of sleeping once more in the pub was a possibility I couldn't afford to miss.

For the moment though, I needed to pass some more time in town before returning to Amelia in the cemetery. That said, I had already discovered something to 'do next' on my own, and so was less concerned about whether she had thought of anything to help me out or not. Still, I was interested in what she would have to say; perhaps digging up more memories of her own, regarding both her and myself as children. After all, that was the whole point of me coming to Kilportach in the first place. I wanted to find those lost people and memories, recover the childhood of which I had lost.

Either way, I decided to head out of the town itself and towards the Wishing Lake on the outskirts. For a start, I wanted to read the Sullivan book without the threat of further interruptions from people, and a 'hidden place' like the Wishing Lake was the perfect spot to do so. Moreover, I felt I wanted to peer at those waters again; this time with fresh knowledge about what happened to myself and my family in the cave below. With any luck, I thought that standing by the rivers edge could help me to focus and correlate my research, and perhaps even force new ideas to surface regarding those questions still unanswered.

Indeed, I had forgotten how synonymous the Wishing Lake was with the very concept of the 'hidden place'. As soon as I arrived, having first passed by Shane Cullen's old cabin and trampled through grassland forever uncut, an immediate sense of somnolence seemed almost to rise from the water itself. Unlike before, there were no interruptions from the likes of Amelia to lessen the quiet which rippled in the lake. The scent of rain was still clinging to the air, and the wet grass glistened with many droplets, making it hard for me to find a dry spot to sit upon.

When I did though, I decided to savour the Wishing Lake's atmosphere before opening the Sullivan book I held on to. If anything, the knowledge I had gained since my previous visit made those calm waters even more astir with reflections apart from the physical world. As before, the lake was unblemished and unusually still, with subtle gleams upon it's surface like illusions adrift on a mirrored expanse. It was comforting to rest my eyes upon; to stare at and wonder what wonderful lore had shaped it's story and it's legend. Yet there was also something of sorrow to it, an unhappiness carried on it's subtle glimmers, as if the offerings laid upon it's bed had infected the water with their mournful wishes.

I sat peering at the lake for a little while longer, before deciding finally to open the book of which Mr Silsbury had kindly lent me. Part of me wondered just how this book could be met with such derision from the old man in first place, not to mention Adam and Amelia having mentioned it. To look at, it was nothing but an old and dusty book, it's pages weak and uncomfortably thin, it's hard blue cover the image of an old bible or textbook. That said, the title, engraved on the cover as *'Grimorium Votum: Translated by Samuel Sullivan',* had intrigued me since I first picked it up.

Without delay, I opened the book to it's introduction, still unsure of just what it's contents were or even how important Kilportach was to it. As it turned out, the book was a collection of *'terrible tomes, hidden texts and forbidden knowledge'* put into a compendium by it's author, Mr Sullivan. A few pages later, and a hand drawn map of the British Isles contained a contents page separated by county, with Kilportach's entry about three quarters into the book. Out of interest, I first turned to a chapter on a town in England, near to the county of where I lived. It revealed a translated and arcane document, littered with drawings and pointed symbols, like something from a book of ritual or magic. From what I read, it seemed to be talking about the moon, and some kind of secret communication undertaken at certain and specific moon-phases. It was certainly nothing that could help me out, and was generally difficult to understand, such was the nature of it's small printed text.

Already disheartened, I quickly turned through the musty pages to reach the chapter on Kilportach itself. It was fairly long, and according to Sullivan's notes at the top, was translated from a grimoire of unknown origin. As before, it's nature was that of esoteric knowledge, and was written in a hoary and abstract fashion, with the book's font cramped and fading away. Even so, I felt an unusual certainty that something there would be of interest to my current questions and research. It was just a matter of discovering, and understanding it.

'Think of the night. We are not taught to dream. But it is possible to wake in the darkest night with illusions stronger than spoken memory. Angelic wildwoods and beautiful flowers, townscapes huddled with strange companions, secret skies above whispering seas. Even as infants first learn how to speak, it is probable that their first true words are in recollection of their dreams. But how could a child, unversed in the travesties of human existence, simply imagine such lucid worlds as embarked upon in their night time journeys?

It was my understanding, long before the incidents I incurred in that place, that during our sleep we do indeed travel; leaving the ambits of grounded existence, and through passages of time replete with tangibility, to the world that was ours before our birth. Therefore, when faced with the pleasantries of morning interaction, the correct question is not 'what did you dream', but 'where did you travel to?' For although the places we visit are in flux and unrest, there is no doubt to those of a certain intellect, that they are indeed to be considered real.

When I first met Aisthra, it was this particular aspect of our lives which fascinated her the most. During that time, I resided in a hovel within her town, and it was there when I found myself seduced by her oceanic beauty. By candlelight we pondered on unknown things, and spoke deeply of many a hermetic verity, the kind of which had, these last years, enveloped my life.

Unkind things were hidden in that town. Upon arrival, I discovered an object resembling in shape that of an adult human body. It's flesh however was rigid and stained, with a bony structure unnaturally bent, thus coinciding more with wood or an unsightly, rotten leather. Assuming it to be a large animal of some sort, and not wishing to touch such a thing with my hands, I kicked it over with my foot to dislodge it from the earth. To my astonishment, it was indeed humanoid in both size and appearance; with a collapsed face not otherwise dissimilar from that of our own distinction. Interestingly, the side of it's skull was split open and cracked, as if killed by the force of a heavy object, wielded by none other than a human animal. Perhaps it was indeed a man, or a hominal ape struck down where it lay as a result of some feral savagery.

Nonetheless, Aisthra shortly took to me to her home; an inland sea hidden by forest and field, known to superstitious locals as 'mian loch a chomhlionah', or the 'wish fulfilling lake'. She told me there of her weary fate, and that although she attempted to help those who called her, their gifts of gold and wooden idols were no longer enough to bind her to them. She had wanted to see the world of dreams; the mutable spheres of enchanted lands which only we can experience and know are real. It was a world of which she had never seen, and yet knew existed in the water she breathed, as brought forth from humankind's offerings to her.

Aisthra also told me that of which unsettled my stomach in a sickly manner. That thing I discovered was undeniably human; and was but one of over a hundred score who now lay without grave nor decomposition. They were, according to Aisthra's testimony, the remains of the people who brought her here; slaughtered in repellent attempts to force her to grant their material wishes.

It seems that our ancestors were not as devoid of intelligent reasoning as modern man assumes them to be. The evidence is abundant; from dolmens erected to the phases of the sun, to stone circles describing the movement of planets, more accurate than anything a 'peasant' could muster. Further to this, these people believed that the human brain was the entry and exit point of the soul. Therefore when we enter the world of dreams, the brain was a gateway or sea mouth for the spirit; both leaving it in order to dream, and re-entering it to awaken. Indeed, it seems even by modern scientific workings, our bodies are but vessels imprisoning us, and it is only during lucid nights when the brain allows us to venture out of these mortal confines. The ancient people knew this too.

That is why those in charge of the colony ordered such sacrifice to darling Aisthra. A truly loathsome and esoteric people, the settlers of what is now a modern town were fearfully led by priests and mystics. It is these people who would gladly murder their own; take screaming captors to the waters edge to present them to Aisthra as their imperative gifts. Some would even cry out to be chosen for sacrifice, seeing their deaths as the greatest honour; a chance for Aisthra to grant their wishes of healing.

But sacrifice alone was not the aim of such barbarism. It was evolution; a greater offering than simply sinking their gold and silver into the water. By cracking the skulls of their ritual offerings, they were 'forcing' the brain to let go of the spirit, to make it enter the world of dreams without the necessity to return to it's host. That way, they were giving to the lake what Aisthra had asked for; the ability to dream for herself.

But beloved Aisthra, I understand you. I know that such dreams, even hundreds of them, are not worthy to grace your seaborne allurement. That is why I returned to her home once more, to not only offer myself to her beauty, but to tell her of my idea to help her.

For her home is under that bottomless lake, in unlit caverns damp and pulpous, where she first enticed me over to her. Thus my reasoning to her was simple and true. She must tell of the people worthy of her grace. Those of whom dream superior dreams, who wake with the greatest memories in the night. She must call them over to her, as she did to myself. 'Show them your home' I said to her, 'Bring them under, so that it is known who's dreams you desire to see'. Aisthra. My love.'

What followed was a number of unintelligible pages, littered with drawings and esoteric mathematics. It seemed that the author was giving guidance; a list of things for those who would follow him in examining the behaviour of this 'Aisthra' character. It had a dark, somewhat fearful aura to it, as if even without understanding it's content, the images were watchful and oddly communicative. Like the rest of the book, it seemed to be concerning magic and ritual, though this time centred in Kilportach, and around the local lakeside folklore.

But the truly shiversome part of the story was in the final paragraph of the monologue. Reading it, I assumed I was seeing things on the page which in reality were obscure and meant nothing in actuality. After all, we can all make out voices in silence, see faces in shadows or things move in the corners of our eye. That said, the grimoire was certainly different to these, not just in it's mood and written tone, but in it's details of Kilportach's most prominent mystery.

To read it, it felt as if I was being granted access to something nobody else had ever been told. It was like a momentary glance into the sacrosanct; a curious feeling of understanding which presented in the body as an uplifting ripple. With it however, a darker sensation was carried on the words; a murkiness of which was unexplained yet omnipresent in the story.

But that last paragraph; no matter how many times I re-read it, was clearly in reference to my own research and the pivotal existence of a cave beneath the lake. In the story, assuming that 'Aisthra' was the name of the Selkie, her home in caverns beneath the water was obviously the same cave that my family was killed in. Had the author of the grimoire been under there too? It was not in itself important to my research, but it seemed like the tragic cavern I entered was following me, perhaps even taunting me, as if it knew I would return to discover it's secrets.

Knowing this though, the rest of the story in the Sullivan book seemed even more unpleasant than it otherwise would have been. If the author's mention of the cave was true, could the rest of the story also be accurate? It was easy to see why Silsbury thought the book was responsible for Lee Buckley's views, and obvious why he would find the work distasteful. But it did make sense. The bodies really did all share the same head wound, and the plaque in the museum clearly mentioned the possibility of ritual sacrifice. Of course, there was no way of telling how much of the book was grounded in anything more than speculation. In many ways, the content of the story was erratic and arcane, seemingly written by a visitor in town who chanced to meet with the fabled Selkie. Though still, I have read such grimoires and books before, and although their material is often difficult to grasp, I have no trouble in believing that their knowledge is true. In fact, the whole thing made me feel distinctly unsettled, a feeling I usually wouldn't encounter upon reading such a theory or story.

It was probably because of the place I was sat. I could easily imagine the screams of those sacrificed, dragged in the night to the banks of the lake, their skulls pierced in the every place I was now sitting. The lake was silent, not unlike something many miles from all human civilisation. Indeed, it was easy to envisage such things having happened there; things now forgotten to all but the trees, and the memories of the lake which still shimmered in unease from that of which it had witnessed.

I could have sat there and thought about it for hours. In fact, I could already feel myself drifting into a trance when I realised the morning was fading fast. I needed to return to Amelia's crypt, to tell her of the documents Jack was going to give me, and to hear what she herself had thought of to help my finally narrowing research.

The Cloud Painter

From the moment I met Amelia, I immediately wondered just what her story could be. How had she acquired her underground home, furnished it with beds and tables and chosen it to call her own? Many would argue that she was mentally unsound; that something had happened to make her live such a reclusive existence. Of course, I personally would seldom reach for knee-jerk intolerance like the unthinking masses. But even so; Amelia's life was somewhat of an extreme. I may have known her when I was a child, but I truly did wonder just what had happened to her, since the cave-in took me away from the town.

That said, as I approached the mournful statue which stood at the top of her transformed crypt, I felt almost as I was returning to someone I closely knew. When I knocked on the door, she answered without her usual hesitation, greeting me dressed in the same brown coat from when I first met her.

I wasted no time in telling her what I had found out. As I explained; the other Lucas Clarke was one of the remaining mysteries, and if Jack's note could shed even a small light on him, it could lead to uncovering the leftover questions. Amelia listened, agreeing with me that the two Lucas Clarke's where doubtlessly the source of a lot of the earlier confusion. I also told her of the Sullivan book, saying I had read it by the Wishing Lake, and handed it to her to ask for her opinion.

"Well, like I said before, I read it a lot of years ago", she said, sitting on the bed and once more flicking through a couple of it's pages. "I used to be really into it for a while. That sort of...world of the past it speaks of, I really understand it. But yeah, some of it's a bit too exaggerated nowadays, I think."

"What do you think of the part about Kilportach?"

"I can't make sense of the symbols and things, if that's what your asking. But the story is similar to the rest of the book; like folklore tales with a bit of an edge, in a way."

It seemed Amelia had no real take on the monologue of the author and his mysterious Aisthra. Then again, apart from the mention of the cave in the lake, there was little of importance apart from it's obviously eccentric and interesting hypotheses. Still, she held onto the book for a number of minutes, reading sections she undoubtedly remembered with a smile upon her face. After a while though, she closed it up, and returned at once to the matter at hand, that of helping me with finishing my research.

"So", she said. "Your going to pick up this note from the pub later on today?"

"Yeah, I think so anyway." I decided to sit on the chair where I had previously sat, and asked her if she had thought of anything in addition to just Jack's uncovered note.

"Two things", she smiled. "Well, one really. The other's just a thought. I mean, what do you know about those murders in the town?"

"The murders?" I wasn't expecting her bring such a thing up. Then again, I had pushed their significance to the back of my mind, being more worried about my headaches and fainting than the threat of the killer on the loose. After she mentioned it though, a familiar queasiness fell into my chest, weighing it down with an uncomfortable sensation of heat. I realised in that instant that I couldn't trust anybody in the town.

"I discovered the first one", I solemnly continued. "It's just...really awful. And the other, Catherine, I mean who would want to kill somebody like that?"

"Yeah, well I don't know anything about it really. But I was thinking, things like that don't happen in Kilportach. The only other time was with Shane Cullen and that was over 30 years ago. I mean, it could be something, right?"

"Could be what?"

"Something you could have a look into. I know it's not easy, but ask yourself; why were those people murdered? You never know, it might be something. I don't know."

"Well, I suppose. But look, the policeman in charge of it isn't someone I want many run ins with. But yeah, I know what you mean."

"OK, so that's that. Now then, onto to the real thing I thought of to help you."

She got up from the bed, walked to the door and opened it up, letting in a stream of welcome cold air. Afterwards, she walked back over to where I was sitting.

"We can go and see the cloud painter. Both of us."

"Sorry?" I stood up, wondering what she was trying to say. As I did, I took in a few breaths of the fresh air from outside of the stuffy crypt.

"His real name is Leon Gould. He's an artist, paints pictures of things that he sees in clouds. He was...well, someone who helped me a lot in the early days."

"I see. And he can help me somehow?"

"Definitely. And anyway, I need to tell him about you, don't I? He's lived in the town for most of his life, and most probably met you as a kid."

"Ah, your right. His name doesn't ring a bell I admit, but if you think he might of known me, then it's well worth a try."

"I still can't believe that you are...you. I bet the cloud painter is just as shocked as I was too!"

"You don't call him by his real name?" I asked, seeing Amelia sounded rather excited at the prospect of telling him of my 'survival'.

"No", she laughed. "There's a reason though I promise. Now then, are you ready to get going?"

"Just like that?"

"Why not? It's quite a long walk to where he lives, and besides, I thought you were eager to work this all out."

"Oh, I am, believe me."

It was refreshing to have such a light conversation with the previously inhospitable Amelia. Clearly, since discovering that I was the 'Edward' she once knew, her inhibitions were put aside in favour of friendship. I was unsure of how this 'cloud painter' could help me, but was more than willing to follow along, even if just for Amelia's sake.

Before leaving, she picked up the Selkie necklace from above her bed, and hung it around her neck. Apparently, she had never went out without wearing it since the day it was given to her by my Mother. I could have easily taken it as a cue to ask her more about my family, but I decided it best to leave it for the time being.

I walked into the main street of town with Amelia, wondering if I should stop by the pub to see if Molly had heard back from Jack yet. Amelia however did not want to go inside, and rather than risk upsetting her mood, I simply agreed to come back later on. She did however speak to me as we walked throughout the shops and street sides. In fact, she told me of buildings that she remembered from her youth, places where myself and her used to play as children. In a way, it was the closest I had felt to actually remembering myself having lived amidst those narrow roadways. She told me of things both expected and eccentric, mentioning that since the town was undeveloped, there was little in the way of modern children's amusements. Indeed, I can still remember when Molly first told me that only two children lived there that time 30 years ago. One of them was myself, it seems, and I spent my days with Amelia making our own games from sticks and pebbles.

She even mentioned of the hunts for 'hidden places', smiling as she recounted nights when we would search for ghosts in the deserted main street. There was no doubt in my mind then; the person she spoke of was definitely myself. It was disappointing though that no memories of my own came forth from Amelia's continued nostalgia. I had no trouble believing that events had taken place; but the emotion that accompanies childhood recollection was still sadly missing from within myself.

"Actually", said Amelia, as we ventured into the outskirts of town, dominated by the backdrop of labyrinthine terraces. "It was not long after we thought you died that my own parents passed away as well."

"Really? That must have been hard."

"Yeah. I was a kid, just like you were. My other family lived in Belfast and also some other city in England, but I didn't want to go there."

"To England?" I joked, noticing Amelia's tone drop slightly into wistfulness.

"Ha, no", she smiled. "I just didn't want to leave, specially not to live with my aunts or uncles. They were just too different from me, even at that age. I couldn't do it. You probably wouldn't get it."

Of course, I did indeed understand what Amelia was meaning. I knew immediately that the Ford family was different from my own, and even as an ill and confused child, I knew I would be unhappy with them. It was peculiar, surreal even, that Amelia seemed to have shared in things that I myself could identify with. Peculiar, and a little bit tragic. I felt a pang of emotion as we walked along; a throb in my chest which quickly dispersed into flutters of longing for an unremembered past.

"So, what happened?" I asked her. At first she didn't answer, instead simply mumbling to take the next right onto another estate in a cramped suburbia. It looked like a street that forever slept; with neat cut grass and flower gardens climbing red bricked walls and closed net curtains.

"I stayed here", she eventually said. "The cloud painter, well, Leon Gould, he took me in as a child."

"Oh, I see!"

"That's right", she said, pausing for a second in the middle of the street. "He was the one who set me up with the grave-home, actually. Got the bed in there, the desk...all of it. Actually, he even gave me those cigars you've been smoking. They were really expensive ones, apparently."

We began to walk again, my mind finally beginning to grow content with the idea of Amelia's converted crypt. At first, she was simply one of many enigmas I encountered in that Irish town, but now I felt I was getting to know her. It was inevitable, I suppose.

"And you know what", she continued. "I could never remember his name as a child, and when I thought I did, I got it wrong. So I took to just calling him 'the cloud painter' instead. It made us both smile!"

"Is it only clouds that he paints, then?"

"You'll see in a minute, were almost there".

We soon turned onto a street of taller buildings, cramped tightly together as if holding their breath to prevent them from toppling over. They were grey pebble dash, and each identical with flat windowed faces, greeting all who passed them with a slumbersome sulk. Dirty curtains twitched as we walked along, most likely hiding threatening locals who stared out aghast at the strangers on the street. At the end of the road, a rusted fence led into an overgrown field. The house next to it, at the end of the serpentine line of buildings, was the one Amelia stopped in front of.

Like the other houses, it met all visitors with a languid sigh, it's grimy white windows pale and weary, it's pebble dashed brickwork unmoved by the passing of life around it. Beside the door, a plastic bin stood full and unemptied, a collection of flies hovering overhead attracted to the foul odour it gave off. It was hardly the sort of place that inspired my confidence.

Amelia pressed the plastic door bell, resulting in a tinny speaker playing a monotone version of the song *'Greensleeves'*. There was no answer. As we waited, I noticed a wooden plaque hung above the door, with neatly carved letters painted in black. *'We Shall Not All Sleep, But We Shall All Be Changed. C 15:51'*.

Amelia pressed the door bell again. There was still no answer. This time, she tried the door handle, revealing the door to in fact be open.

"Odd", she said to me, before opening the door fully and calling inside. "Hello? Are you in there?"

Nothing. At this point, I assumed that Mr Gould had simply gone out, and accidentally left his front door unlocked. Amelia however seemed more concerned, and walked inside the house calling his name.

"Is it OK to go in?" I said, feeling natural resistance preventing me from walking into the house uninvited.

"Oh yeah. I'm here all the time, don't worry about it. He won't mind."

I stepped inside, closing the door behind me as I did. It led into an unusually cramped front lobby, with a set of steep stairs and a number of doors against a white painted and stained wall. I followed Amelia through into the sitting room.

There was nobody there. Amelia seemed more worried than I would have thought.

"Maybe he's upstairs", she said, making her way immediately back to to the door.

"Couldn't he have just gone out, you know, shopping or something?"

"Yeah, I guess", she sighed. "I'm still going to check upstairs though. Wait here if you want."

Before I could speak, she left the room and clambered up the staircase. I realised it was natural that she would be concerned about the man who took her in as a child, but she seemed genuinely upset that he didn't come instantly to the door. Then again, with the murderer of Bridget and Catherine on the loose, it made sense she would want to check he was safe.

While she was upstairs, I stood in the middle of the untidy sitting room, and was taken aback by the nature of the paintings on the walls. There must have been more than thirty framed pictures, each displaying eccentric images hovering amid a clear blue sky. I was expecting paintings of clouds and skylines, but found myself standing face to face with deformed portraits and loathsome caricatures. They seemed to be distortions or shapes in the clouds, drawn into existence with subtle colours and exaggerated features jutting from the sky. Some of them featured troubled faces, their startled expressions looking at the viewer with a mixture of distrust and unhappiness. Others were paintings of imaginary animals; restlessly charging out of the sky, their proportions misshapen by the clouds they were formed from. Some even featured pareidolic houses, trains or reaching hands, all alive in a daytime sky and defined with colour and skilful brush work.

There was even an easel in the midst of the messy room, an unfinished cloud painting sitting within it. It appeared to be some sort of grotesque marine creature, raising from an sea of brilliant sky, like it was leaping from the canvas and into the room. Bulging clouds came together around it, forming fins, gills and a giant gaping mouth. If anything, the paint looked like it could still be wet, but I decided against getting close enough to find out.

It was around another minute before I heard Amelia finally thumping back down the wooden stairs. I turned towards her; a black book clutched tight in her hand, and her expression more calm than the previous worriment. She made her way instantly into the sitting room, and handed me the book before she uttered a word.

"What's going on?" I said.

"He's gone. Left town for a couple of days apparently. Damn it, I thought this might have happened."

Intrigued, I flipped open the book at the page it was marked at. It was a hand written diary, scribbled in a mixture of black and blue pen, and with many words crossed out and then rewritten.

"You read that in here?" I asked.

"Yeah. But seriously, I can't believe he'd leave the front door unlocked like this. And he didn't even tell me he was going!"

I didn't really know how to respond. It was clear that Amelia knew this 'cloud painter' well, and was rightfully worried that his house was left open long after the man himself had fled. More than this, I felt a rush of questions coming forth all at once; about the paintings, the diary, and just what she hoped he could add to my research. For the time being though, I held back. The immediate concern, especially for Amelia, was the unlocked door of Leon Gould's home.

"What can we do? I mean, do you have a phone number for him or anything?" I asked.

"Oh, he's not on the phone. Never has been. But look, it's not that bad really. I just cant believe he'd forget to lock the thing in the first place!"

"So what are you going to do?"

"I have a spare key", she firmly replied. "He gave it to me last year when he'd been ill. Wanted me able to come in to help him, should the need arise, you know?"

"I see. But hang on, why did you say that you thought this would happen? What did you know?"

"Nothing", she said, walking to the other side of the room from me, and standing in front of one of the paintings. "It's just that after the murders in town, I wondered if he'd want to get away."

"How so?" I approached her, standing below a large framed picture, hanging above an old and rugged looking sofa. It displayed a swollen and disfigured face, sat amid a darkening array of rain clouds. It's bloated cheeks and and insensate eyes gave a somewhat cadaverous appearance to it, as if the sky had momentarily gathered in a shrill reminder of '*Memento Mori*'.

"He always thought he knew who murdered Shane Cullen", she said, not taking her eyes from the uncomfortable portrait. "But there was never any proof. You know that. Anyway, he always thought that should anything else happen, he'd be approached due to what he told the people he knew. And now look..."

"I understand. He thinks the murders in town will bring up old memories, right?"

"Yeah. It's in his diary, actually. Read about it, if you want."

I was not accustomed to reading peoples private diaries. That said, I would not fool myself into pretending I would not peek into it, even if simply to understand more about the man who painted those cloud-born images. And of course, if the killer of Shane Cullen was so much as hinted at, then it would be as one more strand of knowledge to gathering the loose ends of Kilportach's own story. It still felt like an intrusion, however.

"I'm not sure about reading his private work, you know." I said.

"It's nothing", she sighed. "Anyway, I'm going to have to go home to get the spare key to lock up. You can stay here, guard the place. And, well...just read it if you want to. I only flicked through it anyway."

I had not thought about retrieving the key. Obviously, it would not feel right to accompany Amelia and leave with the knowledge that the house was unlocked. Kilportach might have been almost a ghost town, but the street was far from the kind of place that inspires a sense of safety within one. Therefore, after a few more small words between us, I agreed to stay inside the house whilst Amelia went to bring back the key.

It was odd, but the second she closed the front door on her way out, I felt markedly uncomfortable within the house. It was not simply the expected sensation of intruding on a place without formal invitation, but something greater; more difficult to pin down. I first assumed it was the paintings themselves, their sullen nature seeming to capture a discernible mood, a suspended moment held forever on canvas. But there was more to it than that. It was almost as if when I moved but an inch, the walls shook off their inert languor, and became conscious of the person who now stood in between them.

I sat on the sofa, aware that without having taken the pill, I was practically asking for a headache to appear. Still, I had not yet experienced any of the 'signs', and for the time being tried to ignore the lowering feelings present in the house.

In my hand, I opened the diary once more to it's most recent entry. Turning back a few pages, it seemed like the diary was not so much a mundane personal log, but the attempts of it's author to correlate feelings and experiences into a written form. In that respect, it was similar to my own chosen way of expression; to put into writing that of which I would otherwise forget or never understand. It was also not a traditional diary, in that there were no dates contained on the pages. Instead, he seemed to have used a standard lined notebook, and presented each entry on a different page without giving the expected times or dates. Perhaps he thought them unnecessary.

Soon, of course, my previous reticence to reading the diary was swept away as my eyes caught the words on the pages. I went back a few days prior to the entry where the murders were mentioned, and began to read an intriguing insight into the world of this Leon Gould.

'Page 22

I have noticed that as I visit different places, the clouds seem to gather in unique patterns dependant on what is happening below them. It is almost as if the sky is mimicking the things it sees below on earth, and modelling them into it's own interpretation. In Kilportach, the clouds gather too often with a threatening ugliness; a sort of mocking grimace which usually means more rain in coming. In other towns, I see things such as strange yet placid animals, murmuring landscapes of mountain and sea, and of course mass arrays of human imitation.

Even so, Kilportach is a good place for an artist to live. It is without the glare of larger towns, devoid of the din of society, which all but blots out the energies dormant in nature. Indeed, it takes a great deal of respect; of understanding of nature to create art such as what I put my name to. I am vane? Perhaps so, but I see my art as more than a just piece to hang on a wall. It is an attempt to capture the tremor of nature; the vibrations which pass unbeknown to most as they walk through the mundane existence called 'life'.

Page 24

I can hardly believe it. Indeed, I have had to write this for the sake of my mind, to convince myself that I am in fact awake. There has been a murder in the town!

Someone called Bridget Brady it seems. I never knew her, but it's not that which will keep me awake at night. I can always leave some floral tribute later. The real matter is the motive of it, and the obligatory exhumation of the past that will follow. Yes, I have no doubt that this is related to before. Such things just don't happen in this town. Well, not without a reason anyway.

I'll admit this has me remarkably unnerved. I have thought for days now that the past was returning, that I'd seen and felt things in the town which were too uncanny to be simply coincidence. In fact, only yesterday I swear I saw Edward Clarke, but fully grown and back in the town as if came to revisit his old homestead. It is possible, I suppose. Despite the memorial, all who were present at the time of the incident know full well that young Clarke was taken into care. Hmm, I suppose I could tell A. about this, but she would never forgive me should I be incorrect.

Page 25

A man called Adam came to visit me today. He said that he was suffering from terminal cancer, and was saying goodbye to the people he met when he holidayed here as a child. I didn't remember him, but he said that had seen my paintings at a roadside exhibition when he was here. Odd, I can't remember ever having done such a thing, but maybe my old brain is finally slipping. Either way, I welcomed him in for a tea and chat, though I'm not sure he understood the nature of my art. Actually, he asked me some things about the past as well. It really is coming back to haunt us. I can just feel it.

Page 27

It has gotten worse. I assumed I'd misheard when first I was told, but I have since made enquiries and know it to be true. There was another murder, this time in broad daylight in the middle of the town!

It's different this time, though. It's difficult even to write this down, but the victim was my old friend Catherine McGuire. God no! This can only mean one thing, and I care not for those who will accuse me of being paranoid, or of overreacting yet again. Catherine was, all those years ago, responsible for identifying the body of Shane Cullen, the only other murder we've ever had. And she knew, as well.

In fact, it was myself and her who sat in this very house, and worked out between us what the idiot police could never do. The man who killed Shane Cullen; it was non other than that ne'er-do-well Lee Buckley, the one I warned him about since the day he arrived. There's no doubt about it; someone is here, in the town. Someone who knows what happened with Cullen, and knows the face of the man who killed him. The murders of the past and present are connected.

Page 28

I knew this would happen. Those murders have brought up unclean memories, the sort of thing that could get a man hurt, or worse. Three decades ago, when I told the police about Lee Buckley's guilt, they said no such man had ever been in Kilportach, and that I was hindering their investigation. So, like a fool, I told everyone I could around the town, tried to gather some form of community spirit to make sure Buckley was brought to trial. Of course, before anything could be done about it, their minds were turned to the next disaster – the underground cave-in which killed a whole family beneath the so called 'Wishing Lake'.

But now, I don't know. I knew at the time that there were people who disliked my knowledge of what Lee Buckley had done. I feel unsafe. Last night I heard strange things outside my door, the rattling of windows and the echo of footsteps. I know it. Someone really has returned to uncover the truth of decades past. Or maybe to hush it up for good. I need to leave here.'

I was fascinated with what I was reading. This 'cloud painter', this Leon Gould, was yet another person who knew about what happened in the town 30 years ago. Unfortunately he didn't elaborate, but it was still enough to persuade the prickle of goosebumps to accompany the reading of several passages. So Lee Buckley was the killer, or according to Gould, anyway. It certainly made sense, although I know not what type of things must have happened to cause a man to turn on his friend in such a way. Still, as Amelia said, there was little proof that Gould really did know the murderer, and it seems the police did not even want to know. In fact, that passage stood out to me as distinctly odd. If the police had statements from the people in the town, they would know that Lee Buckley was indeed present and visiting Cullen when the murder took place. So then why did they tell Gould that there was no such person?

Of course, the part of the diary which stuck with me the most was the mention of myself and my tangled tale. If, as according to Gould, it was known that I was taken into care after the accident, then why is the gravestone standing at all with my name etched underneath that of my parents? I think what the 'cloud painter' was saying is that only certain people knew the truth of the incident. This is why he left the town in fear, thinking that the murders were somehow connected to what had happened back in my childhood.

For the time being, of course, I could do little else but reread the diary, and sit in the house awaiting Amelia's return. Still, although I'd not found the answers I'd hoped to find there, Leon Gould's diary spoke in shrill apprehension of those times 30 years ago in Kilportach. If only he was there to talk to in person. For now, I sat back and peered once more at the paintings, planning my next move after leaving the house. Yes, I would go back to the pub and speak to Molly; and see the note from Jack about the unknown guest known only as 'Lucas Clarke'.

People of the Past

The town of Kilportach, with it's uneven buildings and soundless ambiance, was a place that inspired the deepest thought by simply stepping on it's timeworn pavements. That day, after leaving the cloud painter's home with Amelia, a blanched sunlight had fallen across those rugged rooftops, and I began to think about what had happened since I first arrived in the town.

Doubtlessly, the deplorable murders had cast a shadow not only over my own research, but across the entire population of Kilportach. Indeed, many would argue I was foolish to stay, to carry on with my investigation in the midst of such unrest in the town. But something had forced me to remain in Kilportach, as if the secrets hidden in it's old recesses had longed for me to discover them once again. I understood that feeling, whilst walking towards the small town pub with Amelia by my side. My repressed memory, that which was crushed beneath my brain injury, had no doubt stirred and pushed me forward as soon as my eyes caught sight of the town.

In fact, although the situation accompanying this was not in itself admirable, I was even beginning to understand my ailment. Of course, I fully expected another headache after refusing to take any more of Ryan's pills, and I was correct.

The first 'signs' started almost as soon as I left Amelia and walked into the finally reopened pub. As I turned to close the door behind me, a familiar voice called out my name, seeming to be coming from far away, but at the same time close to my ears themselves. What was different though is that I though I recognised the voice. It was the same one from my previous 'nightmare', where the shape that had also haunted me spoke of my past in Amelia's crypt.

For the time being, I tried to ignore it. I had just walked into the Wishing Lake pub, and was eager to see how Molly was doing, and perhaps even tell her of my latest revelations. Adam was also sat in the pub, just finishing up a fresh meal over at a window table. He welcomed me as soon as I walked inside, and told me that Molly was in the back room, and would be out to see me at any minute.

When she did, of course, she greeted me immediately with a hearty smile, and after drying her hands on a towel she was holding, opened up right away in apologetic conversation.

"Mr Clarke! God I'm sorry about last night, I really am. Was it you knocking? I bet it was, wasn't it?"

"Yeah", I smiled. "Don't worry about it though."

"Oh come on now. I should have known it was you and opened up. I mean, you found somewhere else to go I hope? Tell me you did."

"I did, yes. Not as comfortable as in here maybe, but I'm OK."

"Well thank heaven for that, then", she loudly sighed. "You'll be wanting a drink I suppose."

I ordered a soft fruit juice to drink, not wanting to try anything more heavy, should a full headache start to present itself. As she served it to me, Adam walked over to the bar with his plate, and thanked Molly politely for cooking it for him.

"So, Mr Clarke", he then turned to me. "Having much luck with your family tree hunting?"

I was not really prepared to tell Adam about what I'd learned in Amelia's crypt. He was friendly enough, but I had no reason to explain to him something I thought unimportant to his own reasons for being there. Instead, I simply told Adam that I'd made some good progress, and that after only a few more questions were answered, I'd be leaving Kilportach in a number of days.

"Ah, I see", he said, taking a seat on a barstool next to me. "Well, as long as it's all working out good for you. Actually, you had a Samuel Sullivan book when I saw you in that shop. Have you a had a look in it yet?"

"Oh, yeah, I did actually", I said, taking a sip from the glass of orange juice sat in front of me at the bar. "To be honest, it didn't make a whole lot of sense."

"Yeah", laughed Adam. "Those type of books are all gibberish, aren't they? I think so, anyway."

"Pretty much", I agreed, not bothering to bring up the mention of the cave or the Selkie in the Sullivan book. I doubted Adam would be interested, anyway. "So, how are you getting on in town yourself?" I asked him instead.

"Oh, not so bad", he said. "I managed to persuade Molly to open up again, so that's something. I'll probably be heading off myself soon too, though. Just a few more nights, you know. Actually, my cousin at home has just recently had a baby. So I shouldn't really have stayed this long to begin with. You know, just in case she needed me or anything."

"I see. Is it a boy or a girl?"

"Oh, a little girl, thanks. Yeah, there's not many left in my family now, so she's going to be a whole new start, in a way."

I spoke to Adam for quiet a while longer, and him mentioning his cousins baby managed to at least take my mind away from the pain which had started to swell in my head. Although I admit, I felt a number of times like I wanted to ask him about his visit to Leon Gould. I didn't though, choosing instead to allow him to tell me more about his cousin and her new arrival.

After a while though, Adam settled up with Molly for the dinner, and left the pub to return to his camper van. This was advantageous for me, actually. Alone with Molly, I felt I could open up in more detail about my experience and what I'd discovered. After all, it would have been unkind not to tell her the truth of my identity. She had known me when I was a child, even though; like seemingly everything else in Kilportach, I could not remember her.

That said, it was difficult to bring up the subject to her without it sounding like some kind of delirious joke. I was not trained in breaking things to people, and had usually not found myself in situations which demanded such things to be spoken about. Furthermore, I had no idea how Molly would react.

Because of this, I held back for a while on bringing up the subject, and decided instead to ask about Jack and his note from the B&B he was dropping off for me.

"Oh yes", said Molly. "He did bring something in for you, a couple of hours ago now it was. I put it in the drawer I think, hold on."

She opened the drawer where she kept all her photos, and removed a sealed white envelope with my name written on it by hand.

"There you go", she handed it to me. "Don't worry, I haven't opened it!"

"Thanks", I laughed. I put the envelope in my pocket, not wanting to open it right away.

"So anyway", continued Molly, taking my now empty glass of juice and putting it underneath the bar. "You said to Adam you'd made some good progress with your goings on around town. So come on, tell me. Is it anything good?"

"It certainly is".

Then was my chance to explain to Molly just what I had found in the depths of my own mind. I started slow, and refused to mention things such as the shape or even where I was at the given time. In substitute, I told her of my visit to Dr Ryan, and how soon afterwards I made discoveries in town regarding the name of my foster parents. From there, it became more challenging to convey to Molly. In fact, I felt the same heavy sweat and palpitation which usually accompanies a nervous guilt. I mumbled, unaware of just how to express that I was in fact the child she had thought killed 30 years ago. I told her parts of the things I found out, then upon reaching the most important ingredient, fell short of finding the words to express myself. In the end, I decided to just come out with it.

"What I'm trying to say, is that I actually lived in Kilportach as a child."

"But how?" She leaned on the bar, clearly confused but interested in what I was attempting to convey to her.

"My name was Edward Clarke, you see."

There was an unmissable pause in the air at that moment. She stood still, looked me in the eye with a mixture of bewilderment and sheer disbelief. I looked at the floor, feeling like I'd told her a hideous lie or some sort of embarrassing, shameful secret. Unlike with Amelia, where we were both caught in the residual essence of the event, with Molly I had time to think and prepare. And it must have been hard to believe my story.

"But...wait on Mr Clarke, what about things like Edwards grave? Or even your own birth certificate for goodness sake. I mean, are you sure about this? Really sure?"

"I didn't say it all made sense. But it's true. Something happens when you remember things like that. So yes, I'm sure. And I don't pretend to understand the other things. That's why I'm still here."

"I left town on the day when Mr Cullen was murdered, remember?" she said, her voice turned quiet and deliberately slow. "I only found out later what happened to the Clarke's. But I would never have guessed such a thing could happen. This is big news, Mr Clarke!"

"I know that."

"Absolutely. But how about an even bigger question, though. What will I call you now, eh? Edward, or Leonard?"

I had decided soon after discovering the truth that I would still use the name I was brought up with. Edward might have been the name I was given at birth, and in many ways I was still that person, but I could not truly deal with changing my name. And for most people that I knew in my life, there was no need for them to ever be told that Leonard was not the name I was born with.

After a while, I managed to tell Molly the remainder of my story, including all that I had found since last we met. If anything, she seemed to take the news as largely joyful, and without the scepticism I'd imagined she would express. By the time I'd finished telling her my tale, she was leaning close to me against the bar, an enthralled smile firmly upon her face, as if I was reciting some radiant family memory.

"Well, it's all good news for you then, Mr Clarke, isn't it?"

"You could say that, yeah."

"Actually, I'm feeling much better myself now as well". She left the bar, walking to the fireplace against the wall. It was already full of logs and paper, and was just waiting for Molly to light it up.

"Adam managed to persuade me to open back up". She knelt down, removed two fire-lighters from a box next to the dark stone fireplace, and wedged them into the scrunched paper. "He said the murderer is hardly likely to come into an open pub with people in it. I think he's right too, don't you?"

"Definitely", I assured her, truly not wanting Molly to feel afraid due to the events taking place in town.

As she lit the fire, a friendly and solacing atmosphere rushed in as the flames took hold of the wood. The fireplace was a central point in the pub; covered with horse brasses and copper pans, all polished to a level where the fire reflected in them. One could easily imagine in times gone by, when the pub would no doubt be crowded with people, all swapping merry stories around that fireplace. Now, of course, I was the only guest in that mute public house. I wondered how it managed to stay open at all.

"Anyway Mr Clarke", continued Molly, getting to her feet and returning to the bar. "Would you like another drink or anything?"

"Not for now, thanks."

"Well, give me a shout if you do, OK? I'm just going out to the kitchen round back. It doesn't clean itself, right?"

Molly left me once more alone in the pub. I got up from the rather uncomfortable barstool, and sat down in the place where I had previously slept. Unfortunately, though the crackle of the fire was sufficiently comforting, I quickly found my mind trying once more to focus upon the headache I'd tried to ignore whilst talking.

It was weaker than before, though. I did not feel faint or even that nauseous, with just a sharpened ache in between my eyes forcing me to concentrate uncomfortably upon it. It was an unlikely theory, but I felt for a minute as if the things I'd discovered could have actually reduced the headache's intensity. After all, could not the 'sign' of hearing my own name spoken have been my own consciousness attempting to help me? It made sense, but I knew that I could just as well have been wrong, and that yet another painful experience was only minutes away from presenting itself.

For the time being, I reached into my pocket and removed the envelope that Jack had brought for me to look at. I had no idea what it could have been about, and honestly I had very little faith in it telling me anything that wouldn't lead to more questions. Even so, the other Lucas Clarke was one of my remaining unanswered questions. He was, for all intents and purposes, the most obvious catalyst for the mistake on the original records which brought me to Kilportach.

Inside the envelope, a folded and brittle piece of paper revealed a document from Hawthorn House B&B. It contained a black letterhead with the name of the guest house, along with a silhouette drawing of a flower. Underneath, uneven handwriting was jotted down, confessing the thoughts of the previous owner regarding his guest called Lucas Clarke.

'Remember to tell Kerry about weird behaviour from the guests staying in room 4. On the night they arrived, the man went out and left his young son here alone, and didn't come back until the early hours of the morning. The kid was crying and couldn't sleep. I had to stay up with him until near 2.30am. The next night a similar thing started to happen, but this time he took his son out with him. When they came back, they didn't say anything when I welcome them in, and just walked straight upstairs and locked the door. It's not even like there's anything to do until that late. The pub wasn't even open.

Anyway, another odd thing. When I was staying up with the kid, he asked me why his Father had given a different name when they signed into the hotel. According to the kid, his name is Buckley and not Clarke at all. So the man had given me a false identity! Surely there's no reason for that in a place like Kilportach.

Still, I don't know so much. Last night there was so much noise from their room that I thought they were going to break the floorboards. Shouting and yelling, loud bangs, everything. Honestly I feel bad for the kid. This Mr Clarke/Buckley has definite problems. What on earth is he doing up there?'

I do not know if my stomach sank whilst reading, but a definite change occurred inside me. In fact, it was like a sudden realisation, a somewhat uplifting feeling of levity, which filled my chest like a light being switched on. It was a simple note, written more than 30 years ago, but it created a hurried and lambent sense of understanding.

If Lee Buckley was the other Lucas Clarke, it explained why the police told Leon Gould that no Lee Buckley had been in the town. It would also account for 'Lucas Clarke' been a suspect in the murder of Shane Cullen, especially if Gould's theory on Buckley was correct.

This was excellent news. I sat up straight, all but forgetting the mild headache that was hardly more than an annoyance at that point. I was filled instead with new enthusiasm, an inspirative tingle which entered the body upon every breath of the smoky air.

The other Lucas Clarke had been a recurrent nudge to the difficulty of my family research. But this made sense, making previous questions fit into the story without any stretch of imagination. The only mystery was why Buckley would choose the name of my Father to stay in the guest house. Had Shane Cullen told him about my family before he came to visit? I could not understand why he would. The only other explanation was that, as according to Silsbury, Lee Buckley had asked about the people in town before he actually arrived to visit. Yet even so, why would it be that particular name that he chose to hide himself in the hotel?

Of course, this was assuming that Buckley really was the murderer. There was only the 'cloud painter' to go by on that, as well as the correlation of names regarding the suspect being my Father. Then again, if Buckley was really like the note made him out to be, then he didn't seem like a person you could trust.

As my elation at reading that note died down, I began to ponder once again on a mental check list of questions to answer. I felt like getting up and pacing around, but instead sat back down and tried to still my mind. With the problem of the other Lucas Clarke out of the way, my other enigmas seemed even more baffling. There was the matter of Edward Clarke's grave stone, and of my birth certificate giving details in contradiction to my recently recovered memories. Also, there was still the question of what happened in the cave to cause the disaster and give me the TBI. And what of the recent murders in town, were they connected to my past as well? There was still so much that didn't make sense.

I got up from the chair, called in to Molly for another drink. In a way, I'd made a big discovery that day in the pub. I felt closer, even if only by force of illusion, to reaching the answers for all of my questions. Yet again though, I found myself standing by the empty bar, a fresh glass of fruit juice in my hand to nurse the dull ache in my head. And I needed to think, to figure out what all of my options were, and what I could do to understand these final, curious mysteries.

Session 2

I did very little for the remainder of the day. I left the pub for a walk in the late afternoon, though the weather soon took a turn for the worse as I reached the area around the peat bogs. By evening, my only real option was to return to the pub and settle down with a meal before spending the night there. In the end, Jack came in for a couple of drinks, and I managed to while away an hour or two by talking to him beside the bar.

It was not until later on in the evening when I made my only step towards progress. I had sat for hours and debated how to solve my problems, and finally arrived at what I deemed to be my best choice. So, after Jack had left the pub and Molly was getting ready to close, I used the pub phone to leave a message for Dr Ryan. Of course, the doctors surgery was closed for the night, but I felt better having left a message, rather than simply turning up in the morning.

The reasoning behind it was obvious. Dr Ryan's hypnotic regression was the first time my damaged memories had been woken up and recollected. At the time, I knew almost nothing about my heritage, and yet managed to come up with relevant memories which now I know I could not have progressed without. Furthermore, I was no longer apprehensive of the therapy, seeing Dr Ryan as a kind practitioner and the quality of the results as stunning. Therefore, when I left the message on his office telephone, I made quite clear that my reason for calling was to book in another regression with him.

To my surprise, he rang the pub telephone early the next morning. As expected, the level of work to carry out in Kilportach was slack to say the least, and this worked hugely to my advantage, with the doctor saying I could just call in and he would work with me to suit my schedule.

So, after eating a small cooked breakfast with Molly, I made my way immediately towards the doctor's, actually excited to once more enter my mind of childhood memories.

The other thing I was looking forward to was telling Ryan of what I had since uncovered. In fact, when I subsequently arrived at his office, the first thing I mentioned was the progress I had made. Ryan seemed pleased, shaking my hand with a genuine smile and an almost detectable sigh of relief. For him, the information I was mentioning would clearly make his own work easier, and give him solid themes and names of which to work with in the hypnosis.

Indeed, there was little introduction for our session that morning. Having had the therapy once before, Ryan didn't feel the need to give me the same introductory speech as he did on the first visit to his office. I was already calm, and laid still on the sofa awaiting his words, not feeling troubled but rather inspired.

"Start by concentrating on your breathing", said Ryan quietly, sitting beside me. "As you do, your eyes will start getting heavier and heavier, on every breath. Soon, they will be so heavy that you can't keep them open."

I closed my eyes, holding each breath for a few of seconds as instructed, then releasing it along all tension in my body. It already felt tranquil and calming to me, with only a couple of breaths enough to lull me into a sleepy, warm sensation.

"That's good", he continued. "And you may also notice your body itself is feeling heavier. In fact, it is so heavy that even if you tried to move it, you find that you are unable to. Now take another deep breath in, hold it, and exhale."

A few more breathing exercises followed. Before long, I could feel Dr Ryan's suggestions taking form inside me with remarkable ease. My eyes were leaden and firmly closed, revealing only a field of black, decorated with hazy and morphing shapes. Everywhere in my body, a mute numbness began to slowly develop, increasing in potency with every breath until it felt as though I was hovering above myself.

"It reminds you of old and creaky houses, with foundations so strong that they have survived through countless generations of people. You find yourself standing in front of such a house. It's garden is long and overgrown, and it's windows are large like big, all-seeing eyes."

Like before, Ryan's choice of imagery was easy to conjure inside my mind. I imagined a house of worm-eaten wood, standing slightly crooked with the passage of time, as if leaning over with arthritic discomfort. Unlike the labyrinths of modern suburbia, this house had been granted the gift of consciousness, and the windows, as Ryan suggested, were lead lined and oval, like opening eyes peering at me as I stood at it's driveway.

"You find yourself drawn to the house", said Ryan, his voice now slowing down and becoming more purposeful, therefore charging his words with a somnolent quality. "And as you approach it's large, wooden door, you imagine all the families who have lived there in the past. There have many births and many deaths, and all have happened within those walls, of which you now stand closely in front of."

It was then when I found myself fully immersed in the world that Ryan was painting to my subconscious. Like dreams, where emotions are stronger and stranger than life, I could almost smell the musty wood and see shadows dancing behind those windows. Before long, after first breaking for another breathing exercise, Ryan asked me to turn the handle of the door, and walk into the house that my mind had created.

"Look around you, and see how the old house is decorated. Perhaps it is covered in rich furniture and paintings. Or maybe it is empty and filled with nothing but cobwebs. Either way, you soon notice a huge, dark wood staircase standing in the very middle of the house. It is so long that you can't even see the bottom, with only darkness visible as the stairs lead down."

I began to feel a prickle of elation, seeming to come from the top of the stairs which I knew were hiding my memories below. Would they lead to answers? I was almost apprehensive when Ryan asked me to begin walking down them, thinking for a second that nothing would be there to greet me at their darkened bottom. Yet I carried on, succumbing once more to the slumberous tremors which kept my subconscious mind unlocked.

"On every step, you find yourself taking a deep breath. In, and out. And you notice that the more you walk down the staircase, the harder it becomes to see anything around you. You take another breath, hold it, and let it go."

By the time I reached the bottom of the stairs, I found myself surrounded once again in the amorphous colours and shapes of my mind. Swirling patterns would come into being, then mould into thinner and less colourful shapes, before vanishing completely into the blackness. I was aware of my emotions however, feeling a mixture of the previous excitement, tinted with a slight and prickling fretfulness.

"Take a minute to adjust yourself", said Ryan calmly. "Soon, you will notice that something is below your feet. When you feel it, you will realise the darkness from before has gone, and you are standing somewhere that you know, somewhere you have been before. Tell me, Leonard, where are you?"

"I'm...at home. My mum and dad are eating their dinner. I'm getting ready to go out, even though it's dark outside."

I felt my usual emotions had slipped away, been replaced instead with smaller feelings incapable of thinking the way I was used to. I was still aware of being in Ryan's office, but my thoughts and feelings were taken over by a strong upsurge of familiar sensations, from many years ago in my past. I realised at once that I was back as a child, and was sitting in a room full of bright coloured furniture, a harsh lamp sat by my tall bunk bed.

"Now remember, everything you see is only a memory", said Ryan. "Now, were going to move backwards a little further. What happened earlier on that day, back when it was still light outside?"

"I....it was the day when...No, I can't rememberer anything. I don't know what happened. I really don't."

"You do, Edward. It might just be hard at first, that's all. I can call you Edward, can't I? That is your name, isn't it?"

"...Yeah."

"So, Edward, what happened earlier on that day? And don't worry. Whatever it is, you can tell me all about it."

"Me and my friend...Amelia, we were looking for hidden places all over the town. And we found this one down by the lake. But then later on I...I know I shouldn't have!"

Although I had no intellectual say in the things I was seeing inside my mind, I remember with detail the vivid scenes which sprang into my thoughts like they happened but days ago. At the time, I was aware that I was myself as a child, and even though I knew that time had moved on, all other thoughts were impossible to access. It was like I really was back in that time, seeing the things that my mind had blocked, as vibrant and true as the day they happened.

"Amelia is your friend, is she?" continued Ryan, his voice seeming to be coming from a space above my consciousness, and ringing in my mind with a noticeable echo. Still, hearing his voice was restorative and pleasant, as if when he spoke or asked me a question, it prevented me from becoming lost in the lucid world I was then reliving. "Tell me, Edward, what hidden place did you and Amelia find at the lake?"

"It wasn't even me who found it, Amelia did. A big cave, going right underneath the water. She wanted to inside, but I didn't want to!"

"Why didn't you want to?"

"It was too dark, and it didn't look safe."

"OK Edward, that's good. Now were going to move further on in that day again, just like before. So, what happened next? Take your time, and remember that everything you see has already happened. It is not real, it is only a memory."

"Later on...Mr Cullen started asking me about what we found at the lake. I told him about the cave and then he started asking questions. I didn't know what to do! And his friend was there and he asked me as well. I just...I told them what we'd seen. That's all I did, I promise!"

"Slow down, Edward. Remember your breathing. In through the nose, hold it for a second, and release. Good."

What I saw in front of me was graphic and real. The light of the day was bright to my eyes, the warmth of the sunlight touching my skin with a genuine validity not felt in most memories. I found myself standing by Cullen's hut, two tall men peering over me and asking questions so fast I could not understand them. I do not know if I felt scared per say, but I certainly didn't know what was happening, and thus felt a surge of troublesome uncertainty.

"So, you told Mr Cullen and his friend about the cave. Good. Now then, what can you tell me about Mr Cullen's friend? What did he ask you about the lake?"

I felt an instant flutter of fear fall across my entire body. It was the sort of thing one remembers from their childhood; a helpless emotion, a tearful shriek that shivers at the thought of being in trouble for something out of your control. I could not understand it, still aware of my adult cynicism underneath, but unable to break from the stronger emotion of sheer weakness in front of the man I saw in my mind.

"It was...Mr Buckley. No, I don't like him! He shouted and asked me weird things and I didn't know what I was supposed to say!"

"It's OK Edward, calm down. Breath in, and let it go. Good. Now then, let's move even further on, shall we? Back to your bedroom at night. You said you were going out. Where were you going?"

"I...I wanted to go and see the cave again. Mr Cullen and Mr Buckley made me want to see inside it, even though I knew I shouldn't have gone. I told my...told my parents I was going back to see Amelia again. But I went to the lake."

"You went to the lake, all on your own? And what happened when you got there? Don't worry, you know can tell me."

"I went underneath. It was a hidden place, I really wanted to tell Amelia about it."

"What did you see there, Edward, deep inside that cave?"

A sharp pain swiftly pushed itself into my chest, and the previously lucid memories I saw turned at once into a shivering, darkening blur. I remember feeling my breathing quicken, pulsing in deep and purposeful gulps, in unison with the sound of my heavy heartbeat.

"Edward, what is it? What can you see underneath the lake?"

"It's a Selkie" I quietly mumbled.

"No it isn't, Edward. Come on, look more carefully. What is it really that you saw under there?"

"No, it really was a Selkie I know it was!"

At that moment, I almost broke out of the hypnotic trance. I can clearly remember jumping upwards, the muscles in my body tightening and contracting, as if I had forced myself up from the sofa. I felt a dizzying and nauseous throb, and felt the air of the office enter my lungs with a conscious realisation.

Somehow though, I didn't open my eyes. Dr Ryan then worked on calming me down, going back over the previous breathing and muscle relaxation scenario. It took a while, with the first set of breaths not working to sooth me, but instead feeling course and superficial. After a while though, I began to once more sink into the sofa, and after feeling that similar drop in awareness that accompanies the seconds before falling asleep, I was ready to try once again with the session.

"Don't worry", Ryan assured me. "We are moving forward now, away from the lake, away from the cave. Now then, I want you to take your time, and only speak when you feel your ready. Then, when you feel you are, tell me what happened in the following days, after you went underneath that lake."

I could have spoken immediately, seeing at once a dim yet lifelike memory forming amongst the shapes in my mind. I waited though, waited until I could feel the emotion that coursed through the colours and the sounds of my mind. It was still not pleasant, and once more I found myself unable to resist the primal feelings of my childhood, but I couldn't afford to lose sight of those memories again.

"After I went in the cave", I slowly began to explain. "Everything started changing, and I didn't like it at all."

"What do you mean?"

"My parents weren't the same. They wouldn't let me go back outside, even just to see my friend like before. And they shouted at me, and said I shouldn't have ever gone back to the lake. And then...and then..."

"What is it? Can you see something?"

"I don't know, too much happened at once! My dad said some new people were coming to town, and he had some papers or something to give them. But then Mr Cullen was found...he was killed!"

"Breath, Edward. Deep, and slow. That's good. Now then, what happened with Mr Cullen?"

"Someone killed him". I felt myself writhe uncomfortably on the sofa. "I didn't know what was going on, and everyone was crying and shouting and things. Then my dad said it was something to do with the lake, the cave. But it was me who told Mr Cullen about it! I...I blamed myself. I thought that it was me, that if I hadn't told him he wouldn't have been killed and-"

"OK", calmly interrupted Ryan. It gave me a minute to slow down my breath, which had grown faster and more erratic as I tried to explain what I saw and felt. "It wasn't your fault though, was it? You didn't do anything wrong."

"I know...I just didn't know what was going on. And then soon afterwards, those people my dad mentioned came and stayed in our house."

"Do you know who they were?"

"Mr and Mrs Ford. They spoke with my parents until really late at night. And my dad gave them the papers he had made for them. I don't know what it was about."

"OK Edward, that's great. Now let's take a minute to pause and relax. Imagine the clock, endlessly ticking. You find yourself breathing along with the clock, rhythmically, and peacefully."

As I followed the doctor's instructions, the splintered and hazy memories I saw began to lose their colour and fade away. I returned to the void of abstract shapes in my mind, breathing with such ease that I couldn't even feel my chest muscles moving. In fact, an almost electric feeling had lowered itself into my body, as if my veins themselves were charged with a sort of numb tranquillity

"Let's move forward again, shall we?" said the doctor. "To the time just before you hurt your head. See if you can remember what happened that day. Where are you?"

"It's...night time, and I'm in my bedroom at home. My mum and dad have been wanting to take me away somewhere, saying something to do with Mr Cullen is dangerous for me as well. I don't understand it. Then...I went outside to put out the rubbish bags."

"What happened next? Remember, it's all already happened."

"There was nobody around, and it was all quiet. But then...Mr Buckley came up to me in the garden."

"Mr Buckley did? What did he want with you?"

"He started asking me questions again."

The face of Lee Buckley in my memory was in no way like the man I had seen in the photos. To the unclear world of my childhood mind, the man in front of me was unnervingly tall, peering down at me with squinted eyes devoid of any emotion I knew of. Inside, I detected that same feeling of helplessness, as if it didn't matter what Buckley said to me, I could do nothing else but succumb to his intimidation.

"What sort of questions did he ask?" said Ryan, his voice seeming to have taken on an aura of concern.

"The same as before, about the cave. None of it made sense! And then...he wanted...wanted me to go with him to the lake."

"What did you do, Edward?"

"I tried to go back inside, said I wasn't allowed to go anywhere with him. But he wouldn't, I mean, he took hold my arm!"

I remember a oddly painful flinch, once again causing me to move on the sofa. It was like an insect bite or needle injection, but resonating across my entire body. Afterwards, my heartbeat started to loudly thump, increasingly in speed with a bothersome throb, which when heard in my ears almost drowned out Ryan's voice.

"This is important Edward. You need to stay calm. Nothing can hurt you any more, remember that. But we still need to know what happened. What did Mr Buckley do?"

"He took me there". I had difficulty speaking, my voice trying to shout out loudly and clear, but coming out as a weak and tear filled tremble. "It was so dark, I couldn't even see what was happening."

I had never been familiar with the feeling of acute panic before, but I am sure that is what I felt during the hypnosis. In fact, whilst recalling the memories of the night of my injury, I thought at one point I felt Ryan's hands supporting my body and holding my chest. Was I moving so erratically on the sofa? I am unsure, but all I do know is that what I felt was outside of the usual boundaries of fear.

"That's when it happened", I continued, my words yet again difficult to express in a volume acceptable to be heard. "There's two people in the cave under there...and I'm...I'm..."

"Slow down, Edward, and pause for a moment. I want you to imagine there's a sphere of light in your hand. Bright, blue light. Good. Now then, if at any time you feel too frightened to carry on, squeeze the sphere tightly in your hand, and you will return at once to the present day. Do you understand that?"

Imagining the sphere in my hand was, as I'm sure Ryan intended it to be, a great comfort at that moment. It acted as a reminder of my consciousness, that really I knew that at any time I could open my eyes and break the hypnosis. It was a safety net, and it allowed to me venture further into my childhood, whilst not forgetting that really I was in the doctor's office.

"Yes, I understand", I said.

"Good. So, who are the people in the cave? What are they doing?"

"I don't know, I can't see them. They're speaking. But one of them is leaving, the other one told him go outside."

"I see. And what of the other person? What is he doing now?"

"He's...talking about something, and I don't understand it. And now he's picking something up, and he's..."

I definitely felt the doctor's hands on my chest. I must have jolted upwards with the rush of pain which came from nowhere at that moment. It was like a trapped nerve or hideous toothache, where pressing against it causes a pulse of sharper agony to pour through the body. I was sweating too, I could feel it falling across my brow and enveloping my skin in a hot, uncomfortable prickle.

"What has he picked up?" asked Ryan assertively.

"I don't know what it is...but he's coming towards me with it. Now he's...no, please don't do it!"

In the space of a second, an overwhelmingly strong headache sensation pierced my skull with alarmingly realism. It was as if the insides of my head were shook, or otherwise dislodged from the skull that supported them. Then came the vibration; a ringing feeling of aching pressure, like a thousand dental drills had penetrated my bones at once.

"My head", I shouted out, finding myself in a lucid state of both the memory and present day merged into one. I was not even sure if what I felt was a memory, or whether I was calling out to Ryan about a pain which existed in the present day world.

"What is happening Edward?" said Dr Ryan, his voice almost painful to the ears which still shook with the tension from the torment in my head.

"I've hit my...no, it's him. He's trying to kill me!"

"Who?" exclaimed Ryan.

"I can't see...my eyes are all, I don't know, they've all gone dark. He's doing it again, and now...wait, I think...there someone else here!"

"Tell me who it is. Come on Edward, you have to remember."

Ryan's voice had changed from it's previous calmness to become assertive and somewhat concerned. It also seemed louder, as if he was leaning even closer to me or had forgot his role of relaxing arbiter.

"Who else is there" he asked again, seeing that I was having trouble answering and needing time to even think of the right words.

"It's my mum and dad", I eventually shouted. "And my dad, he's got hold of me. I think...he's...he's forcing me up from the floor. My head hurts. I don't know what's happening. Wait, he's taking me outside, and now there's someone else."

"Another person? Who is it this time?"

"No! My dad's gone back inside with my mum and the man who hurt me. No! I don't want to. I don't want to."

"Edward, remember the sphere of light. You can squeeze it any time and wake up immediately. Don't worry, I'll understand if you do."

I felt my fingers clenching to crush the sphere and force my eyes to open once more to reality. Yet I stopped myself. I wanted to see what had happened to me, to my parents, and I knew that this could be my only chance. I remember forcing my fingers outwards and straight, and telling myself not to open my eyes until at least Ryan ended the session himself.

"The other people", I quietly sobbed. "It's the people who came to stay. Mr and Mrs Ford. But I can hardly see them, my eyes are red...it's blood!"

"Are you in pain, Edward?"

"My head, yes. I passed out, I think. Then Mrs Ford caught me and carried me away. But my parents are still in there!"

"What is happening? What did Mr and Mrs Ford saying to you?"

"They said....they said 'your name is Leonard now'. And they said that they were my new parents. They have something, in their hands."

"What is it?"

"Mr Ford said it's a 'special birth certificate'. But it's not mine! It's all different and I don't like it. I want to go back! Please don't me go away with the-"

My hand clutched down tight on the sphere in my hand, and I opened my eyes with a startled gasp. I looked at Ryan, sitting on the chair and leaning over close to me. Rivulets of sweat were streaming across my face, and I found myself momentarily dazed, before breaking out of the hypnotic trance and sitting upright on Ryan's sofa. It was as if I'd been woken abruptly in the night, and my body had not yet found the strength to catch up with the world passing by around me. One thing was for sure though. During that somewhat uncomfortable session, I had gained innumerable childhood memories, and with them many of the questions I asked had found their answers hidden within me.

Indeed, as I shook hands with Ryan and thanked him for the session, I felt an unmistakeable impression of fulfilment. My research, which I'd assumed to be almost impossible to finish, had reached at last it's final threads, and I felt a sanguine optimism as to it's completion. Ryan's therapy had opened doors which would otherwise be forever locked, and I left the surgery that mid morning, I began at once to ponder the things of which I'd seen in those dark corners of my mind.

Reminiscence

I walked across the streets of Kilportach with a new found enthusiasm towards the place. I had been there in my memories, to a time when the town was both pleasant and mournful, and alive with the childhood emotion of discovery. In fact, some of that blameless fervour remained as I approached the main street after leaving the surgery. It's narrow recesses and weary buildings seemed to speak with suggestions of ancient things, and should I open myself up to their words, even more secrets would show themselves to me.

I did not, of course, venture into alleyways unseen by the town, no matter how compelling their investigation would be. It was easy to forget the shadow in Kilportach, the hushed aura of the streets not what you'd expect from a town coping with two recent murders. Actually, I had not seen a police officer for some time, a realisation which could have been either good or bad. Had the murderer been found and caught? I doubted it, guessing instead that the police had already scaled back their investigation. I had never had any faith in their capability.

As I passed by the pub, I noticed that Molly was standing outside, washing the old windows of the pub. As she saw me walking by, she dropped the chamois leather into a bucket at her feet, and turned to greet me.

"Hello again, Mr Clarke", she smiled. "I bet you think I do everything myself in this pub, don't you? Well actually, you'd be right. Anyway, how are you?"

"Very well thanks."

"Good to hear. Actually, I wanted to see you. Your coming into the pub tonight I take it?"

"I was planning to, yeah."

"Good. It's just that me and Adam were going to have a look through all the old photos. He's leaving tomorrow you see, and he wanted to see them. I thought you might have wanted to join in with us."

I wasn't exactly going to refuse. The pub was still my only refuge apart from Amelia's crypt, and I would not let up another chance to peer into the past of the town. Besides, I would most likely be leaving shortly myself, and if the evening with Adam and Molly in the pub was to act as a goodbye to Kilportach town, I would definitely want to be there myself.

"I'll be there", I said to Molly.

"Excellent, I thought you'd like it". She reached back into the bucket of soapy water, and rung out the leather before getting back to washing the windows. "I'll see you tonight, then."

For the time being, after leaving Molly and the main street of Kilportach, I decided to head towards the cemetery to tell Amelia of what the hypnosis had told me. If anything, it would be a chance to talk it over and make straight in my own mind the things I discovered. Besides, I was sure that Amelia, after all we had done together, would be interested to know that I saw her as a child in my own memories of living in the town.

Indeed, the repressed memories clung to my present awareness as real as anything from only days past. And it all made sense. The birth certificate I brought to town with me was false, most likely part of the 'papers' that my Father gave to the Ford's as they arrived at the house. Therefore, my parents had feared for my safety so much that they changed my name and date of birth for the adoption, as to grant me even further protection. This is why it looked as though Edward Clarke was two years my senior, and why it claimed as I born as Leonard, as if my old self never existed at all.

Then there was the matter of the TBI. Yes, the memories of what I saw in the cave were still impossible to recall, but I knew at least my injury was not caused by an accident, or even the cave-in. Somebody, most likely Lee Buckley who kidnapped me that night, had attacked me underneath the lake, and in the process caused this unpleasant condition. In fact, it made sense that this combination of factors were what made me lose my memories in the first place. After all, what child could stay balanced after all that had happened 30 years ago, even without a traumatic brain injury?

Undoubtedly, when I finally reached the crypt and began to tell Amelia of my findings, she shared with me the same sense of vivacity that I felt myself upon waking from the session. As before, she sat on her bed and allowed me to talk, not interrupting as I slowly explained, and gathered my own thoughts as I told them to her. I spoke with a sort of refrained excitement; feeling strongly relieved to be reciting my findings, yet remaining stoic with the nature of the topic. By the time I had finished, I expected Amelia to burst into an immediate flurry of her own reactions. However, it was over a minute until she spoke at all. She just looked at me, then down at the floor, and seemingly took in what I had told her with a deliberately slow contemplation.

"That's horrible", she finally said. "Someone kidnapped you? Tried to kill you under the lake? God, I had no idea."

"Of course you didn't. I would never have imagined it, myself."

"No, I just mean it's hard to think things like that could happen here. And to you, of all people. No wonder the cloud painter would never tell me what really happened back then."

"It makes sense of a lot of things though, doesn't it?"

Amelia stood up, and begun to pace around the room whilst thinking out loud her own theories of my regression.

"So, you think the birth certificate was like your parents faking your death?" she asked. "As if they knew that something was going to happen to you?"

"It seems that way. Honestly, I aren't sure why they changed my name with the adoption, but it sorts out the problem of the birth certificate. But yeah, obviously the people here thought I'd died with them in the cave-in."

"Yeah, and as horrible as it sounds, they wouldn't have had to find your body to believe that. Think about a cave-in..."

It was not the first time I had imagined the scene of the cave-in after the tragedy had occurred. I could see images of breathlessness, of been trapped in a void darker than anything conceivable. Truly, of course, what Amelia said was correct. It was likely that after excavating the wreckage, the remains of those who were trapped inside would be crushed below the fallen rubble. It was a nauseating thought, tinted with the sort of dreadful emotion which accompanies the witness of death and bloodshed.

"Don't worry, your right", I said to Amelia, now standing up myself and joining her with her museful pacing. "It was only natural to assume I was with them. After all, I wasn't anywhere in the town."

"Mmhm. So wait, who was the other person in the cave, if the man who had hurt you was Lee Buckley?"

"I don't even know if it was Lee Buckley, I'm just surmising. The thing is, I can't remember fully what I saw under there. But yes, there was someone else, but they left the cave before anything happened."

"I see." She came to a pause in the middle of the crypt, looked straight at me. "I have an idea."

"What's that?"

She went to the desk opposite her bed, and opened one of the drawers. She removed a few sheets of plain white paper, and an expensive looking fountain pen.

"When I have a hard time thinking about something, I write it all down", she said, handing me the paper. "So, why don't we try it together?"

"Write down what I saw in the hypnosis, you mean?"

"No. Well, sort of. But I thought we could write down everything that happened 30 years ago, and try to put it all in order. That way, any blanks will be really obvious, and it's guaranteed to make more sense. What do you think?"

It was a good idea. In the past, I had often done the exact thing that she mentioned, and written down my worries or concerns to read over. After all, when taking a pen to a thought, it ceases to exist as simply an idea. It is granted it's own unique mannerism, a consistent mood which will not change with the onset of conflicting emotion or circumstance. Moreover, for me personally, writing down problems was of far more use than the accepted method of looking to others for comfort. How could another human being, no matter how close or experienced in the subject, fully understand your own questions and fears? They cannot.

"That's a great idea", I said, realising that yet again I was agreeing exactly with Amelia's views. "Now then, the problem is trying to put it in order."

"We won't do it here", she assertively replied, before walking to the door and unlocking it. "I thought we could take a walk into town. If you don't mind, that is."

"Oh, of course."

I would usually not want the interference of others whilst trying to concentrate on writing such things, but I knew Amelia was not going to hinder me. In fact, considering we used to know each other until the night of that repellent cave-in, she would no doubt help with the task at hand far better than anybody else in the town. Besides, leaving the crypt to wander into Kilportach was surely the best way to ponder the events, and even if the exercise ended in failure, it would allow the both us to reminisce on the night which ultimately altered both of our lives.

Indeed, as we walked through the myriads of yawning streets, I could once again feel an uncommon equanimity by having Amelia accompany me. It was like a sort of unconscious nostalgia, a latent deja vu of having stepped on those same old pavements with the same companion. The town had not changed, just grown more weary with the passing years, which had stripped it from all it remembered of yore. In a way, one could argue that the town itself brought us together, if not from a wish to reunite us, then to settle it's own wistful retrospection.

"I still have trouble believing your Edward Clarke", she said as we slowly made out way towards the peat bog area of town. "I still remember you just as a kid. Before all this happened."

"I imagine it really is hard to believe."

"Oh, I believe it alright. It's just mind blowing, you know? And to think, the cloud painter said he knew all along that you hadn't died under that lake. I guess he didn't want to tell me."

"Oh yeah, the cloud painter took you in as a child, didn't he?"

I was still intrigued with the enigmatic life of Leon Gould and his bizarre cloud paintings. At the time, Amelia was clearly more concerned with the unlocked door than of telling me about him. Yet whenever she spoke about him or his works, I detected a slight resistance in her voice, as if at any second she would lose her impersonal demeanour, and begin to open up about her childhood.

"Yeah", she said as we walked along. "I mean, some would say he wasn't the type to adopt a child and make it work. But he did. In fact, I owe pretty much everything I believe in to him. And you, of course."

"Me?"

"You know", she smiled. "Hidden places, all that sort of thing. We used to search for ghosts in the town at night, long past the time we were supposed to be home."

I felt an odd sense of yearning as I peered at the buildings, stacked up around us as we approached the bogs, their windows unblinking and following us closely. Had I truly influenced Amelia so? I would never have believed it, save for the noticeable similarities between my world-view and that of her own. Even so, like everyone else I had met in Kilportach, she clearly held her memories close, and recited them to me with a fervid spirit of which I had no choice but respect.

"Kilportach is great for things like that, isn't it?" I said. "It's like the whole town is one large 'hidden place'"

"Actually, the cloud painter said the same thing when I told him about it. He said I was lucky to have seen such places, as not everyone can find them even if they look."

"He really does seem like an interesting person, I admit".

"Oh, he is. And he was always a friend, both to me and my family, even before anything bad happened. Yeah, there was Shane Cullen, the cloud painter, and of course your...wait, hold on a sec." She came to a pause in the middle of the road.

"What is it?"

"It's probably nothing". Her hand reached for the necklace still glinting around her neck. The silver Selkie. "I just thought that, since Mrs Clarke gave me this only days before...you know, well, actually it doesn't matter."

"No, it's fine, tell me."

"I just wondered whether you remembered where you got this from, in the first place? Mrs Clarke said that it was you who gave her it, after all."

"I saw it once in my memories, but otherwise, I'm not sure. Sorry."

"OK". She started walking again, and I followed a few steps behind to match her pace. "I thought that maybe, well, this was what you saw underneath the lake. You did see a Selkie after all, didn't you?"

During both hypnosis sessions, I had not been able to comprehend what I saw beneath that myth laden lake. When recalling the memory, I saw only a creeping and loathsome darkness, a suffocating atmosphere which pushed me away and obscured itself from the reaches of my eyes. I was unsure however if this was due to a further blockage in my own consciousness, or if I truly did see nothing in there but the murmur of an unseen blackness.

"So, you think I found the necklace under the lake, and that's what I meant by seeing a Selkie in there?" I asked as we arrived at the peat bog area.

"Just a guess", she said. We walked along the pavement for a little while, before both deciding to sit on a bench, overlooking the vast fields of waterlogged peat bog.

As always, the bogs created within me a strange and somewhat humbling sensation. By seeing them, the scope of Kilportach's immense isolation was incomparably clear. A tiny dot on a mass horizon of sodden marshland, Kilportach was nothing but a handful of buildings, dropped into the uncharted backwoods of Ireland. Not only this, but the recurrent imagery of the bodies, made even more hideous by the theories written in the Sullivan book, still managed to bring forth a unearthly shiver which prickled along the edges of my skin.

Interestingly, a tractor was parked in the midst of the peat bogs, just as it was on the first night I spent in the town. Around it, a number of people were gathered in conversation, and a few of them seemed to be taking notes and photographs of the earth below. Amongst them, I noticed both Dr Kenny and Ryan, dressed not in their standard medical uniform, but in outdoor gear and what looked like waders. Had another body been discovered already? It was too far away to tell what was happening, but it was clear that the bog land of Kilportach was once more allowing it's unseen secrets to be unearthed.

"So anyway", said Amelia after we had sat watching the bogs for a minute or two. "You've got the pen and paper. Do you want to get started?"

"Yeah, there's just a lot to think about, that's all."

We began to discuss with increasing vigour the order of events having happened when we were children. During that time, we swapped the paper and pen between one another, each jotting down our own thoughts and ideas, then trying to connect them with arrows and lines into some form of tangible diagram. Much was crossed out and written again, and it took more than a couple of complete reruns for us both to be finally happy with it.

By the end, the paper resembled a jumbled mess of scribbled words joined up with arrows, mixed with a couple of untidy doodles we drew whilst thinking and speaking together. The best of them was certainly drawn by Amelia; a pen sketch of a Selkie shedding her sealskin, a few ripples of water glinting behind her. As for the writing itself, it was disorderly and somewhat hard to decipher, but as we held it between us and read it through, it became clear that we had in fact covered the entirety of the fateful events.

'What happened in November 1981?

Lee Buckley visits Shane Cullen in Kilportach
- *Apparently, Buckley and Cullen were friends, and had been researching the Wishing Lake as seen in the letter we found in the hut.*

We found the cave underneath the Wishing Lake
- *While looking for haunted and 'hidden places', Amelia found a cave underneath the lake. At this point, neither of us went inside.*

Shane Cullen asks Edward about the cave
- *This makes sense if Cullen and Buckley had researched the theory of the Sullivan book, where the Selkie's home was 'beneath the lake'. Cullen and Buckley wanted to know if there really was a cave.*

Edward enters the cave on his own
- *I went inside the cave after sneaking out of home on a night. I saw inside a 'Selkie'. Possibly the necklace?*

Shane Cullen murdered
- *According to Leon Gould, the murderer was Lee Buckley, who was staying in Kilportach under the pseudo name 'Lucas Clarke'. Motive still unknown. Possibly occult/Sullivan book related?*

Lucas and Ethel Clarke summon the Ford family to town
- *Obviously sensing the danger in town (and the fact that their son was now involved), the Clarke's decided to send Edward away with a false birth certificate and name to obscure him from Buckley/the murderer. It is unknown whether this was meant as a temporary measure.*

Edward abducted from his home, and taken to the cave
- *Lee Buckley kidnapped me from the garden, and took me back underneath the lake.*

The tragedy in the Wishing Lake cave
- *Edward and two other people gather inside the cave. One of the people leave, and Edward is attacked by the other, most likely Lee Buckley. At this point, the Clarke family*

enter and rescue their son, but are caught in the resultant cave-in.

Edward Clarke taken away from town, brought up as Leonard
- *I was taken away from town with an undiagnosed traumatic brain injury. Memory regression followed.*

"God, it actually makes sense for once", I laughed as I read it. "What do you think?"

"I think we did a good job", said Amelia. "It's weird though, I can hardly remember finding the cave with you back then. I even told you that there were no caves in Kilportach at all. Sorry."

"Don't worry", I said. "It's pretty unlikely that you would remember. To you, it was just another day, right?"

"I suppose so. So look, can you think of anything still unanswered after writing this? I think it's quite conclusive, don't you?"

Amelia's exercise was most definitely a help. By reading it, all of my original questions were answered, leaving nothing of the previous mystery regarding the Kilportach of 30 years ago. The only remaining questions were obvious, such as what I saw inside the cave and who the other person was on the night of the attack. As it stood though, these were of little importance to me. I was astounded by how much I had discovered in town, and had never thought that my own childhood was hiding so much misfortune and pain. Then again, it was like I had thought after first seeing the TBI scan; that blot in my mind was a 'hidden place'. Such places always resound with the memories of olden times, and with them the murmurs of tragedy which were caught in the eyes of the place itself.

Amelia understood this perfectly as I told her how I felt. In fact, after once more reading our untidy notes, and setting off back towards the town centre, our discussion turned onto our shared enjoyment of finding such places unseen by the monotonous passage of the world. We hadn't spoken for long though, when Amelia unwillingly changed the subject by way of a genuine sounding concern.

"By the way", she said as we walked uphill towards the main street. "If you go to any hidden places here in Kilportach, be careful, OK?"

"How do you mean?"

"Oh, it's nothing. Well, actually...I was thinking of Mr Cullen, and how those other people have been killed in town only days ago. Sorry, I just, you know, had a bad feeling."

"I see. Well don't worry, I'll probably be leaving Kilportach shortly. Your idea with taking notes really helped make sense of it all. I've no reason to stay for much longer."

Amelia came to a pause in the middle of the road. She looked at me directly in the eye, an distinct change in expression visible on her face.

"Really?" she sighed. "I thought you'd be staying for longer, but never mind. I suppose not."

"I'm sleeping in the pub, you know. I really can't stay for any longer than I need to. Besides as you say, there's this whole thing with the murderer to think-"

"I know", she interrupted. "I was just happy to see you again, that's all. You might not be able to remember anything, but I can, you know."

"Yeah...I'm sorry"

We began to walk again, yet our steps grew progressively slower, as if Amelia thought that when we parted ways, I would leave the town without seeing her first. I was not accustomed to such personal goodbyes, but I had no real choice with Amelia, and would obviously not leave without telling her. Still, I found myself unsure of how to respond, and so instead stayed silent and kept on walking, turning my mind onto Molly's evening with Adam in the pub.

"Actually, you don't remember what my last name is, do you?" continued Amelia.

"What? Oh, no, I don't think so."

"Ah well. It's Venn, by the way. Not that it matters. But look, you'll let me know before you go, won't you?

"Of course I will, yeah", I smiled.

"That's alright then. Though I do wish you could have stayed for longer."

"Listen", I said. "There's supposed to be some kind of meeting in the pub tonight, the landlady going through old photos and things. I'll be there so, well, why don't you come along? We could talk about the past, or anything you liked, really."

"I don't go in there", she replied. "I've no desire for company, you know? Well not usually, anyway. You're different."

"I know what you mean, believe me. But seriously, the pub is nearly empty all the time. You know that, right? Anyway, you can come if you like. I'll be there all night."

"I'll see". We came to a stop as the roadway split between the main street and the one leading to the cemetery. "I might come to see you. It would make a change anyway, wouldn't it?"

"Sure", I smiled. "You know where to find me, anyway."

I had no idea whether Amelia would visit me in the pub. Either way, it would likely be one of my final nights spent camped on the sofa in search of memories. For the time being, I wandered into the main street itself, intent on passing the day away until the time for me to retire to the pub. A hushed sense of longing seemed to cling to the buildings, as if they too had found some solace in my rekindling of their own omnipresent memories. Therefore I did not pace around the townscape, choosing instead to relax in it's quietude, imagining old times spent there as a child, and awaiting the setting of the pale sun overhead.

Records and Requiems

Since finding out about my lost identity, I found that in many an idle moment my mind returned to the rhetoric of asking 'what if?' Indeed, I have no doubts that should my parents have lived, my childhood would have been a world away from the tiresome upbringing of which I endured. After all, the rural stretches of southern Ireland were a different landscape to the suburban vapidity of the Ford's household. Moreover, the idea of growing up without the headaches was something I could barely even imagine, as was the concept of a real family.

Yet as Kilportach once more sunk into the evening, another kind of feeling presented itself as I walked below the reddish, darkening sky. I would soon be returning to the town's train station, and once more making my way back home, my research in Kilportach now all but complete. I felt irresolute, like my subconscious mind was prickling my thoughts with questions of whether it had all been worth it. For although I had seen many wondrous things in that tiny and uncommunicative town, not everything I'd seen was going to leave a positive imprint on my memory. The murders of two of the people I'd met had cast a shadow not only over myself, but over the entire populace of the town. The abhorrent sight of discovering Bridget was something I doubt I could forget in a hurry, even if the true scope of her death was obscured my own encompassing research.

Yet ultimately, I felt that my time in Kilportach town had surpassed everything I had expected from it. I had discovered the cause of my grievous headaches, uncovered the truth of my missing memories and made sense of the enigmas on the genealogical records. It was more than I had ever hoped to accomplish, and had created within me a new form of healing which I would doubtlessly remember for the rest of my days.

For that, I told myself even before I arrived, that my evening with Molly and her photographs was going to act as somewhat of a finale to my digging into the past of the town.

I arrived just as the final strands of daylight had left the sky with a slight feeling of coming rain. Inside, Molly and Adam were sat at the bar, the rest of the pub still completely empty and the tables not even set for dinner. I walked over to the bar, where Molly had placed an old shoebox full of pieces of paper and countless photographs.

"Ah, there you are", she said. "Let me pour you a drink."

I ordered my favourite, a Tullamore Dew, and was soon enrolled in the conversation her and Adam were having about the town of old.

"Molly was telling me about you", Adam said. "About how you had some hypnosis or something to get back your memories? Sounds fascinating."

"It was." I took a sip of the whiskey. "In fact, I'll never know how I was able to do it, or even how it works to be honest."

"Well", said Adam. "As long as you managed to find what you were looking for. Though Molly said you were actually kidnapped as a child? I mean, how horrible."

"Well, I just look at it as knowing the truth about what caused the head injury that made me forget."

We spoke for quite a while then about my childhood, with me explaining in more detail the things that happened which Molly had not yet told Adam. That said, it wasn't long until Molly had started to show me the photographs in her shoebox. Most were similar to those I saw before; black and white images of old Kilportach in the late 70's when Molly first lived there. She would hand them to me, mostly with a small explanation of it's content, then I would pass them to Adam when I had finished, and carry on slowly with the relaxing whiskey.

There was only one colour photograph, and unlike the others it was an old picture postcard showing the town in days of yore. A number of people were shopping in the main street, which appeared on the photo to be vibrant and alive. Underneath, black capital letters spelt out the caption *'Greetings From Kilportach'*. It was an interesting image, and not only because of it's contrasting view of the town. It also spoke of the history of the buildings and roadways, the town looking almost identical in essence to how it looks in the modern day. The only difference was the feeling of a prosperous and living town which had all but abandoned the Kilportach of today.

It was not long until the night grew old with countless discussions and photographic records of yesteryear. The open fire in the pub continued to be fed, and in recompense bathed the carpets and walls in an amber glitter to compliment the oft wistful remembrances.

Of course, much of what Molly herself spoke of meant little to Adam or myself, but I felt a humbling sensation whilst viewing the images of the town. Some of them contained the portraits of people, residents and visitors to Kilportach caught forever on black and white film. And of course there were the images Molly held dear; those of people like Shane Cullen at his hut, and even one of the pub itself when she first took over as the landlady.

"You should have seen the state of it", she said. "But I think I did a good job of cleaning the place up. Well, I like to think so, anyway."

"I think it's great", Adam said. "Not many places left like it nowadays, right Leonard?"

Obviously, the empty pub was hardly a place that could be considered a thriving business. During my whole time in Kilportach, I had barely seen another person inside apart from Adam and a handful of thirsty locals. Yet for Molly, the Wishing Lake pub was her home and career, and ultimately it was that homelike quality which gave the place it's amicable atmosphere.

However, no amount of decoration or fireside crackle could truly prepare me for what was waiting later on that night. It was a moment unlike any other I'd experienced, and arrived with such a lack of forewarning that the only expected emotion was disorientation. It was like a 'jump' had taken on the form of solidity, and forced itself into the real world with a drawn out and deplorable tangibility.

It began when our conversation had moved away from the photos and onto the sorrowful topic of the murders. I mentioned how in my childhood regression, I had blamed myself for the death of Cullen based purely on an inability to understand what had happened. It was then that Molly brought up poor Catherine, and how a similar thing could have happened with her when confronted with her eventual killer.

"That woman was always as trusting as ever", she said. "And you know, I think it's the same as what you were saying. Even if there were clues, or any signs that she might have been in danger...I don't think she'd really understand it properly."

"Honestly, I just can't make out why someone would murder an elderly lady like that" I said. "I really can't."

"I don't know", continued Molly. "God, it's like everyone who really knew the town has died. There's nobody left here any more, is there?"

The long session of photos and reminiscence had clearly made Molly pensive and heavyhearted. Then again, it was easy to share in her emotion. In the moments of silence between our conversation, there was never a noise from outside the pub, not from people or even the passing of cars. It was as if we existed temporarily beyond time, sat in a public house of memory, at the end of Kilportach's very own lifespan.

It was around that time when Adam reached inside a small jute bag he had placed at his feet. From it, he removed a dark bottle of liqueur without a label, and offered myself and Molly a drink.

"I completely forgot about this", he said. "I was saving it just for tonight, since it's my last night here and everything. Shall I pour one for all of us?"

"Oh I'm not sure", smiled Molly. "What is it, exactly?"

"It's a local drink I brought from home. It's quite strong though, so you have been warned. I'm sure you'd like to try it Leonard, right?"

I of course let Adam pour me a small glass of the unnamed drink he had brought with him to town. It was a tawny coloured spirit, tasting like pipe smoke with an earthy hint of barley around the edges.

"This is brilliant", I said to Adam. "Where exactly does it come from, again?"

"Oh, it's from a local merchant in my home town. Come on Molly, why don't you try some? Just a little bit, eh?"

"Oh, go on then", she said, getting a glass from behind the bar. I am not sure whether she liked it or not, the sharp flavour clearly surprising her upon her first sip of the liqueur. Even so, she thanked

Adam for pouring her a glass, and continued to take small sips of the drink as we continued to talk around the bar.

"Actually, that reminds me", said Adam. "All this talk of photographs, and I forgot to show you mine." He reached back into the bag where the drink came from, and removed this time a small photograph, like the sort from disposable polaroid cameras.

"You remember when I told you that my cousin had recently had a baby? Well, this is her". He passed the photograph to me.

It was a picture of a newborn baby, wrapped in a light pink blanket in what looked like a hospital bed. Her eyes were closed tight, and a small tuft of dark hair stood out against her healthy white skin. I smiled at the photo, and passed it to Molly who would doubtlessly appreciate it more than myself.

"Oh, she is lovely, isn't she?" beamed Molly as soon as she saw the image. "Has she given her a name yet?"

"Oh yes", said Adam. "She's called Lily."

"Very nice", continued Molly, passing the photograph back to Adam who put it back inside his bag.

Unfortunately, I found myself unable to share in any degree of cordiality surrounding the baby or indeed any other topic. I had swiftly developed a hot sensation, a prickling sort of heat which made me at once feel a great deal of tiredness. I assumed it was the first signs of another headache, and tried to keep my mind occupied by joining in with the continuing conversation. I also finished the strong drink that Adam had given me, it's sharp after-taste managing to wake me up, if only for a couple of seconds.

It was no use, though. In fact, it was strange. The usual signs of a coming headache did not present themselves as I would have expected. Instead, I quickly began to feel a great deal of dizziness, which although alleviated by focusing my eyes, returned within seconds and grew seemingly worse. I took in a few deep and forceful breaths, each time managing to regain clear sight for a second, then falling back into this swirling giddiness which came from nowhere and refused to let up.

Around me, I could hear Molly and Adam speaking, and I'm sure they were talking to me as well. However, as I often did when confronted with such feelings, I found myself switching off from the world and concentrating only on the pain I felt. I stared at the bar, seeing the empty glass I had drunk from on top of the polished, dark wood surface.

The more I did though, the worse the things I felt became. I was sure by this time that it was not a normal headache. My entire body seemed to be sweating and hot, with my head feeling heavy as if weighted with liquid and ready to fall at any moment. I also seemed to have lost awareness, if only of the noises and voices around me, which dropped in and out of my conscious mind with an oddly nauseating pulse. I do not know if they were talking to me, asking me if I was feeling OK. They probably were, but I found myself feeling so bizarrely fatigued that I could barely open my mouth to respond.

It wasn't long before I lost alertness completely. Such is the nature of an abrupt change in wellness, as if the body is unable to correlate the hurried onset of malaise. Indeed, I do not know if I once again fainted that night, or if I had actually fallen asleep by succumbing to the profound weariness I felt. Either way, the next thing I remembered was the simmering whirl of coloured shapes which gathered in obscure and unfathomable murk. It was the kind of sleep which accompanies fever; abnormally deep and existing in limbo between restlessness and imperforate numbness.

Soon though, the almost familiar images of memories began to form themselves amongst the murk. It was hazy, nauseatingly so for the first few seconds, but as I accepted what I saw in front of me, more childhood memories seemed to spill forth from the once locked area of my mind.

I was sat in the living room of my house as a child. A large wooden cabinet was stood to my right, filled to the brim with china and silver ornaments. In front of me, my Mother and Father were loudly talking to another man of whom I seemed to know, but could not remember what his name was. He was slightly overweight, with a mid length black beard and an old looking tweed suit.

"I'm telling you", he said to my parents. "He's staying in that bed and breakfast hotel, and he's using your name to hide himself".

"And your saying that he was the one who killed him?" gasped my Mother.

"Yes. It was Lee Buckley, I know it to be true. He's staying here with his young son. Now I don't know how he managed to find your name, but the man is definitely dangerous. You need to be careful."

"But listen", my Father shouted. "Why in the hell would he want to kill Shane? What had he done to him?"

"It's not that simple..."

I found myself unable to concentrate for long, the words of the man fading into a blur, and the image I saw once more losing it's sharpness. Before I knew what was happening, an unpleasant mixture of sounds and shapes began to clot and mould into an painful din. It was another memory, forcing itself into my mind as if demanding I experienced all that is was hiding. This time, however, the things I saw were accompanied by a thumping discomfort; an odious tremor which fell across me like deep seated, uncontrollable anxiety.

At first, I could see nothing but and endless blackness, making me doubt that it was a real memory, and not just a sickened, febrile entrancement. Yet as once again the images began to settle, I found myself standing in front of a man, in the damp cavern I then recognised as the cave below the Wishing Lake. I also knew the loathsome figure who towered above me within that gloom. It was Lee Buckley, and behind him stood a frightened child who cowered in the dark and stared straight at me.

Before I could understand just what was happening, Mr Buckley began to read from a book, muttering some kind of unspeakable language which echoed throughout the humid cave. I did not know what he was talking about, but something about his feverish recital drove a terrible fear into my body. I just stood there, unable to move and hardly breathing, my every muscle shaking with panic.

Then, Buckley put down the book he was reading from, and turned to the child who stood mutely behind him.

"Adam, it's time for you to leave here. Go!" he shouted.

"But...no, I can't" whimpered the child. "I don't want you to do this again. Please don't!"

"I told you to go! Get outside and wait for me there. This is not for your eyes."

The child refused to move from the cave, backing away into the shadowed corners which pulsed with a dark and hoary energy. Buckley took hold of him by the arm, dragging him towards the pinprick of light which led up and outside of that disgusting cave.

"Don't do it dad", he screeched as Buckley forced him towards the entrance. "I'll never forgive you for it. Nobody will!"

"Shut up Adam, now leave me in peace. And I better not see you come back here again. Wait for me outside, OK?"

As the child was pushed towards me and into the moonlight, he looked into my eyes with a feared expression which spoke at once of horror and unsustainable sorrow. I recognised him. It was the same Adam from the present day.

Someone shouted my name. At first, I did not know if it was still part of my memory, or resonating from a different place outside of the confines of my subconscious. At that moment, I existed once more in that shapeless obscurity which has formed the backdrop to my memories. When the voice called again though, it sounded different. It was like before, when the 'shape' I saw in Amelia's crypt began to speak to me in that darkness. It seemed to come from both inside, and outside me, and I knew not whether it was my own consciousness or a physical entity beckoning to me.

"For gods sake, Leonard...Edward! Wake up will you!"

It was definitely real. I felt the tugging of hands across my clothes, lightly shaking my drowsy body into slowly realising it was awake. I felt my eyes were open, and achingly sat up to look around me, still unsure of what had happened, or even where I was.

It soon became clear though. I was on the floor beside the bar, the stool I was sitting on toppled over, the lights all switched off apart from the flicker of the dying fire. Amelia was kneeling beside me, and she helped me back onto my feet with a heavy sigh of genuine relief. I was still tired, feeling sick. What had happened to me?

Unfortunately, I had no time to think about it. The pub was empty, and Molly and Adam were nowhere to be seen.

Quietus

"Amelia, have you seen Molly?" I blurted as soon as I got to my feet in the pub.

"What? Look, just tell me if your alright will you. What happened?"

"I don't know. I just...I don't know. But seriously, where are they? What time is it?" I leant against the bar, my empty glass still standing upon it, glimmering in the amber light from the fire.

"Who?" she said, sounding confused. "There's nobody else here, if that's what you mean."

I didn't say anything then, instead just getting behind the bar and opening the door into the back room. I switched on the light, and nobody was in there. My chest tightened, oppressive thoughts of Molly being in danger resounding along with my pulsing heartbeat.

"What's wrong with you?" exclaimed Amelia, walking around to meet me behind the bar.

"It's Adam, it's...he's Lee Buckley's son."

"What? I don't know any Adam's, Edward."

"Ugh...just, look upstairs or something. No, I'll go." I regained my clear sight in a matter of seconds, though still felt the effects churning in my stomach of whatever it was that had forced me to collapse. Still, I made my way up the stairs, not knowing what or who was up there, but finding myself unable to think of the threat.

"Who's Adam?" shouted Amelia up the stairs. "What is going on?"

I didn't reply. I simply fumbled upstairs, opening the doors in the narrow corridor, looking for Molly or any signs of life. Of course, I might have been grossly overreacting, but the thought of Bridget and Catherine would not leave my still recovering mind. If Buckley was the man it was said he was, could his son Adam have turned out the same? I didn't like to think of it, but at that moment all I could imagine were the worst possibilities for that trusting landlady.

There was nobody upstairs. Most of the rooms were nearly empty, with only her bedroom and bathroom showing any signs of being lived in at all. I stumbled back down the stairs, where the confused Amelia had switched on the main lights.

"Come on please", she said. "What's all this about Lee Buckley's son? I come in here and find you laid out on the floor, and you wake up in some kind of frenzy! Tell me what happened."

"Look, when I was passed out, I saw another memory. That other person in the cave, on that night...it was Buckley's son, Adam. The one staying in the hotel with him, the one who was here just before I..."

"What is it?"

I picked up the glass from on top of the bar. It still lingered with the aroma of the drink, a sharp and sooty scent of liqueur, sharp even to the nose.

"Hey!" shouted Amelia. "Come on, will you. Speak to me."

"Listen", I said. "What if he gave me something in that drink? I started feeling ill just as I was drinking it. And wait, he gave a glass to Molly as well!"

"You mean this Adam character?"

"Yes. Look, I'm sorry Amelia, I'm just...trying to think. Did you see anybody around the town, as you were making your way over here?"

"What do you think? The place is a ghost town. Well actually, I did see a car heading out of town, sort of towards the lake. Why?"

"The lake, I wonder..."

I made my way immediately to the unlocked front door, telling Amelia I was heading outside to try and find Molly and Adam. Clearly she was upset and confused, my ramblings making little sense even to myself at that point. Even so, images of when I went searching for Bridget entered my mind which a shiversome potency.

This time, though, it felt even more dreadful. The lights off in the pub, but the door unlocked. Adam's drink and it's resulting loss of consciousness. The fact I was left there until Amelia woke me up. It just all felt wrong. Horribly so.

"Where are you going?" she called out as I was leaving the pub.

"The lake, I think. Look, come with me if you want. But don't hang about."

She hesitated for a second, as if unsure of whether she was prepared to follow me into the darkness of the town. After a few seconds though, she reached into the pocket of the coat she was wearing.

"Come on then, but we're not going without this". She removed a large torch which she switched on immediately, then followed me outside of the abandoned pub.

The night was cold and drizzling with intermittent spurts of rain. There was no moon, and not a single star in the sky. Therefore, Amelia's torch was the only light as we made our way together out of the main street, and towards the Wishing Lake on the outskirts of town.

I walked quickly, gradually breaking into a run as Amelia followed directly behind me. I knew not if the lake was the right place to go, but I could not stand in the pub and do nothing at all.

"What do you hope to find?" panted Amelia whilst running with the torch. "This Adam, he's not dangerous is he?"

"Could be. You don't have to come, you know."

She said nothing, just continued to silently follow behind me, lighting the way with the erratic glow from the powerful torch she held in her hand.

Images of strange things prodded my mind. I saw Leon Gould's paintings, reminding me of how Adam went to see him and told him stories of having met him in town. I thought nothing of it when I read his diary, but Adam said things to the cloud painter which set him on the path to his eventual desertion. Indeed, Adam said that he met Gould whilst selling paintings on the street sides of Kilportach, something the artist confessed in his diary that he had never done. What else did he say? Whatever it was, it must have unearthed merciless memories for the painter who knew of Lee Buckley's guilt.

By the time we arrived at Shane Cullen's hut, we were both forced to pause and catch our breath in the cold night air surrounding the

285

lake. As expected, the place was silent, with only the voices of nocturnal birds watching the two of us alone in the gloom. A peculiar mood seemed to come from the hut, a voiceless shriek which shook with unease at it's owners past being once more dug up.

We didn't stay around for long, yet slowed down our pace as we trampled through the grass on the way to the waters edge itself. I felt eyes upon me, as if the one I sought was holding his breath, and waiting in the confines of every shadow which clung to the barks of those ancient trees.

"Shouldn't we have phoned the police?" whispered Amelia. "I mean, if you really thought there might be trouble?"

"You think they'd show up?" I quietly said. "We can phone them later, if we really need to."

As it stood, the expanse of darkness which hid the lake at night was almost impossible to see anything within. Even with the strong light of Amelia's torch, any more than a few inches before us was shrouded entirely in moonless obscurity. It was unnerving, my mind filling with primal thoughts which needed no words to invoke trepidation. The nocturnal lake was, after all, sentient with the pulse of bygone secrets, still speaking in tongues not of our world and remembering all that have seen it's waters. And myself too; I could feel it. The place I now walked through was the very same place where Lee Buckley first tried to take my life.

Still, myself and Amelia slowly walked towards the edge of the sacred lake. It seemed deserted, as quiet as one would expect from a 'hidden place' on the outskirts of a town where nothing was alive. I began to lose all sense of hope, imagining that we had chosen the wrong place, and Adam was right now alone with Molly in some other unlit part of Kilportach.

But then, it happened. A 'jump' far stronger than any I had experienced, brought on by an unexpected voice destroying the silence of the night-time lake. It was a scream, calling my name. It was Molly.

Amelia and myself ran forward, her flashlight flitting in every direction to uncover where the horrifying cry was coming from. Then we saw them. At the lakeside.

It was Adam, holding Molly in front of him with his arm tightly held around her throat. In his other hand, a large handgun was placed against the side of her head.

"I told you to shut up", he shouted at Molly, pressing the gun even further to her skull. Amelia pointed the torch straight at them, forcing both Adam and Molly to squint their eyes in discomfort.

"Adam", I tried to shout, my voice hoarse with the difficulty of my mind trying to comprehend what was happening before it. "What are you trying to do? Tell me!"

"Leonard Clarke", he replied. "Or Edward, I suppose I should say. You could have been lucky. I didn't think you really knew anything. Had to ruin it though, right?"

"Leonard, get out of here, go", cried Molly.

"Shut up, like I said!". He tightened the grip on her throat, forcing her to choke.

"Alright, look", said Amelia, standing beside me pointing her torch, directly in front of Adam and Molly. "I don't know what the hell's supposed to be happening, but I don't want anyone pointing guns around. Put it down, will you?"

I was strengthened by her cold and unsubmissive approach. I took a step forward, inching closer to Adam in front of me.

"Keep your distance", he shouted back at me. "I didn't think you'd come round from that drink I gave you yet, not with your so called headaches and everything. Impressive."

"So the drink was poisoned?" I replied, trying not to show emotion in my voice, as to not let on that I was enraged and worried. I could easily have snapped though, lunged forward and tried to attack that madman, but I knew it was impossible.

"Just something to make you sleep", he said. "Like I said, you could have easily gotten away, if I hadn't found out who you really were."

It was nearly impossible to believe what I was seeing in front of my eyes. Adam, who had shown himself previously as dignified and well tempered, was the killer of Bridget and Catherine, the man of whom all Kilportach feared. To think how many times I trusted him, how many times he had stayed in the pub with Molly, telling her that she had nothing to worry about. Who was this man? I looked into his eyes, reflected in the harsh light of Amelia's torch, and saw nothing but an empty, tormented delirium.

"Listen up", said an assertive Amelia. "Your the son of Lee Buckley, are you? And your the one who killed those people in town?"

"That's right." He once more tightened his grip on Molly, forcing her to wheeze and writhe with discomfort. "He dragged me here when I was a boy, forced me to watch as he tore the place up, stopping at nothing to raise some ridiculous myth from his books."

"Wait, the Sullivan book you mean?" I said, not sure just how I could free Molly from him, so concentrating instead on keeping him talking. I felt numb all over my body, as if the muscles had tightened to such a degree that no sickness or dizziness could force me to falter.

"Yes, that and others. You've read those things too, haven't you? I should have known all along that you were one of them."

"One of who? Make sense for once", I shouted at him.

Adam laughed, then took the gun from Molly's head, and pointed it straight at myself instead. In that second, a dark wave shivered across my bones, forcing my feet into the ground and preventing so much as a muscle moving. I was seconds from death. I didn't fear it, but was forced in the space of a single second to prepare for that of which one can never truly know. I stared into the barrel of the pistol. Waiting. Expecting.

"One of the people who knows the past", said Adam, holding the gun with remarkable steadiness and pointing it between my staring eyes. "That's why I came here, why I did it. I'm dying, aren't I? I have only a couple of months to live, to settle that of which my Father started. You think I want a world where my cousin's baby grows up with the stigma of my Father stuck to her? I want to erase the past. Make it forgotten."

"Your mad", said Amelia, signalling Adam to turn the gun away from me, and point it towards her instead. She didn't falter, standing close beside me and aiming the torch right into the pistol he was pointing at her. The light was unsteady, her hands shaking, but she stood strong, and didn't give up. "You wanted to kill everyone so that your name was cleared? Yeah, great thinking there, Buckley."

"Not everyone", he raised his voice further. "Just people who knew what happened back then, people who could talk and remember the past. I want to remove the memories of that time, so that when I'm gone my new family can grow up without having to bear his cross."

"So Bridget and Catherine were less important than that?" I asked him. "And Molly...Why did you do it, Adam?"

"Molly would have been OK if it wasn't for you." She tried to scream, to call out to me from beneath his grip, but she seemed unable to find the breath. "You had to tell her about it, didn't you? About the cave and my Father, and everything that happened. And the others...they knew. That one from the tourist office knew my Father was guilty, she even saw Cullen's body and spoke with that bloody idiot artist. And the hotel, well...she had records, letters, all sorts of things. That's where we stayed, isn't it? Or didn't you find out as much as you thought, hmm Edward Clarke?"

"Of course...but then tell me, why did your Father use the name of my family? Why did he sign in as Lucas Clarke when he stayed at Hawthorn House with you?"

"You really are stupid, aren't you" he said. He took the gun away from myself and Amelia, placed it back to the head of Molly. She tried to break free, managing to catch her breath and scream out, even though it was inaudible through her lack of strength. After a few seconds though, he took his arm from around her throat, and pushed her away from him with such momentum that she fell forwards and onto the grass. Myself and Amelia managed to catch her, lifting her into a sitting position where she began at once to gasp for breath.

As we stood up back up, Adam was pointing the gun at all of us, a barbarous smile now on his face, as if he took delight in the power he was wielding.

"Your all too stupid", he loudly said. "I may as well not have bothered with you. Still, too late now, I suppose."

I was sure at that moment that we were going to die there. Indeed, it is often said that such inhuman things happen with a rapidity so incomprehensible, that our usual feelings have no time to fabricate.

Things such as a car crash, a fire or natural disaster, they each end life with a dreadful ease that makes our human reasoning not fit to grasp them. I felt it that night. I stared death himself in the face, as if taunting time to finish it's business, and have Buckley kill Clarke at the old Wishing Lake.

And yet there was not only me to think of. Beside me, Amelia was intimidating our executioner by aiming her torch into his maddened eyes. I dared not imagine what she was feeling, but just her presence with me created inside a heartless asperity, allowing me to face the lunatic before us. As for Molly, she sat on the ground between myself and Amelia, her hands wrapped tight around her reddened throat, still wheezing uncomfortably and unable to speak. But she was safe. Alive.

"Tell me, Edward Clarke", said Adam, moving a few steps closer to me, and aiming the gun once more at my head. "You really don't know that, in the end, everything here is all your fault?"

"Oh yeah, I'm sure it is", I grimaced. "Come on, what are you going to do?"

"Edward!" gasped Amelia, beginning to show discernible unease at the continuing discussion with Adam Buckley.

"Think about it", said Adam. "When my Father and I first came to town, he had made enquiries about the people who lived here. Oh, you know the sort of thing...he wanted to know about people with visions, people who saw things move in the gloom, got messages from this bloody seal-woman. I'm sure you get it, don't you Clarke? The Sullivan book says that the Selkie called people into her home, those of whom she wanted for herself, those who would guarantee the wishes were granted."

"And this concerns me in which way? Come on, tell me".

"The name of the Clarke's, and most specifically their little son, Edward, was mentioned to my Father by the people in town. Apparently you used to be out in the night, searching for ghosts and who knows what. You even dragged some ridiculous girlfriend with you, and tried to find these 'special' places or something."

"Hey!" shouted Amelia. "You don't even realise that it's me your talking about, right? And I'm pretty sure it was hidden places."

"I don't care, OK?" He shook the gun at her, looking for the first time to be oddly nervous, as if underneath his threatening exterior, his motive was beginning to fall apart. Still, I was afraid for the safety of Amelia and Molly, perhaps even more so than I was for myself. I wasn't affected by Adam's attempt to make me take the blame for his behaviour, but I did feel responsible for bringing Amelia along with me to the lakeside. Therefore, I found myself wanting him to point the gun at me, and away from Amelia and Molly beneath me.

"Adam", I said. "If what you say is true, then answer my question. Why did your Father use the name Lucas Clarke in the hotel?"

"It's perfectly simple", he spat back at me, turning towards me with the gun. "He panicked, thinking he was going to get traced by the hotel. So he thought of a name to cover himself, just something from the top of his head. And of course, your name was on his mind at the time. That's all there was to it. Nothing more."

"OK, so look, are you going to put that gun down now?"

"No chance", he said, inching closer again to me, the barrel of the gun now merely inches from the centre of my skull. Amelia turned, trying to steadily aim the torch, but her grip growing weaker and forcing the light to shake within that moonless darkness. "I want to explain how this is all your fault, Clarke."

"Really? Then go on, I'd like to hear it", I said, still trying to make it look to Adam as if I wasn't affected by his threats. Of course, I found myself unable to concentrate on whatever I may have been truly feeling. All I could feel was a pressure in my chest, as if my thumping heart had toughened the muscle and made my heavy breaths force their way upwards. I gulped, looked Adam once more square in the eye, and wondered just what his next move would be.

"You told Shane Cullen about that cave", he said. "Well, Cullen went to see it for himself, shortly afterwards. That's right, he went under there, exactly the same as what you did. Now, my Father took that as a sign from his abominable Selkie, and the rest you already know. He murdered his friend, smashed out his skull with his bare hands, just as was the fate of those disgusting bog bodies. I was forced to see that, you know. And it was all because of you. You told Cullen about that cave, so you have blood on your hands as well."

I was aware that Adam was deranged, and was trying to make me feel accountable for the murders he had carried out. That said, I did sense a pang of the childhood emotion which haunted me during the regression hypnosis. I had blamed myself for Cullen's death, so much that I told myself I was responsible for his murder and all the misery that followed. But I would not buckle under the trepidity of my childhood fears. I needed to get Adam to drop the gun, if not only for myself then for Molly and Amelia.

"Give it up", I said. "I'm not remotely interested in what your saying. You actually think you can get away with the murder of two people, and not to mention the three of us? Think it through, Adam. Your out of your depth."

"It's not me for god's sake" he yelled. "Why won't you listen? Even the death of my Father himself was caused by the stupidity of your bloody family. Who do you think came running to the cave, making so much noise that the whole damn thing collapsed on top of them? Only you and me were spared. And to think, I thought you were just some paltry visitor, not that same child from way back then!"

"Then go on", I continued, forcing myself to take a step towards him, the gun brushing against the skin between my eyes. "If your so sure about what your doing, then do it."

"No way Edward", said Amelia, pacing sideways so that she was behind Adam, her torch light forming a corona around him. "Besides, I doubt he'd be able to pull the trigger. Not on someone who isn't defenceless, right?"

Adam lowered the aim of the gun, turned to Amelia, then back to myself. He seemed worried, as if an unforeseen flow of second thoughts had rendered his menacing ego powerless. Until now, those he had preyed on were alone and incapable of retaliation. But when I spoke to him, when Amelia circled him and answered him back, he quickly lost his illusion of power. Yes, I was aware that at any time he could snap, pull the trigger on me before I could stop him, but somehow I couldn't make myself think about it.

To my side, Molly had finally got back her breath, and after seeing Adam's first signs of nerves, got to her feet and stood beside me.

"What are you doing?" he immediately snarled at her, waving the gun in front of him. "Don't you realise there's no way you can ever leave here?"

Amelia stepped around him, temporarily blinding him with the torch as she once more joined me at my side. In that moment, all three us stood in front of Adam, who backed away towards the edge of the lake, erratically pointing the gun at all of us.

"Really?" asked Amelia. "I think were all going to walk away fine. I mean really, your going to kill all three of us and think the police won't hunt you down?"

"Shut up!" He uncomfortably shouted, his voice now mixed with heavy breath as if beginning to panic with a dangerous severity. I was stood in the middle of the three of us, the muscles in my body jumping and unstable, my mind fogging with thoughts of death approaching. "I will get rid of anyone who knows what my Father did. Anyone! That way, I can alter the past, erase it from the memory of all the world. You see if I don't!"

"You won't", I said. "You can never get rid of those memories, Adam. Someone will always remember what happened. Just look at me, I thought I'd lost all of my memories, didn't I? Well, they were still there, locked up inside me. It can never be truly forgotten."

"That's right", Molly joined in, her voice croaky and sore from where Adam had strangled her. "There are always things to help people remember. Photographs, paintings, written records. I can't believe you didn't think of that Adam! What has happened has happened. And that's all there is to it."

Adam said nothing, just shook the gun in front of him, his aim trembling and growing more unsteady. His chest was pulsing, forcing audible breaths in and out, and in his eyes was the appearance of madness. I realised then he was breaking down, his mind likely inefficient to comprehended such a set back in his plan. So, like a wild animal he cowered in front of us, looking either on the verge of complete collapse, or of a violent and uncontrollable rage. The fear, of course, came from not knowing which one would come first.

"Put it this way", said Amelia, still pointing the torch as if it too were a gun, into the gaping eyes of the killer. "Even hundreds of years into the future, something remains of all the people who once walked this earth. Look at a cemetery. Even the oldest and most decaying graves are in themselves a memory. There's no way those things can ever be forgotten."

"No, no your all mad", Adam cracked up. "My family's name was ruined by my Father. All I want is to take it away, make it my legacy to baby Lily. Why should she grow up with this town hanging over her? Why should she have to even know about it?"

"Adam!" blurted Molly, trying hard to raise her voice as loud as she could manage. "Have you any idea what you are saying? That girl is already going to grow up with something just like what your Father did! Can't you see it? Her second cousin is a murderer, spending his life in prison?"

"I don't think so", said Adam quietly. He placed the gun against the side of his own head. The barrel was touching his skin, his hand alarmingly steady. "I'm going to die anyway, aren't I? Come on, you didn't actually think I was planning to live, did you?"

There was a frozen moment of startling silence. Amelia dropped her aim with the torch, pointing it towards the ground. All I could see was a silhouette. The shadow of a man awaiting death. I dared not speak, unsure of how to respond to a killer who had turned his weapon against himself. Did I really want to talk to him? In a way, I pitied him, but at the same time I felt an outburst of relief that, even if only for a single moment, the three of us were safe.

I felt Molly move forward, about to reach out her arm to Adam and shout out some sort of words to him. But there was no time.

My ears burst, then fell into silence. A high pitched ringing echoed throughout me, and I opened my eyes to the tepid darkness of the lake. There was nothing there. Adam, who had seconds before threatened our lives and told us his horrific tale, was no more. Thought was impossible, yet as time held it's breath in that pungent moment, a single emotion quivered in the darkness. Were were alive.

It was too fast though, too fast for any of our minds to properly understand it's reality. We just stood there, our eyes fixed on the shadowed mass on the floor, and waited for our senses to catch up with our eyes. Adam was dead, killed by his own hand.

Farewells

The so called 'real world' is a different landscape to the confines of the Wishing Lake in the midst of night. For when standing by those darkened waters, an arcane semblance exists in the air which allows unreality to blend with the senses, and thus all but mute their expected reaction.

It was not until the sun began to rise that I finally took in the severity of the events having taken place last night. I sat on the sofa all night in the pub, remembering the sirens which shattered the night after we mustered the courage to report our experience. And yet even then, it all seemed to have happened outside of existence, as if the whole thing was fiction and Adam would stroll into the pub with nary a word to say. Yet it was real, and harder to fully comprehend than any matter of mentally replaying it could solve. But it did replay, over and over inside my mind until I had to force myself to banish it's memory. My skin still crawled though, replete with the repellent touch of death which lingered still in my every thought.

In the morning, each of us was called to the police station to make separate statements as to what we witnessed. We could not even travel together, with the police picking us up at separate times from outside of the pub early in the day. Of course, I told them everything, going so far as to explain my own research and it's relation to Adam Buckley. The policeman seemed to understand, and was actually relatively civil whilst speaking to me during the session. That said, it was made clear that the statement was for Buckley's suicide only, and should they pursue a case for him as the killer, much more could be required from me. I was not happy with it, but followed along with the police's instructions until finally allowed to leave the station.

The thing I found most difficult to explain was the sheer speed of which Adam took his life. I saw nothing, of course, the sound of the gun forcing my eyes to close and only reopen to see his lifeless remains. What was hard to explain was the change in the air, as if the very aura of the lake had grown swiftly strange with the abrupt visit from death. In fact, it was almost ironic. To the lake, was Adam not just another victim who's skull was broken in front it's wish-filled waters?

I arrived back in Kilportach around midday, the policeman saying he would be in touch should I be required for any more questioning. As it stood, I was simply happy to once more see daylight, and to witness what little life there was that day in old Kilportach town.

In fact, the whole place felt somewhat different that day. Perhaps it was the sunlight, falling over those ragged buildings unaware of the horrors that took place while it slept. More likely though, it was my own reaction in the face of Adam's death. After all, I had managed to survive and face up to his attack, and was standing there on those cracked pavements when hours beforehand I was sure I would die. More than this, an ambience of absolution hovered within me; a mood of closure for Bridget and Catherine. It was like the town had been cured from some crawling illness, and although it could never fully recover, it was vibrant in the knowledge that it's fearful aggressor could no longer strike at it's enshrined memories.

The first train leaving for Cork station had already departed the town in the morning. There was only one more for the rest of the day, leaving the town in the early evening. I would be aboard it, leaving Kilportach to experience it's first night without the shadow of the Buckley's haunting it's streets. In recompense, I would be taking with me my own memories, a gift from the small town of where I was raised, a thing more precious than anything I possessed.

Of course, there was more than simply memories in that town. I had met people, touched their lives with my presence, and in turn allowed them to touch my own. I'd shared in their tragedies, seen things to scar and haunt in my mind, but I'd also witnessed something different. The people in the town had helped me, and I would like to think I helped them too, in whatever small ways I may have done. For that, leaving Kilportach was not only about leaving the place I had found my childhood in, but of going home to my own world and allowing the townsfolk to do the same.

There were a number of hours before the train would arrive. I took that time to say proper goodbyes to the people I had met in the town of Kilportach.

I begun by walking to the doctor's surgery, where I asked at reception to see Dr Ryan who thankfully was in his office. When he realised I was leaving town, he immediately phoned for Dr Kenny to join him in the office to say goodbye. It was unusual, most likely against their official position, but the doctor's seemed genuinely happy to have seen me gain so much since my first visit to the surgery.

"Remember the MRI?" laughed Kenny. "I told you to have it all along, didn't I? Anyway, see your own doctor as soon as you get back, and see about changing that medication for good, OK?"

"Definitely. Thanks Dr Kenny."

"So, going home?" Ryan shook my hand. "Well, I'll admit you've been an interesting patient for me. Something different, you know. Real different."

"Actually", I said. "I don't think I'd have ever achieved so much if it wasn't for your hypnosis, doctor."

"Ha, I told you all along you needed to see him" laughed Dr Kenny, taking his turn to shake my hand and wish me the best for my journey home.

I did wonder, long after leaving the staffed yet empty surgery, if I really had been their only patient apart from the bog bodies in that place. I had never once had to book in an appointment, and the doctor's were more than happy to help every time I so much as passed them by. For that, I truly was grateful for them.

Feeling better after my meeting with Ryan and Kenny, I made my way across the peat bog area to the old museum where Jack was working. The place was open, with a tiny sign stood outside the door with handwritten text in black felt tip. It showed an arrow pointing into the museum, and above it was written; '*come face to face with the bog people. See Silsbury Man, inside the museum*'.

It was difficult to speak to Jack, though. I needed to tell him about last night, to inform him that Bridget's murderer was no longer a threat to anybody in town. It was a challenge. Jack was a kind and humble man, and bringing up such painful topics around him was nowhere as easy as I thought it would be. Instead, I started by simply telling him the news; I would be leaving town at the end of the day and had dropped in simply to say goodbye.

"That's good", he said. "So you've found all that you wanted in our little town have you?"

"I have. Much more than I ever thought I would, honestly."

"Well, it was certainly good to have met you, Leonard. So don't forget us, now will you?"

It was my only real chance to tell Jack about discovering the murderer. I wasn't sure of how to begin, but I mentioned that I could never forget the town, especially after what happened to me the night before. At this, Jack helped my fumbling by mentioning the sirens, saying he had been woken up in the night by the sounds of what he thought were fire engines or police. I said he was right, it was police, and they had came to investigate the suicide of the murderer of Bridget and Catherine. I didn't have the know-how to express the whole story, instead telling Jack the bare minimum details whilst avoiding anything to rekindle bad memories. I could actually feel my heart beating with nerves, both feeling relieved to be telling Jack the news, yet anxious at once more bringing up the death of his friend Bridget Brady.

"So, he actually killed himself?" was Jack's response, his voice changed from the elated tone of before and into a reflective, somewhat wistful resonance. "Adam Buckley you say, that was his name?"

"Yes. I'm sorry, I just thought it was right to tell you this in person."

"Well thank you, Leonard. I won't pretend it's easy to understand what happened to Bridget, it never will be. But knowing that he's, well, gone now...yes, it's a help. So thanks."

I didn't like to leave Jack on such a sombre note, but I would not feel right leaving the town and just letting him find out what happened on his own. It was better for me to be there to tell him, if only to offer what slight comfort I could that the threat posed by Adam could not happen again. Of course, it could not bring Bridget or Catherine back, but to the mind of one plagued by the cruel actions of another, knowing of their fate, no matter how unpleasant, was surely as close to absolution as one could expect in such a situation.

After shaking hands with Jack and leaving the museum, I slowed down my pace and looked over the bog lands, knowing that in only a few hours time, I would pass by them on the train and never see them again. I would not say their presence was something I'd miss, but I did take my time to peer longingly at them, as to take their photograph in the eye of my mind. They were so vast, so replete with dark pools and endless patches of pale green, that I wondered if their secrets would ever be truly unearthed. No, I was sure that they would not. The peat bogs would ever withhold their mystery, allowing but fragments of what they had nurtured to be found by those who found puzzlement in them. But they would know nothing more.

It was similar in principle to the town itself. As I strolled for the last time into the main street, I could feel the unreadable charisma the buildings had cultivated. It was a place I knew I could not find replicated, a town alone in the midst of the wilds, without the knowledge nor care for the world at large, which in turn knew not of Kilportach's existence. There would be many who would find such a town unbearable, and assume it to be strange to live in that place where time yawned and passed with never changing direction.

But the people in Kilportach were friendly and real. I knew this as I walked once more into the pub, intent on saying goodbye to Molly who was no doubt still in shock from last night's abomination. Sure enough, she was sat behind the empty bar, lost in her own thoughts of past and future. She hardly even noticed I had walked inside.

"Oh, Mr Clarke, I'm sorry", she said, her voice tired sounding as though she had not slept a wink since leaving the lake last night. "I've got something for you, hold on a sec."

I took a seat opposite her by the bar. She got to her feet, and walked into the kitchen for a couple of seconds, returning with a gift wrapped bottle of something.

"There you are", she said, handing it to me. "It's nothing special, but still. For everything you've done."

"You didn't have to Molly", I said. "But thanks. So, how are you coping with everything? Still mostly tired, I'd say. Right?"

"You can tell, can't you", she smiled. "But yeah, I'll be alright. And what about you, are you really leaving?"

"I am, yes. I came here to say goodbye."

I tried not to bring up the events of last night, knowing that Molly would not want to discuss them, nor see them as fit for my final discussion with her. Instead, I simply thanked Molly for all of her help, for letting my stay in the pub on a night, and for all of her meals and incomparable hospitality.

"Get away", she warmly smiled. "The food's not that good I know for sure! But yeah...thanks, Mr Clarke. Guess I'm going back to having this place to myself, eh?"

"I guess", I laughed. "But seriously, I won't be forgetting all you've done to help me. I'd never have managed it without you, and this place."

"Oh lord, you'll have me embarrassed in a minute. Oh wait, actually, I have an idea."

"You do?"

She asked me to wait behind the bar, and once more clambered up the stairs to get something from her living room. It took a while, and I could hear the floorboards creaking above, as she moved from room to room in search of whatever it was she was looking for. Eventually, she came down with a large camera in her hand. It looked professional, a huge lens and flash fastened to it with all manner of dials and different buttons.

"I might not remember how to use this, you know. But it's only ever brought out on special occasions."

"That's your camera?" I asked in awe, the lens itself looking as though it would only be available for career photographers.

"Yeah, I know", she laughed. "It was something I bought when I first came back here. Something to cheer me up, you know. Thing is, I hardly get a chance to use it. So, what do you say?"

"You want a picture of me?"

"Of both of us! Come on, it's got one of those delayed action thingies. Well, if I can manage to get it to work that is."

I of course agreed to let Molly take a photograph. For the first few minutes, she fiddled with the settings and took a test picture, then moved the camera to a table in the corner in order to set up our shot. It was clear she wanted it to be perfect, checking the viewfinder and moving the camera bit by bit until she was happy.

Eventually, we stood side by side in front of the bar, holding our smiles for a number of seconds until the flash finally took the picture. And then it was done. Molly had captured another memory, another face in the town to show to her visitors many years into the future.

"Brilliant, Mr Clarke", she said, taking the camera back to the bar. "I can't wait to see what it comes out like."

"It's not often I get my photo taken, actually, Thanks, Molly."

"No, thank you. It means a lot to me, actually, believe it or not. Now then...will you be wanting a drink before you go on your way?"

"I wasn't going to...but go on then. Just a small one."

It was the last drink I would share with her in Kilportach's old pub. It was bizarre, actually. Only last night I was sat at the same bar, sharing a drink with the very man who would try to kill us only hours later. I tried not to dwell upon his memory, instead wanting to remember Molly's pub as the friendly and delightful place she had made it.

I did however share a word with Molly in memorial for those we had both seen lost. The tourist office stood with it's lights turned off, the pavement in front of it empty and barren, the flicker of leaflets forever lost. I wondered what had happened to the painting I had found, the canvas remembrance of two people now both departed from our world. It had lightened up Catherine's final day, connected her to a vibrant past of which all too soon she was to become a part of.

"If I ever see it", said Molly. "Then it's going straight on the wall in here, that's for sure."

I could already imagine it. In fact, I was almost sure in that moment that Molly would successfully get hold of the painting. The canvas itself would make sure of it, if not for itself then to ensure an immortality for the people who were painted skilfully upon it. That way, the memory of those who the town itself cherished would forever look over it's guests and visitors, calm in the knowledge of their endless memory.

I did not stay long inside the pub after finishing my drink with Molly. The sun had departed behind the clouds, and the hour of my departure from Kilportach was growing closer by the minute. I wanted once more to walk through that townscape, to thank it for allowing it's furtive past to be imparted onto one of whom sought out it's story. Besides, there was one more person I needed to say goodbye to.

The cemetery spoke, as it always did, with the voice of one who muses on days of antiquity. The field of uncut grass, decorated with decomposing stones each etched with names and elegies, was the perfect place for me to end my journey. It was still strange though, to see that mournful stone statue which stood at the point where my childhood friend lived. Strange, but somehow welcoming.

My knock on the door was met with an answer almost as soon as my hands could reach it. She was dressed in her usual assortment of creased clothes, including the very same brown coat she was wearing on the first day I met her in the cemetery.

"I knew you'd be coming", she said, leaving the crypt and closing the door behind her.

"Were not going in?"

"If you've come to tell me your leaving, then no." She walked past me and up the steps, and stood in the middle of the cemetery pathway. I followed her, noticing her expression in the middle between contented and sorrowful.

"Well, that is why I came here, yes", I said.

"It's OK", she sighed, turning to look at me. "I just had a feeling today would be the day. Tell me first though, your alright, aren't you?"

"Of course I am" I smiled. We began to walk slowly throughout the cemetery, passing by forlorn graveside ornaments and elderly trees with watchful branches.

"Good. I am too, by the way. I wasn't sure about making that police statement thing, but I suppose I had to."

"Yeah. Hopefully that's the last we hear about it."

She nodded, sighing slightly as we reached the gravestone where my parents were buried. We stood in front of it, peering at my own name carved in stone like a grisly reminder of what could have been.

"So", she longingly said. "This is it."

"Yeah. I'll be on the train that leaves here in few hours. Back home to England."

"I see. So, tell me...what have you thought about being here in Kilportach? About coming home, I mean."

"Well", I lightly laughed. "It's like nothing else out there, isn't it? But yes, if I'm honest with you, I've found it, well...I don't know, actually."

"Well, I've found it wonderful", she said. "Having you here...you've no idea how much it's meant to me. Can you imagine it? I've visited this grave almost every day. And now your here."

"Actually, I can't imagine it", I replied. "But I would like to thank you Amelia. For, well you know, everything you've done for me."

"You don't have to thank me. Just...well, here."

She put her hands around the back of her neck, and unfastened the Selkie necklace she was wearing.

"Go on, take it". She handed me the necklace, dangling it from her hand and dropping it into my open palm.

"You want to give this to me?" I asked, clasping the cold silver in my hand.

"I do. Besides, it was yours to begin with, wasn't it? And, well...it's something you can remember me by."

"I don't know what to say, Amelia."

I looked at the necklace in my hands, the silver Selkie shining with the light of the day. My hand seemed almost to tickle beneath it, as if it was charged with a magnetic quality that connected itself to my very spirit. I once more clasped my hand tightly, the cold silver warming with the heat from my body.

"Are you sure you don't want to keep this yourself?" I asked.

"I am sure. Really I am. I think you were always supposed to have it. Don't you think?"

I was unsure if she speaking metaphysically, or mentioning the one question of which I had found myself unable to answer. The first time I went under the lake, was it really the necklace that I found inside and presented to my Mother as a gift? In reality, there was no way of telling. All I know is that I saw a 'Selkie', and shortly afterwards the chain of events which changed the very town took place. But the truth of whatever I saw in that cave shall be forever concealed in the confines of my memory. I will never know the truth.

"Amelia, thank you".

"So", she sighed. "I suppose in a minute you'll be going, right?"

"I will. I'm sorry, Amelia, I know you wanted me to stay in town longer. But..."

"I know, and it's alright", she said. "I just find it sad how quickly things pass. But I mean, everything is just memories in the end, isn't it? It just feels too soon, sometimes."

"I think I know what you mean", I said. After all, I was standing above the grave of my family, their voices now silent and their lives only a fragment of the mind, a picture of a time that used to be. Even so, I had seen them live, felt their presence during the regression as real as anything the present day could manage. With that and Amelia's companionship, I felt that I really had found my past, just lying in wait in that reticent town.

"Just promise me one thing", said Amelia, turning and making eye contact with me. "Promise you'll always remember this place. Remember the childhood we shared here together. Because no matter where you are, I will always be thinking of it. Remembering it. And you."

"I will. I promise".

"I'm glad", she said, her voice growing quiet and tinged with tristful contemplation. "I'm really glad..."

"Amelia?"

"What? It's nothing. Anyway, I thought you were supposed to be catching a train? Why are standing here talking to me?"

"That's more like it" I smiled, once more enjoining my gaze with Amelia as if to whisper a wordless and poignant goodbye.

So my time to leave Kilportach had arrived. I detected a change in the air at that moment, as if once again I was a simple visitor, merely sampling the town and it's secrets, before departing again into my own home and life. In a way, I was sorrowful to turn my back on that place, leaving all of the people I had met, and returning home from a location which had welcomed me to it with ardent murmurs of my past.

But Kilportach will continue to exist in it's own way. It's people will continue to live out their lives, alone with the strangeness of the town which cradles all who dwell there in it's own immemorial spirit. It is a spirit that is present in it's buildings and streets, in it's endless peat bogs and it's timeworn, enchanted Wishing Lake. For although the town's aura is undoubtedly coloured by the analysis of our mortal minds, it is also true that those very thoughts are influenced in part by the town itself.

And so I began to leave the cemetery, already imagining the train arriving and taking me back to the busy Cork station. Yet as I did, Amelia shouted one more thing to me, forcing me to pause in my tracks once more, and turn around to face my wistful childhood friend.

"Sorry, Edward, I just wanted to ask you one last thing."

"What is it, Amelia?"

"You'll be coming back here, one day. Won't you?"

The Wishing Lake – Mark Robinson

KILPORTACH

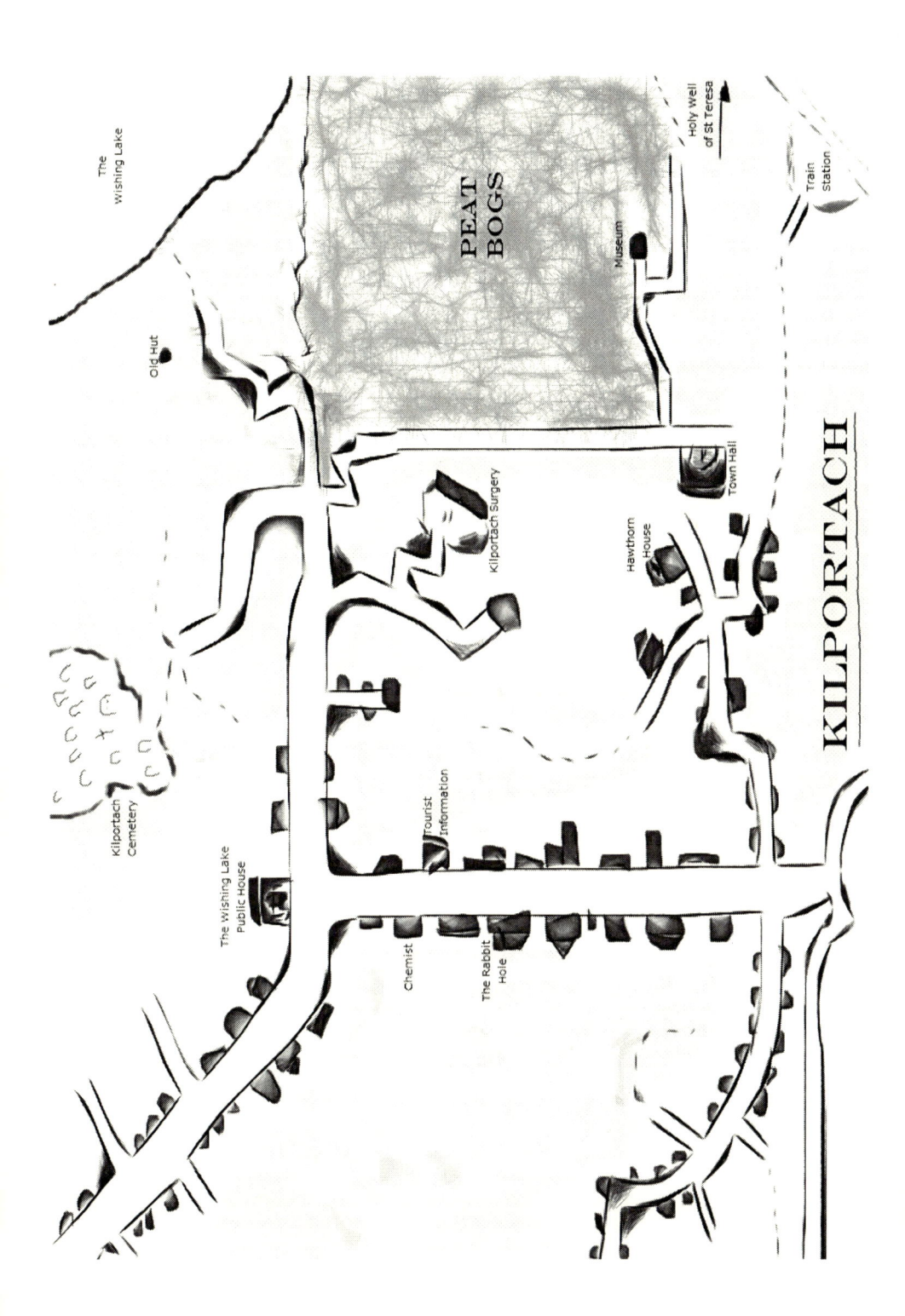